Looking Back on Forever

By: Kat Alexander

*This book contains mature content not suitable for readers under the
age of 18. This book contains content with strong language, violence,
and sexual situations. All parties portrayed in sexual situations are
over the age of 18.*

ISBN-13: 978-1542951807
ISBN-10: 1542951801

Cover by: Cover Me Darling

http://www.katharinealexander.net/

Dedication

To The Killers, the band, not the psychos, whose music inspired this
book.

Part One

*"How do you pick up the threads of an old life?
How do you go on, when in your heart, you begin to understand
there is no going back?
There are some things that time cannot mend.
Some hurts that go too deep...that have taken hold."
~ J.R.R. Tolkien, The Return of the King*

There are moments in time that stand out more than others: your first kiss, a special birthday party, seeing your baby for the first time, an intimate conversation, a first date, even something as little as sitting around a dining room table with friends. This is the story of the moments that stood out after I first laid eyes on Noah Gish.
~ Claire Sawyer

Chapter 1

For My Sanity

~Noah~

"Dude, this is going to be great," Kyle goes on and on as he helps carry my belongings to the guest room, my new room for the next ten months—senior year of high school. "My popularity status is going to skyrocket this year! Cousin to the big, bad city boy. Oh, yeah, girls are going to flock to us. Just wait."

I let Kyle drone on about using me for personal gain as I set the last box on top of the blue covered bed. My aunt and uncle—Kyle's parents—decorated this room in anticipation of my arrival; I can tell. The room used to have white walls with faint pink décor. Now it looks like something Picasso would be proud of: blue comforter, blue walls, blue curtains, blue rug, blue, blue, blue. What the hell were they thinking?

What makes it worse? I hate blue. As a kid, I loved blue. What little boy didn't? But in second grade, as we were making our spring time crafts, the teacher ran out of blue finger paint. I looked around the room and noticed everyone had made blue skies and blue water and the boys, of course, painted blue bicycles, blue T-shirts, blue, blue, blue. It was then, right there, that I made a statement. I would hate blue. Why? Probably because there wasn't enough for me.

So, how do you think I finished my painting? That's right. I was the smart kid. I painted a sunset with fall toned leaves and red, fiery waters. Did my teacher appreciate my artwork? No. She mistook it for fall, not spring, even though I pointed out that there are still sunsets in the spring time. Stupid bitch.

"So … what do you want to do tonight?" Kyle pulls my attention away from the blue nightmare of the room.

I shrug. "What is there to do?"

"I know this isn't New York, but there is always a party or two on the weekends. Chelsea Winds is having one tonight. I thought we could stop in for a few beers. If you don't want to stay, then we can go down to the pool hall or something."

"I can do that. Who's Chelsea?"

Kyle rolls his eyes back with a deep sigh. "She is every guy's wet dream. We're talking blonde, big tits, nice ass, legs that go on for miles." He starts humping the side of my bed. "She gives out, too. I know a lot of guys who lost their v-card to her."

"You hit that?" I ask, thinking I don't want to have sex with the entire town by tapping one chick. That's not kosher.

"Nah, man. She won't give me the time of day," he admits before slapping me on the back and putting his arm around my shoulder. "But I'm sure she'll do about anything to get some info on you, pretty boy." He laughs as we head out the bedroom door. "So, what do you say? Wanna play hard to get so you can help me out some? Give her the cold shoulder for a night, so she's begging me, on her knees, to tell her about you."

I grin at his antics. "What makes you think she'll want to know anything about me?"

Kyle stops and moves to stand in front of me with his hands holding my shoulders back like he's about to teach his son a valuable life lesson. "Uh, Noah, your reputation precedes you. Enough said."

Enough said? What the hell is that supposed to mean?

~

This girl, Chelsea, is the all-American cheerleader stereotype, which is not my type at all. She's gorgeous; don't get me wrong. Kyle's description of her was spot on. However, I like brunettes.

As she follows me around like a puppy dog, I give her the cold shoulder. And no, I don't do it just because Kyle asked it of me. The girl's voice pierces my ears like nothing else. She has a high-pitched voice that sounds like she's screaming when she talks, like she wants everyone to hear her and thinks everyone does (most do). Not I, though. I want to drink my beer and scope out the scene; see who I will be going to high school with in a couple more days.

Kyle's friends are nicer than I expected. Must be the small-town personality. It helps that I'm the "city boy" and everyone wants to know what the city is like. Most of these kids have never been farther than fifty miles from here.

Mostly, everyone wants to know about the typical city sights. On and on, they ask questions about New York. And that's typically how my night goes—harassed from all sides with a girl mauling my flesh, not taking the hint every time I pull a limb free.

I miss my friends. My home.

It sucks to finish the last year of high school in a new town. My friends and I back at home had plans. Our band grew quite the fan club. Most of our senior class and some in the lower grades were following us around from club to club, gaining us lots of attention. We had those "big dreams" to be found before we graduated. Now I am stuck out in Small Town, USA. Breckinridge, Colorado. Population: Forty-six hundred.

Parents suck. My mom and dad are both history buffs. Mom is a professor of historical studies. She took a year sabbatical to tour some archeological digs around the world. Something about some connection between the cuneiforms. Dad, a researcher, of course had to go with her on their quest for knowledge, leaving me to my dad's brother's care, which was the ultimatum: go with them or be sent here.

Everyone thinks I'm crazy not to go with them and finish school online, but what they fail to realize is that I *always* had to go with them growing up, which made me struggle throughout school. A five-year-old in kindergarten turned into an eight-year-old in second grade when my mom took another sabbatical to the jungles of Congo—I must input here that the hippopotamus is the scariest creature on earth, and that internet and tutors do not exist in the Congo. To this day, I am not a fan of the zoo.

Chelsea grabs my arm again with both of her claws as she laughs at something Kyle says, bringing me back to the present.

I pull my arm out of her clutches and hand her my drink so she has something else to hold on to. "Why don't you finish that? I need to step outside for some air." I give Kyle *the look* before stepping away.

"I can come with you," Chelsea eagerly calls out as she stays in step behind me.

I turn back around to face her. "Just stay here and keep Kyle company. I'll be right back."

She pouts, which would look adorable if she wasn't such a clingy slut. "All right," she relents with a smile.

Finally free, I make my getaway.

Kyle and I already planned this. I sneak out from the backyard, drive away in Kyle's car, and wait for him to seal the deal. If Kyle wants to chance that, who am I to stop him? He knows what he is in for.

At seventeen, Kyle has a lot of growing up to do in the women department. Just from hearing him and his friends talk, I know his maturity level isn't that high yet. They still talk about lifting skirts with a baseball bat or pretending to fall so they can grab onto a breast "accidentally." I might only be a year older than him, but that kind of stuff was child's play when I was twelve, not seventeen.

I step outside and circle around a group of kids sharing a joint. One of them tries to offer me the joint, but I decline. The rule with drinking and smoking pot is a lot like mixing beer with liquor. You want to smoke first, then drink.

I make it to the side yard to find a couple loving it up against the side of the house. The girl, another blonde cheerleader type, has her legs wrapped around some guy's waist. The guy's pants have fallen around his ankles as he thrusts into the girl, probably too drunk to realize his hairy ass is on display.

I quickly look away before the guy comes after me with his pants down. The dude is built like a linebacker, looks to be about six-foot-five, maybe two hundred fifty pounds. He definitely doesn't look like he belongs at a high school party.

Already forgetting the scene of fornication, I'm lost in thought, staring down at the blades of grass that are already forming their nightly dew as I walk toward Kyle's car, wondering where I'm going to go to kill time before Kyle calls me to pick him up. We should have ridden separately. I should have brought my bike. That way, I wouldn't have to wait around.

I get into the driver's seat of Kyle's piece of crap Honda and lean my head back on the seat, reclining the chair. I'm tired and want to go straight to bed. I don't even care to unpack tonight. I can take care of that tomorrow.

There is still three more days before school starts. Maybe I will drive around town to scope out the stores. I also need to buy some toiletries. I didn't pack those. Most of my stuff was shipped here with my motorcycle, a present from my dad for my eighteenth birthday last May. For the flight, I only brought a carry-on bag and my guitar. There was no way was I going to ship that. It was bad enough I had to ship my bike and be without it for a week. I still need to check it for scratches.

I shoot a text to Kyle to tell him I'm waiting and to text me back when he is ready to leave.

Damn, I'm tired.

A pounding noise jerks me awake. It sounds like a stampede of elephants, and the world is shaking with its thunderous footfalls. I look over to see a grinning Kyle staring back at me from the other side of the car's window. My heart is pounding so hard it feels like it's trying to break free from my chest. I'm going to kill Kyle for putting the fear of the Congo back in me.

Never take a child to the jungle. They will be traumatized for life.

"Move over, dude. I'm driving." Bastard is grinning like a moron.

I have half a mind to punch that smirk off his face. I need to get him to stop using "dude." That shit gets on my nerves. This isn't some sunny beach escape where surfers are dudeing it up. This is Small Town, America.

I get out of the car before walking around the back then sliding into the passenger seat. No way am I "moving over" the console like some kid.

I'm being an asshole. I know I am, but shit, am I tired. I want to sleep for a day, start over after I wake up, and play Mr. Nice Guy then. Not right now. Too tired right now.

Kyle is oblivious to my tired, pissed off state, bouncing around as he gets into the car and starting the engine.

"Dude—"

"No more *dude*! Got it?" I say harshly. "Call me Noah or cousin or man or something. Just knock it off with the surfer talk. And no *brah*. I hate that shit."

"What the hell crawled up your ass?" Kyle retorts, happy persona now gone. I feel bad for that, but not bad enough not to snip this dude shit in the bud now.

"I'm tired, and I hate the dude shit. Please, for my sanity and our family"—I motion between us—"bonding shit, just stop with the dude." I take a deep breath to calm myself down as Kyle pulls out from in front of Chelsea's house. "I'm sorry, Kyle. I'm tired." I slap myself in the face to wake my ass up then turn toward him. "I take it that it went well with the blonde."

Kyle's face lights up, and I know our little snapping bit is over and forgotten.

"Hell yeah, she was all over me the minute she realized you weren't coming back. At first, she was determined to find you, looking all over the house and outside. Then, when you shot me that text, I told her you took off. After that, she was more than eager to drag me to her room." He gets a smug look on his face at that before his expression sours. "She asked questions about you the whole time she was riding my dick, but I can't complain." He shrugs, focusing out the window as he drives down the road. "I don't even know what she asked or what I said. That chick knows how to—"

"I don't need details. Thanks, though," I mutter as my eyes start to close. I let out a yawn, telling him, "Glad you had fun. I hope you wrapped that shit up. I'd hate to think of it falling off."

Kyle reaches over and punches me in the arm, laughing like I made a joke. I didn't.

~Claire~

"Dad!" I call out. "I'm home. What do you want for dinner?"

It's surprising when my dad is actually home before me. He's the District Attorney for our small town and works sometimes twelve to fourteen hours a day. I usually eat alone, so for him to be home makes it a special occasion, and I want to cook him whatever he wants.

I hear him shuffle around his office before he comes into view. I'm already striding toward him as he reaches out and wraps me in the warm embrace only a dad can give.

Even though he works a lot, he's still the best, most caring dad in the world. I know he loves me; he tells me that every day and shows me by being supportive. He never lets me give up my dreams. He pushes me to be the best at everything I do. He listens to me when I need to talk. He's both my father and the mother I can't remember.

Dad pulls away and kisses my forehead. "I have a craving for your chicken parmesan. Can we do that?" His smile lights up his face. We both love chicken parmesan. It's kind of "our dinner," a favorite we have frequently.

I return his smile. "I think we can do that."

Dad gives my arm a squeeze. "Wonderful." He turns away before stopping and turning back. "Need any help? I have a few more interrogations to read through, but I can wait—"

I hold up my hands. "I got this, Dad. I'm just glad you're home early for once." I head toward the kitchen, calling over my shoulder, "You won't hear any complaints from me."

I hurry through the process of making dinner since it's already past six o'clock, breading, boiling, sautéing, and tossing a quick salad together before putting the bread into the toaster oven. When everything is ready, I call Dad in to eat.

The table is set, and I have laid out all the food in our special serving dishes. Since it's extremely rare that we get a chance to eat together, I go all out, setting the dinner out as special as I can in our formal dining room. This is our norm. A time we make special for us.

"This smells great, sweetheart," Dad says as he walks into the room, then takes his seat at the head of the table.

I finish lighting the last candle before sitting to his right. "Thanks, Dad." I start dishing out a helping of spaghetti onto my plate.

Dad makes a show of looking around the room. "Where's Troy? I thought he would be here with you."

Troy is my best friend, the mayor's son, and my wanna-be bodyguard/thinks he's my boyfriend. He is not my boyfriend. I have never kissed him, but he sometimes holds my hand. I have told him on more than several occasions I don't think of him that way, but he brushes off my words like I'm silly and don't know what I'm talking about.

I have no interest whatsoever in relationships, though a date would be nice every now and then. However, Troy is bound and determined to threaten any guy who even looks at me. The girls all love him and scorn me for "taking all of his attention," not that I care to.

I have been called frigid, yet a whore by scornful girls in the school. The guys became tired of not being able to talk to me, so they call me a bitch or a stuck-up snob, not understanding it's my domineering friend who pushes them away.

Once, when a guy was brave enough to approach me, Troy stormed in and beat him. I had to pull Troy off the poor kid. Needless to say, I didn't talk to Troy for a week. I finally relented to the silent treatment when he showed up at our door, crying big, old, fat tears, and then endured a lesson from my dad about forgiveness and virtue. Our friendship continues, but I lost a bit of respect for him after that.

"I don't know," I answer my dad.

I feel my eyebrows pull together in thought. Troy said he was going to meet me at the auditorium, but he never showed and never called with an excuse. I assume he had to do something with his family. That's usually the only reason he isn't at my side. The man won't go a day without seeing me. It's unnerving.

"How did practice go?"

I smile up at my dad. "It was amazing. I was spot-on today. Signora Gelardi barely criticized me." We both laugh at that statement.

Signora Gelardi is my singing tutor. She came from Italy about twenty years ago, when her daughter moved to the States. She taught music in my elementary school back then. Previously from that, she was a Prima Donna, but her career was short-lived when she became pregnant with her first child. After that, she played small roles until she eventually settled down to raise her family and became a teacher.

She is retired from teaching now but still took me on as her pupil. She has connections everywhere and gave me an amazing recommendation to the Manhattan School of Music in New York City after requesting some acquaintances to fly all the way here to hear me perform at the governor's ball. It was, by far, the most nerve-racking night of my life. It paid off, though, and next year I will be in the city, hopefully working toward my dream of being a Prima Donna.

My dad and I have a great meal together, with me telling him about my classes this upcoming school year, how my tutoring has been coming along, and him telling me about the case he is working on right now.

We are interrupted from cleaning up after dinner by the doorbell ringing. Dad is putting the last of the dishware into the dishwasher as I am taking the linens into the laundry room.

"I'll get it," I tell him as I drop the linens on top of the drier, and then turn around to head toward the front door.

It's Troy. He looks a bit disheveled and reeks of alcohol and something else. His eyes are bloodshot, his pants and shirt are wrinkled, and there appears to be a hickey on his neck. I raise my eyebrows at that.

"Are you insane?" I ask him as I push him back and step outside, shutting the door behind me. "You come over to the district attorney's house after you've been drinking?" I shake my head at him. "I'll be right back," I tell him before he can speak a word.

I go back inside the house to grab my purse and keys, calling out to my dad, "I'll be right back. I'm going to go for a drive with Troy really quick."

" 'Kay, sweetie. Be careful. Love you."

"Love you, too," I say, hurrying back out the door.

I give Troy a disappointed look as I start down the front stairs, stopping when I realize his car isn't here. I turn back to see he has his head down and his hands shoved into his pockets.

"Where is your car?"

He shrugs. "Chelsea's house, I guess. I walked here."

Chelsea lives up the street. Her family owns a couple businesses in town. Dad and her parents are friends, but never me and Chelsea. We have been enemies since for as long as I can remember. She always needed to destroy my toys and such when we were still in diapers. That girl is evil. Really evil.

"Chelsea's house? What were you doing over there?" I'm incredulous. They hate each other. Well, she hates us. Always has. Always will.

"She had a party, and I thought I would go to, you know ..."

No, I don't know, but whatever.

I have never been to a house party, though I have seen what they are like on TV, and from what I have seen, I'm not missing anything. I don't feel that rebellious urge everyone else does to let loose, get drunk, stoned, sleep around—whatever. I like to stay focused. Concentrate on my goals.

I slowly look him over again. "Why do you look so guilty?" He looks defeated, like he did something terribly wrong and will never be forgiven for it. "Did you get into another fight? Get kicked out? Tear her house apart? What's wrong?"

He doesn't look like he was fighting. I mean, he is disheveled like he could have been, but when he fights, there is blood, and I don't see any blood on him.

I pull one of his hands out of his pocket and look at his knuckles. Nope, no cuts, no bruises, no blood. Just old scars from past brawls and slamming fists into walls. The man has a temper, a bad one. I have been thankful on more than several occasions that his temper hasn't been directed at me. I trust him with my life.

He pulls his hand out of mine so quickly that I feel offended and a bit hurt. What's wrong with him?

"Sorry," he says when he sees my look. "I, uh ... I got really wasted really fast and sleptwithNikki." He says the last part so fast and so low I almost miss it.

"Ew." The distaste is out of my mouth so fast that I can't stop myself. No wonder he didn't want me to touch his hand, knowing where that hand has been.

I rub my hands across the back of my jean shorts without him noticing.

"Come on," I tell him, heading toward my car. "I'll take you home and pick you up tomorrow so you can get your car, 'kay?"

He nods solemnly as follows behind me. For such a big guy, he always looks like such a lost puppy when he's like this. That's one of the reasons I love him so much. He makes mistakes a lot, but I honestly feel like he can't help himself. He beats himself up for it for so long. I think it's the pressure of being the mayor's son. So many people hold him in high expectations. He has to watch everything he says and does. He can't make any mistakes. So, occasionally, that pressure builds up in him and he explodes—getting into fights, sleeping with random girls, getting drunk.

"I feel like I cheated on you. Why do I feel so guilty? Why do I feel like I did something wrong?" he says as he buckles his seatbelt. He looks over at me through his lashes, his head still bent down like a dog who had his nose tapped for peeing on the carpet.

That thought makes me giggle. Then I sigh at his words. We have been through this so many times before that I should just record my responses.

I turn the key in the ignition, then drive down the long driveway. "You didn't cheat on me because we're not together. We've never been together, and we won't ever be together. You are my best friend, and I love you, but like a brother, Troy. You're the big, little brother I've never had.

"You feel guilty because you did do something wrong. I know you're always under a lot of pressure, but so am I, and you don't see me getting drunk and sleeping with random guys."

He growls at that statement, and I roll my eyes.

"With your repeated slip-ups," I continue, "we should have another couple of months before you feel the urge to slip again." I smile and grab his knee, giving it a little shake.

He gives me a small smile in return, something rare, and grabs my hand before quickly releasing it. Oh, yeah. Dirty sex hands. Yuck again.

"We need to find something else for you to preoccupy your … unguarded times."

"You."

"Hmm?" I hum, not understanding what he's referring to.

"I need you."

"I'm always here for you. Obviously, that's not working. The one day I haven't seen you practically all summer and you are at a house party—"

"No. Why can't you see that you are perfect for me? You calm me. You make me a better person. Why can't we try us? We're already best friends. Just think about how it would be to be best friends that kiss each other, hold hands, sleep together …"

"I'm not getting into this with you again. I don't see you that way. I'm sorry," I whisper. "You're my best friend. I don't want to ruin that."

He looks more forlorn as I pull up to his house.

Troy takes his seatbelt off before turning to face me, reaching out like he is about to brush my hair out of my face, but then he hesitates when he remembers not to touch me. "I'll always be here for you. You'll see. One day, we will be together. We're made for each other. Just, right now you are so concentrated on that music school … Once you get there, you'll see that we've belonged together all along." With that, he gets out of the car.

I sit there, watching until he is out of sight. Then I whisper to myself, "I'm sorry, Troy. You aren't the one for me."

Chapter 2

Always Sorry

~Noah~

I let out a yawn as I get into Kyle's car, wishing already that I hadn't agreed to ride with him so I could skip school. First day of senior year.

This past weekend went by quickly. I slept practically all day on Saturday, feeling jet-lagged from coming off a flight to ending up at a party. The rest of that day was spent lounging around, unpacking and checking up on my bike. I went for a quick ride around town with it before tuning my guitar and spending a quiet night in my room, playing around with a new song.

Sunday found me jamming with Kyle in the detached garage in his backyard. I was impressed with his skills at the drums. He was better than my drummer in the city. I found it hard to wrap my brain around that, but I guess you have more time to practice without distractions. Kyle admits he started playing when he was seven, which means he has had ten years to hone in on his skills and add his own flare. I'm impressed.

When we pull into the busy school parking lot, I scan the surrounding crowd hanging around the parked cars. Some kids are waving to others as they pull in. Some are sitting in their cars, puffing on their cigarettes, trying to be discreet about it. A few couples are making out, in and out of their cars. I get a whiff of pot coming from two cars down. Yep, like any other high school.

"Come on; I'll show you around school really quick." Kyle climbs out of the driver's seat and throws his bag over his shoulder. "It's pretty simple, really. There are two floors, four hallways. Bottom floor's hallways are labeled A and B. Second floor's, C and D." He grabs my schedule from my hands and points to my first period class as we walk toward the school building. "See? C12. Second floor, front hallway."

I snatch my schedule back from him. "Got it." I'm such a grouch in the mornings.

"No problem," Kyle mutters warily, sneaking a glance at me as I down the remnants of my coffee.

I close my eyes, thinking how I am going to have to buy a thermos to make it through the days. One cup of Joe will not do it for me anymore.

I toss the empty Styrofoam cup into the nearest trash can and take a deep breath. "Sorry for snapping. I can't jump into the swing of things so fast after sleeping in all summer, you know?"

"I got it, dude. No worries here."

I ignore the dude drop as we continue walking into the school, which is packed with bodies. It sounds like an amphitheater with all the voices trying to yell over everyone else. I feel an instant headache coming on.

Kyle looks down at his watch. "Five minutes. I'm down here in hall B. The stairs are right there." He points at a door that is being held open by the sea of bodies going in and out of it. "There's another set of stairs at the end of each hall. Got it?"

I feel like he thinks I'm an idiot when he talks to me sometimes. I know he means well, but this school isn't even a quarter of the size of my last one. The layout is pretty cut and dry. I don't think there is a possibility of getting lost.

"Yeah, I got this." I turn around and head toward the stairs.

On the way up, I'm met with a lot of wandering, appreciative female eyes and lots of scornful looks from the jocks. The scornful eyes, I'm not much accustomed to. New guy syndrome. That's what it should be called. New fresh meat for females' pleasure and males' dislike.

I politely smile at the female hellos and nod an understanding to the males' jealousies before leaving the stairs of sin and making my way down the hall to my classroom. I find it easily and quickly grab a seat in the back, watching all the students file into class.

I like to people watch. People are the same everywhere you go. They all form cliques, whether that be with over ten people or a couple. All of them have their own tastes, usually centered around their music likes or their hobbies. For example, punks like punk music, cheerleaders hang with jocks, skaters, teen pregos, the artists, the drama club, the band geeks, dead heads. See? Cliques: an exclusive group of individuals with similar interests or goals, disregarding outsiders.

So, where would I fit in? Hmm, senior year, new kid, only knows cousin … Guess I'm cliquing with him. Besides, we both like music. I'm sure we can stir something up with that. Maybe one of his friends is a bassist. I have some new music I never shared with my old band. Maybe we can …

That thought is halted the minute *she* walks in. Long, soft waves of brown swish inside the doorway. Below that hair is a petite, *very* petite, package full of curves. Flawless ass wrapped in some tight jeans, tiny waist, full breasts seen at a side profile, outlined in a gray V-neck shirt. Those soft globes peeking out as she inhales. The ideal hourglass figure.

I haven't even seen her face, and I'm already picturing what I would do to her. I want to feel her skin. I can imagine how silky it would feel, how soft and conforming to my grip. How it would feel under my lips. Taste on my tongue. I want to lick her back. Every curve of …

Again, my thoughts come to a halt. My erection stops mid-growth.

Her face. Those eyes.

My heart stops. It literally. Fucking. Stops. I don't even think I breathe.

I'm not a fan of clichés, but from my reactions—my stopped breath, stopped heart, the jaw dropping, eyes devouring, not to mention, sexual thoughts paused … and now my heart is beating like I ran a marathon, quick breathes, heart attack approaching. If I believed in it, I think I am experiencing love at first sight. And from the looks of her—paused mid-step, eyes locked on mine, rapid breathing, mouth parted, now trying not to look at me—I would say she is experiencing the same dubious phenomena.

Her face, if it had to be described in one word, it would be angelic. Her skin is impeccably fair, with a pretty blush to her cheeks. Her eyes are big and doe-like, so sweet, innocent, and the most beautiful shade of blue I have ever seen. They are fanned by the thickest lashes, and the arch of her brow begs to be outlined by a finger. Her lips are the closest to natural red I have ever seen on a girl. And I know it's not makeup; there isn't a stitch of it on her pretty fresh face. Her nose ... I want to press a kiss to that little nose.

What the hell am I saying? One look at this girl, and I am a puddle of mush.

My heart starts back up and everything seems to move in fast-forward for a minute. Kids are rushing to their seats; the teacher is sorting papers into piles, stapling as she goes; books and notebooks are slapped onto desks; bottoms are dropped into seats. However, me and the girl are frozen. She is still standing motionless at the door, and I'm motionless in my seat.

Our eyes meet again, taking each other in slowly. I can feel, literally *feel*, the burn of her gaze as they pass over me. Neck is burning, shoulders, arms, chest, abs, the leg that's sticking out from the side of desk. And then back up. Even my hair feels like it's being singed by her gaze. Our eyes lock again as we both remain in our position, not looking away now.

A shove to her back finally breaks her out of our locked gaze. She mumbles an apology to the ox of a guy who nudged her before he grabs her arm and pulls her to the two empty seats in the front of the room.

Of course she would have a boyfriend. An over-protective ass of one by the death glares he's aiming at me. I stare back silently, not giving anything away as I watch him face the front of the class and sit down.

I remember that back; the back of his head. Those jeans look familiar, too.

I startle as I realize he's a much bigger ass of a boyfriend than first impression. He's the guy who was fucking blondie against Chelsea's house the other night. Son of a bitch doesn't deserve someone like the angel sitting beside him.

What am I thinking? She looks like an angel, but for all I know, she could be the world's biggest bitch.

"Don't even go there," a male voice speaks from my right.

I look over to see the pothead guy from the party the other night. I look at him quizzically.

He nods his head toward the front of the class, toward *her*. "She's unavailable."

"I see that."

Pothead shakes his head. "That's not her boyfriend. She doesn't *do* boyfriends. She's too good for that. That guy … Troy … doesn't see it like that, though. She won't date him, and he won't let anyone near her. They've been friends since kindergarten. His daddy is the mayor, and her daddy is the D.A. They think their shit don't stink."

Not the impression I got, but okay.

I look back up toward the front and spot her looking at Troy, who is staring at the ceiling, tapping his pen annoyingly on his desk, before she glances back at me through the curtain of her hair. She sees me staring at her and quickly looks down, a pretty blush coloring her cheeks.

That move tugs a small grin from my lips. I unabashedly continue to stare at her, waiting for her to look up again. Within seconds, she does.

Another tug pulls at my lips, but I try to restrain it.

Our eyes lock for a few heartbeats, a slow smiling forming on both our faces.

I can't wait to see that smile directed at me every day. Senior year is starting to look better, and I thank God I didn't skip today. I don't think I will skip a day this year. I will even come to school with the flu as long as it means I get to see her beautiful face and that stunning smile and those eyes sparkling with enjoyment at our second staring impromptu.

"Claire," the big guy next to her snaps, and her attention is automatically pulled forward, away from me.

My eyes linger on her hair before I slowly look over at ox-man, who is shooting eye daggers at me. He gives me an imperceptible shake of his head while I raise an eyebrow at him in challenge.

There is no way this guy is going to scare me off from talking to her. He might have scared the rest of the male population away, but that won't happen with me. If I want to see her—and I do—then I will.

I want to make her smile. I want to hear her voice. I need to touch her skin to see if it feels as soft as it looks. I want to run my hands through her hair and curl the tips around my finger as I look into those deeply blue, deeply hypnotizing, big, round eyes.

~Claire~

I have never been attracted to anyone in my life. None. Zero. No one. I haven't even swooned over famous actors or rock stars. Just never have. I have never felt that first amazing rush when your skin tingles, electricity dancing along your skin. Such an amazing, euphoric experience. It's like you are aware of every part of yourself. You imagine you can feel the blood rushing through your veins, feel your heart stop and then speed up, faster than it ever has. A huge adrenaline rush. You can even feel every hair follicle stand up. The moment your breath hitches before you unconsciously hold it because, suddenly, butterflies flutter around in your stomach.

God, it's such an amazing feeling.

I have never felt anything like it until I walked into my first period class on the first day of my senior year, seventeen years old.

I keep an eye on Troy, who is having some words with a boy for doing some unknown discretion against him. I see Nikki down the hall, giving me a smug look like she one-upped me by having sex with Troy the other night.

When are girls going to learn I couldn't care less if he sleeps with them? He's a brother to me. My little, big brother; that is how I refer to him since he's a year younger than me yet so much taller than my five-foot-four frame. He's actually almost a whole foot taller than me.

Standing on the threshold of the classroom, waiting impatiently for Troy to finish his threats and making sure his fists don't start flying, I feel eyes on me.

I turn around to go ahead and take a seat in the front of the class where I can keep an eye on Troy when all the amazing, tingling, electric, heart-stopping, heart restarting, breath hitching, breathing stopped, eventually breathing competing with heartbeats, butterflies, raised hairs feeling overcomes me.

In the back of the room, sitting casually back in a desk chair, is the most striking person I have ever seen. Just ... striking. Brown, thick, wavy hair that any girl would kill for; dark brown, hungry bedroom eyes; a proportional nose; luscious lips; a firm, chiseled, movie star in the making jaw. Those arms, that chest, the leanness to his waist, all accentuated by his tight on the arms, loose on the waist black T-shirt.

His long legs are spread out around the desk in front of him, distinguishable inside a pair of loose-fitting jeans. He looks fit, and not in the scary, natural-testosterone filled way Troy looks. He looks fit in the runner, natural push-ups, no weight lifting, but I can still kick anyone's ass stereotypical bad boy kind of way. He is ... hypnotic.

His eyes draw me in the most. They hold so many emotions, like lust, simmering low and melting to ... wonderment? There is also appreciation and mostly surprise. I have seen lust on a guy's face, but that emotion quickly vanishes as we stare at each other.

Wonderment and surprise are a first for me when a guy sees me. Appreciation, I am well aware of that look.

I never feel embarrassed throughout this whole devour each other act. Shy, yes.

His expression looks how mine feels—star-struck.

His attractiveness lights up the room, too striking in its richness for a girl not to stare. And stare I do ... until Troy nudges me in the back a little too hard.

When I steal a look back at him, I see the most adorable smirk on his face, almost like he wants to smile but doesn't want to give one away to the rest of the room. It is a small smile for me. My smile.

The rest of class goes by excruciating slow. Between stolen glances, I feel his gaze burning a hole in my head. Throughout the entire class, I am highly aware of my body. Every movement I make is slow and concise, not wanting to make a fool of myself. Every breath I take comes out deep, since I keep forgetting to breath. I am so self-conscious. I can't concentrate on anything outside of my body. My thoughts are consumed with stolen kisses, sweet caresses, longing stares, a fantasy relationship with the boy sitting in the back.

As class dismisses, I look back again to see him still sitting there, still staring at me, with that little smirk on his face. I give him a small smile in return and am rewarded with a full-blown smile that shows perfect white teeth and one dimple on his right cheek. It leaves me breathless.

I can't help it; my smile grows even more. I don't know what has come over me. I want to giggle like a school girl, but I don't feel like one. Instead, I feel like we have known each other all our lives and are sharing a secret from the rest of the world.

I haven't even talked to the guy yet, for Pete's sake. I don't know what his voice even sounds like. I need to know.

I need to go up to him and say hi; see where it goes from there. He must be new because I have never seen him. I can ask him about that. That sounds like a good plan. However, what if he's a player? What if these stolen looks and beaming smiles is his modus operandi? He's too gorgeous. He probably knows it, too. No, I can't speak to him. His allure is already too strong.

The goal. Focus on the goal. I don't have time for relationships, or teenage drama and heartache. I don't have time to fantasize about kissing him, running my hands through his hair, and lying next to him so I can look closer into his eyes as he holds my hand.

This school year is going to be miserably long.

"Come on," Troy breaks me out of my thoughts.

I startle a bit at his intrusion, still staring at the gorgeous boy who hasn't made a move to leave, now staring at me with a confused look on his face. I realize that my smile is gone, wiped away into a frown as my thoughts darken.

I turn toward Troy to see him giving a hard look at the guy. I nudge him with my shoulder to get his attention, and then walk past him and out of the classroom. We have different classes next, and I really don't want his company right now. I prefer to stay in my own despairing thoughts, though I know it's inevitable that he will follow me.

As I make it to my classroom, which is only a couple doors away from my first period, I break out of my thoughts to realize Troy did not, in fact, follow me.

I spin around, alarmed at what he could be up to. I know he didn't miss the glances I shared with the boy. I should have been more insistent he leave with me. I know what he is capable of—using force to prove his point if threats don't sink in. And I am positive threats won't scare away the new kid. He seems too … confident.

I rush back to the first period classroom to see that my fears were correct. Troy is bent over the new guy's desk, hands gripping the edge, dangerously low to his face, most likely whispering intimidations. The new guy is sitting upright in his chair now, confidently in Troy's face. He doesn't show an ounce of fear. I see no sweat marring his brow. No shaky hands. He is either incredibly brave or stupid. I hope not the latter.

I come up behind Troy, not letting him know I am behind him. Other kids are walking into the class, eyeing the scene warily. These two guys don't seem to care or see anything else around themselves until the new guy's eyes flicker to me for a second. Then he speaks with a more raised voice.

"People aren't objects. You don't *own* her. From what I hear, you two aren't even a couple. And from what I *saw* the other night, if you really do like her, then you have a poor way of showing it by fucking some blonde up against a house." His voice is so deliciously seductive; smooth, deep, sending chills up my spine, causing my skin to break out in goose bumps. I was right about his confidence; it oozes from his voice. There is a hint of an accent there. He sounds like he's from the north, but there is something foreign about it, too.

"You don't know shit, you pussy pretty boy. As for the chick, she doesn't matter. She knows the score with me and Claire. No one else matters but her, and she knows it. My life and Claire's is none of your damn business. Stay. The fuck. Away from her, or me and you are going to have some serious issues. You feel me?"

"Nope."

As Troy's arm starts to swing back and new guy jumps to his feet with his own fist up, I decide it's time to intervene.

"Troy," I snap.

Troy's fist automatically drops to his side as he swings around to see me standing behind him.

"Claire," he whispers apologetically. "I ... I—"

"I know," I console him. "You're sorry. Always sorry." I sigh with exhaustion over his games. "Let's go." I grab his huge arm, coaxing him to follow me, and he surrenders without a backward glance.

I glance back once to see the new guy still standing where we left him and mouth, *"Sorry."*

He nods once, looking calmer than a moment ago, with his hands clenching and unclenching into fists at his sides. He tilts his head to the side as he watches me leave and gives me small, understanding smile.

So many things are spoken in my *sorry* and his smile. I'm sorry for what Troy said to him; how he threatened him. I'm sorry that Troy was right; he needs to stay away from me. His smile says he understands, but he's not giving up. His smile says he's bound and determined to ignore Troy's threats and my sorry to having to stay away from me. His smile says he won't give up until I am his.

Chapter 3

What the Hell Have You Done Now?

~Noah~

Well, this day has been ... intense.

You would think the most intense part was being threatened by an ox-man who called me, and I quote, "cock chomper." Why did he say I was a cock chomper? Because, and I quote, "I was too pretty not to want his cock shoved down my throat." The guy has some serious sexual issues to have made a comment like that. Sick fucker.

That wasn't the most intense part of my day, though. It was the connection I felt shared between me and Claire.

God, her name is as sweet as her beautiful face and her voice ... My heart stopped for the second time when her soft voice cracked through mine and Troy's inevitable fight. It was soft, even when she was trying to be harsh.

When she talked to Troy in a defeated voice after his excuse of an apology, I wanted to wrap her in my arms and protect her from the harsh world. She was the epitome of innocence. I could see it in her eyes, hear it in her voice.

Despite her innocence, there is sadness surrounding her. Something in her life isn't right. Is it Troy? Does he give her a hard time? Hurt her? Does she feel overwhelmed by him? Or is there something else? She's the district attorney's daughter. Is he hard on her, expecting more because of the low-life's he sees daily?

"Earth to Noah," Kyle calls out, interrupting my thoughts. He's sitting behind his drums, holding some of my music sheets. I was almost reluctant to show him my music, having not shared it with anyone else. However, since I am stuck here for the next ten months, I might as well make the most of it.

I adjust the strap on my guitar, flip the switch to turn the amp on, and mumble, "I'll start," before striking a chord.

Just a few chords in, and Kyle is already testing the waters, finding a beat with heavy bass to compensate not having a bassist. It sounds good deep. When the song ends, I automatically move into playing another one, lost to the music.

I don't even know how long we practice, but it's at least five songs through when I hear giggling coming from the other side of the room.

I open my eyes and barely hold back the groan and eye roll when I spot Chelsea sitting on a weight bench, making herself at home, staring at me with hungry eyes. She has a friend with her, another blonde. Nikki, I think her name is. I met her briefly at lunch today when Chelsea plopped herself onto my lap, disturbing my lunch and conversation with Kyle.

Lunch. That was another disaster. Kyle went on and on about playing gigs around town, really excited and too focused on that instead of playing for fun. I had to bite the inside of my cheek to keep myself from saying something to him. I don't want to hurt the guy's feelings.

I was moving around the food on my plate, wishing I had asked Kyle if we could go into town to grab some lunch. I didn't, though, because I hoped to catch a glimpse of Claire, which I didn't.

It was while I was lost in thought when the blonde dropped into my lap, causing me to grunt. I didn't even have to look to see who it was. I automatically shot Kyle a look that was a plea to help me out, but all he did was roll his eyes. Great, I couldn't tell if he was upset or amused. I mean, Kyle banged this chick a few nights ago, and here she was, back to flirting with me.

With that thought, I dumped her into the seat next to mine where, completely unfazed, she adjusted herself and started her clinging by gripping my bicep and running her hands through my hair.

The whole lunch hour consisted of removing her hands from me to her pressing her tits against my arm. When I turned my back on her to take a deep breath away from the stench of her perfume, she would put her claws back on me.

Meanwhile, it looked like Chelsea set her friend up with Kyle. I guess I could keep up the pretenses of a nice guy until he got laid again.

Back in the garage, I ignore the uninvited girls, used to having groupies hang out at practice back at home. Kyle, on the other hand, is having a hard time concentrating, missing the beat. This will be a serious hurdle to overcome if he aspires to play live anywhere.

Halfway through the next song, I notice Kyle never jumped in with the drums. I look back to see what he is doing, and all I see is blonde hair and two sets of legs. Nikki is straddling him and giving him a serious make-out session. Don't these girls realize they are interrupting something?

I roll my eyes, flick a pissed off look Chelsea's way, and continue to play through the song. Once I'm done, I flip off the amp and pull the guitar strap over my head.

As I make my way to the case to put the guitar down, I hear Chelsea from directly behind me say, "What are you guys up to?"

Seriously? Did she just ask that? Is she that dumb or maybe blind and deaf to not see and hear that we *were* practicing?

I want to retort with a, "What the hell does it look like?" but instead I answer, "Just playing around," with a shrug. I don't want to deal with this chick.

"You sound amazing," she coos.

Does this chick know any other adjectives? My mother would have a coronary if I ever brought her home.

"Thanks," I mutter, snapping the guitar case shut, and then stand up with the case in my hand. "Dinner should be ready, and my aunt doesn't like for us to be late, so ..." *You can leave now.*

I walk past her, but she grabs my arm with a light laugh. "Are you shy or something, Noah? You don't have to be shy around me. I'm a sure thing when it comes to you. And I will make you feel *so* good."

I can't help myself. "I'm sure you would. All I have to do is ask Kyle or any other guy in town." With that, I walk out of the garage, not even bothering to see the look on Chelsea's face. I can imagine, though, after the way she let go of my arm so fast and took a step back.

Poor Kyle; he won't be getting any from Nikki.

I walk through the back door and into the kitchen, taking a huge whiff of the delicious smell coming out of the oven. Aunt Katy is at the stove, stirring something in a pot. She turns around when she hears the door shut and gives me a warm smile.

"Pot roast?" I ask.

She smiles. "Yep."

"My favorite." I grin back at her.

Kyle takes after Aunt Katy with their light brown hair and slim figures. However, Kyle has my family's dark eyes, whereas Aunt Katy has light hazel eyes.

"NO-IE!" Abby, my three-year-old cousin, squeals as she comes barreling into the kitchen. She races toward me as fast as her little legs can, and I quickly pick her up before she crashes into me.

"AB-BY!" I cry out the same way she does.

She giggles as I start to throw her into the air. She's so cute with her ringlets of brown hair; her chubby little cheeks; and those big, innocent brown eyes. I call her my little birth twin since we share the same birthday. She was so excited to find out we were going to celebrate together this year, telling me she was going to be the princess and I was to be her white horse. Yeah, that's not going to happen.

"Down, pweeze, down." She lets out a cross between a laugh and a cry when I throw her up one more time, catching her before she hits the ground.

As soon as she's on her feet, she scurries back into the living room to return to her favorite doll, clutching the ragged-looking thing to her chest. Cutest little girl ever.

"You're so good with her." Aunt Katy says as she walks past me, carrying a few trays.

I shrug. "Can't help it. She's too darn cute."

She smiles at that. "Will you go get Kyle and tell him dinner is ready?"

I cringe, and she notices, giving me a questioning look.

"I'd rather not?" I try to say gently, and it comes out as a question.

She puts her hands on her hips, which looks funny because she put oven mitts on to take the roast out. "Why not?"

Shit. How do I answer that?

I give her a shy smile, one that I know makes the girls back home melt. "Um, well, you see ..."

"Spit it out, Noah. Are you two fighting already? Dear Lord, the fights you two got into when you were little. Neither of you wanted anything to do with the other. I never understood it."

I don't remember what she's talking about, so I just shrug. "No fighting," I promise. "He, uh ... Some people stopped by, and I don't want to talk to them. I don't like being rude; it's just that this one girl gets on my last fuc—ever loving nerve. If I go out there, she will—"

"I get it, Noah. And watch your mouth." She looks thoughtful for a minute before a mischievous grin creeps up. "Do you think I should go out there?"

Aunt Katy is always thinking of ways to humiliate Kyle. She's fun and loves a practical joke, but this one might backfire on her. If she goes out there, there is no telling what she will walk in on. I don't want to subject my aunt to that.

I blanch before recovering. "I think we should let him eat a cold dinner."

Katy nods. "That's probably the wiser decision. Mark isn't going to be too happy about it, though. He likes to discuss school. You know, he's like your dad when it comes to history." She turns around and finally retrieves the roast from the oven.

Don't I ever know. Mom and Dad only *ever* talk about that. Unlike my parents, Mark is a software engineer. He likes history, especially battles and wars.

"Well, I guess it's a good thing I'm here. I can distract him with the Peloponnesian war."

Aunt Katy laughs then calls the family, sans Kyle, to the table for dinner.

~Claire~

"You missed the high C at the end," Troy snaps once Signora Gelardi hits the last key on the piano.

Really? What does Troy know about music?

27

I sulk, shooting him a death glare before turning a questioning look at Signora Gelardi.

"He's right. You're not here today. Your brain seems scattered, and you're not focusing on the music."

I sigh and nod in understanding, hating that she agrees with Troy. She never agrees with him. In fact, she hates him and has told me several times to not allow him in practices. Though I tell Troy he's not welcome here, he doesn't listen. He thinks he's being supportive and that extra criticism is good for me. I disagree. You can only beat someone down so much before they snap. And today, I want to snap.

Troy has been a jerk all day, ever since his run in with Noah—I learned his name from Troy. Apparently, Troy cornered Chelsea and demanded to know who he was and where he came from. This knowledge was imparted to me at lunch, where Troy spent the hour staring daggers at the back of the guy's head while mumbling profanities under his breath.

I tried to calm him down, but he wasn't having it. His swearing grew worse when Chelsea and Nikki came to their table, and Chelsea sat on Noah's lap like she belonged there. I smiled when I saw Noah immediately drop her into the chair next to him and brush off every advance she gave. Chelsea couldn't take a hint, though, and that made me see red.

When her hand slipped under the table and up his thigh, I thought I would jump out of my seat and … I don't know what I would have done to her, but it wouldn't have been nice. However, Noah none too gently threw her hand from his lap had me calming down.

"That's because her thoughts are on some new kid at school," Troy snipes, giving me a scornful look.

How dare he!

"Troy, you need to leave *now*." I am seething, hands clenched into little fists as I stand on the stage of the school auditorium, looking down at Troy's now heartbroken face.

"I want to look out for you—"

"Leave. Now," I say deceptively calm.

I can't deal with him right now. I can't deal with the drama. They are right, and I am wrong, and I can't deal with it. I need to get Noah out of my head, and I need to clear the air of the drama it's causing. Troy staying here doesn't help matters.

"I'll call you later, okay?" I try to relieve the heartbroken look on his face. The guy is a huge bully, but when it comes to me, he has such a sensitive heart.

Troy nods, and then I watch him leave.

Breathing a sigh of relief, I turn my attention to Signora Gelardi.

She's looking at me thoughtfully. "Is he right? Are you losing your passion? Is your passion turning toward something else? You can't have both. You know the mistakes I made. Don't follow my lead on this." She shakes her head dejectedly, like she already knows the answer.

"No, of course not. I don't even know the guy." I take a deep breath and close my eyes. His face flashes through my vision. "Troy is jealous because he saw the two of us looking at each other. I mean, he's the new kid in school; everyone notices something like that. He shouldn't care that I noticed, too."

Signora Gelardi continues to shake her head. "No. I see what Troy sees. You're wistful just talking about him. You blush." She stands up from behind the piano and comes over to stand in front of me, staring right into my eyes. "I'm sorry to have to agree with your friend, but I think this boy is going to be a distraction for you. If you treasure my advice, as you say you do, then stay away from him. That's all I can say."

~

I get home later than usual after going back over the songs I messed up earlier in practice. Signora Gelardi was right. After I determinedly got Noah out of my head, my singing was back. I hated that also meant Troy was right.

I groan out loud at that thought as I walk through the empty house and into the kitchen, feeling a bit miffed at more than them being right. My dad isn't home yet, which really bothers me because I'm home late and it's already past eight o'clock.

I consider calling him, but if he's working this late, that means he is extremely busy and a call from me will hold him up that much longer.

I sigh as I open the refrigerator and pull out the leftover chicken parmesan, throwing a clump of it into a bowl before reheating it in the microwave.

As I wait for the food to heat, I look back over the pamphlets the Manhattan School of Music sent with my acceptance letter.

I can't wait to be there. To be on my own. To be able to perform.

Being on stage has been a fantasy of mine ever since I was four years old, performing in my first ballet recital, before I discovered my voice.

I can thank Signora Gelardi for finding me. She picked me right out of the crowd of elementary students and has encouraged my singing ever since. She found opportunities and competitions in all the surrounding states for me to participate in, and I loved every minute of it. The feel of all eyes on me, my voice echoing throughout the room, filling others' hearts, moving people to tears or smiles. It's a euphoric experience, a high I can never get enough of.

My food reheated, I sit alone at the table to eat. My thoughts start to wander to my mother, wondering what it would be like if she was here when I got home. I can only imagine the woman I have grown to look like would be in the kitchen, keeping the food warm for me and Dad. Maybe, if she was still around, Dad would make a better effort to want to hurry home.

That thought always depresses me, like I'm not good enough. I know that's not it, though. Dad loves me with his whole heart. It's coming home to the memories Mom left behind when she ran off with my dad's college roommate right after I was born that hurts him.

You would think that a mother couldn't abandon her newborn child. You would think a mother would want to know her little baby. You would think a mother would want to see how her baby grows up; get to know her. You would think wrong.

Almost eighteen years later, and not one little word from my mother. We don't even know where she lives—nothing. It hurts, but I think it would hurt more if she one day decided to show back up. I would rather think my mother died than imagine her living with a new family of her own.

I shove my half-eaten plate away from me, suddenly feeling too tired to eat anymore.

I go through the motions of cleaning up before heading to my room, but when I'm halfway up the stairs, the doorbell rings.

I moan in exhaustion, wondering who is here at nine o'clock at night.

Opening the door, I'm not surprised to see Troy standing there. Though I am surprised to see that he looks drunk … again.

Leaning against the doorframe, his head down and shoulders slumped over, almost taking up the whole doorway, his jeans and T-shirt look more disheveled than they did the last time I saw him, which was only a few hours ago.

I stand in the entry with my arms folded over my chest, glaring at him. "What do you need, Troy?"

"Can I come in?" He finally looks up at me with bloodshot eyes, reeking of alcohol.

I sigh and drop my arms, swinging the door open wider to accommodate his size.

He walks in with his head back down, staggering a bit. I ignore him and walk past him to the living room. I feel him follow me as I sit in the chair, forgoing the couch in case he needs to lie down for a while—more like pass out. Dad is going to kill him when he gets home.

"I can't believe you drove like this. What has gotten into you lately? Sit down and talk to me."

He's still standing, now next to me, staring at the couch. He looks from the couch to me and back again before his eyes rest on mine, and he holds his hand out to me. "Sit with me, please."

I stop myself from rolling my eyes, holding his hand as he pulls me up and walks me to the couch. I don't want to do this right now. I want to go to bed.

We sit on the couch together with him still holding my hand, which isn't unusual, but right now, I have a bad feeling, and with him pestering me the other night about being together, I don't think holding hands is an option right now.

I pull my hand out of his, and to make the blow gentle, I pull my hair up into a bun on top of my head.

"You're so beautiful like that." Troy smiles shyly at me, touching a few escaped tendrils along my cheek. I again refrain from rolling my eyes.

"What do you want, Troy? I want to get you home before my dad shows up and sees you like this. And I want to go to bed. You really stressed me out today, you know. I wish—"

My words are cut off when Troy lunges at me, pinning me to the couch with his huge body. His mouth is pressed hard against mine, not moving, just pushing my head into the couch cushions forcefully. I'm completely thrown off by this, not able to move for a minute.

When realization hits me, I'm mortified. I do not want my first kiss to be by him. I keep thinking that, if I kiss him, I'm kissing everyone at school. He recently had sex with Nikki, who had sex with half the football team, meaning I'm kissing Nikki, meaning I'm kissing half the football team, who have slept with numerous other kids at school, meaning everyone has slept together. I don't like that one bit. I don't like the knowledge that everyone is connected in this way and that makes me now connected to all of them.

I shove against Troy's shoulders as I feel his mouth begin to move, his tongue slipping out of his mouth as his lips part. I struggle against him, wanting to yell but too afraid to open my mouth and have his tongue enter.

I mumble incoherently, practically screaming as I struggle to get out from underneath him. He grabs both of my hands, pinning them above my head as his hips hold me in place, his erection digging into that part of me that no one has touched. I am frantic now, not wanting to feel him against me that way. It feels so dirty, so wrong. I am in no way attracted to Troy. He feels like a perverted relative right now.

Tears start coursing down my cheeks as I try bucking him off, instigating a groan of pleasure from him. Oh, God.

He trails his lips away from mine—thank God—and starts licking and nipping his way down my neck. I take the advantage and start to yell at him.

"Troy, get off me! I don't want this! Can't you see you are scaring me?"

"It's okay, baby," he starts to coo against my neck. "This is the way we're meant to be. You'll see. You'll enjoy it, and then you'll know we're meant to be. I love you so much, Claire. Pretty Claire ..." His voice trails off as he starts to suck on my neck. It hurts. Oh, God, it hurts.

I start screaming so loud my throat burns. He now has both my hands pinned above my head with one hand, his hips still holding me down, while his free hand starts to grope my breast, massaging it through my shirt.

I feel so dirty. I hate this. I hate *him*!

"Stop! Please, please stop! You're going to regret this, and I'll never speak to you again. I hate you! I hate you! Get *off* me! Dad! Daddy, please help me! *Somebody*!" I screech, my voice breaking as he starts to slide his hand down my waist.

"Come on, Claire," he breathes against my mouth, his breath rancid with alcohol. "Stop being so dramatic. Calm down. Relax. You'll love it, but you have to relax for me, baby." His hand now drifts lower as he raises his hips to allow his hand to get closer to my mound.

Oh, no! No, no, nonononononono!

I scream as loud as I can, desperate. He releases my hand and covers my mouth as his other hand starts massaging me down there. I claw at his face, his head, pulling his hair out, beating my fists against his back. I continue to strike out at him any way I can, but it doesn't affect him as he continues to touch me, moaning like my hits are giving him pleasure.

I can feel snot dripping out of my nose as tears continue to pour out of my eyes. I'm still screaming my voice out behind his hand. I'm so scared. This isn't the Troy I know.

Suddenly, thankfully, mercifully, Troy is thrown off me. I see him fly over the back of the couch, causing the couch to tilt backward before it settles back down. I crab crawl backward until I hit the arm of the couch where I curl up in a ball and continue to cry.

My dad is home! My savior.

He's standing over Troy as the jerk incoherently mumbles apologies. He stays lying on the floor, groveling at my dad's feet, telling him sorry repeatedly. My dad ignores him, his phone already against his ear, already connecting with Troy's father.

"Come get your son *now*." My dad's voice is deathly calm. I have never seen him like this. He sounds calm, his face looks calm, but his whole body is trembling.

He never takes his eyes off Troy as he stands over him, telling him, "You, stay on that floor. Don't move an inch. Do you understand me, boy? I will throw your ass in juvie so quick if you defy me. You come near my daughter again, you're gone. *Do you understand*!" he roars, and I flinch. I have never seen my dad lose control.

"Y-y-yes, sir. I'm sorry, sir. So sorry." Troy turns toward me. "I'm so sorry, Claire. I wasn't going to do anything. I swear. I just—"

"Shut up! Don't talk to her. Don't look at her. Just stay on that damn floor and shut up until your dad gets here!"

My dad turns to me then. I'm sure I look a hot mess because his angered look turns to one of complete sadness. He looks so lost, so scared when he sees me.

He doesn't spare another glance at Troy as he comes to me, dropping to his knees in front of me and pulling me into his embrace.

"Daddy," I choke out as I cling to him, my sobs choking me as I bury my face in my daddy's neck.

He starts to shush me, caressing my hair that has come undone and is now tangled down my back. Then he pulls back and looks me over, probably assessing for how far Troy went.

I shake my head at him. "He didn't do anything, Daddy. You got here before—" I choke on another sob, thinking about what Troy, my best and only friend, tried to do to me.

He is so sick. Why couldn't I see that? Why did I refuse to see all the signs? Why did I continue to be friends with him, knowing all the problems he had? He could have seriously hurt me. He could have knocked me out and had his way with me. All the "could have" scenarios run through my head and my sobs renew.

"Oh, God, Daddy. I was so scared," I hiccup the words out.

My dad continues to sooth me until we hear, "What the hell have you done now?"

The mayor is here.

Dad gently pushes me back against the couch, looking me

directly in the eyes when he says, "Stay here, sweetheart. I'm going to talk to Mr. Couer outside. I'll be back soon, okay?"

I nod then watch the three men walk out the door, Troy in front of them with his head down, his dad breathing down his neck, as my dad stoically walks them out the front door, turning back once to look at me.

Chapter 4

Is He Asking Me Out?

~Noah~

Kyle and I have been rehearsing my songs for two weeks now. We finally found a bassist, too. Well, Kyle did, since I don't know anyone around here. She's an older chick who graduated a few years ago named Cynthia, but she likes to go by Cyn. She's a cool chick, and I would totally dig her except for her bleach blonde hair and her huge biker boyfriend, Max, who works at a tattoo shop in the next town over. Now, that guy is scary and makes Troy look like a little kid.

Max is a tank with his shaved head, body covered in tattoos, and eyes that look black and soulless. I hung out with him and Cyn this last weekend; had him ink in a tat I have had outlined on my side forever.

More news is that we got a gig. I can't fathom this town having a place that would welcome a band. It's too kosher here, too clean. Yet, somehow there is a bar here, that has a stage, that signs on high school kids. Well, the bar is a restaurant, albeit a very small restaurant. So, yeah, our first gig is tonight.

Chelsea finally took a hint and has been latching on to Troy. These kids really get around. To say that Kyle got a chance with Nikki would be a lie.

I'm now walking into the lunch room after running home for some leftover enchiladas. Going home also gives me a chance to make another cup of coffee to get me through the rest of the day, and I get Abby off Katy's back for half an hour.

The bell still has five minutes left when I sit down next to Kyle, who is talking to his friends. He's psyched out over the gig tonight, telling everyone about the songs. He's even gotten a couple of girls latching on to every word he says. Well, until I sit down. Now they are trying to get me to talk about it, but I have nothing to say.

I swing my attention away from the table and scope out the cafeteria scene. Turns out, the chick I'm obsessing over, Claire, is in our lunch hour, but she has been MIA for the past couple of weeks. Apparently, she and asshole Troy had a huge falling out. Rumor has it—and this town is all about their rumors—Troy's dad, Mr. Mayor, was called out to her home to escort his drunkass son home after Mr. D.A., aka Claire's dad, had a few choice words about Mr. Mayor's son, telling the mayor to keep his son away from his daughter or charges will be filed. It makes me curious to know what happened and if the rumors are even true. Per a nosy neighbor who heard screams coming from their house before Mr. D.A. showed up, they are.

I swear, if that asshole touched her, I will kill him. She's too innocent to be defiled by a sick shit like him. And I know she hasn't. She still has that beautiful innocent look in her eyes. Plus, she stands up to him. A woman hurt by a man in such a way would not be able to hold herself up the way she does.

In first period, they ignore each other. Well, Claire ignores him. The day after "the incident," he tried to sit next to her, and she just shook her head at him. The shit lowered his head like a wounded puppy and made his way across the room from her. And that's where they have been sitting every day since.

While in her presence, he continues to look at her with longing, trying to get pity out of her. The moment she is no longer in the room, though, he is a completely different person: flirting with the girls and laughing with his buddies like he doesn't have a care in the world. I wish Claire could see him in his element.

Claire and I have still been playing flirty eyes. Neither one of us has approached the other; we haven't talked. Despite that, I can't help staring at her. I'm drawn to her in a way I have never been drawn to a female before. At the same time, I don't know how to approach her.

It's been two weeks of innocent looks, and I feel like I lost my window. I should have gone up to her the next day; maybe asked her if she was all right after the Troy incident. But, I couldn't. I didn't want to embarrass her by bringing it up, and now too much time has gone by. Furthermore, I have never come on to a girl like her.

She's so much more than anyone I have met. Besides, I don't want her to lose that innocence in her eyes. I don't want to take that away from her. I want to cherish her. I want to protect her, hold her, simply kiss those pouty lips. I don't want to show her any ugliness. I don't want her to see any ugliness. Just beauty.

God, I can't believe my thoughts when I think about her.

The bell suddenly rings, and I find myself steered through the halls by Kyle's friends. I back myself out of their clique and lean against one of the walls at the corner of two hallways. This is where I stand every day, waiting to see Claire come out of the library she's been hiding in during lunch.

I sip my coffee out of the new thermos I bought myself a couple weeks ago. It's still hot, the bitter taste awakening me. I stare at the library door, burning a hole in it until I see it open and brown, waist-length hair backs out of it. She's holding the door open for the librarian who is pushing a cart out. God, she's so special.

I watch the two of them say a few words to each other and smile before Claire closes the door. Then her gaze touches mine when she finally turns around to head toward her next class. The moment freezes for me when she gives me a smile that touches her eyes. We have been at this game for the past week. Yeah, I'm a stalker, but what else is there to do in this small town?

I take another sip of my coffee, hiding a grin behind my cup. I know she sees it when her own grin grows. Then, the magic of the moment is over when she turns the opposite corner and is gone from my sight.

"Noah, you have got to be kidding me," my cousin's voice pulls my attention to him.

I just stare at Kyle to get to the point.

"You can't go there, man. The last guy to do it was sent to the emergency room. I'm warning you; don't mess with that girl. It's like a rule in this school: Claire Sawyer is off limits. It's rule number sixty in the student handbook." He nods his head like it's a fact.

"I've heard the warnings." I shrug. "Not in my handbook.

Besides, I haven't even spoken to her. I ..." I let my words drift off. I don't want to talk to Kyle about this, about what I feel for a girl I haven't even spoken to.

"I know, man." Kyle bobs his head as if he knows what I was going to say, like he feels the same things I do, which he can't. No way. If he did, he wouldn't be flirting with so many other girls.

"She's like the chocolate golden egg and all the other girls are a dud, sent to the furnace," he continues.

"Don't compare me to Veruca Salt. I don't have to have it now, just ..." I sigh. I can't believe I'm talking to my cousin about this, and in *Willy Wonka* comparisons. "... someday."

Kyle gives me a studious look, his eyebrows pulled together. "You're gone. Done for." He suddenly throws his head back and starts laughing. It sounds like a hyena—I hate those ugly things. "I can't believe"—he gasps for breath—"you of all people are falling in love."

Asshole.

I turn away from him and quickly walk down the hall, disappearing into my classroom. I can't believe the one time I open myself up, I get joked on. I should prove a point to him not to be such a jerk by not showing up to tonight's show, but I can't let down Cyn. I need to think of some other way to humiliate Kyle. Jerk needs to learn not to piss off a city boy.

~

I called Cyn and asked her to find some embarrassing drumsticks. When Kyle isn't looking, I swipe his drumsticks from his case so he shows up to the gig empty-handed and has to use whatever embarrassing sticks Cyn finds. The girl loves a good practical joke and even texted me a picture earlier, showcasing her find.

How about these? the text says with a picture of pink leopard-print sticks.

I laugh out loud as I text back, *Perfect. Thanx.* I can't believe she found something like that.

"What's so funny?" Kyle asks as he gets out of his mom's truck, the only vehicle that will fit his drum kit.

I climb off my bike and stick my phone into my back pocket. "Nothin'. Just Cyn."

Kyle laughs. "I like that chick. She's crazy. The shit that comes out of her mouth ..." He shakes his head.

Cyn is crazy cool. She's hilarious at practice, even making me laugh, something I don't do much around people. And she's a good buffer from groupies. A girl shows up uninvited, which they all are, and Cyn picks up the leaf blower and chases them away. Blows them away, as she puts it.

I really love that girl already. I wish I could take her away to the city with me when I go back, but I'm sure that would offend my bassist there. Maybe the band won't even be together when I get back. Only time will tell.

Cyn would fit in perfectly. She has that no-nonsense attitude and can hold her own with the best of them. Plus, with Max next to her, yeah, they would fit in perfectly.

Me and Kyle start taking his drums into the bar—I mean, restaurant. Setting them up is such a pain in the ass, but we do it in less than thirty minutes. That's when Kyle starts freaking out.

I maintain control of my features as Kyle starts going through his bags, looking for his sticks.

"Oh, man. Oh, hell no. Please don't tell me—shit. Noah, man, I forgot my sticks. Shit! It's going to take me half an hour to get back home and back here."

"No worries, Kyle. I have an extra set you can borrow," Cyn says with a wink in my direction as she walks up with her bass already strapped across her chest. "We go on in ten. We don't have time for you to drive across town and back. You'll have to deal with these. They're my favorites, so be gentle with them." She hands Kyle the pink leopard-print drumsticks.

He looks at them with a horrified expression, not reaching out to grab them.

I can't help it. A laugh bubbles out of me before I can stop it.

Kyle looks at me like I have lost my mind.

Cyn starts to laugh along with me, while Kyle's face turns red, even his ears. He's fuming.

"Fuckin' asshole." He grabs the offending drumsticks then turns away from us to hide behind his drum kit where I'm sure he's hoping no one will see his newly acquired sticks.

"Thanks, Cyn," I say, trying to quiet down my laughter. "That was great."

Cyn shrugs, smiling at me with the biggest grin ever stretched across her little face. "That was totally classic. Did you see the look on his face? Oh, my God, we should do that more often. What did he do to piss you off, anyway?"

I drop my head and shake it. "Nothin'. Just doesn't know when to shut up."

I drop down to my knees, pulling my guitar out of its case. My baby. My cherry red, Gibson Les Paul, the best that money can buy. She's my red-headed slut. I love to finger her, and she loves to be fingered by me. No woman can compare to my redhead.

I attach the strap before walking to the front of the stage. The place is packed. No doubt the owner doesn't like the fact that there are a lot of high school kids here, but he can't complain when I see a lot of them have food in front of them or sodas in their hands in cocktail cups, like they look more grownup drinking their diet colas from Long Island glasses.

Max is here, sitting in the corner booth close to the stage with a table of his friends all decked out with their tattoos. I nod my head to him as I turn on my guitar, and then turn on the mic.

Kyle and Cyn decided we *had* to have a name for our band. Kyle wanted School Victims, but I shot that down, telling him it was too macabre. With all the school shooting these days, heaven forbid we have one at our school, and then are blamed for instigating it by our music. We settled for Cyn's choice: Characters. It was simple, wouldn't piss anyone off, and definitely defined the three of us since we all have different personalities.

I step up to the mic and say, "We're Characters. Thanks for coming out to see us." Then I strum the first chord, and we jam away.

The crowd eats it up, though it's hard to tell if they like us, or if they are excited that something new came to their small town. Older couples continue to drink their alcoholic beverages and communicate with each other while bobbing their heads to the beat. The younger crowd stands around or sits on the small stools at the circular tables placed in the middle of the room. A group of girls from our school start moving toward the stage and dance provocatively with each other, Nikki and Chelsea being two of them.

I look over at Cyn and roll my eyes. Just the other day she chased Nikki out of Kyle's garage, so she is well-acquainted with her.

Cyn shakes her head and mouths, *"How do you do it?"* I know what she's saying. How do I put up with it?

I shrug at her and continue singing through the first song.

Once the final chord is struck and the sound rings out, continuing until it grows faint and is overtaken by the cheers and clapping that follow, I don't miss a beat, I don't soak up the attention, I hit the notes that start up the next song, only allowing a few seconds of cheers before I begin another song.

We play eight more songs; three are our own and five are cover songs that blend well with my music style. We only have five songs total that are complete, so we need to work on some more if we get more gigs.

Once the set is over, I thank everyone for coming then grab a towel off the amp to wipe the sweat off my forehead and neck. Stage lighting is always hot, add to that the number of bodies in this small bar/restaurant, and I'm a sweaty mess. I can't wait to get on my bike and feel the cool air against my damp skin.

I reach toward the edge of the small stage to grab my water bottle, but Chelsea snatches it up before I can. I watch as she opens the bottle and slips her tongue under the lip before swallowing a gulp.

Ignoring her, I turn around to see Cyn holding out a new, cold bottle of water for me.

"Thanks," I tell her before spinning off the lid and chugging down a few gulps.

Cyn looks over my shoulder and shoots death glares at, I'm assuming, Chelsea. "That girl doesn't give up, does she?"

"Nope." I pull off my baby and lay her gently in the case, rubbing a resin cloth over the freshly made prints on her body. Once she's clean, I close the case and pull the strap over my head.

"Come here. Play along," Cyn says before wrapping her arm under my shoulders so I'm forced to move my arm over hers. She walks us toward Max's table, and I feel her place her hand in my back pocket where she grabs my ass.

Max lifts his eyebrows at Cyn.

"I'm keeping the horny groupies away," she explains, nodding back at the swarm of girls.

"I'm going to help Kyle tear down, and then talk to the manager," I tell Cyn, pulling out of her hold. Then I shake Max's hand and promise him I will be back when he says he wants to introduce me to his buddies.

Kyle and I take a shorter amount of time tearing down than we did setting up. While we are taking the kit apart, the manager comes over to us, shakes our hands, and then asks if we can make this a weekly gig. Of course, Kyle is all over it.

I call Cyn over, and she shrugs and says, "Sure." Then we make our way to the manager's office and sign a contract. Every Friday night, we will play here.

~Claire~

These past two weeks have been bad for me. I'm completely alone now, but I won't give in to Troy's pouts. I see how he is when he thinks I'm not around. I see him flirting like he hasn't a care in the world. Why he pretends with me, I have no idea. I don't get why he acts.

Why can't people be themselves one hundred percent of the time? Why act one way around certain people, then an entirely different way around others? It doesn't make sense to me. Be one way or the other. Don't act. It's all an act. Everyone in this school is putting on an act, and that's why I don't associate with any of them.

Well, everyone, but Noah. He doesn't seem to pretend with anyone. I watch him. He's not much of a talker; he doesn't put up with crap from anyone—I knew that from the first day. He seems real. It makes me wonder how he acts at home. Is he still broody, never smiling? Or does he smile more around familiar people?

I know where he's from. I know he's here to stay with his uncle's family. The Gish's are a nice family. I don't know about Kyle, though he seems like he wants to be like all the others at school.

Noah is just different in my opinion.

And now there is talk around school about what an amazing guitarist he is. How his singing is so soulful. The girls have been gushing nonstop about the performance his band played Friday night. Apparently, a band he put together with his cousin and some hot, older girl. Is she his girlfriend? I shouldn't care, but I do, and so does every other girl in this school. Evidently, he was seen holding the girl after the show and left with her.

Why do I want to cry at this knowledge? This isn't me. I don't want things like boyfriends, relationships, teenage drama. I have dreams, ambitions outside of this little town. I want to perform in the opera. I want to sing onstage and bring emotions out of people with just my voice. This … This *crush* is not me. I can't want that, not after working for so long and now having everything I want at my fingertips. Noah is simply a blip on my radar that will pass quickly. Blip, blip, blip, and then he will be gone.

"Did you see his abs when his shirt lifted up?" a girl at the table next to mine starts fanning herself dramatically. I know for a fact the two girls gossiping are supposed to be researching their science lab and not talking about the elusive Noah Gish.

I have my head in a book, studying for a test in my next class. The library is where I spend most of my lunch these days. I don't have anyone to sit with in the cafeteria, and I want to avoid Troy at all cost.

Despite their angst against getting their work done, I hope they don't stop talking. I can't help soaking up any piece of Noah I can learn.

"God, he's so yummy. I wanted to lick the sweat off him. And the way his wet hair fell into his eyes while he played …" the other girl sighs, and then the two of them giggle quietly while looking around to make sure their teacher didn't notice.

"He'll probably win homecoming king and prom king," the first girl says, and then they both nod in agreement.

I want to snort. Noah doesn't look like one to care for the school's courts. He probably won't even show up to the dances. Well, that's what I can make of him in the small amount of time I have observed him.

"Too bad he has a girlfriend."

"Yeah, and she's older."

"She's probably in college."

"I didn't notice her drink, though. Maybe she's not that much older."

"How old do you think Noah is?"

Girl number one grins widely. "I heard from Casey, who heard from Stephanie, that Chelsea Winds was telling Nikki Corry that she got a glimpse of his transcripts. He's eighteen."

Freshman two questions, "How did she see his transcripts?"

"She volunteered to run the front desk during study hall."

Of course Chelsea would do something like that. That girl knows no boundaries.

"She is so smart. I wish I had study hall so I could get a peek at his transcripts. I bet he's been expelled from schools for drug trafficking!"

I want to snort again, although I wouldn't be surprised to learn something like that from him. He's so quiet. He seems like he may have something to hide.

Just then, the bell rings, breaking up the girls' conversation. Their teacher starts calling out their homework assignment as I gather my own belongings before heading out of the library where I know Noah will be waiting, watching me.

I know I keep telling myself not to like him, that I don't have time for relationships, but I can't help liking—no, loving—the attention. No one else has ever made me feel this way. When other boys asked me out—or tried to before Troy got to them—I never felt a thrill like I do just knowing Noah watches me, giving me his shy, little grin.

For a guy who supposedly has a girlfriend, not to mention the attention, even seemingly unwanted, of every girl in this school, his shy smile tells me this connection, or whatever it is between us, is as new to him as it is to me.

I walk out of the library and there he is, like he has been for over a week now, looking gorgeous in his worn jeans; tight T-shirt hugging his arms, his chest, stopping right below his belt. I bet if he stretched

45

his arms up, I would see those abs that the freshmen girls were talking about. Yeah, he does fit the rocker role very well. I wish I could hear his voice. I bet it's deep and raspy when he sings.

Also in the hallway, not too discreetly making out, is Troy and Nikki. This is not the first time I have seen him like this, but it is the first time so blaringly out in the open. It makes me wonder if he's tired of acting like the wounded puppy around me. I want to say good riddance, but years of friendship does make me sad and grieve a bit for what we did have.

Just thinking about what he wanted and picturing me in Nikki's place disgusts me to no end. Remembering his hands on me, pinning me down to the couch, not taking no for an answer causes nausea to bubble in my tummy. Yeah, good riddance.

Then I belatedly realize I must pass them to get to my next class.

I turn away from their public display of affection to look back at Noah who is now also watching the couple make out. He's wearing a stony look on his face, like he doesn't like what he sees. Does he like Nikki? Were they previously together and now he feels scorned? No, that can't be it. I have only ever seen Chelsea throw herself at him. Nikki was used to distract his cousin. I have seen their act too many times. Then what has Noah looking at them with such malice?

And cue in Chelsea, hair swaying back and forth as I'm sure her butt is doing the same in front of Noah, trying to gain his attention yet again while he is still looking scornfully at Troy and Nikki.

Chelsea's holding her books in front of her, pressing them tight against her breasts so they push out of the top of her shirt as she comes right up to me, something she hasn't done in a very long time.

"Claire, how have you been?" she asks a little too sweetly with a smile on her face and an evil glint in her eye.

"I'm fine. What do you want, Chelsea?" I really do try to be pleasant with her, considering we grew up in the same neighborhood and her family has been to holiday parties at my house for years, but really, it's so hard when this girl bleeds out so much hate toward me.

"I just wanted to gloat," she admits with that smile growing in delight.

"Gloat about what?" I start to walk toward my next class, keeping to the opposite wall of the groping couple.

"The fact that you are all alone now. Your one last friend has left you because you're a cold, frigid bitch," she sneers, her smile leaving her face, as she keeps up with me. "I hope you learn to warm up. Otherwise, you'll remain alone when you go to your fancy school, and Daddy isn't there to—"

"Back off, Chelsea," *that* deep voice comes from behind us.

"Noah. Hey, baby. I was just having—"

"Girl talk? Or fun taunting people who are superior to you so you feel the need to bring them down so you can feel better about yourself?" He stares at her like she's the most despicable thing he has ever seen. It kind of frightens me.

I don't know why I don't walk away. Instead, I'm frozen as a small crowd of stragglers slow their walk, wanting to catch a glimpse of the altercation.

"No!" Chelsea's eyes widen in shock that he would call her out.

"Then what? Tell me what you were telling her," he demands, taking a menacing step toward her.

This is so much different from what Troy did do to guys who tried to talk to me. For one, he never looked attractive when he scared boys away; he angered me. Two, Troy never intimidated girls; he excused their taunts. Having someone who doesn't even know me stick up for me humbles me, so I remain where I am, wanting to see where this is going. I also want to stick around to thank him; finally talk to him.

"We were talking about the homecoming dance. You know, who we want to—"

He puts his hands up, effectively cutting her off, before glancing at me, his face softening. Then he once again turns those dark, angry eyes on her. "What does saying 'you're a cold, frigid bitch' have anything to do with that?" He shakes his head. "You know what? It doesn't matter. I've wasted enough words on you. Don't speak to her again. Don't speak to me again. Don't even look at us. And spread the word to the rest of your asshole friends." He looks her over like she's the most revolting thing in the world.

I am quailing inside at the mention of *us* as Chelsea spins around and starts tromping the other way as dramatically as she can. Now I have a chance to talk to him, and I'm going to take it—I look up at wall clock—for the next two minutes I can.

"Thank you," I tell Noah as everyone starts making their way back to class. He never takes his eyes off mine, and it's a bit intimidating. "She's always been like that. I ignore her. I know they aren't true"—I shrug—"so it doesn't bother me. But thank you, anyway. No one has—yeah, thanks." I walk past him, feeling extremely childish for rambling one minute then not being able to put two words together the next. Real mature.

"Wait. I've ..." His hand shoots out, and he gently grabs my upper arm, his fingers rough and callused. Warmth seeps into my skin at the contact.

He laughs and shakes his head at himself as I turn back toward him, watching him in confusion.

Why is he laughing? And wow, he has a nice laugh. Throaty. And his smile ... A real smile. I'm gone. I'm gone, and it's all because of a high school boy. Crap, this interaction is going to take even more of my focus away. I should have run the moment he called Chelsea out.

"My band has a gig on Friday nights at Jeremy's, the restaurant. You should come sometime."

My mind goes through a jumble of thoughts. Doesn't he have a girlfriend? Is he asking me out? Is he just being nice because of the Chelsea incident? No, I'm certain that's not it. What's going on here? Does he feel the connection I do?

Sometime between his laugh, my thoughts, and him telling me about his gig, he runs his hand down my arm until he is holding my fingers gently, causing goose bumps to cover my arms.

I'm having a difficult time breathing, gulping in air as I nod my head a few times. "Yeah, I've heard. Congratulations. It's not my scene, but maybe I'll stop by. Sometime ..." I sound like an idiot, my sentences choppy.

A smile like none I have seen on him lights up his face. He has the straightest, whitest teeth. This close, I can see the depth of his eyes. They are breathtaking. So deep, so dark, like pools of dark chocolate with flecks of gold. And there are a few light freckles along his nose. It's quite adorable.

"Well, I hope to see you there," he states.

Before I can respond, he lifts my fingers and kisses the tips before turning and walking away, leaving me standing there, gaping after him as the final bell rings.

I'm late for class for the first time ever.

Chapter 5

Hearing A Band Play

~Claire~

It has been almost three weeks since my encounter with Noah. I don't know where to go from here. It feels like too much time has passed. So, I'm alone. Alone except for Signora Gelardi, who can, in fact, tell that one hundred percent of my attention is not on music.

We wasted an hour one session on her lecturing me on how I am too young to throw away my dream for a "pathetic school love," as she put it. I wouldn't go that far, but she seems determined that she sees more than I do. She says this will be my downfall, that I won't make it to Manhattan School of Music next year because I will throw everything away and be pregnant by this time next year. She's a little overdramatic.

So here we are now, at another singing practice, inside a soundproof room in the basement of the theater in town. Signora Gelardi makes me sing the same song repeatedly, until the fifth time, when I get a "much better." Then I look at my cell phone to see that it's after eight. According to the whole school, who are still talking about Noah like he's a god, his band is just starting. I want to finally go down to the restaurant and see him.

I haven't had the nerve before now. Every week, all week, I talk myself into it, telling myself that it's only one night, and then my nerves betray me at the last minute. If I went there with someone, it probably wouldn't feel like such a big deal, but I have no one. I will be an army of one against most of the school, by myself as everyone watches me walk through the doors, watching being a teenager, hearing a band play, something I have *never* done.

And what if Noah is with someone there? Will I be able to handle seeing that? Will everyone think I'm a fool because my knight who stood up for me was only being chivalrous, not appreciating seeing someone get picked on, that it didn't mean more than what my heart is telling me? Will I be the talk of the school on Monday when everyone sees I thought something more than what it is between us? Was his kiss only an act of kindness? Has he done that to other girls who fawn over him, girls who will be there tonight? Oh, God, I'm scaring myself out of it again.

I can't go, but I *have* to! Now is the time to be young, to experience more of life than school and Signora Gelardi. If I don't start being young now, then maybe I will be the same, boring, social outcast when I get to the Music Conservatory.

I'm going to hear a band play.

"Signora, it's late, so I'm going to head out now."

Signora gives me her no-nonsense look. She can see how jittery I am and knows something is up, yet she's not going to mention it. Her look tells me all she wants to say.

"Four o'clock on Monday," is all she says as I grab my sheet music and stuff everything in my bag with the rest of my homework for the weekend.

"Good night," I call out as I make my way out the door.

When I get home, the house is dark except for the foyer light we always leave on because we always seem to get home when it's dark.

I'm too wound up to eat, so I quickly head up to my room where I throw on some mascara and a light lip gloss. I take my hair out of its bun and brush it out. Now it looks wavy from being up all day.

I remain dressed in what I wore to school—a white T-shirt and dark skinny jeans—but I kick off my converse for a pair of knee-high brown boots and throw on my matching fitted leather jacket. It seems to fit the M.O. for hearing a band play, right? And it's not something I haven't worn before.

Ready to go and not allowing myself to think about what I'm doing, I write my dad a note and leave it on the foyer table for him. Then I lock up the house, hurry to my Jetta, and then make my way across town to Jeremy's. On the way, I play my favorite playlist, acting like I'm on my way to school like normal, except it's not normal, because it's night out, not morning.

What am I going to do when I get there? Will I even be able to leave my car? God, what if someone comes out and sees me sitting there like an idiot? No, I have to go in. I promised this to myself. I will go in, sip on a soda, sit in the back, and watch. I don't have to talk to anyone.

And now I'm pulling into the crowded parking lot. Wow, this place is packed. The whole school and then some must be here tonight. I didn't even think this place was large enough to accommodate so many people. And I find out they aren't when I see a line out the door. I'm already late. What if I don't even get in to hear them? At least I know I tried, right? I made the effort to be young and fun.

Thankfully, the line only has five people in it, and they all seem to be together. They are an older crowd who are talking about Noah's band. Evidently, the band is pretty talented because these people are from a few towns over and came all this way to hear them.

I am more and more intrigued as we watch older couples leave the restaurant, and now the five people in front of me are allowed in after the bouncer checks their IDs and puts paper bracelets around their wrists. There are a few more people behind me now, but I don't turn around to see if I know them or not.

When it's my turn to enter, the bouncer looks at my ID then stamps my hand with the under-aged mark, and now I'm in.

The restaurant is set up with booths along the front and far side of the room, with tables and chairs scattered in the middle. A bar sits along the wall to the left as you walk in, basically entering from the side of the building. At the back is a small stage, just enough room for the drums and a few people to stand in front of it. A dance floor encompasses the space in front of the stage. On a normal week night, tables are covering the dance floor, but not tonight.

There are so many people around that I literally bump into people as I make my way to the back of the room. The band is playing a cover song to my favorite band, and the way Noah sings … it sounds like his own heart is being gutted. Even his voice cracks like he's feeling the emotions from the song. It's mesmerizing.

His voice isn't raspy like I imagined; it's clear, yet a little throaty at the right times to make it more emotional. He's simply remarkable, commanding the attention of everyone. And as I look around the room, he does indeed have everyone's attention.

He's wearing his usual torn jeans and a gray T-shirt that is drenched in sweat, sticking to his skin. I can see drips of sweat break from his hairline, sliding down his face and the sides of his neck. His hair is slicked back from sweat, but a few tendrils cling to his forehead, and his hair in the back is curled from perspiration. He has a cherry red guitar sitting low on his hips, his fingers gliding over the neck while his other hand holds a pick, strumming the strings.

I don't even notice the other members, completely caught up in him.

Just then, he looks up and I swear right at me.

My breath catches in my throat as he continues through the ending of the song, singing directly to me.

~Noah~

Finally talking to Claire felt like a huge weight lifting off my chest, but that was close to three weeks ago. We are now in mid-October. Now that weight feels like it's adding on again as each day passes and Claire and I are back to flirty looks and shy smiles.

I shouldn't have kissed her hand.

It's frustrating. I waited in vain during two shows for her to show up to no avail. She's the only face I want to see out in that crowd. I want her to hear my words. I want to watch her face as she deciphers the songs about her.

I can't make this girl out. She's like no one else I have ever met.

Chelsea and her sidekick finally gave up on me. They are both now standing at the back of the crowded restaurant. Troy is still hooking up with Nikki by the looks of him pawing at her right now, and Chelsea has apparently gotten back with her on again off again boyfriend—like she's capable of a relationship—the quarterback. James, I think his name is. Cool guy. Of course she got back with him in time for homecoming. Two guesses who won that. I heard my name was in the running. I thought you had to agree to be a nominee?

While the crowd begins to grow, I sit back and sip on a Coke with Max while scouring the crowd for any sight of her like I have for the past three weeks.

"Who are you looking for?" Max asks from beside me, gripping his beer mug. I could go for a beer right now. I'm so stressed over Claire never showing up.

"Claire."

Max already knows about my infatuation with her. I guess I get a little talky when I'm drunk.

"What are you going to do if she shows?"

Kiss her. Take her in my arms and never let go. Just *be* with her.

"I don't know. Haven't thought that far." I pick up a straw wrapper and start tying it into knots until it breaks.

"Want me to bring her over here? Make sure no one messes with her?"

I give him a look up and down, and then pointedly look around the table at his friends. "I think you'll scare her out of here."

"No, he won't," Cyn chimes in from his lap. "He can be pretty charming when he wants to be. Even has a nice smile when he shows it."

Max grins up at her, and then she lowers her mouth to kiss him chastely.

Huh? She's right. He looks like a completely different person when he smiles.

"Thanks, Max," I consent. Then I describe her to him.

He gives me a nod as I stand up.

I reach out to take Cyn's hand, pulling her off his lap so we can get this show started. She's dressed in a short leather skirt with chains and a cut up Ramone's T-shirt that shows off her small waist.

Kyle gets up from across the table, and then we all make our way to the stage to loud cheering.

I look out over the crowd again, searching every face for hers. She's still not here, but wow did this crowd get big over the last few weeks.

We play for over half an hour before I turn to a cover song, one that works well with my voice and the emotions I have to force out.

Heart break. Past love lost. It feels almost real when I sing it tonight, thinking about how I lost my chance with Claire, regretting not approaching her these past few weeks, losing my chance with her.

My voice breaks at the right time before I lower it to deliver the next line, and when I finally open my eyes to look out at the crowd, my eyes meet hers.

She's standing beneath one of the recessed lights in the dim room, it glowing over her head like a halo, bathing her body in soft lighting. It would be impossible to miss her with her standing right there, dressed for sin in those tight pants, a simple white T-shirt, and a leather jacket. That jacket makes me think about taking her for a ride on my bike. No, that's moving too fast for a girl like her.

I can't believe she's finally here. I want to smile at her, assure her I know she's here, but I can't lose the vibe of the song, and I'm pretty sure she knows I know she's here.

When the song ends to an abrupt applause, I don't take my eyes off Claire, watching her clap with the rest of the crowd as I lean over and whisper in Cyn's ear, "Tell Max she's in the back, under that light."

Cyn looks out over the crowd then jumps off the stage and hurries to Max's table while I start the next song that has a long guitar solo, giving Cyn time to get back on stage. It's the first song I wrote about Claire, so it's ideal to play it now, now that she's here.

Cyn jumps back on stage and starts without missing a beat. I keep my eyes on Claire as I watch Max approach her. She's still watching me, so she startles when Max puts his hand on her forearm. I watch him lean over to whisper in her ear, and then she looks over at me with a question in her eyes. I subtly nod to assure her it's okay to go with him. I see him give her that rare smile, and she smiles at him in return before he pulls her through the crowd, his hand around her wrist, back to our table.

I can't take my eyes off her as I watch the guys scoot over, giving her room to sit down. She doesn't look the least bit intimidated by Max and his friends, thank God. Or if she does, she doesn't show it.

A waitress comes over and takes her drink order, and then I have her full-attention again. I hope she listens to the words I'm singing to her. I hope she hears how I don't feel worthy of a girl like her, but I can't help wanting what seems out of my reach. That I watch her every day, too much of a pussy to talk to her. That I have never been so terrified of anything in my life than her rejection.

Once the set is over, I don't waste any time. I'm like an eager kid chasing the ice cream man. I jump off the short stage, guitar still strapped across my chest, leaving Cyn to say our good-byes and thanks. I hear some guys laugh, and I get a few claps on the back in congratulations on the show as I make my way to *her*. Her attention is already riveted on me.

"You made it," I state the obvious. The waitress hands me a bottle of cool water, and I thank her as I wait to hear Claire speak.

"Yeah, I finally decided to give my teenage years a chance." She smiles up at me.

Wanting her to myself, I grab her hand and pull her up, leaving her no room so she crashes into my chest. Then I lean down to her short frame and whisper, "Come on."

I drag her along with me, back behind the stage where Jeremy, the owner and restaurant's namesake, gave us a storage closet for our equipment. My guitar case is on one of the chairs, so I swipe it off and onto the floor, and then lead Claire to the now vacant seat. Then I watch her take in the room.

"The owner lets us keep our things back here so we don't crowd the stage. He learned that lesson our first gig." I shrug, not knowing why I felt the need to share that.

She nods, not giving anything away, not saying anything. It's so frustrating, yet relieving. I'm so used to chicks yapping my ear off. That's probably why I never talk; never felt like I could get a word in, anyway. No, that's not why I don't talk, just an excuse.

We can't stay mute the entire time, so as I lift the guitar from my body, I ask, "What did you think? Of the music?" I clarify, smoothing my shirt back down. I notice she's staring at where my shirt had ridden up, so I turn around to put my guitar away before she can get embarrassed by getting caught checking me out.

"You guys are really good. It's hard to believe you haven't been together as a band that long."

I keep my back to her as I wipe down my guitar, placing it in its case gently as I shrug at her reply. "I already had most of the songs written. Kyle and Cyn are talented. It didn't take them long to pick up on them. It flowed." I zip up the case then turn back to see her watching me.

"How long does it usually take to learn a song?"

I like how she seems genuinely interested, but then I remember she's into music, too, just not like mine.

I place another chair in front of her, straddling the back of it. "It depends on the complexity of the song. Usually, I play and they follow. Sometimes we don't agree to how something sounds, so we change it up a bit." Folding my arms on the back of the chair, I rest my chin on them. "But, to answer your question, typically two to three days. Though we are practicing a few songs at the same time." I smile, and she returns it with one of her own. "Do you play anything?"

She looks down, her hair framing her face. I want to reach out and feel how soft it is. It's so full and wavy right now.

"Um, I have been taking piano lessons since I was a kid, but singing is my passion." She shrugs. "I dabble with writing music. You can't be around music all your life and not know something about creating it." She peeks back up at me, and I grin again, which makes her blush.

I love it. She's so adorable and sexy and beautiful. I can't believe I'm finally talking to her; that we are together in the same room, alone, having a conversation.

She says singing is her passion. I wonder what she sings to.

"So, you like singing? What do you sing? Do you like the musical kind of singing? Are you a pop kind of girl? Or are you into the death metal, thrashing, screaming your voice out?"

She laughs and replies with, "None of the above."

This piques my interest.

I scratch my head. "No musicals, no pop, no death metal … um, rock?"

She shakes her head with a playful grin on her lips.

"Don't tell me you rap?" I ask in mock horror, leaning away from her as I hold the back of the chair. It makes her laugh, and then she bites her bottom lip to stop herself. I grin at hearing her laugh. It's unlike her voice—throaty and sensual. "I gotta admit. I'm at a loss here. What do you sing?"

She blushes again and ducks her head back down. "Please promise you won't tease me. It's not something a lot of people around here take seriously, but it's who I am and I love it. It's my life, my dream, and it's what I'm going to study when I go to the Music Conservatory."

"You're going to the Music Conservatory?" I ask in surprise. When she nods, I ask, "You already got in?" She nods again. I'm amazed and intrigued by this girl now. Plus, I'm ecstatic. She will be in my city, only a stone's throw away from my neighborhood. "So, tell me."

"Opera." She whispers the one word, and I'm stunned. Completely blown away. Never would I have guessed this petite, gorgeous girl would sing opera of all things.

"Wow," is all I can think to say. Like I said, I'm stunned.

She peeks back up at me from beneath her long eyelashes. "You're not going to tease me?"

I shake my head. How can I tease her because of something like that? She said it was her life, her passion. That's the way I feel about my music. I wouldn't want someone to tease me, so why would I do it back? Besides, I get enough shit from my parents about music not being serious.

I wonder if my parents would take me serious if I went the Music Conservatory. Probably not. I would have to study history or literature for that to happen. They would probably be disappointed if I studied medicine.

Her shyness now gone, she beams at me. "I knew there would be something different about you. Most people think I'm a snob and tease me." She shrugs, her smile falling. "I don't think they understand how I take my goals seriously. They don't understand the dedication I put into the future I have mapped out. I don't believe in concentrating only on what's happening today; I concentrate on five years from now and work every day to get to that five-year goal." Her grin comes back. "I'm sorry, I'm being too serious."

I break out of my daze of staring at her mouth and shake my head. "No, I think that's admirable. My parents want me to be like them, but that's not the future I see for me, so it's hard for me to plan my future when I know someone won't be happy about it, whether it's me or them."

She nods. "I can understand that. I'm sorry."

I jump out of my seat, needing to lighten the mood. "Let's get out of this room." I grab her hand and help her out of the seat. "We usually head to Max's after the show. I would really like it if you came with me."

"Max?"

"The guy who brought you to the table?"

I see recognition alight her eyes as I open the door and lead her out, past the stage, and over to our table where Kyle and Cyn are now sitting. We need to start taking down the drums before we leave, but I want to spend more time with Claire first. I'm afraid if I let go of her, she will leave and none of this would have been real.

I help her sit down and turn to Kyle to tell him we need to start loading up when all hell breaks loose.

Chapter 6

Bliss Wrapped in Hell

~Claire~

Noah is not what I expected. He has manners, holding my hand as he helps me sit and stand. He didn't laugh or tease me about my opera dreams, something I am overly grateful for. He seems understanding. He makes me laugh. He makes me blush. He makes me feel fun. I'm having a good time with him.

When Max first came over to get me, I was a little freaked out. He looked so intimidating, and I was in a room full of people who couldn't care less if he took me in the back and stashed my body somewhere. However, I felt a lot better when he told me that Noah had sent him and that I should sit at his table until the show was over. Noah's nod of assurance made me feel even better.

Sitting with Max and his friends was entertaining. I vaguely listened to them all talk, cracking jokes about one another as I focused on the music, on the words Noah was singing, on him.

Between songs, I noticed I was getting a lot of condescending looks. Girls were blatantly staring at me, whispering to one another and pointing at me and Noah. I ignored them, keeping one hundred percent of my attention on Noah. His focus was entirely on me, as if he was singing each song to me personally. I wanted to swoon like the girls in the movies.

Noah holds my hand all the way back to his friends' table. The bassist, Cyn, is sitting on Max's lap, kissing him, dispelling the rumor that she is with Noah. Kyle sits in the place that I was sitting in earlier, but he gets up when he sees us coming, making room.

I sit there and watch as Noah turns to his cousin, but something in the opposite direction grabs my attention, and I turn to see Troy barreling through the crowd like a linebacker, taking out all the people in his way as he charges straight for Noah.

"Noah, turn around!" I scream.

~Noah~

I hear Claire's frantic voice and turn around in time for Troy to collide with me. We both fall to the floor on our sides, and the wind gets knocked out of me.

Chaos sounds all around us. I hear people yelling, idiots chanting, "fight, fight, fight," chairs scraped along the floor, music muted in the background.

Troy gets a few jabs to my ribs as I try to break his hold around my neck. This guy is seriously trying to kill me. I stop trying to break free, and instead throw my elbow into his face, hearing a satisfying crunch. He immediately releases me, and I jump to my feet, getting into a defensive stance, watching him between my two fists as he gets up, blood gushing out of his nose and turning his white dress shirt red.

"I told you to stay away from her, you pussy." He wipes at the blood coming out of his nose, smearing it across his cheek. "You take *my* girl into a back room, just like that, you piece of shit. She deserves better than that."

I don't say anything. I follow his movements as he hops around. This guy knows how to box. I can tell by his posture. However, I know I have been in more fights than him, and I'm always the one who walks away. I'm not cocky; it's the truth. I grew up where you have to fight to live. He's grown up where everything is given to him. I can control my anger, and I have patience. This guy is a loose cannon. There's no telling what he's going to do.

Well, I can control my anger until I hear, "Deserve to have you try to rape me on my living room couch, Troy?" Her angered voice breaks on the word rape, but by the time she says the asshole's name, she's seething.

Calm and controlled, she shows no fear to the man who used to be her only friend. She shouldn't fear him; she has me now. She doesn't need assholes like this in her life.

61

"This asshole tried to hurt you?" I hear Max ask.

I don't hear a reply from Claire, and I don't take my eyes off Troy, but I do feel Max and a couple other guys stand at my back.

I'm seeing red now. The world is tinted in it.

I feel Max start to move toward Troy, so I grit out, "I got him." I want this shit for myself. I want to hurt him for hurting Claire. I want to destroy him the way he wanted to destroy Claire's innocence.

Rumors of her attack now proven, I take a step toward him. He throws a sloppy punch at my head, but I duck and get two hits to his ribs, payback for throws he got into me when we were on the ground.

He blocks my third hit, and his elbow nicks my lip. It isn't a hard hit like I think he has in him, but I immediately feel my lip split open.

I hear Jeremy yell at us to take it outside, but we ignore him. This might ruin our chances to play here anymore, but that's a risk I'm willing to take to protect Claire, to make this asshole realize I will be in her life from now on, that he's not getting close to her again.

Troy drops all pretenses of boxing. He drops his arms and goes in like he's going to wrestle me to the ground again, using his brute strength to take me down. What an idiot. This guy really needs to learn how to street fight.

As he charges toward me, I throw my arm back, and then throw a right hook into his temple. The idiot falls down into the crowd and people move back so as not to fall down with him. Blood is all over the floor now. The whole thing started and ended in maybe two minutes, but it feels so much longer than that.

I turn around to see Claire against the table and behind Max and his friends. They are already protecting her, like she belongs with them. I like that. I like to know she has more people who will defend and befriend her if she so chooses.

I walk toward her and the men part, giving me the path I need.

"Are you okay?" she asks, lifting her hand to my face but dropping it before she touches me. She turns toward the table and bends over to grab something.

I lick my split lower lip, tasting blood, as I stare at her ass bent over that way. *Don't think it. Don't think it.*

"Yeah, I'm sor—"

62

"Don't you dare apologize," she says as she turns around with a wet napkin. "He came after you." She presses the napkin to my lip, making me flinch at the ice-cold feel of it. I realize she wrapped an ice cube around the napkin.

I reach up to take the napkin from her hand. "Thank you."

"Thank *you*," she says back immediately. "He deserves worse than what you did to him." Her eyes get all sad as she says, "I-I can't believe I thought he was my friend. He was all I had."

I take one of her hands that she's nervously twisting, winding and unwinding her fingers together. "I want to be your friend, Claire. And not like him. I would *never* hurt you like that," I swear.

She nods, tears in her eyes, but she won't allow them to fall. "I would like that." She gives me that beautiful smile of hers.

"Noah, I can't have shit like this in my restaurant, man. You need to pack up your shit and go," Jeremy interrupts.

I turn around to face him, dropping Claire's hand and the napkin from my lip, touching her hip as I do. Jeremy is giving me a stern, don't-fight-me-on-this look. I notice a lot of people have left. Some kids from school, including Chelsea who is giving Claire a death look, are surrounding Troy, trying to get him up. Max and his friends are watching him like a hawk, waiting to see if he makes another move.

"Are you kidding, Jeremy? *He* came at *me*. You can't take this out on the band. Kick his ass out, ban him from here, and I promise nothing like this will happen again." I step up to him, letting him know I'm not backing down from this. "I bet I have over thirty witnesses who will tell you he came at me. Don't do this, Jer." I can't mess this up for Kyle and Cyn. They love the gigs.

Jeremy steps closer and whispers, "He's the mayor's son, Noah. I can't kick him out. His dad will use this as an excuse to shut me down."

Hearing what Jeremy said, Claire says, "And I'm the D.A.'s daughter. I'll tell my dad what happened. This is because of me, so I'll make sure they won't give you any trouble."

I give her an incredulous look and snap, "This is not because of you. The guy is an asshole, would-be rapist with some serious anger issues. That's not your fault."

"No, but it's because of me he attacked you," she argues, looking defiantly back at me.

I shake my head at her, not knowing if I want to kiss her to get her to stop arguing with me or shake her. I don't want her thinking anything about him is her fault. I don't want the two of them tied together in any way.

I finally notice Kyle and Cyn taking apart the drums. I need to help them.

"I'll be back," I tell Claire, ignoring Jeremy who is still standing there, and make my way to help Kyle and Cyn where I will unfortunately have to tell them the news that the asshole ruined our Friday night gig.

~Claire~

While Noah helps move the equipment out of the restaurant, I tell Jeremy that I will talk to my dad and have him call. I stress that the incident was in no way Noah's fault, and that I don't like the idea that Troy gets special favors because he is the mayor's son. I also stress that my father wouldn't like to hear about that, either. And, as District Attorney, he would expect equal justice, no matter who you are. Jeremy finally relents, walking off as he mumbles something about mistakes and ruining businesses.

As we talked, I noticed Troy leaving with his entourage, not looking back once. No, I didn't like to see him get in trouble, but he brought this on himself. Every punishment he gets, he deserves. He will be lucky if my father doesn't insist that assault charges be pressed against him this time. I have a feeling Troy is one strike away from jail time, if my dad saw fit. In fact, I'm surprised he didn't insist with the sexual assault.

A lot of the younger crowd is gone now, no doubt going home to make curfew. Being a responsible teenager has its perk. I don't have a curfew. My dad and I have always had the agreement that I let him know where I'm going and everything is fine.

Max and his friends are back to drinking at their table, so I make my way back to them while I wait for Noah to finish up. I feel weird waiting for him, like maybe I caused too much trouble and now he won't want anything to do with me. I think about going, foregoing the embarrassing encounter that is sure to happen. I have too much baggage; caused too many problems for him already.

I turn around to head out the door when I bump into Noah.

"Whoa, you okay?" he asks, settling his hands on my hips to stop me from stumbling back. I can't make out his freckles in the dim lighting, and his eyes look almost black, soaking up the darkness of the room.

"Yeah, sorry. I was heading out."

I watch his face drop at my words. We are still standing really close to each other, too close for just being friends. I would never let Troy stand this close to me, the toes of our boots almost touching, breaths practically mingling. I have to look up, and he has to look down when we are this close. I imagine we look like a couple by how we are standing, his hands still gently gripping my hips.

"I thought you agreed to come with me," he whispers.

"Holy hot chemistry, Batman!" I hear Cyn say as she walks past us with Max and friends, winking at me as she passes.

"Ignore her," Noah demands, bringing my attention back to him. "Why did you change your mind? Is it because I snapped at you?"

My brow furrows. I thought he wouldn't want to waste any time with me after I caused so much trouble for him, but he looks and sounds hurt, and his body language tells me he isn't put off by the drama. I decide I need to go with honesty since I expect nothing less from him.

I swallow hard. "I didn't think you would still want to hang out after what happened with Troy. And I promised Jeremy that I would get my dad to call him. If I do that, your band will still be able to play here and Troy won't be allowed back."

"You'd do that for us?" He finally takes a step back, releasing me from his hold. He looks around the restaurant then back at me. "That would mean a lot to Kyle and Cyn. They love this gig."

My eyebrows knit together in confusion. "And you don't?"

He shakes his head. "It's not for me. I only want to play, but they like performing." I start to ask why, but he continues, grabbing my hand and leading me out the door. "Come on. We can talk later. I'll follow you to your house."

I stop suddenly, and he has to take a step back to fall in line with me since our hands are still joined. "You want to come to my house? I thought we were going with them." I gesture toward his friends, wondering why he wants to go to my house. Is this it? Does he think I don't want to go with him? I'm confused; a million questions flying through my head.

He looks at me like *he* can't figure *me* out. "You said you promised Jeremy a call from your dad tonight, right?"

I nod. I told him I would. Does he think I won't?

"Okay, well, you have to get home, and I'm not done hanging out with you, so we'll kill two birds with one stone."

~

Twirling my keys around my finger as I lean against my car, I wait while Noah gets off his bike. Of course he has a motorcycle. It totally fits his persona.

This guy is going to break my heart. I can already foresee it. I foresee him taking everything from me, stripping me bare and leaving me with nothing—no soul, no heart, no sanity. It's in his quietness. It's in his almost desperate interest. It's in the energy that pours out of him, feeding me with nervous emotions. He radiates an eagerness that appears new to him.

I have watched him for two months now, and I have never seen him openly talk to someone, or even reply with more than a couple words, yet he singled me out, spewing more words to me than I ever saw him say to anyone else. He has girls throwing themselves at him, and he brushes them off, yet he singled me out. He decisively asked his friend to pull me aside, protect me while he performed, probably knowing I was out of my element. I have never seen him take a girl aside and talk to them, yet he grabbed me the minute he could.

I thought about all this on the drive home. I somehow don't see this as normal behavior for the composed and contained man before me, who at this moment is taking off his helmet and setting it on the seat of his motorcycle.

He looks up at the house then over to me where I am still leaning

against my car door, lost in thought on how to proceed this …
whatever it is between us.

"You sure your dad is awake? It's got to be close to midnight."
He looks back over at the house, and I turn to follow his eyes.

"Yeah, he works … all the time. He'll be up." I'm still looking at
the house as I talk, so it startles me when he grasps my hand and gently
pulls me toward the house.

"Let's get this over with before I get thrown out of here. I want
to spend more time with you, but I'm sure that won't happen once your
dad hears the story." He's still focused on the house as we walk up the
stairs to the front porch. It's dark, and he isn't looking at me, so I can't
gauge his mood by seeing his eyes. However, his self-deprecating
words tell me he doesn't think my dad will allow him in.

I open the door and tell him, "My dad isn't like that. You'll see."

We walk into the foyer, and I set my keys down on the table.
Noah is still by the door. He closes it gently then leans against it,
putting his hands in his pockets. He doesn't even glance around the
room, his eyes focused on me.

I turn away from him and start walking toward my dad's office,
calling out, "Dad?"

"In here, honey," I hear him call from his office, just where I
thought he would be.

I walk into his office, with its floor to ceiling bookshelves along
one wall. His desk is at the back, in front of huge bay windows that
look out to the side yard. There are two high back lounge chairs placed
in front of his desk. The other wall is decorated with pictures of us
throughout the years, even one of my absentee mother in the hospital
with me the day I was born … before she left us. Poor Dad brought
me home alone, his wife running off in the middle of the night from
the hospital.

"Did you have a good time?" Dad asks as I walk around his desk
to give him a hug.

"Yeah, I did … until Troy ruined it." I let go of him and step back
around his desk, moving toward the doors to see why Noah didn't
follow.

"What did he do now? Are you hurt?" He follows me, and I know he's scanning my body for injuries.

"I'm fine, Dad, but Noah—"

"Who's Noah?" he cuts me off, his brow furrowed.

"I am, sir." Noah meets us at the office door, his hand extended to shake my father's.

My dad takes it, looking at me with a raised eyebrow. I know I'm going to get extensively questioned later, lawyer style.

"Call me Jonathan, please." He releases Noah's hand. "Troy do that to your lip?"

Noah touches his split bottom lip like he forgot it was there.

Before he can answer, I tell my dad, "Troy attacked him, unprovoked." I make sure to point that out, knowing he would end up asking for details. Then I tell him step-by-step what happened, including talking to Noah in the storage room, letting him know what Troy assumed. I have nothing to hide, so why not be honest?

When I finish, I tell him, "So, now Jeremy is telling Noah that his band can't play there anymore. That he can't ban Troy because of who his father is. I told him if I could get you to call him, you would assure him that nothing will happen if he bans Troy and gives Noah's band another chance. It's only fair."

While I talk, Noah remains silent, sitting in the chair next to me while my father leans back against his desk, arms folded in front of him. Now Dad stands up straight and puts a hand on Noah's shoulder. Noah looks up to him, but I can't discern the look on his face. He's been expressionless this whole time.

"Thank you for giving that asshole what he deserves." With that, my dad walks around his desk and sits behind it, picking up his cell phone from next to his laptop. "I take it you have the number for Jeremy's?" He looks at Noah, who nods his head and spits out the numbers. While he waits for the line to connect, Dad looks at me and says, "I'll call Mayor Couer in the morning." That's our dismissal.

I get up and Noah follows with a thank you to my dad. Dad nods his head in answer as he begins speaking to Jeremy. We make our way back to the foyer and instead of going to the door, Noah sits on a step to the staircase. I don't question him; just sit down next to him.

"Your dad seems pretty cool," he admits, looking down at his hands resting between his knees.

I bump his shoulder with mine. "Told ya."

He looks over at me and gives me a soft smile that I return.

"So, where's your mom? We're not going to wake her up or anything, are we?"

His question throws me off, and I feel my smile fade. He looks like he's about to say something, maybe apologize, so I hurry up and answer.

"She took off after I was born."

"Shit. Sorry," is his reply.

I bend over and start to finger the laces of my boots. "Not your fault. Dad says he never saw it coming. He always tells me that she seemed so happy when she was pregnant with me. He thought she was kidnapped or something. Turns out, she didn't want us anymore."

We are silent for a few more minutes, both considering the bomb I dropped, and then he asks, "Want to go for a walk? You have a pretty big lot." He's referring to the two acres our house sits on. Our backyard is massive, with enough trees to make a small forest. Everyone in this neighborhood has a large yard. "I don't get enough of nature, living in a city," he adds quietly.

~Noah~

We have been walking quietly around her backyard for a few minutes now. Not uncomfortable silence, though, more like in our own heads kind of silence. I don't know what she's thinking, but I know I can't stop thinking about touching her.

Her skin is so soft, her hands so little. I love feeling her little hand in mine, swallowing it up in the curve of my palm. And I have yet to touch her hair. I still want to know if it's as soft as it looks. And her lips, so red and plump. I can imagine them slightly open as she sleeps, curving into a cute pout as she exhales.

I shake those thoughts from my head and take in her backyard. She has a full deck, filled with an outdoor dining set, a grill built into an outdoor kitchen with sink and mini fridge. I have never seen an outdoor kitchen before. Her lawn is large with manicured grass, hedges outlining the border against a small fence that encloses the grass area. At the back of the yard is a small gate that opens to a stoned pathway leading toward a wooded area. That's where we are heading now, walking through the gate and into the tall trees.

Claire breaks the silence as I hold open the gate then latch it closed.

"So, why do you not like performing?"

I look back at where she waits for me then make my way toward her, taking her hand in mine again. "It feels like something personal. They are my words, my thoughts, and it feels like I'm opening up for people I couldn't care less for." I shrug one shoulder, not looking at her as I watch where we step through the woods. The air smells so clean here.

"Then why share them at all? Can't you play someone else's songs?" She's not looking at me either as we walk. I can see her looking ahead, staring at seemingly nothing.

I wonder what she feels about me holding her hand. She's never tried to pull away or hesitated when I reach for it.

"I don't know too many people who can write music. At least, no one in the band back home can. And we play cover songs, too. Still, that seems personal because they're songs I pick. No one ever has input into what we should play. They just want to perform." I don't know if I answered her question, but I feel like I opened myself up more than how I feel I do on stage.

All of a sudden, Claire's whole demeanor changes. She bounces on her toes, drawing my attention to her face. She turns toward me, her face all alight in smiles. I can't help smiling back, though I'm a little confused to what we are smiling about.

"Can I tell you why I like performing?" she asks.

I give her a nod, curious as to why she would feel so happy about sharing something that I abhor.

"I love watching the audience's faces. I love making them smile or cry. Or, when the song is about hate, I see their faces fill with the emotion. That's my favorite part—conveying emotions to people with just my voice."

I think about what she says as she continues. This is the longest I have ever heard her talk at once, and I don't want her to stop.

"I don't think you should worry so much that people are relating the songs to you, but that they are relating the songs to themselves. I don't hear a song on the radio and think, *that person's love life sucks.* I hear it and feel how that would feel if I was in that position."

"Really," I mumble, trying to see it from her point of view. God knows it will help me feel better about performing if I don't think I'm gutting myself out there for other's amusement.

Claire stops and drops her hand from mine. "I'm sorry, Noah. I didn't mean anything by it. I don't want to tell you how you should think. I didn't mean to offend you."

I step back to where she is, watching her twist her hands in front of her while her head is slightly down. I tip her chin up with my index finger and squat a little until I am eye level with her. She's so short. "I'm not offended. You made me think differently about it. I was wrapping my head around your perspective. I've never thought about my music that way. I think the same about others, personifying it with myself, just not when *I* write the music."

She nods, looking straight into my eyes, and I drop my finger slowly, caressing her chin before it falls. "Okay. Thank you."

"For what?" I look at her in confusion and notice her eyes drift away from mine, staring past me.

"For …" she lingers on the word, "not being mad. For continuing to be my friend. For not leaving me alone." Her eyes glaze over.

I know she must be thinking about Troy or possibly her mother, though I don't understand how she would miss someone she never knew.

She turns away from me, heading back toward her home, and I watch her, feeling like shit for this night turning out so bad.

This girl hides so much of herself behind her self-assured persona. She never seems to let anything past her defenses, but apparently, a lot already has. She's holding in so much, and I want in there. I want to break down her walls and bury myself inside her.

One night, and she has already changed my outlook on performing. What else could she give me? More importantly, what can I give her in return?

I catch up to her when she reaches the gate. "Wait." I grab her wrist to stop her from retreating further. "I feel bad that this whole night has seemed so …" I search for an accurate term to describe the nightmare yet pleasant dream tonight has been. Because yes, a lot of shit went down and conversations turned sad, but I got spend it with *her*.

"Bliss wrapped in hell?" she offers.

I smile wide. That's exactly how tonight feels, but that's not what makes me smile. It's the knowledge that she feels precisely the same way. That through all the shit, she found bliss in being with *me*.

"Exactly." I grab her tiny waist then lean back against the fence with my legs spread in order to accommodate her short physique. Claire only comes up to my sternum when I'm fully standing. Right now, she is up to my chin.

I have never been with someone so little, so this is going to take some minor adjustments. Well, I have never been with anyone, not in this sense.

She stands a few inches from me, not knowing where to put her hands, until she finally settles them on my wrists. My thumbs have a mind of their own, making circles on her waist under her jacket, slowly moving her shirt up until I'm touching her soft skin. I see her shiver at the contact.

There is a slight breeze, blowing tendrils of hair across her face. She releases one of my wrists to swipe them back then brushes her hair behind her ear before settling her hand back down. I smell pine sap and dead leaves and fresh dirt, cut grass, and Claire, a warm vanilla scent and mint.

I think I'm making her uncomfortable, but I can't tell if it's the good kind or the bad, before she chooses that moment to whisper, "I think I should go inside now." She stares into my eyes as she says it, but then glances down at my lips.

She wants me to kiss her. I know this, but will she deny it? I want to test the waters.

I lean in while also pulling her the few inches forward that separate our bodies, and she tilts her head up, letting me know she wants this.

I can't mess this up. I want to give her something that she will never forget, but I don't want to scare her by being too forward, too rough.

She closes her eyes, and I feel her minty exhale against my lips that are only a breath away. Closing the gap, I press my lips gently against hers. They are as soft as I imagined.

I release her waist and move my hands up to cup her face, while her hands remain on my wrists. Then I move my lips slightly to kiss her upper lip before placing a longer one on her fuller bottom lip, feeling her apply pressure as she returns the kiss. Slightly opening my mouth, I taste her bottom lip, and her lips open to take a breath.

I glide my thumb across her cheek as I move my other hand into her hair, feeling its soft silkiness. Tilting her head back a little, I gently introduce my tongue, and hers meets mine shyly, hesitantly, telling me this is the first time she has been kissed like this. I only allow my tongue a tiny taste before pulling it back in, kissing her lips again.

Her hands release my wrists, drifting up my arms and into my own hair. She gets braver now, softly tasting my lips with her tongue before I part my lips for her.

It's so hot to know I am the first to give her this. I can't get enough. I can stand out here forever, kissing her like this.

I'm sure she can feel my erection against her belly as our breaths mingle, coming out fast and hard, as our kiss grows hungrier. I can't move this fast with her, though. As much as I want to remain like this forever, I have to slow down for her.

I pull back and look at her face. Her eyes remain closed for seconds longer, her lashes fanning her reddened cheeks. Her breasts rise and fall fast from her heavy breathing as they remain pushed up against me. She's so gorgeous.

She finally opens her eyes and meets mine. Her lips part for a second like she is about to say something, but I beat her to it.

"I should let you go in."

Her face falls for a second, and she looks down at my lips.

I think I said the wrong thing, but if I stay here another second, I'm afraid I will ruin any future kisses by getting close to pulling a Troy. I would never force myself on her, but I don't ever want to go so far as to where she would have to tell me to stop.

"Can I pick you up tomorrow? Maybe go out for lunch?" I ask.

Her eyes shoot back up to mine, and she gives me a shy smile. "I would like that." She nods. "Yes."

I can't help the smile that comes over my face at knowing we have plans. I hope we always have plans for the tomorrows.

Her eyes widen at my smile like I shocked her. I take advantage of it by kissing her again.

It's not for another half an hour before I finally get on my bike and pull away from her house, her taste on my swollen lips.

Chapter 7

Live in the Moment

~Claire~

It's been a few weeks since that explosive make-out session in my backyard. My first and, as far as kissing goes, I am incredibly grateful at how amazing it was. It was gentle yet scorching; smooth yet electrifying; tender, tentative, exploratory yet all-consuming. It was the sweetest, most affectionate anyone has ever treated me, and I am addicted.

However, Noah has not kissed me the same since that night; just gentle kisses on the lips, nose, cheek, forehead, and once under my ear that made me clench my legs together. That little, seemingly innocent kiss left me a panting mess. He knew how it affected me, too. His eyes widened in shock before giving me an almost shy smile. I think my reactions to him shocks him.

The day after that kiss, Noah picked me up and met my dad again, where they talked for a good half hour, something I was grateful for because Dad really seems to like him. Then Noah took me to the next town over where they have nicer restaurants, driving his aunt's truck since he guessed there was no way I would get on his motorcycle with my dad watching.

We had a comfortable conversation, getting to know each other better, asking mundane questions like favorite color, bands, foods, and such. We fell into each other so naturally it was like we have known each other all our lives, making me regret waiting so long to even talk to him. A whole month, and then some, lost.

He shared stories about all the places he has been to in the world. One minute he would reminisce like it was the greatest time he had, and then his mood would turn somber. That's when he admitted how he fell behind in school, that he should have graduated by now, that he was ready to be done with this chapter of his life.

That saddened me because, if he hadn't been held back, then we would have never met.

A girl from our school was dining with her family at the restaurant. And by the apt attention she was giving us—and by her fingers furiously typing on her cell phone—I knew the whole school would know about this come Monday. I was not mistaken.

These past weeks have been filled with nothing but stares and comments about me now being a whore—how else could I have gained Noah Gish's attention? It was disgusting. But I never mentioned it to Noah. I saw how he fights, and I don't want him getting expelled for sticking up for me.

Speaking of fighting, Troy's father has him on a probation of sorts. Not legally, though Troy cannot leave the city limits and has every faculty member in the school watching his every move, per his father's request. Let's just say that Troy hasn't even looked in mine or Noah's direction.

Though he may not be looking at me, I have noticed some strange behavior with him and Chelsea. By all appearances, Troy is still with Nikki, yet I caught him and Chelsea in heated conversations over the past couple of weeks, heads close together, voices lowered.

She is once again no longer with James, but she hasn't appeared to move on to anyone else, either. She has been forlorn, looking depressed when she thinks no one is looking, and her attitude toward me has escalated ... when Noah isn't around. She has even gone so far as to shove me with her shoulder when she passes me. So mature.

Since our first date, mine and Noah's relationship has slowly progressed. A kiss has gone from hesitant to second thought, like it's ingrained. Conversations have gone from curious, get to know you to saying what is deep inside our thoughts, our feelings, and opinions about anything and everything. It's magical watching and living this connection.

Now it is Halloween, and though it falls on a Wednesday, Noah and his band are performing tonight—yes, my dad fixed that complication for them.

I'm supposed to meet Noah at the bar after my lesson with Signora Gelardi, who is none too thrilled at the new addition in my life, lecturing me almost as much as she teaches. She's relentless in telling me how off I am when I sing, even when I know I have not made one error.

"Again," Signora Gelardi snarls, pounding on the piano keys.

I ignore her attitude and take a deep breath as she starts the introduction to "Casta Diva" from *Norma*, an aria, which is a prayer to the Druid gods to bring peace during Rome's occupation. The high soprano notes are a testament to how much my skills have grown.

As the notes grow closer to when my part starts, I close my eyes and feel the music. I want to get out of here as soon as possible to make it to Noah's gig on time. He has been at his own practices while I attend mine, leaving us little time to be together, though we do go on dates almost every other night, eating dinner together since he learned my dad isn't home often to eat with me.

One night after Chinese take-out, I pulled out my history book and learned that Noah has a photographic memory. Since then, he has been tutoring me, not that I need it, but it is fascinating to pick his brain.

I keep waiting for him to make a move, to start a make-out session like our first and only. He doesn't give. We will sit close together, my legs draped over his as we share a book to study from. He will play with my hair, wrapping the long strands around his fingers. He sometimes rubs circles along my back where my shirt has ridden up. And he also likes to play with my hand, mesmerized by how tiny my fingers are, or so he says. Regardless of all the contact he gives me, I still haven't felt his tongue against mine in weeks.

I never realized what sexual frustration was until Noah came into my life. I never experienced my sex clenching in need until Noah kissed me. Never had an inkling to experience sex until Noah.

I have only known him for weeks, yet I want to give him everything. And that scares me. Is that how others feel?

Noah scares me, but at the same time, he frees me. He makes me feel so alive. He makes me want to live in the moment. At this moment in time, I feel like I could give everything up to be with him. Say screw everyone and everything, jump on the back of his bike, and ride off into the sunset. And that scares me.

I don't want to be *that* girl. Because then I see a future of living in trailer parks, barefoot and pregnant, while my boyfriend—because we will never get married in this scenario—plays his guitar in bars, coming home smelling like cheap beer, stale cigarettes, and cheap perfume.

This is the visual that grounds me. That is not a future that looks happy.

Even if living in the moment feels fantastic, I have to remind myself of the bigger picture. And if Noah was to push me, and not act like the perfect gentleman he has been, then I don't think I would care for him or want him as much as I do.

~Noah~

I know I shouldn't be here. I should be helping Kyle and Cyn set up for the show, but when I found out where Claire has her practices, I had to come and watch her.

I asked her to sing for me last week, and she immediately turned red and dropped her head. We were sitting on her couch. I had my feet kicked up on the coffee table, watching her lying back on the couch, reading the book that was assigned to us with her feet in my lap. She was humming something that wasn't familiar. The melody sounded like an opera song. Even humming, she sounded amazing, clear, mesmerizing.

"Sing it out loud," I suggested, thinking she would. I mean, she performs in front of people; what was there to be shy about?

"What?" Claire dropped her book into her lap, looking at me in confusion. I guessed she didn't even realize she was humming.

"You were humming. I want to hear it."

Her face automatically flushed, and then she tried to hide it behind her book. "No."

My mouth dropped open. I couldn't believe how self-conscious she got around me. I wanted to tease her; make her feel comfortable enough so that she would share this with me. I shared my music with

78

her, and she knows how I feel about that.

I scooted up the couch, her legs still draped over mine. Reaching out, I lowered the book that was practically plastered to her face. "Why not?"

Her flush disappeared when she looked me straight in the eye. "I will feel embarrassed."

"Why?" My brow furrowed. I knew that was how she felt, but I still didn't understand. "You sing in front of other people, so why not just me?"

"It's different," she mumbled, looking away.

"You were the one telling me that you like to sing to see people's reactions. You were really adamant that singing *in front of people* is your favorite part, so ... give it to me. Feed me emotions," I encouraged with a grin.

"That's what I'm afraid of with you," she told me. When my smile turned into a look of confusion, she continued, "I'm okay with admitting that I'm insecure enough to wonder what you are reliving, or who you may be thinking of when I invoke emotions in you. I don't want to see that on your face and have to wonder. I want to wait until I'm secure in you, in us, and in where this"—she gestured between us—"relationship is going. I mean, this is a relationship, right?"

Her insecurity was endearing to someone used to confident women who knew what they wanted, who knew they were beautiful and flaunted it. This *girl*, because she is still a little girl in so many ways, is more beautiful, more put-together, successful, and just more than anyone I ever met. However, her loneliness, insecurities, and her brutal honesty make me respect and worship—yes, I worship this girl—her unlike anyone in my past.

"I hope this is a relationship," I answered, swallowing down the strong, overwhelming feelings I had for her. "And I understand where you are coming from. But, Claire, I can promise you that when I do hear you sing, *you* will be all I feel."

And it's true.

I can hear her voice from right outside the auditorium as I make my way toward the doors leading in. I don't know what she's singing, but I know it's in Italian.

Her voice is out of this world. I have never heard anything like it. Where her talking voice is small, gentle, yet soprano; her singing voice is overpowering. Her range moves from the sound of tiny, metal wind chimes, but strong enough to make your eardrums vibrate, to a low, soulful tenor that sounds so aching in emotion. I have to see her.

I crack the door open and get my fix. She is standing on the stage, her arms outstretched as she hits a high note, her eyes closed and head tilted back. She's dressed in what she wore to school today: black, skin tight pants; a black shirt that comes off both shoulders; a fat, black belt; and red fuck-me shoes that I would love to have wrapped around my neck, or digging into my ass.

Being in the spirit of Halloween, she dressed up as Sandy from *Grease*, minus the teased hair—thank God. Which means, I guess I'm Danny, since I'm in my jeans and leather, donning the classic black T-shirt—not on purpose, I must add.

I have never done the whole Halloween get-up. Not since I was eight years old when my parents told me I was too old to dress up. I'm surprised Claire got into it, considering she doesn't participate in anything school-related, including dances, something else we have in common. However, Halloween is her favorite holiday.

I couldn't keep my hands off her at lunch today, running my palms up and down the soft, shimmery material of her pants that hugged her better than any skinny jeans, marveling at how someone so short can have such long, sexy legs.

"No!" The sound of a shout from an older lady, whom I guess is Signora Gelardi, takes me out of my wandering thoughts. "Again!" She proceeds to play the piano again, shaking her head at Claire in disappointment.

I think her tone is a little uncalled for. I didn't hear anything wrong with the way Claire was singing. She sounded flawless, never missing a beat, and her voice transitioned smoothly. But what do I know? Opera isn't my thing.

Claire gives her tutor a look that shows her own agitation at the woman. It's a look of infuriation I have never seen on her before. She always looks so serene, like nothing ever gets to her, so seeing her show anger is new to me.

She looks irresistible with her blue eyes narrowed into icy slits toward her singing tutor, her little fists resting on her tiny hips. She looks totally sexy in that pose, with that look, in that tight, hot, little outfit. I am so lucky she is mine. I only hope I don't screw anything up with her.

This relationship stuff is all new to me. I have never been so open with anyone before, never felt so comfortable spending all my time with someone, and definitely have never cared what a girl says. I was all about instant gratification before, letting a girl talk until there was an opening to get her on her back. That was all I wanted in a woman. Until Claire.

She has this aura around her that I am completely drawn to. There is no denying our attraction to one another; everyone sees it. There is so much more to it, though. This goes beyond sexual attraction. This is a mental and emotional connection. It's like there is this tether that connects us. If I close my eyes and follow the pull from my chest, from my soul, it will lead me directly to her. She feels like my lifeline, my other half, the part of me that has been missing since birth. There is no other way to describe it.

That said, I hope I'm not going to get kicked to the curb by being here.

She has her eyes closed again as the song pours out of her fluidly. I understand a little of what she's singing. I know it's Latin.

Without realizing it, I have come through the door and am now standing in front of it. As another high note flows past Claire's lips, I quickly sit down in the back row, scooting down in the seat with my legs sprawled out in front of me to accommodate my height.

I chuckle to myself at the irony of hiding out, starting to sweat at the fear of being discovered and those doe eyes looking at me in anger, or worse, disappointment. Not to mention, with the way Signora Gelardi barks at Claire, I would hate for that bitch to try to bark at me. I would put her in her place so fast that woman would be stuttering for the rest of her life. I can't do that, though. That's a surefire way Claire would never talk to me again.

"Will that be all for tonight, Signora?" Claire's question brings me out of my thoughts.

"Yes, but first I would like to know who intruded on our practice."

I see Claire's eyes dart from Signora Gelardi to the auditorium doors before scanning the rows of seats. Confusion and maybe hurt and betrayal that I wanted to avoid cross her features as I start to sit up in the chair.

Yep, when her eyes find mine, there is definitely hurt and betrayal there. I let her down, and now I feel like shit.

"Hi." I give her a little wave and a shamefaced smile as I stand, undecided if I should move toward the stage or make a run from it.

I think Claire sees my unusual awkwardness because an amused expression comes to her face. Thank God the disappointment is gone. The girl could crush my hopes and heart with a few words if she told me to get the hell out.

With that reassurance, I make my way down the aisle and toward the steps leading up to the stage as Claire descends them. I give her another sheepish smile before pulling her into a hug.

"I'm sorry. I couldn't help myself once I found out where you were." That's the last time I will apologize for sneaking in here, and now that I said it, I won't feel guilty about it anymore.

Claire pulls away but keeps her hands on my shoulders. "It's over and done with. Though, don't expect me to trust you again." Her eyes narrow teasingly before they grow alight with amusement once more. "But now you must suffer the wrath and inquisition of Signora Gelardi. This will be punishment enough. I would apologize beforehand, but you deserve it."

I love her playful mood, but if I were her, I would be more concerned with what *I* may say to Signora. After hearing her bark at Claire, I want to put her in her place.

We walk over to where Signora is standing next to the piano, arms crossed, brown eyes narrowed with intimidation behind her small, rectangular glasses. She is taller than Claire, but still much shorter than me. Regardless, her intimidating stance makes her appear taller. She has an air of superiority about her that would make most men turn into cowering, quivering little boys. Not me. I grew up with my mother. Nothing else on this earth is more frightening than her when she is in professor mode.

"Signora Gelardi, this is Noah. Noah, this is my tutor and once a great Prima Donna, Signora Gelardi. *Behave*," she whispers the last part, but I don't know if it's intended for me or her tutor.

I hold out my hand for a handshake, but Gelardi scoffs at it.

"I have no interest in meeting you, or you taking her time away from me. At least *Troy* knew not to do that." Her accent is thick, and she slips into Italian often, but I understand every word she says.

My face feels hot and grows redder with every word that continues out of her bitchy mouth. Not able to hold my anger back, damning my pride, I shoot back, "While I care about Claire, I don't like your prejudice toward me when you haven't even met me. She's here for every one of your damn practices. I haven't taken her away from that, have I?" Not waiting for her to answer, I continue, "As for Troy, what do you think would have happened with your *time* if he had succeeded in raping her?"

I see the shock on her face that she quickly tries to cover, meaning Claire hid that tidbit from her, which makes me mad at myself for breaking that confidence, even though the whole town knows of the rumor. Whether they believe it or not is another story.

"So don't use that idiot over me," I continue. "Don't judge me or our relationship. And don't interfere in *our* time after she is done devoting most of *hers* to you."

There is a very loud quietness in the auditorium after my angry speech as Gelardi stares at me with unquestionable intensity before turning her eyes to Claire.

I, too, look at Claire, suddenly nervous to see what her reaction is. This is the second time tonight I gave Claire a reason to reject me, and it tears me up inside.

Claire is in an eye-lock with Gelardi. They both appear to be communicating in some way. Finally, I see Gelardi shake her head minutely. Then Claire turns to me, looking disappointed, but whether it is with me or her tutor, I don't know.

She squeezes my hand that we continued to hold throughout the confrontation. I remember feeling her hand tightening around mine during Gelardi's tongue lashing, but I didn't realize that the assuring hand was still grasped in mine until now.

~Claire~

Without a word, I pull Noah away from Signora Gelardi, and we make our way out of the theater. I hear her collect her music, and it reminds me to do the same, but I just want to focus on getting out of this auditorium and away from—Noah said it right—Signora Gelardi's prejudice.

I am more disappointed in her than I am in Noah. They are both hotheaded, but Signora attacked first, despite my warning to her to act decent. Noah was only defending himself, and he was right. He hasn't done anything to take my time away from my music, though I would have rather Signora not know why I'm not talking to Troy anymore. Regardless, it would have been a matter of time before she heard about it.

When we get outside, Noah pulls against my hand, making me stop abruptly. I look up at him as I try to clear the worry from my thoughts and get back into a happy place, not wanting to ruin the night. It is Halloween after all, and it's supposed to be a night of fun, mystery, and entertainment.

Noah grasps my waist with his empty hand and pulls me toward him. I have to tilt my head back to look at him when we are this close.

"I'm not sorry for what I said back there. I know I can't help myself during a confrontation, and though I would rather use my fists to get my point across, I will never hit a woman. I don't think that beast in there is a woman, though, so it was close." His mouth quirks up a bit, but he quickly recovers, trying to be more serious. "I think you know by now that I don't like most people, but she is seriously the worst I've met in a long time, besides my mom.

"I don't know what you are thinking right now … about us," he clarifies, "though you're still holding my hand. But I think I should stay away from her from now on. I don't want to jeopardize your relationship with her, or your tutoring. Period."

I sigh in exhaustion. This night better turn around soon.

"It's going to be fine. She's … who she is. Nothing is going to

84

change her ways. She thinks I'm distracted and needs to find someone to blame. That's you. I love the woman, but I'm glad you put her in her place. I think she is really surprised that you stood up to her. Believe it or not, you impressed her. Though she will never admit it." I smile at the memory of her speechless, staring at him then me like she was trying to figure out another avenue to argue.

Noah bends down and kisses me on the lips, lingering, but no tongue. "I promise to wait out here from now on. No more confrontations with the beast."

I laugh as he guides me over to my car where his bike is parked next to it. When we get there, he hands me a good-sized box that is strapped to the back of his bike with bungee cord. It's not wrapped, just a cardboard box with no stamps or print telling me what it could be.

"What's this?" I take the box with a confused expression, shaking it gently, but I don't hear anything move inside.

"Just open it."

Noah is always so direct. He looks a bit nervous but excited also. It makes me even more curious to know what he is giving me.

Since we don't have much time left before his show starts, I hurriedly rip off the tape then set the box on the hood of my car so I can pull out the bubble wrap, exposing a white motorcycle helmet with a tinted shield mask.

"Uh …" I'm at a loss for words. Does he really think I'm going to get on the back of his bike?

He's grinning now, possibly amused by my shock. He pulls the helmet out then grabs the now empty box, tossing it into the back of my car. Then he swaggers back over to me, locking eyes with mine.

"Let's put this on you." He lifts the helmet to the top of my head.

"Noah, I can't—"

"One ride. Let me take you to the show tonight. If you don't like it, you never have to ride with me again. Okay?"

I swallow hard and nod, shaking with nerves as he pushes the helmet over my head.

The tint is so dark I can barely see, but then Noah lifts the visor, and that's when I notice there are two screens on the face, the inside one without tint.

I look up at Noah who is looking down at me with a smile that reaches his eyes.

"You look so adorable. Don't be nervous. I won't let anything happen to you." The helmet muffles his voice, but I can hear him clearly enough. He takes off his jacket and holds it out for me to slide my arms through before zipping it up for me. "I want to kiss you right now."

I want him to kiss me, too, like our first kiss.

"Got your keys?"

I hand them to him and continue to stand by the trunk of my car as I watch him lock up my car.

"Do you need your purse or anything?"

I shake my head, but he pulls out my cell phone from my purse, anyway, and tucks it into his back pocket as he comes back over to me and grasps my fingers in his, locking them together. Without another word, he pulls me toward his bike, not letting go of my hand as he lifts his leg over the bike and straddles it. Then he pulls me over and guides me behind him, wrapping my arms around his waist.

"You need to hold on tight. You can hold on to your wrist."

I do as he says, scooting closer against his back until our bodies are flushed together. Heat pools down low, making me throb at the connection and friction. I can hear my own breathing pick up.

Noah stills for a beat before continuing with his instructions. Clearing his throat, he tells me, "Now lift your feet and place them on the outside of these pegs."

I see where he kicks one of the foot pegs, and then slowly lift one foot then the other to rest on them. Noah is fully supporting the bike now, and that scares me to death. I imagine all these scenarios in my head where we get into head-on collisions, hit a deer, lose control of the bike. So many nightmares run through my head, and I cringe at the phantom pain of being in them.

I don't want to die. I especially don't want to die slowly in excruciating pain.

"Claire? Claire." Noah's voice pulls me out of my visions of blood and gore.

"Yeah?" I squeak.

"You'll be fine, angel." And with that, he starts the motor and backs us out of the parking space.

~Noah~

Claire's soft body is pressed against mine, her breasts moving against my back with every bump in the road. I can feel her heat against my lower back as I nestle into it unconsciously. Her long legs are parallel with mine, and I can feel her thighs contracting, squeezing mine when we take a turn.

I have never had a girl on my bike before. It's turning me on so damn much. I want to take her on this bike and put myself out of this misery. Rid myself of the ache.

Through the torture, I can tell Claire is having a great time. She is relaxed, leaning more into me and loosening her death grip. I had really hoped she would enjoy this freedom of feeling the wind whip past you, like flying. The freedom makes you feel like you can overcome anything, leave everything behind, be yourself, and have no one tell you where to go or what to do. It's only you and your thoughts.

I hear her laugh, which causes me to laugh. Then I lean down into the bike, bringing her with me as I accelerate. I won't do anything reckless when she's with me, but I was driving like a grandma before, so now that I know she's relaxed and loving it, I can let go and pick up speed.

When we get to Jeremy's, I pull the bike behind the restaurant and into the employees' parking lot. The place is already packed. It's only Wednesday, but it is Halloween, and Jeremy is hosting a costume party tonight. The crowd is going to be unreal. I just hope Max is up for the job of babysitting Claire for me tonight.

I turn off the bike and feel Claire, on shaky legs, try to climb off. But before she can get anywhere, I scoot back, throwing her back into her seat. She lets out a small yelp in surprise as I grab her red-heeled foot and pull it around me, grabbing her waist to guide her around until she is straddling my thighs. Then I take off her helmet, dropping it to the ground, before I grab either side of her face and kiss her like I need her to breathe.

She lets out a gasp at the sudden assault, and I take the opportunity to plunge my tongue into her mouth, tasting her again for the first time in weeks. She moans as her hands come up to grip my shoulders while I slide my hands into her tangled hair.

I inhale her scent deeply through my nose before tilting my head to deepen the kiss. I don't know why I have waited so long to kiss her like this again. Yes, I do. Because I get consumed in it.

Her lips are so soft, her mouth so innocent. She kisses with tentativeness, yet with a poise that would have me believe she does this on a regular basis. Her passion rivals my own. I have never experienced the near combustible attraction that shields the rest of the world from me when I am with her like this. It's like time stands still and locks us in a single moment. A bubble that no one can penetrate.

She moans again and squirms in my lap, pressing herself against the hard bulge in my pants. My frenzy grows. I want to relieve her. I want to relieve me. I want to strip us down and fuck her on this bike.

My hands have a mind of their own. They move through her hair, following the trail to her firm ass where I grip each globe, enhanced by her tight pants, and pull her against my erection, giving her the friction she needs. She gasps but doesn't pull away or try to stop me. My mind has completely shut down, only thinking of pleasuring her.

I pull her with me as I scoot back, and she grinds down on my erection. It amazes me that someone as inexperienced as her still has the instinct to know what would alleviate her arousal. It makes me wonder dark thoughts about her, which *really* increases the frenzy in my body. The visual is not what I need right now.

I press her back against the bike, her legs still draped to the ground and her arms now locked around my neck. I remove my hands from her ass and glide them down her legs to behind her knees, never removing my mouth from hers. Drawing her legs up around my waist, I scoot in to feel her heat. We both moan at the connection.

I grind myself against her, never stopping contact where we both need it most. I swear to God I am about to come in my pants.

I break away from her mouth with a gasp of air, trailing kisses down her jaw to her ear where I bite her lobe before moving to her neck. We are both breathing so hard right now, our chests rising and falling against one another's.

I return to her mouth when my name escapes her lips.

I can't hear her tell me to stop right now. I don't want to. But her arms are pulling me closer, telling me the opposite.

I let go of her knees, not knowing where to go, yet wanting to go where I can't. Encircling her hips, thumbs digging in under her pants, I stop myself from going *there*, sliding one hand back to her thigh. Then I travel up her ribs, lifting her shirt and exposing her little waist. Then I stop again, right at the curve of her breasts, knowing this is uncharted territory for Claire.

God, it's so frustrating to restrain myself. But I will do it, because this girl is nothing like the others. She needs slow, needs someone to be tender with her, needs someone to show her love first.

"Noah," she gasps around my mouth. "I need … I can't …" She's frantic with her need, pressing against me urgently.

Sweat is beading on her forehead, so I gently wipe it off before pressing my forehead against hers, staring into her wide eyes. "I know. Relax and let go. You're holding it in."

"Touch me," she begs, arching her back and pressing down on me harder.

My hands are back in her hair, working the tangles out with my fingers. "I am," I answer, grinding, kissing.

"No," she mewls, trying to grab my hand.

Jesus Christ.

I interlock our hands, misinterpreting what she wants, until she guides my hand down to her core.

"I can't." My voice breaks.

I know her frustration. I feel it, too. But I have experience reining it in where she doesn't.

I can feel her whole body coiled tight, her legs gripping my sides, digging into my ribs. Her arm still around my neck is taut, and her hand interlocked with mine is squeezing my fingers.

"Please, Noah," she begs again, so I pick up the pace, grinding into her fast, aligning the length of my cock right against the apex of her thighs, pumping my hips through the thin material of her soft pants. I'm so close, dry humping like I did with girls when I was thirteen.

"Stop ... holding on," I grunt out, not knowing how to explain this to her.

"Noah," she whispers, her brows drawn together like she's thinking.

I want her to stop thinking and simply feel, so I bend down to her neck and lick a line up until I reach her lips, then plunge my tongue back in, mating with hers.

Claire moans, her body quivering and shaking with torment, finally finding her release.

I lift up from her body, watching as her eyes roll back before she shuts them. Her legs have gone limp again, resting over my thighs. Her hands are staying busy, though, one stroking down her belly, the other pulling her hair. Then the hand on her belly brushes over her breast, groping, while the hand in her hair moves down over her face where it ends its movements at clutching her neck. It's the most erotic display I have ever seen.

Claire is completely undone. Her eyes are still closed as she comes back from wherever she has been. I sit silently as her breathing regulates. My own comes down, though my dick still hurts. She looks like she's about to fall asleep on my bike.

I lean over and press a gentle kiss to her lips, and her eyes open in response as I pull away. Then I pull her up into a sitting position before getting off the bike so I can easily help her down.

Just as she swings her leg around the seat of the bike, we hear clapping. Two sets of clapping.

I turn to see Chelsea and Nikki walking toward the back door with big smiles on their faces. Chelsea is dressed like an angel, with wings on her back. Her clothes are styled more like Tinkerbell than any painting of a Biblical angel. Nikki is her contrary, dressed as a devil, with horns on her head. Her clothes, or lack thereof, are more suitable to her theme, dressed in practically nothing, like Chelsea. Both girls scream attention and loose morals. Neither have the detachment I preferred in girls in the city.

"That was better than porn," Chelsea comments, her eyes taking in every detail of my body with a look of lust. Her tongue peeks out from between her teeth before they both turn around and walk into the restaurant.

Chapter 8

Max's House

~Claire~

I sit with Max and his friends, Ryan, Seth, Matt, and Calvin, as the Characters play one of their newest songs. The audience is enthralled, most eyes riveted to the stage.

Cyn is dressed as a ballerina, a contrast to her usual dark and distressed clothes. She looks cute in her pink leotards and purple tutu, her blonde hair pinned back in a classic ballerina bun, with pink and purple threads weaved into her hair.

My eyes zero in on Kyle's pink zebra-print drumsticks as he beats away. From observing his personality, I never imagined he would be caught with something so feminine. I shrug to myself, bringing my eyes back to Noah.

Watching him play is a titillating experience. The way his hands move, commanding, controlling, yet lightly strumming while the hand on the neck glides. His eyes are closed as he sings; neck arched up; sweat dripping down his face, down his neck, to disappear under his black shirt. His voice is different than when he talks. It's not as deep, but so sinful with his moaning lines. He's a lot more open than I think he knows, baring his soul and communicating to more people than he does talking in a month.

His voice purposely cracks on the next line, bringing me back to the parking lot.

I am so embarrassed. I can't believe the things we did; humiliated that out of all people, Chelsea was the one to witness it. I know by tomorrow the whole school will know, not that I care about that. I'm more concerned that our private moment, that my first ... orgasm was witnessed by her. She will take our moment and paint it red.

"Are you guys coming back with us after this?" Max questions.

I look over at the big, muscled, tattooed man. Max is misunderstood. He looks like a hardcore tattoo artist, but under the exterior is an intelligent man. Noah doesn't know this about him, but Max is a geneticist. He finished school a year ago, his tattoo shop paying his way. He loves the research and does it in his spare time, but remains a tattoo artist. This is why I never discriminate—you never really know a person by their looks. The same goes for Noah.

"I don't know." I raise my voice to be heard. "Noah hasn't mentioned it."

I grab my phone off the table and look at the time. It's already after ten, so the show should be ending soon. We have school tomorrow, but I allow myself until midnight before thinking of going to bed most nights. If we go to Max's house, then we can hang out for at least an hour. I would love to see the place and get to know everyone better. I have been here the past three Fridays and sat with this crowd, but the music hasn't allowed for much conversation. I know their names. I know what they do for a living. And I know they are fiercely protective of those they call friends.

"Happy Halloween," Noah says, ending the show before he unstraps his guitar and disappears into the back room.

The audience, dressed from witches to toilet paper rolls and everything in-between, breaks out in applause and screams for more.

I continue to sit with Max as the band quickly goes through the motions of breaking down the drums and unloading them through the back door, while people—mostly girls—try to talk to the band. Kyle is verbose with ladies, but Noah disregards them, answering with one word replies. If he wasn't so hot, his attitude would chase his fans away.

My soda is gone before the band is done packing up their gear. Ryan offers to get me another, but I shake my head. Then Max is asking to get out of the booth.

I scoot out, noticing all the men getting up from the table, so I grab my phone. Then Max tucks me into his side, picking up Cyn's bass as we walk by. I turn and notice all the guys grab something from Kyle's pile of drums.

We continue out of the restaurant through the back door where Noah, Kyle, and Cyn are on their way back in.

"We got the rest of it," Calvin says, coming up from the rear.

Noah pulls me from Max, entwining our hands together. "Thanks."

Cyn comes up to Max and kisses him thoroughly while trying to dislodge her bass from his grip. Max wins, smiling down on her. "I got it."

She rolls her eyes at him before turning toward me. "Noah was telling us that you sing. You going to do a duet with us one of these nights?"

I look up at Noah in what I can imagine is a look of horror.

He glances down at me before narrowing his eyes at Cyn, who looks back at him coyly, pressing herself into Max's side for protection.

Noah's jaw ticks before he tells Cyn, "I haven't asked her yet. And now she'll probably never agree. Thanks, Cyn." He turns us around and heads toward his bike where he gently places the helmet on my head wordlessly.

Max's friends and Kyle are still loading the last of the drums into the truck when I look up to see Max and Cyn followed us.

"Nice." Cyn smiles, her words sounding underwater due to the helmet. "He finally got you on that thing?"

I lift the second visor and answer Cyn with a wide smile, "I love it! I don't think I can go back to my car now."

Noah grins. "Unfortunately, you have to. I can't ride my bike to school. Otherwise, I would pick you up on it every day."

"I asked Claire if you guys want to hang out at my place for a while—we're having our own Halloween party—but she says it's up to you." Max is stretching the truth.

Noah looks down at me again with his eyebrow cocked up in question.

I nod. "I've never been there. It would be nice to actually hold a conversation with everyone without having to yell."

Noah smirks. "Don't get your hopes up about that. There will be music, and it's always loud." He looks over at Max. "We'll follow you there."

I text my dad to let him know I will be home late, and then Noah takes my phone and stuffs it into his pocket since I don't have any. Then he takes his jacket off and puts it on me once more. I worry that he will be cold since the temperatures have been frigid lately.

Noah seems to read my mind. "Don't worry about me." He lowers the visor then gets on the bike, holding my hand as I swing my leg around and get on behind him.

The ride to Max's place is long. This is the time I start to wish we had my car so the ride back would be warm and more comfortable. Then I start to worry about how long we will stay. I was thinking until midnight, but then that will make me getting home around one. I might only be a month and a half away from turning eighteen, but even so, Dad won't be happy about me coming home *that* late. And already I feel so tired.

I yawn as Noah turns off the bike in the driveway of a large, brick factory building where there is a large garage housing numerous bikes in stages of repair. The front of the building has a neon sign that says *Madness Tattoos* with open windows that look into the shop, displaying walls showcasing tattoo art.

Max, with Cyn riding behind him, and his friends pull their own bikes into the garage. Then Kyle pulls up behind us. We wait for him to catch up before Noah pulls me into the garage where we move through another door that opens to a stairway. There is a door to the right that I assume opens into the back of the tattoo shop.

We all climb the stairs, loud music already pumping through the walls, muted by the closed door at the top of the stairs. When Max opens the door, lights, music, and rowdy voices flood out. There are people all over the open floorplan.

I quickly scan the room that consists of a modern kitchen, living room with bar in the corner, and a pool table dividing the kitchen from the living space. The kitchen has the longest breakfast bar I have ever seen, curving around two sides with ten stools, with an industrial-sized refrigerator and stove. The living room has three couches forming a U, plus other chairs strategically placed around the room.

The men all greet each other with handshakes and back pats,

including Noah and Kyle who must come here often. I get a lot of questioning looks. The looks from the women make me wonder if Noah knows any of them intimately, which makes me feel self-conscious.

Noah wraps his arm around my waist as he leads us to a group of chairs close to the bar. He sits in one, sinking low into the deep cushions before pulling me into his lap. I scoot until my back is against the arm, my butt falling into the comfortable cushion, and my legs draped over Noah's. It's a position we adopted many times at my house while we study, so it makes me feel slightly more comfortable in this house full of strangers.

Kyle is talking to a group of people. I think they are asking about me, because they all look over as Kyle points at me once. I scan the rest of the crowd, seeing a whole bunch of drinking, talking, making out, and people playing pool.

"Not what you expected, is it?" Noah threads his fingers through my hair, working out the tangles the wind caused. The gesture is comforting.

"I didn't know what to expect. I knew there was going to be a party, but I didn't realize Max had so many ... friends." I look at a black-haired beauty who has been eyeing us since we walked in. "Do you know her?"

Noah follows the direction of my eyes then quickly looks away. "That's Sassy. She's been hitting on me since the first night I came here."

"She's beautiful."

"She is," Noah acknowledges, which makes me look back at him, feeling hurt. "But I haven't *seen* another woman since the first time I saw you."

"You haven't ... dated anyone since you got here?" I have to ask. I know Noah isn't a virgin. He told me that he has never had a girlfriend, but he also didn't deny that he slept with many women; women much older and more experienced than me. Women who started coming on to him when he was fourteen. Women like Sassy.

I like the open honesty between us, yet I admit that it makes me feel inferior. How can I hold someone's attention who is much more experienced and probably expects more than I know how to give? I can't help thinking that it's only a matter of time before Noah gets bored with me. That he will want a more. How can he want a virgin? And how can I compete with women like Sassy, who even now is flashing bedroom eyes at Noah.

"No," Noah answers, pulling my attention away from Sassy once again. "Kyle tried to hook me up with Chelsea the first night." He shivers, mocking a look of disgust. "Then I saw you. And I haven't stopped looking ever since."

I smile as he leans in to kiss me. His lips linger on mine before he nips my bottom lip.

"I couldn't stop staring into those large, blue doe eyes. Staring at your long, soft hair, wanting to touch it. I wanted to kiss this little nose." He leans in and does just that. "And don't get me started on your body." He runs his hands down my arms, then he grips my hips. "You look so tiny, but you have these long, amazing legs." Both of us stare down at my legs. I see Noah swallow, his Adam's apple bobbing, before his eyes come back to mine, tension overtaking him, making me aware he is nervous. "I have to admit that your hair and then your ass were the first two things I noticed when you walked into the room." His eyes start to get that hungry look. "Then your little waist and huge—"

I smack his arm gently as I watch Cyn and Max make their way toward us. Max sits on the chair across from us.

"What are you guys talking about?" Cyn asks, plopping down on Max's lap and adjusting herself into the same position as me.

"Nothing," I answer at the same time Noah says, "Claire." I give him a death look, which makes him chuckle before he kisses the tip of my nose again.

"Oh, are you talking her into singing with us?" Cyn assumes.

"I'm working on it," Noah answers before ignoring her as she starts to sing her rendition of opera. It makes me laugh. "Would you ever consider a duet with me?" he finally asks.

I look down at our hands that are in a dispassionate game of thumb war. "I don't know. I guess it would be fun, but I don't sing to the music you play."

Noah lowers his thumb over mine, winning the battle. "I'll write something you can sing to," he promises.

Our thumbs start battling each other again, mine always stretching away from his offensive moves. "You going to write an aria," I tease.

"I don't know what that is, but I'll find out. I've had a song in my head all night that I would love to hear you sing."

My thumb snags his, though I know he let me win. His thumb is twice the size of mine. "I'd love to hear it." I release our hand from the game then run my fingers over the calluses on his until our hands line up.

Noah watches our hands before closing his fingers over mine, swallowing my hand whole. He tucks me closer into him, wrapping his arms around me, and I rest my head against his shoulder, closing my eyes.

"It doesn't look like I'm going to get much talking to Max and his friends tonight," I muse, listening to all the sounds in the house. "I like being here. His house feels comfortable, though I don't know anyone."

"You didn't look comfortable when we walked in." I feel Noah's lips at my forehead, caressing back and forth.

"Mmm ..." I snuggle closer to Noah, tucking my face into his neck. "I was overwhelmed. I didn't expect so many people to be here. It's like the crowd at Jeremy's relocated here."

~Noah~

Claire falls asleep in my lap as Max and Cyn start debating some topic Cyn is learning in school. I feel her gentle breaths on my neck, and her arms have relaxed around my neck. I shift in the chair slowly, lowering myself so Claire is more reclined.

"That's her?" Sassy asks after making her way over.

Claire is right about her. She is beautiful. Her black hair is in small dreads that flow halfway down her back. She has ice blue eyes framed in dark lashes, and heavy eyeliner that only makes her eyes stand out that much more. She's tall, probably five-ten, with a swimsuit model body. She is my type in every way, except I saw Claire. No one comes close to Claire's perfection now. Like how I now see that Sassy has bony hips, her lips are too thin, and her nose is too long. I don't think I would have noticed that before I saw Claire.

I nod my head in answer.

"She's gorgeous," Sassy says as squats down, audaciously studying Claire's features up close. "She's a little too good for you, though. Doesn't really fit in here."

I nod, knowing Claire's too good for me, yet ... "She fits in where I am." Claire might be too good for this crowd, for me, but Max likes her, she's my girl, and I won't come here without her. That's my logic of her fitting in.

"I'd like to meet her some time. I want to know the woman I lost to." Sassy is a tad unstable.

I shake my head at her. "You can't lose what you never had. Isn't that the saying?"

She shrugs. "I would have. Maybe someday," she says in fake wistfulness before pushing up from her position, her leather pants squeaking with the movement. She gives me a wink before sauntering off.

Max and Cyn watched the whole exchange without saying a word. Now Cyn watches Sassy saunter off with a deep frown on her face, while Max eyes me in warning. Does he honestly think I would hit that and ruin what is growing with Claire? His look is surely telling me that.

"You guys can take the third bedroom on the right," he tells me, looking at a still passed out Claire.

I shake my head. "Can't. I need to get her home tonight. We have school in the morning."

Max waves his hand like it's no big thing. "I get up at six. I'll wake you guys. As tired as she is, you don't want her riding on your bike," he reasons.

"Wasn't going to put her on my bike. I was going to have Kyle drive her while I followed." It's too cold out to ride. I about froze my nipples off on the way over here.

Max gestures toward the bar where Kyle is chugging a beer. "Kid is staying here, too. If you're underage, one drink and you're stuck here for the night."

I curse Kyle under my breath. It would serve him right if I took Katy's truck and left him here. Then he would have to answer to why he was drinking. But then that would leave my bike here. Who knows what he would do to it in retaliation?

Crap. What am I going to do? Jonathan Sawyer is an okay guy, lenient and trusting of Claire, but how will he feel if she doesn't come home tonight? Will he blame me? I need to call him. No—I look at the time on my watch; it's already after twelve—I will text him. That way, if he's asleep, he will get the message when he wakes up. If he's still up, he can call me back.

I nod at Max, and he gestures with his head toward the hallway that leads to bedrooms. I pull Claire closer to me, securing her in my hold, and then get to my feet. The girl can't weigh even a hundred pounds by how light she is.

She sighs against my neck, and I feel her arms tighten around me. I don't know if I woke her or if she's instinctively holding me.

I make my way through the crowd that parts when they see me and make my way down the hallway. All the bedroom doors are closed. I'm afraid what I will find when I open the door Max designated as ours. I can only imagine walking into a couple having sex.

Surprisingly, the bedroom is empty and clean, and the bed is dressed in sheets and blankets that don't look rumpled. There is one nightstand, a dresser, a TV mounted to the wall above it, a bathroom, and a closet.

I close and lock the door, using the light coming in from the window to guide my way. The sounds out in the main room are muffled now, still present, but subdued. I pull the blanket and sheet away from the bed before lying Claire down. She automatically curls up, facing away from me. I take her shoes and belt off, but then stand there, debating whether to take her pants off or not. I would want someone to do that for me if I was in this situation.

That logic cements my decision, and I eagerly go to her buttons, finding that they are snaps and open at a tug.

I expose the front of her panties, finding red lace. I bite my bottom lip to stifle the groan building in my throat. I figured virginal white for her. Or pink with a floral print. I did not expect this.

I slow down my breathing that has escalated in the few seconds it took to expose her panties and guide my fingers into the waistband of her pants, pushing the material down her legs. Claire stirs and starts to kick her own pants off when they reach her ankles. Then she turns over onto her belly and gropes at the blankets. I quickly pull them over her, needing to cover that marvelous ass of hers and not wanting her to wake up.

Turning away from her sleeping form, I pace the perimeter as I text her dad.

Not what a dad wants to hear, but we're in Carson. Claire fell asleep. Taking her home in morning in time for school. No alcohol, no drugs involved. I drove my bike. Claire's car is at theater. Don't feel safe riding back when she's tired. Call if you have any concerns with this. Noah.

That sounded good, right?

I toss Claire's phone onto the nightstand then take off my jacket, tossing it onto the floor. My shirt, boots, pants, and socks follow. I usually sleep in boxers, but ever since moving here, I have to wear sleep pants to bed because little Abby likes to wake me up in the morning. Baby girl would be traumatized if she encountered my morning wood.

I look over at Claire's phone just as it beeps and lights up. Her dad decided to text instead of calling. That's a good sign.

"To be trusted is a greater compliment than being loved." George MacDonald.

Wow. Claire's dad ... I don't even know what to say to that. I know it makes me want to deserve that trust. What I did earlier tonight with Claire was too much too fast. I need to rewind and go back to my no touching rule. Otherwise, it's too easy to lose control.

I put the phone back down on the nightstand then turn the bed covers down before sliding in. Claire's still lying on her stomach, her face toward me. I lower until I am eye-level with her and stare at her face, watching her sleep. Her hair is tumbled around her face, obstructing my view, so I push it back, causing Claire to shift in her sleep. I freeze, then slowly bring my hand back to my side of the bed.

Claire sighs in her sleep, her mouth parting as she lets out a breath. Her eyes are moving beneath her lids. I hope she's dreaming about me. Her arm is stuffed under the pillow with her hand sticking out. I reach for it and hold on, the only contact I allow myself for tonight.

~

That small contact didn't work out the way I intended.

I wake up to hearing Max tapping on the door. The sun is already out, lighting up the bedroom. I have hair in my face. Claire's head is tucked under mine, resting on my dead arm. Our legs are intertwined. My other hand is resting on her hip, and her arms are tucked between us underneath her chin, almost like she is in prayer.

I swipe her hair out of my face, brushing it down her back before pulling her into me. I don't want to get up yet. I don't want to leave the confines of this bed, where she is in my arms, trusting me.

Claire stretches, her arms coming over her head as her legs tauten and stretch downward. She looks like a cat. She yawns in my face before quickly covering her mouth, which makes me laugh, and her eyes dart open, meeting mine. It only takes her a second to register that she is not at home.

She darts up into a sitting position, the sheets pooling at her waist. Her hair is in disarray, her eyes have smeared mascara under them, and her shirt is only on one shoulder. She looks absolutely delectable.

I lift my knees to hide my erection, waiting to see if she will get up and display her ass. At that thought, I start to worry about what she will say or do when she realizes I took them off.

"Where's my phone?" She looks around the room and spots it on the nightstand next to me. I move to hand it to her, but she is already stretching over me, dangerously close to my erection. "My dad is going to kill me. Oh, it's only six; maybe he's still asleep."

"I texted your dad for you," I tell her as she fumbles with her phone, worriedly biting her lip.

She looks over at me before returning her attention to her phone. "Dad loves using quotes when he doesn't know how else to respond."

I take it she saw our conversation last night. "Where are we? Are we still at Max's?" She doesn't wait for me to answer. She shakes her head. "I can't believe I fell asleep like that. I'm so sorry. Is your uncle and aunt going to mind?"

"Me? No. Kyle, though, is another question altogether." I stretch then rest my hands behind my head, watching, waiting for Claire to blow up at me for not waking her up. For not taking her home. For texting her dad. For not wearing pants. For sleeping next to her.

She rubs her fingers under her eyes. "He's still here, too?" She looks down at the dark smudges on her fingers. "I look a hot mess, don't I?"

"I think you look cute," I tell her honestly.

She looks over at me, her eyes scrolling down my body, stopping at the tattoo on my lower ribs. "Is that the only tattoo you have?"

"Yeah." I look down at it as she studies the Latin, leaning in closer to read it. *The unexamined life is not worth living.* It's Socrates."

"What does it mean?" She pulls away from reading it and sits back up. She's cross-legged now, the sheet pooling dangerously low to the edge of those red lace panties, but she doesn't even seem concerned. She must know that she's sans pants by now, right?

I sit up and lean back against the headboard. "To me, it means to learn from your mistakes; have no regrets by thinking through your choices."

Claire yawns again, nodding in understanding, before tearing the sheet off her and getting up, giving me an absolute, undeterred view of her ass. Her panties are barely concealing her; I can see through the lace. She bends over to pick up her pants, completely innocent in the storm she's brewing inside me.

"Claire?" My mouth is dry.

"Yeah?"

I watch as she turns around, putting one leg inside her pants then the other, giving me a full view down her disordered shirt. She hops up to pull her pants up, snapping the buttons before adjusting her top. She finally looks at me.

"Don't bend over in front of a man like that in just see-through panties."

Her face instantly turns red, the blush bleeding up her chest to her cheeks. There is horror and embarrassment in her eyes.

She quickly turns away, bending down once more to pick up her shoes and belt, before busying herself with putting them on.

I lunge across the bed and snag her around the waist, pulling her back down, then leaning over her as she tries to divert her tear-filled eyes.

"Why are you crying?"

"Embarrassment, I guess. Shame, maybe." She closes her eyes and inhales through her nose.

"You have nothing to feel embarrassed or ashamed about. It was sexy as hell. Your confidence is very, very sexy." I kiss her neck, nipping, which makes Claire giggle. "That's better. You need to be more conscious of your actions."

Another soft rap comes to the door.

"We're up," I call out.

Looking down at Claire, I see her smile once more. "I didn't mean to hurt your feelings," I whisper, wiping the freed tears from under her eyes.

Her smile drops. "I know. I … I guess I haven't really been around people my own age to pick up on … that. I mean, I know about it. I just wasn't thinking." Her smile returns. "Maybe it's you. I'm more open when I am with you than with anyone else."

I stare down at her lips, wanting to continue what we did on my bike. "I hope so." I kiss her, but keep it short. If I linger, I won't be able to pull away. "I need to get dressed. And coffee. I seriously need some coffee."

I roll off her and toward the other side of the bed where my clothes are laid out across the floor. Claire's eyes are on me the entire time I get dressed. I don't turn around, letting her look without feeling she shouldn't.

"Noah?"

"Claire?" I already know what she is going to say.

"I see what you mean about bending over. You shouldn't be allowed to do it, either."

I can't stop the laugh that bursts out of me.

Chapter 9

How Can Something Explained as Evil Be So Beautiful?

~Noah~

A week later, I meet Claire outside her classroom door, and she greets me with a smile.

"Aunt Katy baked homemade macaroni and cheese last night. I missed it, so I'm eager to get there and have some before Abby eats it all."

That causes Claire to giggle. "Abby is cute. But if she wants to eat all the mac and cheese, I don't think you stand a chance against her."

Claire has been to my aunt and uncle's house a few times now. Sometimes I endure eating in the cafeteria with her and sometimes I leave her alone in the library while I go home for lunch, but sometimes I want those few precious moments when we can be alone, even during a five-minute car ride.

Mark and Katy love her, and Abby simply adores her. She spoils Abby rotten, so Abby loves when Claire shows up, occupying all her time with her dolls and new drawings she has to show her. Katy fawns over Claire. They could spend hours talking girl code if I wasn't such a jealous bastard for her attention.

"No, I wouldn't, would I? But I have you with me as a distraction. She won't think twice about sharing her macaroni." I grin.

She gives me a look of mock horror and slaps me gently on the arm. "You're using me for macaroni and cheese?"

I laugh out right, loving how simply we fall into easy banter. "Guilty."

"Now you'll have to contend with me *and* Abby." She crosses her arms over her chest. "There will be no mac and cheese for you."

I try to pout like I'm hurt, but I can't keep a straight face long enough, laughing again at our game. "Come on, angel; you're going to deprive me of my mac and cheese?"

"Maybe." She laughs now.

We keep up the banter until we are pulling up to the house, where Abby is already running toward the car. "Cware!"

Of course I'm not here when Claire is around.

"Cware! Cware! I pway dwess up like fawee! Wanna see my wings?" She's wearing them over the dress Aunt Katy put her in this morning, spinning a three-sixty to show Claire before launching herself into her arms and giving her a big hug. Claire spins her around, making her squeal. "Let's go pway in my room." She wiggles her way out of Claire's arms, so Claire sets her down, and then Abby is tugging at her hand.

We follow Abby into the house as I tell her, "Claire is being mean to me today, Abby. She said I can't have any mac and cheese." I give the little girl my pout as Claire gasps at me.

Abby looks at my sad face, and her own face falls before she looks at Claire. "Why No-ie no get mac and weese?"

Aunt Katy chuckles from her spot at the oven, already reheating *my* macaroni and cheese.

Claire shoots me the evil eye before she smiles at Abby. "Because I thought *we* were going to eat it all." Claire tries to get Abby to side with her, but Abby doesn't understand the game yet.

"But Mommy said No-ie begged for mac and weese this morning. That's not nice not sharing." Now Claire is getting the evil eye as Abby wags her finger at her.

Me and Katy laugh as I pick Abby up and start tickling her, telling her she's right.

Aunt Katy walks over to Claire and gives her a hug. They exchange pleasantries, and then Aunt Katy is pulling the leftover macaroni out of the oven, and her and Claire put them on plates for the four us. I put Abby in her booster seat before getting up and making her a cup of milk. I pour myself another cup of coffee and get Claire and Aunt Katy a can of soda. Then we are all sitting around the table, digging into the leftovers.

"Katy, this is fabulous," Claire gushes at her first bite, covering her mouth as she talks around the mouthful of food.

I grin at her. "Told ya."

~Claire~

I place a couple dishes in the sink as Noah announces that it is time to leave. I quickly try to rinse off the dishes so we don't leave a huge mess for Katy.

"I got this. You need to go," Katy says as she comes up behind me.

"Thanks," I tell her, drying my hands off on a paper towel.

"Ready?" Noah asks from behind me as Abby crashes into my legs, wrapping her arms around them.

"Bye, Cware. No-ie says you play with me next time!"

"I promise, Abby." I turn to Katy. "See you soon."

"Bye, Claire. Noah, I expect you and Kyle to rinse out the trash cans when you get home from school."

Noah rolls his eyes after he turns away from her, his hand in mine, pulling me out the door. "Got it!" he calls back before muttering under his breath, "That's disgusting. Kyle is alone in that one."

I visibly shiver, agreeing with him. Cleaning out garbage cans is nauseating.

He opens the car door for me, and I slide in then watch him as he comes around the car. He is so gorgeous, wearing another pair of faded jeans; a faded blue, soft T-shirt; and his jacket. His hair is windblown with drops of rain from the drizzle that just started, making the temperature much colder. Soon, the snow will start to fall. I give it until my birthday.

He glides into the car and starts the engine before turning to me, a big smile on his face. "You'll never forget the mac and cheese, will you?"

I love him like this. So carefree and happy. His smiles are so rare, only given to me, Abby, and his aunt Katy. I start to wonder if he shares them with his mother, too, but then I remember his comparison to his mother and Signora Gelardi. Yeah, I don't think he likes his mother much.

That leads me to wondering about his mom as puts the car in reverse and pulls out of the driveway. I know she's a history professor, but that's about it. I don't know what she looks like, though Noah must resemble her, because his uncle has lighter features, and Noah is all dark. I want to ask him about his parents, but he is in too good of a mood to sour, so instead I play along with him.

"Definitely not. That was the best macaroni and cheese I've ever had. I have to make it for Dad. He loves cheese. You'll have to come over and test it out; determine if it's as good as your aunt's."

He raises my hand in his and brings it to his lips. "Count me in."

I smile back at him as we drive back to school in comfortable silence. I want to ask about his parents, especially his mom. He's never mentioned his dad, either, so I'm equally curious about him.

"What are you stressing about?" Noah breaks the silence, and I realize we are sitting in the school parking lot.

I bring my attention to him as he puts his hand on top of my own that I have been worrying, a habit of mine. "Nothing. Just thinking."

I know Noah doesn't believe me, but he doesn't pry, either. I love that about him; that he lets people have their own thoughts. He doesn't share often, not with other people, so he won't pressure someone else to do the same.

We stare into each other's eyes for a minute. I could get lost in his. They are so dark brown, turning black the longer I stare into them. He drops his eyes down to my mouth in hunger. I have noticed that about him. His eyes are usually dark brown, the color of stained oak, rimmed in black. However, when he's angry or … aroused, the black in his eyes engulfs the brown, demonic in its intensity. How can something explained as evil be so beautiful?

He wants to kiss me, and I want to let him, so I bridge the gap between us and caress his lips with mine. I think this is the first time I have made the first move.

I watch his eyes smolder as I sway my head side to side, gently, barely touching as I glide my lips across his, never really kissing, just

... contact. His breath passes his lips, caressing against mine, and I close my eyes before pressing more firmly against his bottom lip. The sound of our jackets cracking, our breaths, and the gentle splatter of rain is the only noise heard.

I start to pull on his jacket to bring him closer to me, but he pulls away, making me lose contact with his jacket, his lips. I watch as he runs his hands through his still lightly wet hair, messing it up further. Then he looks at the dashboard clock, looks back at me, and then quickly looks out at the rain.

"Claire, I get so caught up in you that I quickly lose control ... like the other night. I don't want to do that with you. I want ..." He stops midsentence, grabbing the door handle. "We need to get inside. Class starts in five minutes." With that, he opens the door and leaves me to myself.

He stands against the wet car door for several seconds, taking deep breathes, I notice. When I still haven't emerged from the car, he finally comes around and opens the door for me, taking my bag in one hand and my hand in the other, practically forcing me from the car. Then he shuts the door and presses up against cold, wet metal.

Noah kisses me like he kissed me last week on his bike, like I'm his reason for everything and he can't go another minute without taking something from me that gives him life. He drops my bag to the ground and cups my face, tilting it at an angle so he can get to me better. I grip the cool leather encasing his arms and hold on tight as he sinks into me, breathing me in as I breathe myself out. The kiss doesn't last long, but when he pulls back, I swear my vision blacks out in my peripheral and I see stars.

Noah slips his hands from my face, following a path until he comes to my hands. He grabs one before reaching over for my bag, and then he leads me into the school.

Once inside, I slip my hand out of Noah's and reach for my bag.

"I'll walk you to class," Noah protests.

I shake my head. "I'm going to the bathroom first. I'm sure my hair looks like a nest from the rain."

He relinquishes my bag, and I put it over one shoulder. Then he smooths my hair down. "You look beautiful."

I smile at him. "Maybe that was a modest way to tell you I have to pee."

Noah laughs, causing several people to look our way with curiosity. His laugh is so infections that I laugh with him. Then he pulls me into a hug, engulfing me in his tight embrace. I feel him press his lips to the top of my head before letting me go.

I walk in the direction of the bathroom without looking back, aware that he could be watching me and conscious not to make a fool of myself.

The bathroom is empty when I enter, the bell ringing overhead. Oh well. I go to a stall and do my business when I hear someone storming in, slamming the bathroom door open before slamming a stall door open. Then there is the sound of retching.

Sympathy for whoever it is comes over me. I finish up my business, wash my hands, and then wet some paper towels before walking over to the stall where the person is vomiting again. When the toilet flushes, I slowly push open the door and pause at what I find.

Chelsea is sitting on the floor, crying as she wipes her mouth off with the back of her hand. Her other hand is covering her waist. Her crying stops as soon as she sees me, and she adopts the hated look that she reserves only for me.

"God, you're the last person I want to see me like this," she comments.

I hand her the wet paper towels, and she snatches them out of my hand.

"The feeling is mutual," I tell her. "But I'm here, helping, so take the kindness."

"I don't need your help," she seethes. "I need your ex-boyfriend to man up and take responsibility for what he did to me. But noooo. I tell him I'm pregnant and he's the father, and he walks away from me. God, how could I have been so stupid? I'm on birth control. We used condoms. Well, guess what? *It didn't work!*" She laughs maniacally. "Even better, *the condom broke!* I mean, shit! Who the hell gets pregnant the one time the condom breaks while on birth control?" She stands up now, getting in my face. "I'll tell you who. *Me!*

"Is this karma, *Claire*? Is this what I get for being a nasty bitch

111

to you? Is that what you're thinking right now? That because I wanted to take everything you have that I got what I deserve? I knew Troy was in love with you, so I had to have him." She points down to her belly. "I have him now, all right. I have his *kid*, and now he's stuck with me! But noooo! I tell him and instead of being there for me, he just walks away and won't even talk to me!"

Tears pour down her face while I stand there, fear gripping me. Fear for Troy. Fear for his baby. And yeah, even fear for what the future holds for Chelsea.

"I hate you! I hate you! *I hate you!*" She starts hitting me, but she's crying so hard that her hits are feeble. That doesn't mean it doesn't hurt a little. And I let her because this girl has always hated me, though I never understood, and she needs to get this off her chest. I shush her and coo that everything is going to be all right; empty words, but meant to relax her. They do, and she pulls out of my embrace, leaning against the bathroom wall with her arms protectively over her belly.

"And I saw Noah first. He came to *my* party. But he didn't want me. He pawned me off on his stupid cousin. No one wants me, not the way they want you. Why? What do you have that I don't? I'm the pretty one, the popular one. But it's you who gets all the attention. And you don't even want it!

"Every guy I've been with, I've caught ogling you. Why, Claire? Why can't one guy like me better? Why can't I be someone's world, like how Noah looks at you? Shit, even James looks at you. And you know what? Turns out that he's gay!" My eyes must reveal my surprise because Chelsea starts nodding. "Yeah, he uses me so his parents won't find out—taking me to school dances and couple functions. I found out after homecoming. Messed up, isn't it?" She doesn't wait for me to answer; she's on a tangent and needs to get a lot off her chest. "Even more messed up that a gay man has the hots for you."

She shakes her head now, still glaring viciously at me. "Just go. Leave me here. I don't want you looking at me like that. I don't need your pity."

"Is there someone I can get for you? Nikki? The nurse?" I have to help this girl. Chelsea is only seventeen, and now she's pregnant. I wouldn't wish that on any girl, especially one who doesn't have the support of the father. I'm going to have to talk to Troy; convince him to man up and protect Chelsea. If she really is having his baby, he needs to be there for her.

"Just. Go."

There's nothing else to say. There's nothing I can do to make this situation any better, at least not from this end. So, I leave. I leave her sobbing as she leans over the bathroom sink, one hand clutching her waist.

Babies are supposed to be happy occasions. They are supposed to bring their parents joy. Birth is supposed to be a new beginning, an end to the old, a new chapter in lives. Births are supposed to be a sign of hope, of things to come, of togetherness and connecting.

I know differently. I know babies can also bring fear, and the want for a different path in life. I learned with my own birth that some people mourn it, loathe it. Some people run from it. They run from their babies because they can't stand the responsibility of nurturing another life form.

I hope that Chelsea isn't like my mother. That she will grow from the experience and learn compassion from it.

Chapter 10

This Isn't About Me

~Claire~

Another month passes by with the same routine, only broken up by dates with Noah. It seems that we are together every moment that we aren't occupied by school, band practice, or my lessons with Signora Gelardi, who has been even more abrupt with me and tries to extend my hours with her.

Thanksgiving weekend is the longest timespan I spend away from Noah, and I am miserable. Dad and I were invited upstate to a senator's home. Mayor Couer and his family were invited also. This gives me an opportunity to talk to Troy, something neither Dad nor Noah can prevent. I need to help Chelsea.

I am over the rape thing. Well, not over it. But now that I know what Chelsea is going through and what must be going through Troy's mind, I want to be supportive to my one-time friend. I *need* to know what he thinks about the situation, if his parents know, if he plans to do anything. I *need* to know that I at least tried to convince Troy to do the right thing.

Maybe I'm a sucker, but Chelsea's declaration of no one wanting her really got to me. I know what that feels like—my own mother didn't even want me. Therefore, I need to make this okay for her. I *need* Troy to be at her side, for her and their baby. I need to give Chelsea a reason to want her baby and find happiness with her new direction in life.

Once dinner is finished and the guests depart the formal dining room to gather in the formal living room, I pull Troy away, and we head toward the back of the house where I know from being here before that there is another less formal living room.

I sit on one of the worn-in chairs, and Troy plops down on the couch. Nervous to have this conversation with him, nervous to be alone with him, even when my father is only a few rooms away, I unconsciously start playing with the edge of my dress, raveling the edge around my fingers one by one. My hands can never stop moving when I'm anxious. I wonder if this is a trait I get from my mother.

"How have you been?" Troy breaks the uncomfortable silence.

I glance up at him before looking back down at my hand's activities. I can't look at him while we have this conversation. "Fine. Good." A smile involuntarily springs up at thinking about Noah. "Better than ever," I sigh out.

Troy nods out of my periphery. "I'm glad." He doesn't sound *glad*.

I glance at him again, and he catches my eye.

"Really, I am." He reclines back, his large body sinking into the cushions, his eyes never leaving mine. "I really am sorry ... for pushing you. I was a mess that day. And—"

"Please stop," I beg. "I don't want to talk about that." My hands have frozen in their twining. I make a conscious effort to remain still and calm, although my heart is racing. "Troy, I want to talk about Chelsea, not us."

"Why do you care about her?" He looks at me incredulously.

"Because I know." I see the shock on his face before he hides it behind a scowl. He looks toward the doorway as I continue. "I know she's pregnant. And that it's yours. Well, I guess it could be someone else's, but she's claiming it's yours."

Troy is still looking at the doorway. I see him swallow hard. Then he whispers, "Why would she tell you that?"

I laugh, but it's not a humorous one. "It's not like she came over and informed me. I caught her throwing up in the bathroom. She wasn't happy at being seen like that, especially by me. She went ballistic on me, spewing all the hate she feels toward me. And she told me what was going on. How she told you, and all you did was walk away. That's not fair to her, Troy." He's now looking at me, and I stare into his eyes as I tell him, "She's scared. Angry. She needs help. If there is a chance you are the ... father, then you need to help her, be

115

there for her. I know what it's like not to be wanted. Don't do that to her, to the baby. She needs support from wherever she can get it."

"Will you forgive me if I help her?"

I stand up in indignation. "For God's sake, Troy, this isn't about me!" I'm trying to keep my voice down. "You messed up. You both have. Take responsibility for your actions. Talk to her. Can you imagine how scared she is right now? She's seventeen and pregnant. Is she going to keep the baby? What if she aborts; do you think she wants that on her conscience? Do you want that on yours? How are her parents going to feel about this? And all the gossip that's going to occur at school; can you imagine the field day this is going to be? Chelsea thrives on popularity; how is this going to affect that for her?"

"Why are you so worried about her? I am—was—your best friend. How do you think *my* parents are going to respond? My dad is the goddamn mayor, and his son knocked up a girl. I've already been in a shitload of trouble. My dad has been taking me to recruiters to ship my ass away from here." He nods his head when he sees the shock on my face. "Yeah, consider me gone the minute that diploma touches my hand. Marine Corp, babe. I'll be gone for months to MCRD then to MCT. So, yeah …"

He sits up again and runs his hands over his face, continuing, "I don't know what to do for Chelsea. I mean, you know how she is. And then we were sleeping together behind Nikki's back. Nikki's a nice girl, but not the forever kind. Neither is Chelsea, for that matter. We were having fun, trying to see how long we could go before Nikki caught us. I can't be stuck with a person like that. If I help Chelsea, then I'm practically claiming the kid is mine. What if it's not?"

"Then you get a paternity test once the baby is born," I counter. "It's not rocket science, Troy."

"Claire, are you in here?" My dad steps through the doorway and freezes when he sees me with Troy. "What are you guys doing in here? Claire, you okay?"

"Yeah, Dad. Just talking," I answer with a warm smile as Mayor Couer and his wife follow in behind my dad.

Mrs. Couer starts gushing that we must be friends again. It's understandable to everyone that she's had a bit to drink.

"Come on, Claire. Senator McFee is asking if you would sing for us tonight." This is Dad trying to keep up appearances in front of others while getting me away from Troy.

I nod and stand up. Troy stands up, too, and when we walk around the couch to join our parents, I tell him, "Please, do the right thing. Talk to her."

He meets my eyes for a second before looking away, a tick working in his jaw.

~Noah~

"Oh. My. God. Noah, you are killing me with this teenage angst shit you got going on. It's been three days. Just *three* days. Get over it already. God, you're like this sappy, in love, little—"

An empty can of some motor fluid hits Kyle upside the head.

"Shut up." I tune a string on my guitar and start off where I left off, working on the duet for Claire.

Yeah, it has been three days since I last saw Claire, knowing she was off to spend Thanksgiving weekend at some senator's house ... with Troy. Of course I know her dad will never leave her alone with him, but still. What if Troy sneaks into her bedroom? What if he comes up with some elaborate ruse to drive away with her? What if he touches her again? Finishes what he started?

I know she's concerned over the Chelsea being pregnant thing. Why? I have no clue. The girl hates her. But that's Claire, always thinking about others. Damn, I don't deserve her. Regardless, Claire already told me that she plans to talk to Troy. I argued that it isn't any of her business—really, I didn't want her anywhere near him and will say anything to get my way—which led to our first serious argument. And that was right before she left. So now I'm freaking out because I haven't heard from her since. No phone calls. No texts. Nothing.

What if she breaks up with me, and all for a stupid argument that has nothing to do with us? My chest hurts just thinking about it, and I can't help rubbing the spot now, losing where I am in the song. Claire has become my whole world in the month and a half we have been together. Jesus, has it only been that long? This is unhealthy.

My phone rings, and I hurriedly pull it from my pocket, hoping it's finally Claire. No such luck.

"Hey, Mom."

"Happy Thanksgiving, Noah," my mother greets in her monotone voice.

"Yeah, you missed that, Mom. It was yesterday."

"Yesterday, I was in conferences all day, so I'm telling you now." I ignore her excuses. "Where's Dad?"

"Probably buried in five-foot stacks of books. He says to tell you Happy Thanksgiving. He's always busy. You know how he is. But he did say that he is going to try to visit for Christmas. You know I don't celebrate, so I'm going to stick around here. There is this—"

"I gotta go, Mom. Thanks for calling." I hang up before she can get another word in. I hate listening to her go on and on about her research when she doesn't listen to one damn thing that goes on in my life. I would love to ask her about her work, but only if she took the time to ask me about my life.

I strum the guitar as I think more on my parents. Dinners at our house are the two of them talking about work and me remaining silent. It's like I don't even exist for them. Dad has never taken me camping or fishing or hunting—not unless it was for pure survival, which the guides did most of the work—or sports events. He takes me to libraries. My earliest memories are of sitting in a stuffy, old library, playing under the table, using books as blocks, stacking them up to build my own world. When I got older—I'm talking eight to nine years old—Dad would have me read out loud while he worked: Aeschylus, Sophocles, Euripides, Greek, Greek, Greek. Mom was never around; only home for dinner before she would lock herself away in her home office.

I know my parents love each other. They have camaraderie, a kinship in shared interests, thoughts, and theories. I think they are more friends than anything else. I'm not sure. I see my parents kiss each other on the cheek, sit close together, but never more than that. Mostly they talk and talk and talk.

And people wonder why I don't follow in their footsteps.

I block out thoughts of my parents and start humming the tune to the song, trying to find something that matches the chords. Kyle is working on the drums, following my lead without me even realizing it. I have been so lost in my own thoughts that I forgot he was here.

Cyn is staying with her family this weekend. We have no gig until next week, so she's taking some time away, which works for me because I really need to get some new songs written.

My phone rings again, and I look down from the weight bench I'm straddling to see that it's Claire. Finally.

"Claire." Her name comes out with the relief I feel.

She is quiet for a minute before she says, "I'm sorry ... for the fight."

I glance up at Kyle who is watching me too avidly. I mumble for Claire to hold on then go outside, closing the door securely so Kyle can't eavesdrop. Then I make my way over to Abby's play set and settle on a swing as I tell her, "It wasn't a fight. Just a disagreement. It happens." I downplay the whole thing. I don't want her to know how freaked out I have been over this. "How has your weekend been?"

"Miserable. Dad's been watching me like a hawk; the wives have been drunk or dragging me along for Black Friday shopping; the men boast about their achievements; and I've spent most of my time listening to the senator's fifteen-year-old daughter go on about her friends, her boyfriend, makeup, clothes—you name it. She never stops talking." Claire giggles, and it brings a smile to my face. "What have you been doing?"

"Missing you," I admit, rocking to-and-fro on the swing. "Katy made her mac and cheese again as a side for Thanksgiving." I hear her hum her approval and promise her, "I made sure she saved some for you."

"Thank you."

"Besides that, I've been playing with my guitar, and not getting any rest from Kyle. Oh, and Abby drew my portrait last night. Do I really have one ear bigger than the other?" This gets more than a giggle from Claire.

"No, I think your ears are proportional."

"I thought so, too, but Abby insists one is twice the size as the other." My face hurts from the grin I'm wearing.

119

We go on to talk about other things, most importantly that she will be back tomorrow. We make plans to hang out at her house. One thing we don't mention is Troy. I don't think either one of us wants to take the chance of getting into another argument about him. Though it is killing me not to ask how she is handling spending the weekend with him.

After we say goodnight, I head into the house.

"Want some?" my uncle Mark asks when I walk in through the kitchen door. He is making himself a turkey sandwich with cranberry sauce on top.

"Sure," I say, making my way over. I'm an eighteen-year-old male; we can always eat.

We prepare our snacks without talking, something we both have in common. Abby is singing along to some cartoon in the background. Katy is taking a nap. This whole weekend has been quiet. It's nice.

"Did your dad call?" Uncle Mark asks as he starts putting the cold items back in the fridge.

"No, Mom."

Mark grimaces. "Ouch."

"Yeah." And just like that, conversation is over. We sit down at the table, eat our sandwiches, and then we clean up.

In my bedroom, I lie out on my bed and pull out the notebook I keep all my lyrics in, staring up at the ceiling while I try to think of the words I want to use for the duet.

I want the song to tell Claire how I feel, to express what she means to me. However, I can't find the words. I know what I want her to say and feel, but that's presumptuous, isn't it? Why is this so hard? Why am I second-guessing myself?

I turn the page of the unfinished song to the next clean sheet of paper. I need to write a song about something that's not us. Maybe I will take a page out of her book and write about some movie or TV show we watched together. No, that's so immature.

Then I have it.

The conversation we had about music, about singing to a crowd. I know how we both feel about it, and I can make it a duet where we are arguing the points of our discussion.

With that decided, my thoughts start to flow on the paper, adrenaline pumping at the idea. I overlap the chorus so that we are both singing, but not the same thing, only keywords being sung together. Now I have no more trepidation over sharing this with Claire.

I finish the song's lyrics in about twenty minutes then go on to the next page. The song opens a floodgate in my mind, and now I have all these other ideas in my head.

I end up writing until I fall asleep, sometime in the early morning hours.

Chapter 11

Birthday Snow Day

~Claire~

Chelsea never came back to school after Thanksgiving break. I guess spending a weekend with her family couldn't hide the fact that she has morning sickness. That or she told her family about her pregnancy.

The rumors about her pregnancy started on the second day she didn't show up. Nikki was the first to blab, telling everyone James, the gay quarterback—though she didn't say gay, and I think only me and Chelsea know about that—knocked her up. I wonder if Nikki will ever find out it was her own "boyfriend" who did. Either way, she must be some friend to go behind Chelsea's back that way.

Now Noah and I are old news. No one pays attention to us anymore. There are no more snide comments from Chelsea, no more leering from boys who think I put out now, no more girls coming on to Noah. Everything is peaceful and quiet; the way I imagine school should be.

Today is my eighteenth birthday, though I still don't think he knows. I never told him.

Noah spent most of the day with his family while Dad took me out to an early dinner and gave me a white-gold necklace with a music note pendant. It is simple, sweet, and pretty. I love it, and I loved spending the time with my dad.

On the drive home, I texted Noah to let him know we were on our way, so when we got back around four, he was already waiting beside his aunt's truck. It was a cold day, so it was normal for Noah not to drive his motorcycle. He was taking his aunt's truck more and more lately.

As soon as I see him, I turn toward my dad, who is still pulling up in the driveway. "Don't tell Noah it's my birthday."

Dad frowns at me. "Why not?"

I shrug. "I feel weird about telling him. I don't want to make him feel bad for not knowing or feel like he should get me something when it's my fault."

Dad puts the car in park, mumbling, "I won't say anything."

I open the car door. "Thanks, Dad."

Noah meets me halfway. He's dressed in his normal jeans, boots, and jacket, but he has on a button-up shirt over his T-shirt. A beanie sits on his head and over his ears, hiding all that luscious dark hair of his. His eyes look darker with the black beanie pulled down to his brows, making him look almost predatory. I can see how much his soft freckles have disappeared with the coming winter.

I'm dressed in a sweater dress, with a long coat over it. My boots, with their heels giving me extra height, are still not tall enough to accommodate Noah's height. I have to stretch up on my toes to throw my arms around his neck.

He picks me up to squeeze me tighter, and I snuggle into his neck. Then Noah puts me down and gives me a huge smile, something mischievous in his eyes. I know that look. He's up to something.

Last time he had that look in his eyes, I had just accidently knocked his water bottle over into his lap. It looked like he wet himself, and I couldn't stop laughing at the look on his face. I tried so hard to stop while running toward the kitchen to get him a towel. The look on his face when I got back to the table was the same he is giving me now, before he took what was left of his bottle and mine, and proceeded to chase me around the house, attempting to pour the bottles onto my pants. Unfortunately, he won, having longer legs than me. He caught me in the living room where he tackled me to the ground and not only poured the water on my pants, but all over me. Two perfectly good waters wasted on drenching my front from head to toe. I didn't mind. I still couldn't stop laughing. But that is why I am worried now.

He looks me from head to toe, and then fingers the new necklace Dad gave me. "Pretty." There is that look in his eyes again.

"Thank you."

Before I can say anything else, he tells me, "You need to change. Something warm. I want to take you somewhere."

I study him for a minute. That look in his eyes … " 'Kay. Give me five minutes."

I change into a pair of jeans, leaving my knee-high socks on underneath, and a warm sweater before putting my boots and long coat back on. I check my reflection and refresh my lip gloss before grabbing a thick scarf on my way out of my room. I make it into Dad's office as Noah starts thanking my dad for something.

"Thanks for dinner, Daddy. I'll see you later." I walk over to give him a kiss.

"Love you, Claire." Dad hugs me tightly, whispering in my ear, "Happy birthday, baby girl."

"Thanks, Daddy." I hug him tighter before letting go to meet Noah at the doorway.

"Ready?" he asks, and I nod. Then Noah says to my dad, "Have a good night, Jonathan. We won't be out too late."

Dad waves him off. "Just be careful. That's all I ask."

" 'Course." Noah grabs my hand and leads me out to his aunt's truck where he opens the door for me before getting in on his side.

"Where are we going?" I ask as Noah puts the truck in drive and winds his way down the driveway.

"It's a surprise. In fact"—he lifts his bottom and pulls out a bandana from his back pocket, handing it to me—"I want you to wear this until I say you can take it off."

I look down at the bandana in my hand then to him. "Are you kidding me?" I laugh. I knew he was up to something.

Noah has that mischievous look in his eyes again, with that cocky grin on his lips.

~Noah~

Claire looks petulant before donning the bandana over her eyes.

I grin, though she can't see it. She thinks she is pulling a fast one on me, but I have known for a month now that it's Claire's birthday. Truth be told, I ran into Jonathan when he was buying the music note necklace she is wearing now. Well, he was trying to buy her some gaudy pearls when I ran into him and asked him if he had a date or something.

"No, Claire's birthday is next month. I'm trying to find something nice to buy her, but the older she gets, the harder it is to shop for her. It feels like I went from buying her a Barbie house to jewelry from one year to the next." He shook his head, still staring down at the pearl display case.

"When's her birthday?" I asked, moving down the cases, looking for something more Claire, more simple.

"December fifteenth," he answered absentmindedly.

I paused, seeing the perfect gift for her. Then I pointed down to the small necklace I knew Claire would wear every day. "You should get her this one."

Jonathan came to my side and peered down to where my finger was pointing. "That's perfect."

And it is. I'm glad I was a part of picking something out for her that she can keep forever. Now, the harder part was finding something to give her from me.

I searched every girly place I could think of, bringing Abby with me to get a girl's input. I found some things that were fine for Christmas, but not her birthday. For her birthday, I wanted something memorable. It needed to be extra special, not the dress—yes, I shopped in a girls' clothing store—or the crystal thingy that Abby thought was so pretty, or the compilation of opera scores I printed out onto old parchment and had bound together for her. Those were Christmas presents. I needed something … something that was me. The predator in me needed to mark my territory.

So, to go with the gift her dad had already picked out for her, I went online and bought a white-gold guitar pick pendant with her birth month and day engraved on one side, but this year is marked. I figured it would look good under the music note.

However, I wasn't satisfied with that. I wanted to do something memorable, too. I wanted this day to be all about us. And that's where we are heading to now.

I drive off the main roads and onto a gravel path. Uncle Mark told me about this place. He used to take Aunt Katy here before Abby was born. He said it was the most isolated place in the area and is great for stargazing. There is even a fire pit he made years ago.

I came here earlier in the day, after calling Claire and making plans to meet her. I really wanted to know how long I would have to prepare everything before picking her up. I didn't want to show up at her house with a truck laden with everything we need. I didn't want to give her any clue as to what I was up to.

I pull to a stop and shut off the truck. I can see Claire tilting her head, trying to peek from underneath the blindfold.

"Where are we?" Her voice breaks the silence of the cab. There are no other noises inside or out of the truck. Everything is almost eerily quiet. All the animals are hibernating and all the birds have flown south. "Can I take this off now?"

I don't answer her. I get out of the cab, watching to make sure she doesn't pull the blindfold off, and open her door. I unbuckle her seatbelt, and then guide her out of the truck. But before her feet touch the ground, I scoop her up into my arms, making her gasp in surprise and wrap her arms around my neck.

I place her on a log and tell her, "Don't move. Don't take off the blindfold yet. Promise?"

She nods, wrapping her arms around herself.

It's cold as hell out here, and I need to start the fire fast. Everything else is already set up; I just need to add flame to the tinder.

Once that is done and the fire starts crackling, I place the metal screen cover over the flames. I notice Claire's head tilting again, listening to all the sounds around her. She now reaches out tentatively toward the warmth.

I make enough noise so she knows I'm walking toward her before pulling her up gently from her seat, leading her toward the tent I have already set up. Inside is a mountain of pillows and blankets that would make a sheik proud. I want her to be as comfortable as possible tonight.

I sit down on the ground and pull her down with me before pressing her back to lie down, me on top of her. I kiss her deeply, breathing her in, as I remove the necklace. Sitting up, I then place the pendant on her necklace and watch as it slides down the chain and falls behind the music note. Then I take the blindfold off Claire, and she blinks up at me, adjusting her eyes to the brighter light. It's almost dusk now, fall seasoning into winter, making the days shorter.

I smile down at her. "Happy birthday, Claire."

She gasps. "You knew? How?" She finally looks down at the necklace, and I watch as she clasps the new addition, reading the date on the back.

"Your dad. I've known for a month now." I connect the necklace back around her neck.

"Thank you," she says as she looks down to where the necklace has settled. "I love it." She looks around. "Are we going camping?"

I shrug. It wasn't really the plan, but if it happens, it happens. "We could. It's a little too cold, though. I was planning on stargazing in the middle of nowhere. I wanted to spend somewhere quiet with you, where there is no one around."

Claire smiles at me, but says nothing. Then, she gasps out, "It's snowing,"

I fall onto my back beside her, looking up through the sheer cover on the top of the tent. Well, guess there went stargazing. I should have checked the weather forecast before I planned all this. Although, watching the snow fall around us is almost like watching a meteor shower.

I remember seeing one once when I was in Africa with my parents—you don't see meteor showers in the city. I was only eight and totally captivated by the falling stars. The village children were scared, but I wanted to seek out a fallen meteorite. I was too scared to go in the jungle by myself, but it didn't stop me from trying to coax the other children to come with me. It didn't work. There was a language barrier. So, my attempts at being a future meteorite hunter were smashed, like the meteors when they fell to earth.

~Claire~

Noah looks lost in thought as we lie here, staring up at the falling snow. It's snowing heavily, and knowing these parts, we will have an

127

inch on the ground within an hour.

I roll into Noah's side and snuggle my face into the crook of his neck, draping my arm over his chest. "This is a perfect birthday. I'll always remember it. Thank you."

Noah turns his head, and we gaze at each other for a while before he whispers, "Same here."

I lift my head, and we meet halfway, kissing. I haven't kissed anyone else, but I must say that Noah is a very fine kisser.

I pull him closer, and he turns so we are both lying on our sides. I wrap my arms around him, pulling him closer and closer, never close enough. Noah runs his hand down my side inside my coat, and that's when I realize the coat is in the way. That's why I feel like I'm not close enough.

I sit up abruptly and pull my coat off, deciding to take my boots off, too, since we have all these nice snuggly blankets around us. With that done, I sit astride Noah's lap, and he sits up, meeting me with his mouth.

His hands are at my waist as I strip him of his jacket, needing to *feel* him. He lets me, and then returns his hands to my waist, gripping so tightly. His grip makes me brave, letting me know he feels this overwhelming need. I need the pleasure that I have only shared with Noah; that I only want with Noah. And I need it now.

I run my hands underneath his two shirts, feeling the warm, soft skin of his back. Noah groans in my mouth at the contact, then breaks his mouth from mine to run it up my jaw to my ear to my neck. His movements are slow yet stuttered, like he wants to move faster, harder but is trying to control himself.

His ministrations make me drop my head back, looking up at the snow collecting on top of the tent. Somewhere in the back of my head, I hope that the snow doesn't find a way to drip inside and ruin the warmth of the blankets. I hope the snow instead creates an igloo around us, trapping in all the heat and giving us a cozy place to just exist.

Noah licks a trail up my throat, sending delicious shivers up my spine. I grip him tighter, pulling his chest into mine, grinding down on him and trying to recreate the friction that caused that explosive orgasm he gave me months ago. I want his hands on me. I want him to touch me ... finally. Why he hasn't, I don't know. It's beyond frustrating. It makes me feel inadequate, like I'm not good enough.

With that thought, I slowly slide my fingers from his back to his front, nervous to what I'm doing, uncharted waters. I move from the top of his chest, feeling his hardened nipples. I stop there, sliding back and forth across them. Then I press back against his chest, forcing Noah to lie back.

"Claire." Noah says my name reverently. He has that predatory look in his now black eyes.

"Can I take your shirt off?"

Noah doesn't answer me; he grabs the hems of both shirts and pulls them over his head before discarding them to the side. I take the opportunity to touch every inch of his bare chest, running my hands over his tattoo, massaging the tendons where his neck meets his shoulders, tentatively skating the tips of my fingers at the rim of his pants, which makes him take in deep breaths. Noah lets me explore every inch of him, his breath escalating until I have my fill.

When I lower my head, wanting to kiss every inch exposed, he stops me.

"Uh-uh."

I give him an almost pouty look, but rejection is swift to cross my features. Before I have time to dwell on it, though, he wraps his arms around my back and rotates us so that I'm now lying down and he is straddling me. It makes my breath escape with a gasp, and then I feel breathless at this new position.

"Do you trust me?" he asks. I can see the fierce determination in his eyes. I can see his arousal. I can also see hesitation and trepidation. He's worried about pushing me too far, rushing. I remember what he said before. *"I get so caught up in you that I quickly lose control. I don't want to do that with you."* I guess that hasn't changed for him, but my hormones are telling me to plunge, even though my brain says it's too soon.

I have only known Noah for two months now, but it feels like forever. Looking back on forever, there are so many moments between us: sharing almost every meal together, spending hours sitting comfortably together, movies, Jeremy's, conversations with my dad and his family, dates, motorcycle rides, walks, kisses, waking up together, the fight with Troy, and now this. So many memories in such a short time. Memories that have lasted a forever of time, yet only two months.

So, yes, even though it's only been two months, there has never been a time when he has shown me I *couldn't* trust him. Not one time has he said or done anything that would scare me or make me fear him. He has only protected and cared for me. I trust him with my whole heart. I trust him not to use me and leave me when it's all done. I trust him.

"Of course," I promise.

~Noah~

Her "of course" sears through me. The level of trust she has in me is astounding, because I barely trust myself. But, for her, I will be worthy. I don't want her goodness, her tenderness, her soft touches, or her attention to go away. I would do anything to keep them with me. She gives me more than anyone in my life has ever given me. Herself.

I can't smile now, though I want to. This moment is too intense. So, I nod.

"Okay. Close your eyes."

I watch as her eyes flutter shut, as she takes a deep breath and lets it out, as her head falls back and snuggles into a pillow, as her face tilts up toward the falling snow. She looks like she could be sleeping right now. A sleeping angel with her white, cashmere sweater that makes her face look like porcelain with that hint of rose to her cheeks, her eyelashes fanning down, her contrasting shock of deep brown hair and red lips. Flawlessness.

I want every moment she has with me to be something special, for her to feel savored and cared for. I start by slowly tracing my callused fingertips along the edge of her shirt where it meets the seam of her pants, just like she did to me. Her abdomen quivers at the touch, and I watch as goose bumps form over her skin. My fingers meet in the middle before moving back to her sides where they start to move upward, taking her sweater with me, exposing her tiny, soft belly.

I lean forward and leave whispers of kisses over the exposed skin, dipping my tongue into her belly button before sliding upward until I meet her bra. Then I lower back down, blowing a cool breath on her skin. She shifts underneath me.

I slide my hands up more, lifting her shirt above her bra. I have to swallow down my rising lust when I see her white lace bra, her pink nipples exposed through the thin, webbed material. Dear God, she's killing me with this sexy underwear. Is this all she has? Or does she wear these things for me?

There is no helping myself; her breasts are right there for the taking, practically exposed to me. I go right in, lowering toward them as her nipples seem to tauten further the closer I get. I slide my hands down the side of her breast, curling them around her back and lifting her upper back as I lower my mouth over one nipple, sucking it into my mouth through the thin bra.

Claire gasps and arches even more into me, moaning as I nip the bud. Then I do it again, and she gasps my name, cupping the back of my head with both hands, holding me there. The action is causes her shirt to fall, so I take her hands and hold them over her head. When I know her hands are going to stay there, I find the clasp on the front of her bra and release it. The cups fall to the side, exposing her breasts.

I don't know if I'm more of an ass or a breast man, but seeing Claire's, I'm a breast man in this moment. There is just enough there to cup in my hand as I move to the neglected breast.

There is massaging, nipping, pinching, sucking for what feels like minutes but could be hours as Claire moans and writhes underneath me. Somehow, her legs have gotten loose from between mine, and she's now straddling me as I kneel. Her shirt and bra are completely off, her arms are wrapped around my neck, and she's grinding on my erection in such a delicious way.

Her breasts are abandoned as I make my way to her collarbone then up her neck, kissing, nipping, sucking on every inch of skin my mouth encounters. I tug her hair back so that her neck is arched. I want to take a picture of this moment. Her long hair sweeping the blankets, her eyes closed, her mouth parted on a moan, wearing only a pair of jeans. So sexy.

She slips her hands between us, and I feel her trying to undo my pants. That's when everything's gone too far.

~Claire~

Noah makes me feel so needy. I want to take this further with him. I want more than the kisses and simply touches. Though this is further than we have ever gone, I want more. I want everything. I want to see Noah unhinged. I want to be unhinged. I'm eighteen years old. We are where no one will bother us, in this ideal setting, with the snow piling on top of us and all around us, darkness now upon us, and I want Noah. All of him. I want him to be my first. Now, in this moment.

I move to unfasten his pants, and that's when Noah puts a halt on our make-out session.

"Claire, no. Not yet."

"Yes," I whisper against his lips as we still move them together.

Noah grips each side of my head and disconnects our lips, staring me straight in the eyes as we try to catch our breaths.

"Not right now," he says slowly, with determination, yet I can see the want in his eyes.

With my hands still around his neck, I lean back and bring him down with me. We resume our kissing as I press him to roll over until I am on top of him. He got to do what he wanted with me, and now it's my turn.

Kissing my way down his neck and collarbone, I start to mimic the way he taunted my breasts, sucking and nipping on his hardened nipples. He sucks in air through his teeth, just like how he does when he sings sometimes. It's the most erotic sound I have ever heard, making me clench with need.

I wander down his hard belly with one hand, following the trail of hair from his belly button down to parts I have never seen, gliding my fingers along the seam of his pants before I bravely move over them to where I know his manhood is. I'm curious what one feels like, looks like in person. I want to know what Noah's is like.

As my hand meets the hardness in his pants, Noah quickly jerks up, making me tumble to my side. I lie there, looking up at a now angry Noah.

I didn't want to upset him, not today. We have only argued a handful of times, and we always feel like crap for days afterward. I don't want to get into an argument today, not on my birthday. Everything has been so perfect.

"Dammit, Claire. I said not right now!" He's fuming, furious.

"When then?" I ask him in the same tone. I don't mean to snap back, but this is new to me ... and frustrating.

Then his face falls, anger gone. He looks defeated, torn. It's so overwhelming how he can switch his emotions so quickly. He's so capricious. And this is my doing—this anger to lost. I immediately deflate also.

Noah comes back down, lying gently against me as he tenderly plays with the tendrils of hair near my face. "I don't know for how long you will want me—us. I don't know what tomorrow brings or the next." He pauses, not looking at me but the tendril of hair. "But I do know that, when I'm with you, I feel different—better. I feel alive and like anything is possible. I know that I want to share so much with you. And I want you to experience everything ... with me." He looks at me now. "But I can't do that fast. I have to take my time with you. Have to." He presses a kiss to my lips as he grinds his erection into my hip. "Get me?"

I nod, but I'm still confused.

"You do want me, though, right? I mean, soon we can ... do this?" God, I'm so nervous right now.

"Fuck, Claire, I want you more than I want my next breath. I can't wait to *do this*. I want you so badly, and you make it so difficult to be good, to savor each second. I want to do this slow, take it one step at a time, give you one taste at a time. I don't want to dive right in. I want you to experience each sensation that builds up to that."

I hear every word he says, watch his mouth as he says it, but one question is echoing in my head that needs to come out.

"How many people have you had sex with?"

Noah instantly shuts down and looks guarded.

Craptastic, and right when he started to look like he was getting in a better mood.

He pulls off me and covers me with a blanket before moving to the other side of the small tent. "Don't ask me that. Not tonight, Claire."

My eyebrows shoot into my hairline. "That bad?"

Noah shakes his head, but not in answer, more like frustration. "You know I'm not a virgin. The number of people shouldn't matter. I've either had sex or I haven't, and you know I have. I've never had sex without a condom and my last test—three months ago, after I got here, I should add—came out clean. That's it, Claire. End of."

"Sorry. I was curious. You can understand me questioning and being self-conscious because I *haven't* had sex before, can't you?"

He nods, wearing a wary expression.

"So, because I'm with you now, and we're talking about sex in the future, you know that makes me nervous on how I would … perform compared to your—"

"I've been in your shoes before, angel. But, when it comes to performing, how you perform, to me, is all in here." He touches his chest over where his heart is. " 'Cause I can already tell we're going to be atomic together. You already affect me with an intensity no one else has. You already respond to me on a level that borderlines live porn." He smiles, and I blush at his words. "To me, there is no comparison. You are in a league of your own, love."

I nod, understanding where he's coming from. That doesn't mean I like it, but I respect that he wants to wait.

"I need to get some air." I rip the blanket off and proceed to put on my boots before stepping out of the tent.

"Uh, Claire? Your shirt?"

I don't look back at him as I answer, "Don't need it."

The cool air is what I need to thaw off the burn in my body.

Chapter 12

Not So Happy New Year

~Claire~

I think Noah is sometimes at a loss with what to do with me. For example, after I left the tent shirtless on the night of my birthday, he chased me down, which ended up in a freezing snowball fight, and my breasts felt like they were going to fall off. It seemed like a good idea until Noah had to hurry me into the tent then proceeded to dress me and wrap me in every blanket before putting me in the truck and turning the heat on full blast. Really, I don't know what came over me, except that I needed to cool down from the hormones.

I came down with a cold the next day, which should have had nothing to do with the night before, a coincidence. I attempted to go to school, and Noah drove me right home and packed me into bed, shaking his head at me when I insisted I was fine. Colds aren't contagious.

In the end, we spent the day there, draped with two boxes of Kleenex thrown haphazardly all around us since Noah asserted that he was staying with me. It was another one of those memories of forever that we made together, filled with eating chicken noodle soup, a TV show marathon, watching him write his lyrics, dozing off, and just being together. Despite the cold, or maybe because of it, it was a perfect day.

A week later and a few days before Christmas, I met Noah's dad … then proceeded to tell him off. I really don't know what came over me then, either. I was so angry at him and his endless chatter about all things Mr. and Mrs. Gish. From the moment we picked him up at the airport, the man would not stop talking about himself. It was such an opposite from Noah that I was dumbstruck at first. Then I attempted interest because this was me getting to know one of Noah's parents, but then I was incensed.

Why hadn't he asked one question about Noah? There was nothing, and that made me go off on him.

Noah followed me home, angry at me for driving off upset and through the snow, like I needed another father. I pointed that out to him, and he yelled that he didn't need another mother, since I was acting like a protective one. That fight ended with a whole lot of apologies and the back story to Noah's life with his parents. It makes sense to me now, why he is usually so quiet. Still, I don't like his father, or his mother now, either, and I haven't even met her.

We ended up back at his family's house later where I apologized to his father. The rest of the time I spent in a somber mood, not talking, hanging out in the kitchen with Katy who told me she was proud of me for everything I said. Turns out, I'm not the only one who sees that Noah's been ignored most of his life.

I thought Noah would have resembled his mother, but no. He's the spitting image of his father. Same height, hair, eyes, facial features. The only difference is his dad is on the slighter and paler side, spending most of his time in libraries and museums.

Christmas was spent quietly at home with my dad. I was glad for it. It had been a long time since we spent a holiday alone. Though Noah did come by that night to swap presents.

He got me a lot more than I got him, which embarrassed me. He gave me an armful of gifts, and all I could think to get him was a composing software program that cost me way over my budget. But when I saw the look on his face and the fact that he couldn't stop reading over everything he could do with it, it was so worth every penny.

It seemed that Noah couldn't decide what to get me, so he gave me a lot, including a lingerie set that I was so glad I hadn't opened in front of my father. Of course, this prompted a whole conversation on my weakness for lace and pretty things. Noah even insisted on looking through my underwear drawer, which turned into a tickling match when I tried to stop him. In the end, he won, to my mortification.

His dad left the very next day. He didn't even tell Noah good-bye. Just left before Noah even got up. Per Mark, his dad ordered a taxi to pick him up and drive him the whole hour to the airport. Noah acted like it didn't bother him, but he was moodier those few days after Christmas. I tried getting his mind off it by taking him sledding, something he had never done before. Kyle and Abby were with us, and we ended up having an amazing time. By the time we were done, we were all soaked and cold, but so happy about it.

Then the shadows came into his eyes again, and I had to think of something else for us to do to occupy his mind. The rest of the week was spent playing with Abby, listening to the band practice, and playing in the snow. They were the only things I could think of to get my Noah back. He was always serious and quiet, but this was too much. I just wanted him to be happy.

Now it's New Year's Eve. The night I promised Noah I would sing the song he wrote for us. We practiced a lot over Christmas break, and I was so nervous every time I sang in front of him. I can sing to a crowd of thousands, in front of the Manhattan School of Music panel, but Noah … His opinion matters more than anyone's. He can make me blossom or wilt with one look. That's how highly I regard him. Messed up, I know. I know the depths of how ingrained he has become to me.

The night starts off so great. Jeremy has booked a few more bands, and one of them has an extra drum kit that they leave for use at the bar, so Noah and Kyle don't have to pack the drums back and forth anymore. There is a huge crowd, music has been playing since eight o'clock with the newer bands rocking the crowd, and the line for the door is wrapped around the building. It amazes me that such a small town can have something like this.

The Characters go on at ten-thirty. Of course, I don't get to sing the duet first. Oh, no, Noah wants to prolong the wait. He wants to get the audience in a frenzy, and then throw me in their faces. Not like half of them will care. I will probably get booed off the stage just for being me, which makes me so nervous I could throw up.

Sassy, the girl I was admiring from Max's house, is sitting next to me at the table. I know she likes Noah, but I can't help being drawn to her. She has something about her I wish I had. She knows she's beautiful and sexy; her confidence radiates from within her. Maybe some of that will come off on me. I really need her confidence right now.

One of the guys has his arm around her shoulders, snuggling her close to him. She rests her arms casually on his thigh while her eyes haven't left Noah. Her eyes never seem to leave Noah. This should bother me, but it doesn't. I think it would if they had ever been together.

Ten minutes to midnight, Noah looks right at me, and then pointedly at the mic next to him. I leave the shelter of the booth, making my way toward the small stage. I can't look at Noah, though I see him watching me. Instead, I look out over the crowd, at the people who all hate me because I have dreams. In any case, that's what it feels like to me.

The song's intro starts before I make it to the second microphone. I can't stand still while I sing, so I take it off its stand and bring it to my lips. I chance a glance at Noah to see him still watching me as he strums.

Cyn is on the other side of him with a huge smile, giving me encouragement. I confided to her during one session that Noah makes me more nervous than anything. She suggested blocking him out. Like I can. I'm constantly aware of him, a tingle that dances along my skin whenever he is in proximity and causes my stomach to feel like it's full of butterflies. I hope I never lose that feeling around him. It's energizing, yet not helpful right now.

I focus on the crowd, watching them watch me, watching them focus solely on me, the new addition, for one song. There is curiosity in their gazes, some disdain, but mostly everyone wants to hear what we are about to give them. I don't linger on one person's face for too long, not wanting to focus too much on what certain people are registering on their faces.

Noah's singing part is first, and I look over at him as he sings about not sharing personal feelings. We sing the chorus together, and then it's my turn to sing about how his personal is my personal. He makes the song sound like more than a conversation we had about performing. He makes it sound like one person fearing a relationship, while the other person tells them to dive in, that she will always be there to guide him through. It's a very powerful song, especially with the soul-scorching chords that build and build until they drop at the end, like a climax to a suspenseful movie.

The song ends to rapturous applause, and then someone starts counting down from ten. The whole crowd joins in the countdown as the ball dropping is broadcasted through the TVs over the bar.

I feel Noah slide up next to me, his lips brushing the sensitive spot behind my ear. "Three, two, one ..." he whispers, and in the next second, he spins me around and crushes his lips against mine.

I get lost in his kiss. Nothing else exists. All the noise from the crowd cheering in the New Year fades into the background. It's just me and Noah and this all-consuming kiss we share. His tongue caresses mine, one hand at the back of my neck, the other pulling me toward him at the small of my back, the kiss lifting me up to my tip-toes.

Then, the night takes a turn for the worse

~Noah~

Max's house is once again the after-party. There are more people here than ever, everyone happy, drinking, having a great time.

As soon as we come through the door, people are patting me on the back, congratulating the band. Claire gets a lot of attention, too, which she beams and graciously thanks them for all their compliments. Eventually, we get separated when a group of women start questioning Claire on her singing experience.

I am corralled toward the bar where I decline a drink. We took Kyle's car over here, but considering he's already tossing an empty beer bottle into the trash before opening another one, I'm assuming the DD position tonight. Claire never drinks, but I would never expect her to be the driver.

I listen to those surrounding me talk while watching Claire. I can never take my eyes off her. Never want to. Therefore, I see it when Sassy hands her a glass with something pink in it. And it doesn't look like pink lemonade.

I watch as Claire shakes her head and tries to pass it back to Sassy, but Sassy says something and waves the glass back. Claire looks unsure, but I see the moment she makes up her mind and takes a sip. She says something to Sassy, and Sassy beams. Then Claire is taking another much longer sip. I want to kill Sassy for pushing her to do something out of character. I want to kill her twice when she looks up, catches my eye across the room, and winks at me. I don't know what her game is, but it can't be good.

I start heading over there, thinking she better not have drugged my angel's drink, but then I am bombarded by my cousin, who has obviously had more than the two drinks I saw him with already. Didn't we just get here?

"Hey, cuz. Happy new year, man." He comes in and gives me a man hug. You know, the heavy pats on the back. He reeks of cheap beer.

"You might want to slow down, Kyle. I'm not dragging you into the house later. And I'm not taking shit from your parents if they find out you're drunk."

He holds up his beer. "This is only my fourth one. I'm good. I'll sober up in an hour."

I mentally roll my eyes at him as I look over to where Claire is standing. She's still talking to Sassy, plus a few other women. She stands out amongst this crowd in her blue jeans and periwinkle, short-sleeved sweater over a white tank top. She's got on these sexy, white kitten heels with her pink toe nails peeking out. Her hair waves down her back, loose, and as I watch her throw her head back in a laugh, her hair extends past that little ass of hers.

"I need to go check on Claire," I tell Kyle, moving past him.

At that moment, Claire looks up and beams a smile my way. I love seeing her smile like that. Like I'm her sun, moon, and all her stars. She controls me and breaks me with that smile. I can't help smiling my cheesiest smile back at her when she bestows it to me. Every time, it's like we are in our own world.

Is this love? You bet your ass it is.

I make it to her and bend down so we are eye-level. "Hey, beautiful."

"Hey, yourself." She grins then bites her bottom lip.

"What are you drinking?"

Now she looks unsure of herself. Dammit, I hate bursting her happy bubble, but double damn, I have never seen Claire drink anything alcoholic.

"Um, a Sea Breeze, I think?" She looks over at Sassy.

"Yeah," Sassy answers. "It's vodka and grapefruit juice."

I don't even look in Sassy's direction, giving her the cold shoulder. "Since when do you drink vodka?"

Claire turns away from the other women who are all up in our business and lowers her voice. "Never. But Sassy insisted I try it, and I really like her. I didn't want to offend her."

I steer Claire away from the women. "Trust me, angel; she's stirring up trouble."

"You think?" Claire has this innocent expression on her face and looks heartbroken at the idea that yet another person is against her. "But what trouble could one drink do? I don't even feel anything. Well, except a little fuzzy-headed."

I chuckle at her. "Oh, she doesn't plan on stopping on one drink."

I don't want to tell her that my fear is she's going to get Claire wasted to a) embarrass her, or b) come on to me when Claire is passed out or locked in a bathroom puking. I see the way Sassy still stares at me even after our "never going to happen" talk. I see the wheels turning in her head when she looks at Claire. I see the vindictiveness behind her smile when she talks to Claire. Sassy is bad news.

"I really like her," Claire repeats.

"I have no idea why."

She's about to say something else when I kiss her, something I have been dying to do since we got here. There is always so much going on in our lives that we never seem to have enough time for just us. I simply want to make out with my girl, kiss her senseless, and gulp down her moans.

I love her soft moans, so free and without conscious thought to hold it in. I can't wait to finally fill her up, but waiting is a personal goal of mine. I want the moment to be perfect, the night to be flawless, somewhere where it's only us, where we don't have to worry about someone hearing us or coming home soon. Somewhere I can savor every inch of her body all night and the next morning long, and I want it to happen after she has had the most memorable night of her life.

For now, I back her against a wall, in a room full of people, lost to everything but her little, pink tongue and soft lips that eagerly meet mine.

She nips my bottom lip, and I groan. As if it's orchestrated, but really is natural to us by now, I lift her up by her ass, and she wraps her long legs around my waist. Now I can feel every inch of her up against me.

Our lips barely part for breath, both of us breathing through our noses, not wanting to stop. She tastes like grapefruit, vodka, and Claire. Tasting her will never grow old. I want to taste more of her, wondering if she's as sweet down there as she is up here.

I groan again at that thought, my lips and tongue getting more forceful, bruising her lips with mine. Claire doesn't back down, though. No, she meets me, bruising my lips as much as I'm bruising hers.

"Damn, Claire. I didn't know you could get down like that. I always thought you were a goody-goody virgin." We ignore Kyle as he continues his slurring monologue. "Remember last summer when we came up to visit you guys for a week? I kid you not, you had what? Like five hot as shit women in like a six-day timespan. Shit, probably more." By this point, we aren't kissing anymore. Claire is hanging on to every word. What is Kyle doing? "Dude, every time I turned around, you had another chick on your lap. Then you disappeared moments later. Then you returned, and there's *another* chick on your lap."

And now Claire is no longer in my arms, but she's still up against the wall, arms folded over her chest, head down. Damn, my stupid drunk cousin.

I spin away from her and seethe through my teeth, "Shut up!"

Kyle blinks drunkenly at me, holding up his hands in surrender, yet another beer in one of his hands. Idiot. "Just saying, dude. Never seen Claire like that. She's hot."

I want to sucker punch him in the mouth. I want to knock him

142

out. As an alternative, I tell him, "Fuck off, Kyle."

The fact that he keeps saying dude is enough to tell me he's too drunk to know what he's saying. Asshole probably won't even remember this moment tomorrow. If he does, I *will* sucker punch him then, when he's sober and can feel the pain.

I turn back toward the wall to find it empty of Claire. Where the hell did she run off to? Shit, she's pissed.

I scan the crowded room, but I can't see her. She's so damn short she gets swallowed up by the sea of bodies. Then I start walking the perimeter of the room, looking around and between everyone. I still can't find her. Maybe she's holed up in the bathroom.

With that thought in mind, I head toward it.

Sassy steps in front of me. "Trouble in paradise?"

"Back off, Sassy." I make a move to walk around her, but her hand comes down on my arm. I freeze and glare at her.

She takes a step toward me, her breast caressing my arm. "If she's hurt by something you can't change, then maybe she's too immature for you." She steps even closer. "What she thinks is so bad she runs away from it, I chock up to experience and a damn good time." I know now that she hung on to every word Kyle said and watched every reaction Claire had. Bitch.

She tries to kiss me, but I back away, swiping her hands off my arms aggressively. "And you are exactly the type of woman I would use—insignificant."

I spin away from her to find Claire at the bar, taking a shot of clear liquid with Cyn. Fuck! What is this night turning into?

~Claire~

"Looks like Noah was right about Sassy," I say to Cyn as I turn away from watching Sassy suggestively brush up against Noah.

I admit it. When Kyle talked about how many women Noah had in a week, I was crazy with jealousy, but more hurt. I calculated how many women he slept with in one week to a year, two years, though he's been having sex since he was fourteen. I don't want to calculate that. The number of women Noah slept with comes out to the hundreds. So, yeah, I am jealous and hurt that my boyfriend shared himself with so many people, yet he keeps insisting on holding off with me.

Has he even gone so long without sex before? Is he going behind my back with Sassy? Is that why Sassy looks so comfortable next to a seething Noah, because she's used to his anger?

I take a shot of whatever Cyn hands me and cough until tears run down my face. Crap. How do people drink this? This is nasty. Like swallowing fire. I really don't understand the appeal of drinking.

Cyn laughs and slaps my back before handing me another shot. My head already feels fuzzier from that shot, and for some reason, her laughing is so funny that I laugh along with her.

"Sassy is a sore loser. She always wants what she can't have." She looks toward where I assume Noah and Sassy still are. "Ouch, that burns."

"What?" I ask, not wanting to look at the scene behind me. Not wanting to see my boyfriend with another woman he could be having sex with behind my back.

It's not just me, right? I mean, if a guy is used to getting it, but doesn't do it with the person he's with, then he's getting it from somewhere else, right?

My brain is shot from the alcohol. I know I'm being irrational, jealous, petty, and simply feeling rejected.

"Noah just threw her hands from his arms none too gently by the looks of it. Shit, he spotted you. Quick, lick this then take another shot." She thrusts another shot glass in my face that's lined with something. Ew, salt. "Let him see you having a good time. That will throw his ego down."

I obey her, not coughing so much this time, putting a smile on my face and laughing at nothing as she shoves a lime into my mouth. Mmmm ...

I am definitely feeling the effects of the alcohol now. My tummy is all nice and warm, and I feel lighter, like I shouldn't let anything bother me.

I should dress more like Sassy. Wear my pants lower and my shirts even more so. I think I have nice breasts. Noah seems to love them. Maybe I should show them more often, be more liberal with my appearance. Maybe get my nose pierced or something. One of those cute, little, barely-there diamonds to stud my nose. I love my button nose.

What if I cut my hair? Chop it all off up to my chin and give it one of those sexy styles. A sexy, bedhead look. Noah will be thinking about sex then. Well, sex with me, hopefully.

Cyn fills up two more shots. "Together, ready?"

I hold up my shot and lick the salt off the lip like she does. Then I tip my head back and swallow the contents. Now it really doesn't burn going down. Cyn shoves another lime wedge in my mouth as she sucks on her own.

"We need to talk," I hear Noah say from behind me.

Instantly, tears come to my eyes and the shots are forgotten. I know what those words mean. It's breakup time. He's going to tell me he wants Sassy. That he doesn't want a virgin, and that's why we haven't had sex. I know it.

I drop the necklace I was unconsciously sawing back and forth, the one Dad and Noah gave me. Then I shove away from the bar and take a step back. When the room spins, I hurriedly grab the bar, but then Noah steadies me, pulling me into his chest.

"How many shots did you give her?" Noah snaps at Cyn in that dominating, no-one-can-touch-me way I can never get enough of.

"Uh … four?" I hear her answer, though one ear is pressed to Noah's chest while the other is muffled from Noah's arm wrapped around my head.

Then there is that moment of quiet anger that Noah pulls off well. Then, "She's never drank a day in her life, and she's what? Maybe one hundred pounds? That's at least five drinks in an hour."

"She was sad. You pissed her off," Cyn throws at him.

"Which is the worst time to drink!" Noah seethes. "How the hell am I going to talk to her now?"

"You break her heart, I'll break your skull," Cyn snarls.

That quiet, anger-filled moment again. "Break her heart?" he finally asks with a scoff. "I guarantee she'll break mine before I ever break hers."

"I don't feel so good," I whimper. That warm feeling in my tummy is now turning into a storm, alcohol somersaulting in my stomach. I'm starting to sweat being held so close to Noah.

I try to push away from him, but he holds on tighter. I get my arms loose and start struggling out of my sweater, and Noah takes a hint, finally freeing me. I get the sweater off and throw it away from me, not caring where it lands.

Now that I'm not being held by Noah, I start to sway again. Oh, no. I don't like this feeling.

I stumble back to the bar and suck on another lime. I need fluids.

My hair is plastered to my forehead and the back of my neck with sweat. I can't stand the feeling, so I dig into my pockets and miraculously hold on to a hairband as I twirl my hair up into a bun and secure it.

Feeling so much better, I sigh as I suck on another lime.

A bottled water is presented to me, and I hurry to break the seal of the lid and guzzle it down. Just as quickly as it appeared, it disappears.

"Not too much too fast. You're going to get sick."

I turn and glare at Noah, who is spinning the lid back on the bottle. "Another thing you're an expert on, I'm sure," I spit at him. Alcohol makes you stupid and brave, spewing out words before you even think.

I hear Cyn say "whoa" and giggle.

Noah's eyes get dangerously small, the black swallowing up the brown. "What is that supposed to mean?"

What is that supposed to mean? That he's an expert on drinking, as well as sex, as well as what's best for me, as well as knowing when the time is right and how to take this slow. He's an expert on turning down his girlfriend and holding her back from experiencing something that she's never given a thought about until him. And an expert on withholding his past and being evasive when I ask questions he doesn't want to answer.

"Is that how you really think?" Noah's menace is directed at me for once.

Crap, did I say all that out loud?

I snap my mouth shut so nothing else spews out, feeling the burn of embarrassment grow in my cheeks. I can't believe we are arguing in front of everyone like this. First, Kyle informs me how many women Noah's been with. Then I watch Sassy walk up to him like she's oh so familiar with him. And now this! I think I'm going to be sick.

I push past him and stumble my way across the room. I feel too hot, too sick, too embarrassed. I want to leave this party. I want to get away from everyone who heard what I said. I want to re-do this night. I want to go home and cry into my pillow. I want to be alone right now and wake up like this night never happened.

I feel the tears burn my eyes as I rush past the crowd, feel the burn in my throat of liquid poison coming up. Oh, God, I'm about to be seriously sick.

I make it to the blessedly empty bathroom in time to throw up the contents of my stomach. The vile liquid, along with the chicken tenders I had at Jeremy's, are dispelled into the toilet as I hear the sound of running water. The puking won't stop, and now I'm full-out sobbing on top of it all. My ears are ringing, and my head is cloudy, and the room is spinning, which makes me vomit again and again.

I vaguely hear Noah crooning that it's going to be okay as a wet towel is pressed to the back of my neck. It feels so cold and good, and now I want to soak in cold water to rid my body of this heat, sweat, and now stench.

Noah flushes the toilet, and I watch the disgusting, putrid contents swirl down the drain. I hear someone tap on the bathroom door, and then hear Cyn talking to Noah. I don't pay attention to what's said; I keep my focus on the now clean toilet bowl, feeling my stomach churn again before I'm dry-heaving.

"Drinking sucks." My throat burns.

Noah hands me a glass of water. "Don't drink it; just clean your mouth out."

I clumsily reach for the cup, but I'm too weak to grasp it, so Noah holds it to my lips, cupping the back of my head to keep me steady. I gurgle some of the water into my mouth and spit it out into the toilet. Then Noah is dragging me up, but when he tries to pick me up to carry me, I protest. The room spins, and I know I need to feel my own feet on the ground before I get sick again.

"Come on," Noah says, holding me tightly as we shuffle out the door.

I keep my head down, too embarrassed to see if people are watching me, as Noah leads us down to the room we stayed in before. He tries to put me on the bed, but I protest.

"I want to take a bath. Can I take a bath? I'm so hot. I want to cool off." I don't even know if I make any sense, but Noah must understand because he leads me to the bathroom where he helps me slide down the wall and onto the floor beside the tub before he turns the water on.

He says something that doesn't register. I nod my head, and then he disappears.

I clumsily kick my heels off then unbutton my pants. I'm still too hot and this cold floor feels so good. I want to press my skin to it.

I somehow manage to get my clothes off, finally feeling the cold against my skin, curling into a ball and pressing my face against the cold tiles. The sound of the water lulls me into a place of peace.

~Noah~

I get back from checking on Kyle who, between realizing how much he hurt Claire—which he apologized for—and Cyn verbally and physically attacking him for his stupidity, is in a much sober place, to find Claire curled up naked on the bathroom floor. It's a shock to say the least, her lying there, only her necklace adorning her.

How did this night end so fucked up? Is this a precursor to the rest of year? God, I hope not.

I'm still a firm believer in Claire not needing to know how I used to be. That doesn't matter to how I am now, how I am with her. And she doesn't need others telling her. On another note, we will be in the city after summer, and if we are still together, she is going to be hearing a lot more. I might as well tell her something, but not tonight. Definitely not tonight.

"Claire? Angel? We need to get you off this floor."

She doesn't respond, so I scoop her up, making sure not to look at her body too closely. She's drunk, passed out. I won't take advantage of her that way.

"No …" she moans. "Cold. Water." I guess she's not passed out completely and still wants that bath.

She's struggling out of my hold, so I say and do anything to appease her. "Okay, okay."

I gently lower her into the water and hear her sigh in contentment. The water isn't completely cold, just lukewarm. I don't want her getting sick like she did after her birthday.

The smell of lavender permeates the air, a bath oil nearby that I put into the water. She settles in as I settle on the floor beside her, needing to be close in case she goes under. I stare at her face, not letting my eyes wander any lower. Her eyes are closed, mascara lines streaming down her face from her previous tears. Her mouth is formed into a frown, and she looks like she's about to cry again.

I grab a washcloth from off the rack of towels and wet it before wiping off the mascara streaks. All disheveled and drunk, she is still so beautiful.

"Why do people get drunk?"

I continue wiping her face as I answer, "Different reasons. For fun, for loss, to forget, to remember. Why did you?"

"I was mad, sad. To forget." Tears stream down her cheeks. "I'm sorry."

"You don't have to apologize. If it was you …" I swallow that bitter taste down. "If someone was saying that shit about you, I would have lost it."

"Too. You were supposed to say you would have lost it, too."

I grin. "Yeah, I would have lost it, too."

She sighs and slits her eyes open. "Even now, naked and alone, you haven't even looked below the neck, have you?" More tears fall, mixing with the growing cold water. It seems like I can never do anything right in her eyes.

I shake my head. "Not when you're drunk."

"I feel better now." A brittle smile comes to her lips. "Can I have some water and toothpaste or mouthwash if there is any in here? My mouth tastes like acid."

I hand her the bottled water I brought with me. Then I get up off the floor. "I'll find you a toothbrush for when you get out." I open some drawers until I find a tube of toothpaste and an un-opened toothbrush.

I hear water stirring around and turn back to see Claire standing in the bathtub. I look at her. I mean, I *look* at her.

Her body is amazing. I have seen the top half before, and I have even seen most of the bottom half, but never have I seen her fully naked. She is all supple curves. Long legs, slim waist with just enough hips not to look too thin. Her torso is proportional to her hips; breasts flawless slopes with pink nipples that are hard nubs right now. And if she turned around, I would see a perfectly round, two handfuls of impeccable ass.

I rush to get her a towel and wrap it around her body before helping her step out of the tub. Her steps are surer, but she still leans heavily on me for support. Towel secured, she immediately heads toward the toothbrush like it's an oasis.

"You okay for a minute?" I need to get away from her for a second, calm myself down.

She nods, one hand gripping the counter while she furiously brushes her teeth with the other hand.

I leave the bathroom door slightly open, keeping an ear out in case she needs help, and then start pacing the room. Denying myself is hard enough, but denying her, someone I care about so much that my heart literally aches and swells with her moods, is pure torture. I keep reminding myself that we are only a few months along in our relationship, and if I get my wish, we will be together for much, much longer, so taking this slow is justifiable.

I sit on the bed and bury my head in my hands. This was not how tonight was supposed to turn out.

I hear the bathroom door creak open and lift my head to see Claire silhouetted there, still naked. She is really trying to kill me. Every day that passes, she gets more and more brazen. Still innocent as hell, but with a siren's determination to sink me in her depths. I don't know how much longer I can hold off without hurting her more and more. I tried explaining, and she tried understanding, but she doesn't get it. I *need* to be right with her.

"Claire ..." I start to warn her off, not knowing what to say when she is drunk.

"I know. No sex. Got it. Check. Yep ... But that doesn't mean we can't do other things." She walks up to me and stops when there is only a breath of air between us, my lips *this* close to her breasts. "Don't turn me down right now, Noah. Between what Kyle said to seeing what a backstabbing bitch Sassy is, I can't handle another blow." Claire swearing is a rare event that turns me on that much more. "Just ... just assure me that you do want this. I need that assurance from you right now."

I grab her hips and swing her around, sprawling her out across the bed next to me. Then I grab her hand and press it to my erection. "Is this the assurance you need, Claire?" I grit out, mad at myself for being so weak around her. "I'm like this *every* moment you are in the room. And *every* moment I think about you when you're not."

She caresses the length of me, causing me to suck in a breath, before lowering her hand away from me. *Not when she's drunk*, I remind myself. Claire, of course, has other ideas.

She straddles my hips, her beautiful tits bouncing with her movements.

I close my eyes to control myself, but even behind my closed lids, I have the picture of her on top of me to contend with.

When I feel her hands at the button of my pants, I grasp her tiny wrists to stop her progression. Then I sit up quickly, nose to nose. "No." I hate that damn word.

Claire, in all her intoxicated bravery, doesn't back away from the steel in my warning. "I. Know. No sex. Again, it doesn't mean we can't do other things."

"Claire, I don't feel comfortable doing anything with you when you—"

"I said don't turn me down right now!" She slaps my chest and pushes me back down on the bed. Leaning over me, she whispers, "I want to see it." Then she giggles. "That sounded really lame."

I crack a smile, frustration melting. "Pretty much."

Okay, I think as she returns to unbuttoning my fly, *if she's in curious mode right now, I can deal with that.* I'm the sober one. I'm the one in control. If Claire gets out of control, I can talk her down, appease her in some other way.

That thought doesn't really make me happy right now because, again, she's drunk.

My zipper is down, and she delves her hand inside when I broadcast the latest thought that hits me. "Claire, you won't regret anything tomorrow, will you?"

That must have been the catalyst to her emotional night because she stops and immediately breaks down into sobs. I'm up and holding her within seconds as she shakes in my arms.

"I'm … sorry," she wails. "I'm not … used to being insecure and jealous, b-but … I've never felt more so in all my life. I excused your past because I wasn't in it. It's now that matters, right?" She doesn't give me time to answer before continuing. "But then Kyle comes up a-and says that, and then all I'm thinking is how many women you've been with. I calculated like *three hundred* and that was being generous." Her voice rises at that, but then she lowers her it again. "I compared … never mind. And then I see Sassy coming on to you, and all I could think is that for someone who was used to getting it every day to nothing, it must mean you were getting it from someone other than me.

"I'm so insecure when it comes to you. And now jealous … Yeah, I think I already said that. I don't want to be one of those girls. I *trust* you. I do. You've never given me any reason not to. We're with each other *all* the time, so when could you …? I'm rambling. Sorry." And then she starts sobbing again.

I move us up to the headboard and tuck us both underneath the covers, shoes and all.

She is right about the women, but *three hundred*, and *that being generous*? Yeah, that's getting way out of proportion. The week Kyle was talking about was during the summer. Most of the time, there was school, homework, band practice where, yeah, things could get out of control, but not that extreme. In fact, during and after practice, I'm not in the mood. That's still the case.

On average, there was only one woman at a time who lasted around two months before figuring out they weren't getting anything more from me. And sometimes I had sex with other people during those two months. So, yeah, added up, that's still a lot of partners, but I am nowhere near the one hundred marker, never mind three hundred. Huh, I never really thought about it. But now that I am, I would say I'm just over the fifty mark. Still seems extreme putting a number on it.

"You know how I feel about us, right?" I ask, needing the assurance.

She nods, sniffling her tears as she reaches up to grab the guitar pick I gave her.

"That you're the first person I've ever opened myself up to. That you're worth waiting for. Worth taking time with. You're the world to me, Claire. You're all I see ... All I see." I kiss her teary cheek and then her forehead before snuggling her against me, resting my head on top of hers.

"When it's your first time, I want it to feel like it's my first time, too. I want to be awkward and nervous, yet excited and feel like I can't wait, which I can't now," I quickly add, because it's true and she needs to know that. "I want our first time to wash away the past. Do you understand that?"

She nods again, no longer sniffling, only listening closely.

"I want it to be the start of us. A different start, one filled with intimacy and desires, sharing ourselves fully."

Claire yawns. "I want that, too," she mumbles, closer to sleep.

I continue to hold her, listening to the sounds of the party quieting down, her breathing becoming steadier. Claire's face is buried in my neck, my chin resting atop her head, the smell of her hair my own calm.

"I want that so much, Claire," I whisper, hoping tomorrow is better and that the new year is happier than this night, and that tonight isn't an omen of what's to come.

Chapter 13

I Forgot All About Them!

~Claire~

Months pass: January, February, March. We don't talk about New Year's Eve. Ever. It's as if it never happened. As if my insecurities are locked away in a vault. As if I hadn't gotten drunk and made a fool out of myself in front of all those people.

Valentine's Day came and went, but needs to be mentioned as the sweetest. We are talking breakfast in bed; a flower sitting on my desk in each class; and two dozen flowers hand-delivered by Mister Perfect himself, dressed deliciously in a newer pair of jeans, a white button up shirt, and an open vest, no tie. He took me to a small Italian restaurant where they served a seven-course meal with a handsome piano being played by an older gentleman who took requests. It was perfection.

Troy informed me after the Valentine's day weekend that he went to visit Chelsea. We still don't talk, and he always makes a point to only talk to me when Noah is there. I don't know if it's a guy respect thing, or maybe Troy knows he's walking the tightrope and doesn't want to catch me alone just to have accusations thrown at him later.

Troy told us that Chelsea is now five months pregnant. He wasn't at school Thursday or Friday because he went to be with Chelsea during the ultrasound to find out the sex of the baby. Turns out they are having a girl. Troy beamed when I congratulated him. You could see the male pride coming off him.

Being responsible for a mother and your child seems to have matured him quite a bit. Troy is already more soft spoken, not aggressive at all. The tension and anxiety I used to always feel radiating off him is now this peace and control he has always strived to reach.

He told us that him and Chelsea are not planning to marry or even have much of a relationship. They agreed to remain friends and stay in each other's lives as much as possible for the baby. You can tell that Troy is willing to do anything for his baby girl. He's already so excited to meet her.

When all the congratulations and my questions were out of the way, Troy shook Noah's hand, gave me a kiss on the head with a weird pat on the back, and then walked away like the conversation never happened. I looked at Noah, and he gave me a shrug, as if to say, "I don't know what that was either, but okay."

A few weeks later, we had dinner with my dad for his birthday. Noah helped me pick out a new briefcase for him. A sleek, black Burberry Brit briefcase, going half and half on it since it cost over five hundred dollars, and that was a steal. Good thing I had money saved up. I tried to argue Noah out of his half, but when Noah decides on something, there is no backing him down.

Noah and I spend a lot of weekends at his uncle's house. Katy is so much fun to talk to while Noah and his band practice. If I'm not watching the band, then I'm talking to her as we cook or play with Abby. Katy is fast becoming the mother I never had. Even Signora Gelardi, who has been the only woman in my life until now, doesn't come close to comparing to Katy, who hugs me often and talks to me as I imagine my own mother would. She has even taken me shopping with her, and once we went to get our nails done together, with little Abby with us, getting her nails painted a hot pink with "diamonds" strewn over them. That was a fun day.

Prom is next month, and though I never thought in a million years Noah would want to go, he asked me. It seems silly to go, surrounded by my peers who have never been nice to me. Plus, the thought of going to prom, of Noah going to prom, is strange.

Noah is so rugged, appearing older than his eighteen years, far more mature than the kids at our school. Him dressed up in a tux is hard to picture, though when I do, he's stunning. I bet he ends up wearing nice slacks and maybe a tie, but never a tux. I just can't see it.

Katy went with me to find a dress. Our small town doesn't have much to offer, so we made a day of it and visited a lot of boutiques in Denver. She convinced me to go with a shorter dress due to my lack of height. It is midnight blue, strapless, accented with beadwork, and made from chiffon. It is sweet, yet sexy with an open back. There is a full, flirty skirt that reminds me of something a ballerina would wear. The skirt would be short on anyone else, but with me, it's the ideal length, hitting right above my knees.

Embarrassing, but gratefully, she brought up the sex talk, starting with, "I hope you guys are using protection." Just like that, all out in the blue. One minute we were talking about fabrics, and the next, she threw that bomb out there.

I blushed, of course. No words came to mind. I knew everyone assumed we were having sex. We spent enough time together, especially alone. But having someone come out and mention it … I didn't know if I should be more embarrassed that we had or hadn't had sex. If I told her the truth, would she even believe it? There was only one way to find out.

"Um, we haven't—I mean," I started, worried that she would assume that meant we hadn't been using protection, "we haven't had sex."

She looked at me, like *yeah, right.* "Claire, it's okay to talk about it. I know you are still in high school, but legally, you both are adults. I want to make sure you both don't jeopardize your futures when an unexpected baby comes into your lives."

That was when everything spilled out. I told her how Noah kept putting me off, how I felt about that, the fight we had over it—everything. We ended up at a small café, talking about it over coffee. She listened, pressing a sympathizing hand over mine. Then she told me, "Claire, it sounds like Noah is in this for the long haul. What's six months compared to six years, sixteen, sixty? This is a blip on the full scale that is your life. Take your time, enjoy the innocence, enjoy being simple, because when it's gone, there is no going back, no do-overs. Take your time so there are no regrets. You always remember your first time. Enjoy the buildup, enjoy the suspense because, in the end, that's always the best part of any experience." And that made me feel better, for a while, anyway.

Now it's spring break, and I am sitting in Noah's room, waiting for him to get out of the shower. No one else is home. Kyle took off right after practice, while Katy, Mark, and Abby went to go see a new Disney movie.

His room is so ... blue, which he hates, and I think it's funny. It's plain; nothing characteristic of Noah. There is nothing that stands out as *him*. No posters, no trophies or awards, no knickknacks. Nothing but school books and his song notebooks, which he keeps under his bed, and a few pictures of us that sit on his dresser. His room is clean, way too clean for a teenage guy.

Wanting something to do while I wait, I drop to the ground beside Noah's bed and fish around for his notebook, wanting to read any new lyrics he's written. It doesn't bother him that I love to read his words. Sometimes he's even enthusiastic over sharing one with me, wanting to get my opinion on wording. I smile at that thought.

I don't immediately feel his worn notebook, so I drop to the carpet to see what I am blindly reaching for. The notebook is north of where I was reaching. I finally slap my hand down on it and slide it toward me when a manila envelope catches my eyes. It's up against the wall at his headboard, like it fell off his bed.

I drop down onto my belly and wiggle my way toward it, wanting to set it out for him in case he did lose it. Unfortunately, the thing is upside down and open, and when I yank it, papers slip out of the envelope like a stream. No, not papers.

Pictures.

Pictures of Noah and some woman.

Pictures of Noah and some woman having sex.

Pictures of Noah and some woman having sex on a couch, on a chair, over a table. His hands touching her everywhere. His mouth on her neck, her shoulder, biting, sucking, licking.

I reach for the pendant he gave me like that will center me, or maybe assure me that what I'm seeing isn't the truth. And maybe it's not because the look on his face in these pictures is one I have never seen before. He definitely has that arousal look I so love to see in his eyes, yet he has a look of detachment. This is not the Noah I know. And I am not like this woman. A woman he obviously wanted.

She has dark hair like me, but not as long. Besides that, there are no other similarities. This woman is a few years older than me, tall, thin, all the right proportions for a model. They look like a perfect couple in all their naked glory. Who is she? Most importantly, why does Noah have pictures of her? Why is he keeping them? If this is what he wants, then why is he pulling the celibacy act with me?

God, *is* this what he wants? I haven't imagined us being together like this. I always imagine looking into his eyes as we make love, everything tender yet passionate, slow yet needy. This. This is raw. This is hardcore sex. He looks like he wants to hurt her, and she looks like she would love it.

When were these taken? Who is the girl? This must be from the city, right? I can see band equipment in the background, band posters advertising a venue. The venue is a place Noah has told me about, where his city band frequented. If this is before us, then why does Noah still have them?

God, this insecurity is choking me. We have been together for six months today, though neither one of us had mentioned the fact. We still have been playing it up that today is special, dropping suggestions and hints that we will be alone tonight, and this is what slaps me in the face? I wanted tonight to be special. I wanted to tell him I'm one hundred percent sure I'm in love with him; been sure since almost the beginning.

Noah's been the one putting off sex. Then I see these pictures that show him not denying someone else, and it makes me feel inadequate. Is he afraid if he goes all the way with me, I will disappoint him? Has he been holding off in fear of us not being compatible that way? I know he said that isn't a worry, but what else is there? We are adults; I shouldn't have to be continuously shut down when we are in a relationship and I'm so willing. I'm sick of this. This is my decision, too. He can't be the one to make all the choices in this relationship.

Are we even really in a relationship? I can't not think this when I see the evidence of one of Noah's priors. He gave himself to her, and others. What makes them different from me? What do they have that I don't have? I mean, I get the not rushing, but I think I can make my own decision to lose my virginity to him. I don't think most adults wait this long in a relationship before having sex, casual or not. This is ridiculous.

Anger sets in as I go through all twenty-five, full-color photographs, thinking angry thoughts directed solely at Noah and his "pure values" on our relationship. I'm tired of waiting, yet I really don't want to think about having sex with Noah in the aftermath of discovering what appears to be his self-created porn. God, Kyle was right on New Year's Eve night. Noah really was a manwhore.

Hands clasping my ankles makes me scream and jump, causing me to hit my back on the bed frame. Noah drags me out so fast and, because it's such a surprise, I'm still gripping some of the photos when I'm out from underneath his bed.

I flip over to see Noah in only his jeans, water dripping from his hair and down his torso. He's wearing his mischievous, playful grin until he sees what I'm clutching in my hands. That grin falls fast and panic overcomes his features. Then, as quickly, his indifferent face comes up.

~Noah~

Panic. Heart racing.

Shit! Those pictures came to me in the mail months ago. A so-called gift from the boys back home. That bitch had a video of us fucking all over the back room, and the guys printed out stills of the video to show me "what I'm missing being here."

I forgot about them, forgot they even existed. As soon as I saw them, I had every intention of burning them, but Katy and Mark were home. I had to wait until they went to bed before tossing them into the fireplace. Obviously, that was forgotten.

I don't know how to explain this. I have to tell her the truth, but how do I explain what the pictures entail? She knows I have had my share of women. She knows some of the things I did in the city, how I was. But she didn't have to *see* it.

She has been giving me a hard-enough time about waiting on sex as it is, and now it's thrown in her face that I did it with random women. Now she's seeing the evidence of my flagrant ways on full display—tits, ass, cock shots, and all. What am I going to say to that? How is she going to take this?

I am so goddamn angry at myself, at her for finding those photos. Again, at me for forgetting them. Goddamn motherfucking shit! I don't know what to say. And there she is, sitting on the floor, holding those goddamn photos, looking up at me with anger and hurt.

I swallow hard and look away from her as I snatch the pictures out of her hands and tear them up without looking at them. I then proceed to get on my hands and knees and crawl under the bed, gathering up the rest of the pictures.

"Are you going to say anything?" Claire's small, controlled voice reaches me.

I make the choice not to answer right away, army crawling back out from under the bed where I make my way to the trash bin in my room and toss the pictures and envelope inside. Then I carry the bin out of my room, making sure to grab Claire's car keys and a lighter, pocketing them as I pass the kitchen. There is no way in hell I am letting her leave before we talk about this, but I'm not ready to talk right now. This is a situation of fucked-up proportions, and I need to calm down before I open my stupidly forgetful mouth and let stupidly unforgettable words come out of my stupidly forgetful head.

I head out the back door and make my way over to the fire pit, dumping all the trash out of the bin. The lighter serves to do what I should have done months ago. Squatting, I set alight some papers that were at the bottom of the trash, effectively incinerating all the papers and pictures. I stay in that position, watching an army of ants running away from the heat.

I still haven't calmed down enough, and my thoughts are running rampant on what to say and how she will react. When are we going to have the blowout? When will she leave me? When will she realize she's so much better than me and I don't deserve her? She's now seen who I am—who I was. She's now seen how I lived before her. Is this going to be the tipping point, where the scale of pros and cons will tip in favor of all my cons and she will run from me?

Fear has my heart pounding against my ribcage. I can't fully breathe. I think I'm having a mini panic attack at just thinking about losing the best thing that's happened to me. I can't let her go. I have changed for her, become a better person. She brings out the best in me. She brings me comfort, listens to me, understands me. I can't lose her. It's only been six months, but the memories are seared into me forever. She makes me smile, laugh. I haven't ever felt this free in my life.

"Noah?" I didn't even hear her come up behind me, so lost in my thoughts.

I continue watching the ants scurry here and there, still not knowing what to say. Damn it all to hell. She probably thinks the worse of me now.

I can't look at her when I say, "I'm sorry you found those. I meant to get rid of them the moment they were sent to me, but I ... forgot."

"You *forgot*? And who sent them to you? *Her*, the woman in the pictures? Is she waiting for you to come back?" Claire's voice break as she tries to control her emotions. I can't tell if she's crying or incredibly pissed. She's trying to be firm, but failing miserably. Either way, I regret those emotions I put in her.

"The guys, the band—they meant it as a joke. The woman ..." I shake my head. "I don't even know her name. She was someone I ... was with my last night in the city."

Claire starts pacing behind me. I can hear her steps squash through the wet grass. I'm still not brave enough to turn around and look at her, to see the disappointment, anger, and sadness in her eyes. I don't want to see those emotions targeted at me.

"Do you realize how hurt this makes me? What's been going through my mind? That you were keeping them to look at repeatedly. That she was someone you miss." She huffs out a breath. "And then there's the sex. You don't even know her name, yet you had sex with her? We've been together for six months and nothing! Do you know, understand, comprehend how that makes me feel? I've been feeling inadequate, like you are holding this off because you think I will disappoint you or something. We've had this argument, but that's still how I feel, Noah. Don't we feel more for each other than you do for a woman you supposedly don't even know her name? Aren't we more than that? If so, then why? Why not give me something you so freely gave to *just someone*. It makes no damn sense to me!" Claire swearing is never a good thing. The closest thing she says to swear words are darn and crap.

If only I can get her to see that she means more to me than a quick fuck. I don't understand how someone who was closed off from relationships suddenly has this desperate need to take our relationship to the next level. I have been trying to make her feel cherished and loved because she is. I don't want her to think that, the moment I sleep with her, I will leave, or that our relationship will change, or anything like that.

"Please, Claire," I try.

"And then I think about *how* you were having sex with her. Is that what you want? Is that something you need? You looked so angry in those pictures, like you wanted to hurt her. Is that something you expect—"

"Claire, stop!" I jump to my feet, standing in front of her within seconds and towering over her petite body. "What you saw in those pictures is in the *past*. I've told you and told you, I didn't give a damn about any of them. It was all about *me*." I pound on my chest, and Claire takes a step back, dropping her guitar pick pendant that she was no doubt sawing back and forth, her newest anxiety twitch. "Me and *my* selfish wants. What you saw has nothing to do with us, with how we will be. I could *never* treat you that way. Don't put your expectations or what you think mine are based on what you saw."

I turn away from her and run my hands through my hair, pulling so hard it hurts. "Dammit! I wish you hadn't seen that. I swear to God, Claire, I forgot all about them! I don't *want* the reminders of how I was. I don't *want* to go back to that person."

Claire lets out a sigh. "I understand. But it still hurts. And I wanted tonight to be about us. I wanted to ..."

I turn around to see Claire looking down, shaking her head.

"You wanted tonight to be the night." God, I wanted prom night to be a surprise, but now that probably won't even happen, so I might as well tell her. "Look, let's go back inside. We can talk in there. Unless ..." She looks up at me, and I try to school my features into apathy. "Unless you want to go home now." I drop my head back down.

It takes a few seconds for Claire to respond. "No. I think it is time to talk about this. I need to understand why you keep holding off." With that, she turns and marches back inside the house.

~Claire~

At this point, I'm numb. The anger, the betrayal, even the embarrassment at finding those pictures and pouring my desires out are completely gone. I'm numb, not even caring at this point what he has to say.

I make my way into the living room and sit on the couch. Noah likes closure, and I want to get this conversation of excuses over with so I can go home and go to bed.

Noah comes in behind me a few moments later. He looks distraught. He looks like his eighteen years and not the mature twenty-something I first thought.

He sits down on the couch, away from me, on the other side, a whole two feet of space between us that feels like so much more. His hands are in his pockets as he sits, his long legs stretched out before him, facing forward, and not angled in my direction at all, which is similar to the way I am sitting, but my arms and legs crossed. Petulant and tortured; that's how we look right now.

"I'm going to come out and say all this in one swoop, and excuse me if I sound like a broken record," he says in a monotone voice. "My past is my past. There is no changing that. Those pictures were a crude joke, and I am sorry you found them. I'm sorry it even happened; that the bitch videotaped us without my knowledge, that the band thought it would be funny to send them." He removes his hands from his pockets and finally angles his body toward me. "I can apologize repeatedly, but it happened. It's over. I don't know what else to say to you."

I remain silent, staring at the cold fireplace. I know I should accept his apology, that I'm being irrational to something that happened before me, but it still hurts. I still feel rejection.

Noah scoots closer. "As for us, I already had a date in my mind for when I can give you what you want. I don't want to have sex here, in my uncle's house, or even at your house where your dad could come home at any time. I want us to have our own space and as much time as we need. I want the entire night to be perfect for you, Claire. As perfect as you are to me. I don't want your first time to be in my bed where we hear someone come home and have to jump up and get dressed before Abby or someone comes barging in. That's not what you deserve, angel."

I soften a bit, knowing what he says is possible. It has happened before when we were making out. My dad would come home while we were kissing on the couch, and I would feel so embarrassed for being caught. Or the time Abby came in and jumped between us, asking if we had run really far and that was why we were breathing so hard. I don't want that to happen during sex.

Curiosity piqued, I finally turn toward him. "What date did you have in mind?"

"Prom." No hesitation.

I roll my eyes and turn a little from him. "You have to be kidding me. That's so cliché, Noah. *Prom*? You know I don't even want to go. And I know deep down you don't want to, either. I say we skip prom, do something else exciting. I really don't want to be around all those people. It's not on my bucket list."

"Honestly, it's not on mine, either, but it's a special night. I know girls like to dress up pretty." He scoots even closer and starts playing with my hair. "We can go out to a nice dinner, dance, maybe have a few laughs at the idiots around us. Then we get the hotel room ..." He lets that linger.

I can imagine the picture he's painting in my mind. Dancing with Noah would be pretty special while dressed up and feeling pretty next to Noah's gorgeousness. But then I picture going to the bathroom and hearing petty talk from the girls at school, hearing them talk about Noah. Then I see those pictures in my mind again, and those girls replace the woman in the photographs, listening to them say what they want Noah to do with them. My imagination is running away from me.

"I really don't want to do it, but"—I turn toward him and set my hand on his—"if it's something you have planned, then I'm there."

The corner of Noah's mouth twitches, fighting back a smile.

164

"Really? So, you're not upset anymore?"

I pull away a bit. "Oh, I'm still upset." That comes out sounding like a lie because a nervous chuckle comes out. "But knowing you have something planned, something I'm holding you to"—I point a finger at him—"makes it a little better." I lean into him, resting my head on his chest. Noah brings his arms around me, holding me so tightly. "I really wish I hadn't seen those photos." Suddenly, the urge to cry overcomes me, and I feel a tear silently slip out.

"Me, too, angel. Me, too."

Chapter 14

Little Demons and All

~Claire~

Today is Noah and Abby's birthday. He promised to pick me up on his bike. Since the weather has gotten warmer, he uses every excuse to ride, and I don't mind because I love it, too.

Of course, being that Noah's birthday was coming up, Kyle made a big deal about it at school on Friday, teasing us about what a "good" girlfriend gives her boyfriend on his birthday. Kyle ended up with a busted lip for that.

We were standing near my car after school. Noah had his arms wrapped around my waist, lifting me up in a big hug and giving me a modest kiss before I got in my car, when Kyle came behind me and whispered loud in my ear, "I know this *good* girlfriend will be very *bad* for her boyfriend's birthday."

Noah dropped me back to my feet and gave Kyle the look that says *you are so dead*, but it didn't deter Kyle. He was in a playful mood and on a roll with his antics and rude comments.

Kyle held his hands up, shaking the hair out of his eyes. He had let it grow out ever since Noah moved here. "What? Just saying. I know what I'd want my girlfriend to give me for my birthday." He did a gesture with his hand, pushing it down toward his crotch while pumping his hips forward.

I closed my eyes and turned red in embarrassment, turning away from Kyle's vulgar imitation. I'm not that naive. I knew what he was suggesting, though Noah has never allowed me to do that for him.

Needless to say, later that night, when I showed up for Characters' show, Kyle had a fat lip, with a split right down the middle. Noah simply looked at me in all innocence, shrugging before glancing across the table at Kyle who was avoiding all eye contact with anyone.

For Noah's birthday, I had something made for him. I found this designer who made Thai Karma bracelets. It's a wrap with five bands of leather braided in a Celtic design. Our initials, CDS and NJG, are branded underneath the thickest leather piece. I hope he likes it.

I hear the doorbell ring while I'm slipping on my ankle boots, and then I hear my dad answer the door. Being a Sunday, he's home for once; practically the only day out the week he takes off, and that's not always.

I take one last look in the mirror, checking to make sure all the buttons are done up on my baby blue dress and that the leather belt is straight before I grab the parcel containing Noah's gift then make my way downstairs.

Dad, knowing Noah likes to read classics, got him an older copy of *The Count of Monte Cristo*. I know it's one book that Noah hasn't read yet. I wanted to see his face when Dad gave it to him, but I can already hear my dad telling Noah about the book in his office.

"Do you like it?" I ask, coming through the doorway.

"Yeah. I read *The Three Musketeers* and have been planning to read more from Dumas for a while now, so thanks." Noah is standing over the book in its box, turned to the title page, wearing his rare, shy smile that tells me he really appreciates the gesture.

"Don't thank me. That was from Daddy. I have my own present for you."

Noah turns to my dad and holds out his hand to shake. "Thanks again, Jonathan."

"You're welcome." Dad smiles at Noah, shaking his hand, and then moves to his desk.

We know Dad's innuendoes, so we head out of the office, Noah carrying the book away with him.

"Is that for me?"

I look up to see Noah eyeing the box in my hand with an eager expression, something I haven't seen on his face before. "Yep. Do you want it now or later? I'd rather we were alone when you opened it."

Noah looks like he's debating hard about this. Then he breaks into one of his rare, genuine smiles. He bends down and whispers in my ear, the caress of his voice making goose bumps rise, "Do we have to be behind a closed door? Is it something dirty? Maybe something you're saving for prom?" He runs a finger along the length of my low collar, caressing the skin at my breast, before he backs up and looks at my face, silently laughing because he knows he got to me.

I shove the box into his waist, halting his laughter at my expensive. Noah's been talking dirtier and dirtier to me. Surprisingly, I like it.

"No, you pervert." I walk toward the living room with him following. "You lost your choice. You can open it now. And hurry. I know Abby is waiting for us."

Abby decided to have a knights and princess themed party since having all princesses wouldn't be fair to Noah. No one could stop laughing when she informed us of her theme, all of us picturing Noah dressed in a knight's costume for his little cousin.

"Happy birthday, Noah."

~Noah~

Claire surprises me in ways I have never imagined. After the picture fiasco, she acted like it never happened, going from calm fury to excitement over prom night, though she still doesn't want to go to prom. Regardless, I will make the night memorable and perfect for her. She has no idea what I have planned.

Most girls would let the entire incident simmer, using it as leverage to throw in your face at any and every opportunity. Or they would dump you, realizing you aren't the perfect man they thought you were. That you are now tainted, and they can't look past your imperfections. At least, that's how I imagine other relationships would end. Not Claire, though. She takes you as you are and accepts it.

I look down to where I have already taken off the twine and wrapping and am now opening the box. Inside is a lot of tissue paper, and snuggled inside of that is a lot of leather strings and beads. What the hell is this?

I must look confused because Claire laughs. She drops her

pendant that she was nervously sawing back and forth and grabs the box from my hand before moving to sit on the couch. I follow her as she pulls out the object.

"Hold out your hand."

I give her my right hand, but she takes my left instead, and then wraps the—well, now I know what it is—bracelet around my wrist.

She flips my hand over to connect the two end pieces as she explains, "It's a Thai Karma bracelet." She meets my eyes for a minute. I'm watching her mouth move as she talks. "I thought it was interesting, and it reminded me of you. Not the Thai Karma part but, you know, the leather. And it looks rugged, like you, not feminine or anything too emasculating." She flips my hand over. "I had your initials branded on the inside ... with mine." She looks self-conscious now, her head lowered as she releases my hand. But I won't let her shy away from this. I want her to own it. So, I kiss her.

Her mouth parts instantly, and I delve in with enough force that she falls back on the couch.

"Thank you, angel. It's perfect." I place another kiss on her lips. "Like you." I kiss her again, longer this time. She's breathing fast through her nose now, her hands hurrying along my back, not knowing where to settle. I have a hard time when we are like this.

I break away from her and prop my elbows on either side of her head, looking down at her face as her eyes slowly open. "You know I adore you, right?"

Her eyes melt at my words. "Adore: to love and respect someone deeply, to venerate and worship. Or do you like me very much? Or maybe you're feeling excitement over your gift?" She quirks an eyebrow at me.

We recently had a paper on the difference between adoration and love. Adoration is such a stronger word than love. Love is more of a sexual attraction, whereas adoration is celestial, encompassing more than a strong affection for someone and feeling romantic about them. Adoration is everything she cited and more. It's something holy, a reverence for someone or something.

I will never adore another person the way I do Claire. Love? Maybe. But never adore.

She's in smartass mode right now, showing off what she learned. I need to set her straight.

I begin to tickle her ruthlessly as she squirms and bucks underneath me, laughing freely. Her laugh is infectious, and soon I'm laughing with her as she begs me to stop, trying to grab my wrists to still my fingers.

As I continue to tickle her, I tell her, "Adore. Love. Deeply respect. Definitely worship. Every part of you." I stop tickling her and lie down next to her on the couch. "Your big blue eyes, the little freckles dotting your nose, your beautiful hair. I really adore your beautiful hair." I push back said hair from her face then lean in to whisper, "The noises you make when I make you come." I graze the back of my hand from her breast to her hips and down her leg, watching its progression. "I worship this succulent, little body."

"Succulent, huh?"

I look back up into Claire's eyes, seeing the heat and arising humor. She's still flushed from being tickled, or maybe it's remnants from kissing, or maybe it's where my words are going.

I caress my way back up her leg, under her dress, to the damp panties below. "Mmhmm, very succulent. I can't wait to taste it."

I love how my words affect her. Her breath catches before she remembers to exhale, her eyes dilate, her chest starts to rise and fall faster.

Seduction is the key to making her first time the most memorable. As we get closer and closer to the date, I give her more and more, just enough to drive her insane. I have caressed almost every inch of her body, except inside, and I have sucked on her tits until she was crying out my name.

Claire has tried and tried to go down on me, but I don't think I could take that without wanting more and giving in to her. She's giving me hand jobs, her small hand wrapped around my cock, me grasping her tiny hand until she mastered the technique. Teaching her things has been the biggest turn on of all.

My fingers brush against her lace covered folds, barely touching.

"Noah," she gasps.

I pull my hand away before leaning over her again, kissing her one more time. "We gotta go."

~Claire~

When we make our way inside Mark and Katy's, the noise level is through the roof. There is no order, just chaos.

A bunch of three- and four-year-olds are running amok. I watch as they eat fruit and sandwiches before dropping them when something of interest catches their eye; pop balloons; and the boys are galloping around on toy stick horses while the girls are shouting off orders, dressed up as princesses, waving their scepters and hitting some of the kids. It's madness.

I cringe, having never been around so many little kids. Noah doesn't look any more comfortable than me. We are both standing inside the door, eyes darting here and there, taking in the madness that has become the Gish's home.

I turn to apologize to Noah, feeling bad that this is his birthday, too. Then I start to laugh.

The look on his face is priceless. His eyes have this wide, awestruck, someone-just-knocked-me-upside-the-head look about them as they dart around the room, taking in the boys jumping up and down on the couches, having already knocked a lamp over; the girls who are fighting over a tiara, crying that it's theirs while a broken tiara lies between them. One kid has even taken it upon herself to fingerpaint with ranch on the wall. What makes it hilarious is that his mouth is dropped open, speechless. I can't stop the giggles that turn into full belly, my-abdomen-muscles-actually-hurt laugh that bubbles out until I am holding my waist, doubled over.

Noah slowly turns toward me, watching my fit, as I let go of his hand, needing it to hold my aching stomach muscles. I literally drop to my knees in laughter, still watching him as he closes his mouth and takes on his composed look. However, he is fighting a smile now, his mouth twitching, mirth in his eyes as he looks down at me. It's too much. I can't stop laughing. The picture is ingrained in my mind's eye now, frozen, a mental picture that I will relive from now until eternity.

Katy comes into the room then, slips of papers stuck to each of

171

her fingers and tape up her arm. I think it's pin the tail on—I look at the wall where the furniture has been pulled away—dragon. She looks around at the chaos, looks at us, then turns her head in every direction, spinning three-hundred and sixty degrees, before she bellows, "Kyle Liam Gish! I told you to watch these kids for two minutes!"

I can't help it, my laughter escalates. This entire scenario is too much. All too much.

~

Katy gets the party and the kids back under control. Kids being kids, hearing and seeing a grownup in their vicinity, they all calmed down at once. Either that or they really wanted to play pin the tail on the dragon. Every one of them stopped what they were doing and lined up in front of Katy, the perfect picture of calm and order. Well, except for their shouts of, "Me first! Me first!" that echoed throughout the house.

Turns out that Kyle was in the room the entire time. He was behind the recliner, picking up pieces of what looked like eaten carrots. Ew. Honestly, I think he was taking his time doing it, not able to handle the chaos. He immediately jumped up when he heard Katy calling him, chewed up pieces of carrots cupped in his hand, and ran to the safety of the kitchen, muttering how he will never have kids.

Meanwhile, Noah lifted me off the floor, shaking his head at me in mock disappointment, while his eyes still held that joyfulness, which sent me into more giggles. After that, we were recruited to different stations. Each of us taking charge of a game while the kids rotated. Overall, it was fun.

Now Katy and I find ourselves alone in the kitchen, cleaning up from all the food, while the guys put together the new princess bed Mark and Katy got for Abby. Abby is passed out on the couch, princessed out. It's hard being a four-year-old.

Katy is telling me about Kyle's birthday parties when he was little and how much of a disaster his sixth birthday was. It makes me laugh and makes me think of Noah's birthday parties. Did he even have one? I know he had to travel a lot with his parents, but what was his home life like?

"What was Noah like as a kid?" I blurt out, cutting her off in her story about Kyle throwing up birthday cake all night after sneakily eating it all because he didn't want to share it with the other kids.

Katy hesitates before she takes a platter off the counter and starts rinsing it. "He was a quiet kid, like he is now." She does a one shoulder shrug. "Mark and I always tried to talk his parents—Sarah and Anthony—into letting him stay with us when they left the country, but Sarah refused. She might not show it, but she really does love her son. I can see that Noah doesn't think so. She shows it differently. She never let him out of her sight when he was little. Same goes for Anthony. They always wanted to be parents, but when they became one, I don't think they knew exactly what they got themselves into."

She glances at the doorway before picking up another dirty platter. "When they visited, he used to fight with Kyle all the time. Kyle is so outgoing and energetic, and I don't think Noah was used to that. He never had playdates, never got to play with neighborhood kids, never had or did anything like other kids."

Cleaning up and dishes are forgotten as I hang on to every word she says, needing to hear about Noah from a third-party perspective.

"But he was always so smart. He would rather sit with the grownups than play with Kyle, and you could *see* him soaking up every word, analyzing. He would get this look in his eyes like he was studying you, learning from you. I have never seen that look in another child's eyes."

I smile at that. I have seen the look she's talking about in a couple of random candid pictures of his childhood she has of him. He wears that same look now when he reads or sometimes when he's people watching. It's like you can almost see his mind at work.

"What are you guys talking about?"

I turn around to find Noah leaning against the doorway, hands in his pockets. I wonder how much of that he heard, if he is mad we were talking about him. From the smile in his eyes, I don't think so.

Katy looks over her shoulder at him, her hands elbow deep in suds, and answers teasingly, "You."

Noah's eyebrows come together, and there is that look we were just talking about.

I look at Katy who looks back at me, and we both start giggling.

Noah shakes his head at us.

"You said we had to leave by five, and it's ten till now." His words stop my giggles.

Crap. Mark and Katy haven't even given him the gift yet. I can't believe four hours have passed already.

I look at her in alarm, and she winks at me before grabbing a dishrag and drying off her hands.

"Mark!" she calls out to him, and we hear an answering, "Yeah?" back from Abby's room. "It's time to give Noah his gift. They need to leave."

We hear a few choice curse words as Mark seems to stumble over pieces of the bed. He makes his way out of Abby's room, Kyle following behind him. Katy moves to the far cabinet and reaches up to the top shelf, coming away with an envelope in her hands, which she hands to Mark who holds it out to Noah.

"Happy birthday," he keeps it simple.

Noah backs away like the envelope is going to attack him. "You guys didn't have to get me anything." Nowhere is the guy who seemed so eager to get presents at my house. I wonder if he acted like this with my dad, too, and I missed it.

"Noah, just take the damn gift," Kyle says laughingly.

Katy slaps his rear. "No swearing."

"You guys have already done too much," Noah insists over my giggling at seeing Kyle's mom spank his butt.

Mark steps forward and slaps the envelope into Noah's unwilling hand. "Will it make you feel better if we tell you it was Claire's idea?"

That seems to change his mind by how fast his head whips in my direction, and that smile comes back in his eyes again. "Really?"

I shrug. "Just open it. I might have suggested it, but it's Mark and Katy's gift to you."

Noah looks at everyone in turn before peeling back the flap and peeking inside. He fingers the two pieces of paper then snaps his head back up. "Really?" he repeats, which makes us all laugh. Plus, there is total surprise in his eyes. "Tonight? Really?"

I have never seen him look so excited before. It's endearing. Plus, he's speechless again. I wish I could take a picture of his expression, capture this moment of rare speechlessness, and then a flash goes off. Katy just did.

"You always cover their songs," I tell him. "And they happen to play tonight, so we decided it was the perfect gift for you. Which is why we need to leave now, because the concert is a two-hour drive away."

~Noah~

I can't believe how quickly this day has turned around. From a four-year-old's crazy birthday party to two concert tickets to my favorite band, playing tonight, on my birthday. I didn't even know they were touring. Attending concerts was one of those things I wrote off when coming here, yet here we are, pulling up to the venue, in my aunt's truck, with Kyle in tow since he bought his own ticket.

Claire is wearing the cheesiest grin on her face. She is so enthusiastic, this being her first concert, which is hard to believe since I have been to so many I lost count. She's been so incredibly happy today, the happiest I have ever seen her, laughing all day, having as much fun with the kids as the kids themselves.

I must admit, watching her play with the piñata even had me laughing. She was so afraid to swing the bat hard the kids hit harder than her. And her playing Marco Polo … She was a big kid out there.

Kyle is talking a mile a minute about the last concert he went to as we walk up to the entrance and have our tickets torn to stubs. Claire is tucked under my arm, looking around at all the people, while I guide us to the grassy area.

The concert is at an outdoor amphitheater, probably the first one this year since it just started warming up. There seems to be only a few hundred seats; most ticket holders relegated to the lawn behind them. Still, from where I find us a place to sit, we have a good view of the stage.

The people around us seem to be together in large groups. They have blankets spread out, holding plastic cups full of beer, their phones blasting out music. It's all feels hectic with the energy everyone is giving off. It washes over me, fueling my own elation and eagerness,

175

especially on seeing how Claire is going to take this all in.

She is still all smiles, turning her head every which way. Sometimes she nods at something Kyle says, yet you can tell she's not really hearing him. I'm not listening, either. I am watching her.

She looks like spring in her light blue dress that shows off the swells of her breast that are currently hidden by her light jacket, and her heeled ankle boots give her bare legs a longer look about them, made even more so by the short length of the dress that cuts off at mid-thigh.

We sit on the blanket Kyle thought to bring with us, and I situate Claire between my legs. Then I lean into her, grabbing all her hair before moving it over her shoulder so I can rest my chin on her other shoulder.

She presses her cheek against mine. "You talk about my first time with you all the time. Here is another one to add to that list," Claire says softly.

I pull away and look at her questioningly, wondering what other firsts she is referring to.

"First boyfriend, first kiss, first, um … orgasm," she whispers, glancing quickly at where Kyle is sitting and watching the stage hands set up the first band. "You made me late to class for the first time—"

"When?" I don't remember that.

"When you asked me to Jeremy's in the hallway."

I smile at that memory. God, that feels like forever ago, though the memory is implanted in my brain like it was yesterday. Back when Claire was an untouchable angel that ghosted through the halls at school, and I would wait to catch glimpses of her, always thinking I missed my chance to merely talk to her. Never did I think then that we would grow to become one of the most amazing connections I have in my life.

"Which leads to first time hearing a band play in a bar," she continues. "First time on a motorcycle, getting drunk …" She makes a face at that, and I internally grimace with her. Yeah, that's a memory we both wordlessly decided never to talk about again. "First date … There are so many. Cooking together, studying together—there are so many little things that all add up to you being my boyfriend, my best friend, and making this past school year the best I ever had. I didn't even realize how alone and empty my life was until you." She frowns at that.

Kyle stands up then and declares he's getting a round of drinks for us. I'm sure he was listening by the tilt of his head and the fact that he is never silent for more than thirty seconds. I don't care if he was. Though I am glad he didn't crack a joke about any of it.

While Kyle gets our drinks, the opening band starts up. A lot of people get up and start dancing or jumping around to the beat. Claire and I stay seated, listening together. Sometimes we sing along. Other times we tune them out and start talking again, making comments about the people around us, the band, and music in general. It feels like there is this invisible bubble around us. Nothing penetrates our space, sounds become muted background noise, until we stop to listen, and then the music feels like it gets turned up ten decibels.

Half an hour later, Kyle finally shows back up, telling us that he ran into a couple of guys he knows. He hands us a couple of bottled waters and sits back down, bopping his head to the beat.

Twenty minutes after that, the opening band introduces the main act, and Kyle jumps up and starts cheering and shouting, turning on his phone's flashlight app and waving it in the air.

I guide Claire up so she can see as the band comes on stage. She has a huge smile on her face now, turning her head to look back at me like she wants to make sure I am seeing what she's seeing. I can't help smiling at her joy, kissing her forehead on instinct to express my happiness in hers.

We dance, we sing, we listen, and we watch, always connected in some way. It turns out to be the best concert because I get to experience something with her, something mundane and something I have done and seen before, but it feels different, because I get to see it through her eyes.

Chapter 15

Better Than Prom

~Claire~

Noah is filled with surprises for me tonight. I am ecstatic, yet so incredibly nervous, because I know the time has come. My legs are shaking and my grip on him is tight as we dance to our favorite songs, alone in a hotel room. As Katy once said to me: the suspense is the best part of the experience. But right now, the suspense has me nauseated.

When Noah showed up at my house in his tux, which I could not believe he wore, my dad took the appropriate pictures, and then we took off in my car with Noah driving. He drove us an hour away into the city, which was farther than I thought we would go since we would have to drive back to town to the only nice facility a prom could be held—the country club. But nope, that wasn't in his plans. Noah took us right to a hotel where we dined in its small restaurant—well, I pushed my food around—and then we went straight up to our room.

Our room … Wow. Noah must have been here earlier in the day because, when we walked in, his iPod dock was playing on repeat, and petals were strewn across the bed, floor, and even the Jacuzzi. It was a pretty room with the rose petals mixed with lilies and lavender.

With my head lying against Noah's chest, my eyes closed, I listen as Noah gently sings in my ear. We are gently rocking, me holding on tightly with my hands wrapped around his back as he rubs soothingly up and down my naked back.

"You know I adore you, right?" Noah asks me this all the time now, his way of saying he loves me.

I nod, my throat too tight with nervousness to speak.

I feel his body shudder with a chuckle against my cheek.

"Backing down now that the moment is here?"

I shake my head this time then finally gain the courage to loosen my grip on him, looking up, up, up into his face. "No." My voice cracks on the word, and Noah's eyes soften.

I might be nervous, but I am not backing down on this. I love Noah with every fiber of my being. I can't see my future without him in it. We click like I have never seen anyone do. We have this connection that feeds each other. We know what the other is thinking and feeling without words. We are two halves of the same whole.

Noah cradles my face, his lips lowering to mine, and I grasp his wrists as our lips connect in a sweet kiss. He pecks my lips once, twice, three times before I raise up on my tiptoes and throw my hands around his neck, crushing our lips together. My nervousness buries itself when I'm like this with Noah. I don't think about anything else; just feel when I am in his arms.

We kiss and kiss before Noah slowly picks me up, and I instinctively wrap my legs around him. His hands are under my dress, gripping, pressing me closer to him as he backs me into the wall, all while ravishing each other's mouths, our tongues mating like it's for the last time as the music fades into the background.

Then Noah lowers me to the ground where he proceeds to lower himself until he is on his knees in front of me. I try to catch my breath, bracing myself against the wall, my brain shut down to all thoughts, except "keep breathing," as he undoes the straps on my heels and takes them off one at a time. Then he circles each ankle with his hands and gradually slides them up my legs.

We watch each other, our desire reflected in each other's eyes. Noah's look intense, the black consuming his eyes, but there is consideration there, too. Well, there is until his devilish smirk comes out, and then his head disappears under my dress.

I gasp out in surprise as he kisses me *there*, something he has never done before. I can feel his fingers gripping my hips underneath my dress. My legs would have given out on me if he wasn't holding me up. This is already territory we have never gone before.

I hear him inhale, his nose pressed *right there*, and I feel a wave of embarrassment heating up my already heated cheeks, which swiftly disappears as he glides his hands back down my legs ... with my panties. My breathing picks up, and I brace myself against the wall as I step out of them, my legs shaking so badly.

Noah brings his hands back up to my hips and pins me there as I feel his tongue on me. The sensation makes me jump, thrusting myself against his mouth, something he must appreciate because he lets out a groan then starts swirling that tongue around. I can't even control my movements as I rock into it.

He moves one hand down to the back of my knee and lifts it up over his shoulder. Then, with that same hand, he presses a finger against my opening before I feel it slip inside.

His tongue presses harder on a bundle of nerves that causes me to gasp out and moan. I reach out for something to grip, but there is nothing, so I brace one hand against the dresser next to me and grab my own hair with my free hand.

Another finger slips inside of me, and my moans escalate. I'm moving against his tongue and fingers, the familiar tingles starting, an orgasm on the rise.

I distantly hear the song change, a faster paced one, and Noah's ministrations pick up pace. He presses his tongue harder against my clit, licking and sucking as he continues to stroke inside me.

My body is flushing. I feel the rise of heat start in my belly and work its way up to my face. Sweat beads my forehead as Noah replaces his tongue with his thumb, pressing, pressing, pressing.

His head comes out from underneath my dress. I feel him watching me as my eyes roll back and the moans continue to escape. Then I open my eyes and bite my bottom lip as I watch him lick his own, which are wet with my arousal. He looks so damn beautiful with his hair now tousled.

My legs start to quiver with the release that's right on the brink of exploding. I concentrate on Noah's fingers that are still caressing me inside and out. He starts talking, and my release finally hits me at his words.

"You look so beautiful. Seven months, Claire. Seven months of buildup. Seven months of dreaming of tasting you, wanting to lick inside you, savor your taste in my mouth. You don't know how close

I was to giving in so many times."

I grasp his hair as I come, sliding down the wall with his fingers still inside me. I bite my lip to muffle my cries before Noah is kissing me, my taste on his tongue.

He slips his fingers out of me, and then he's standing up, pulling me with him. I lean against the wall again as I watch him step out of his shoes and take off his socks. He already took off his jacket and tie when we entered the room. He starts unbuttoning his dress shirt, his eyes always on me. Then he's taking it off, and the belt goes next.

He steps toward me at the same time I step toward him. As soon as I am within his grasp, though, he turns me around and unclasps the one strip of fabric holding my dress up in the back. We both watch as the dress falls to the floor, which seems to signify that this is it, the next step, a warning that there is no turning back, not now that I am completely naked and Noah is the one who initiated it.

My back still to him, he removes the two pins holding my hair back from face then brushes all my hair to the side, completely baring my back. I feel him press against me, his naked flesh connecting with mine.

"So beautiful," he murmurs, caressing my back softly with the back of his fingers, eliciting goose bumps.

I turn around to face him, my eyes level with his lower chest. I look up at him as I reach for his pants, waiting for him to stop me like he has so many times before. He doesn't, not this time. This time, I'm able to unbutton his pants, pull the zipper down, and then I'm sliding his pants and boxers down his long legs. When I stand back up, we are both utterly naked.

Noah moves in and presses our bodies together, starting another dance as he wraps his arms around me, holding me so close. I can feel his erection pressed between us, against my waist. I've felt and seen it before, but not like this, fully exposed, feeling hot and heavy against me.

I don't know what to do next, so I let Noah lead. He slowly dances us in a circle before taking my hand and spinning me away from him. I laugh as I spin back toward him, and then he's dipping me with a kiss. I continue to giggle into his mouth, feeling his own smile growing against mine.

"I adore you."

"I adore you, too, Noah."

~Noah~

My heart swells as I hear those words coming from Claire. She might not realize it, but that's the first time she professed she loves me back. Usually, it's the "I know" response. However, whether she says it or not, I *do* know. Still, it's nice to hear.

I grin as I lift her up from the dip then raise her arms around my neck. We share another kiss, this one less playful as I back her up toward the bed, then press her down before climbing between her legs.

Kneeling, I kiss up her legs, then up her waist to her firm breasts. I lave one nipple at a time, sucking and nibbling them both to hard peaks as Claire arches her back, forcing each breast farther into my mouth. Then Claire grips my cock, and I almost come immediately.

I sit back and hold her hand still. "Claire, don't."

"You always say that."

I clench my teeth through my words. "I'm so close to coming now that, if you move that hand, I'm—"

She dares to squeeze, causing me to suck in a breath.

She moves up onto her own knees, hand still gripping my cock. "Let me ..." She blushes and lowers her head, not completing her sentence.

Intrigued to that telling blush, I ask, "Let you, what?"

"I want to please you like you did me." She won't meet me eyes as a deeper blush rushes to her face. Then she whispers, "Show me?" and finally looks me in the eye.

I'm torn. Claire is always so curious, and it's been fun to teach her, but what if I can't hold back? What if I traumatize her, and then no more head in my future? The minute she puts her lips around me, I will probably explode. I don't know what to do here. However, the time for holding back is gone. I told Claire no so many times before that I can't do it now.

I nod, and Claire's eyes widen in surprise before this look crosses her face that is unfamiliar—lust. Real lust. Then she drops her eyes from mine to stare at my cock. I see her appraising me, her eyes windows to every thought. She's eager to please, surprised by my girth, determined to do this right, yet scared she will fail.

She scoots closer to me, and I release my hand from hers. Then she leans over, her hair curtaining her face. I reach out and gather her hair into one fist so I can watch her as her little, pink tongue comes out and licks the bead of pre-come from the head.

I hiss from the contact, followed by an immediate groan when her lips close around me then slides down the length. At feeling that, I almost come.

Claire lifts her head back up and immediately slides back down, sucking, and I feel her swallow. It feels amazing. She then comes back up and releases me, gasping for breath before she takes me back into her mouth.

My grasp on her hair tightens as I try to hold back, gritting out instructions. Then I feel her exhale through her nose as she speeds up. I am so close to the edge. So damn close.

I pull her head back when I feel the buildup, my orgasm about to explode. "Claire, I'm coming."

She sucks hard, and I do mean hard, and then I'm coming, my cock jerking and pulsing in her hot mouth. Claire stills, her hand on my cock tightening, like it's grounding her, while I groan and collapse back on the bed, my head hanging off the end of it.

Unable to move just yet, I feel Claire crawl over me until she is at the precise alignment of our two bodies.

I open my eyes and lift my head to see her lying over me, her chin resting on her crossed arms over my chest, watching me.

"Did I do it right?" she asks point-blank.

I laugh, letting my head fall back. "Did I come?"

She pokes me in my side, and I jump. "I'll take that as a yes." She pokes me again, and then I'm rolling us over until I'm on top of her.

"Yes, angel. You were perfect."

Her smile hits me like a freight train, making me feel how I felt the first time I saw her. My breath halts, my heart stops, and then my heart is pounding to the point I can hear it in my head. Time stands still, and the world becomes centered around her. Just her. This is the moment in time, the last thing I want to see, to remember, when I leave this earth.

Then her smile turns coy and sensual with those eyes looking so heavy. I created a seductress.

This new her has time stopping once again. I love her so damn much.

I can't wait anymore. I'm still hard, already desperate for another release. I want her right now.

Claire seems to know what's on my mind, seeing the hunger in my eyes. God, she knows me so well.

She pulls my head down until our lips meet in a scorching kiss, opening her legs for me to settle between. Then I move my hand between her legs, slipping one then two fingers inside. She's so small, so tight; everything about her so petite. I don't want to hurt her. I think I would shed a tear myself if I did.

I slip a third finger inside slowly, feeling her walls relax and accept them. So warm and wet. So ready. I can't wait anymore.

Claire and I decided to forgo condoms, despite what happened to Troy and Chelsea. She's been on a contraceptive for years to relieve the pain of her periods, and we are both clean. Besides, I want nothing between us.

Pulling my fingers out, I then guide my cock to her opening, leaning on one elbow while I continue to kiss her. Her hands are in my hair, pulling at it when she feels me rub against her then slip the head into her opening.

I bring my arm back up to rest next to her head, pull away from kissing her, and simply look down at her, seeing flower petals throughout her hair: white lilies, purple lavender, and red roses.

When she meets my eyes, I ask her hoarsely, "Are you ready?"

She nods, looking tentative yet determined. So precious, and now I am about to take that precious innocence away from her.

Maintaining eye contact, I start pressing forward, sliding into her warmth. It's so tight. The journey feels like forever as I work my way in.

"This is going to hurt, angel. I'm going to stop as soon as I push through," I promise.

She nods again, looking at me with nothing but trust and adoration. "I'm ready."

She wraps her arms around my neck, and I thrust into her hard, sinking all the way in. She gasps and pulls my head down, burrowing her face into the crook of my neck. I feel her shivering, and it scares the crap out of me.

"Claire, are you okay?" I choke out, smoothing her hair back. I was so afraid of this.

Claire nods again, her answer muffled into my neck. "Give me a minute. It burns, but the pain was quick. It's fading. Just ... don't move yet."

"I'm not moving until you give me the word. We're going to take this slow, angel. I never want to cause you pain." I say the words, but my body wants to contradict them. She feels too damn good.

I kiss her face, making my way down until she lifts her head. Then I kiss and suck on her neck. She moans, and then grinds against me, making me return her moan.

Her walls are constricting around me, gripping and releasing, making my own cock throb in reply. Ignoring it, I continue to pepper her with kisses as she finally relaxes.

"Okay, I-I'm ready," she moans out when I suck on her earlobe.

I pull back. "I'll go slow."

She nods again as I pull slowly out of her, watching her face for any signs of pain. Not seeing any, I push forward and see her eyes roll as she moans.

"Don't stop," she whispers with a gasp.

Thank God, because I don't think I can hold back anymore. I want to live in her forever.

I continue at a slow pace, holding myself over her and watching her perfection as she meets my every thrust. The she moves her hands from my shoulders down to my ass, grasping it, egging me on faster, harder. Her nails dig in, but I couldn't care less. The pain feels so good.

Wanting to give it to her like she's asking, I drive into her. She gasps out my name, her breathing picking up, as I sink in even deeper than before, being cautious not to be too rough.

"Do you like that?"

"God, yes. Don't stop," she gasps out, her usually soft noises becoming louder.

Spurred on, I raise up, unable to look away from her face as I pick up the momentum. Sweaty, flushed, eyes glazed over, flawless. I wish I had words in this moment to give her, but I can't express enough how wonderful she feels under me. No woman has ever felt so good.

She wraps her legs around my waist as I watch her breasts bounce, hair spilling over them and off the end of the bed, her body glistening with sweat.

I lean back over her and suck a nipple into my mouth before making my way up her neck, and then devouring her mouth, swallowing all her gasps of pleasure.

Her little hips come up to meet me in sync as I rest on my elbows, moving my mouth to her ear. "I wish you could see yourself right now. You look gorgeous. I adore you, Claire."

"Noah ..."

I know what she wants. I can feel her tightening. Thank God, because I need a release.

I reach down to her clit, applying pressure as I circle my thumb around the nub. Almost immediately she lets go in a hoarse scream, her body convulsing as I fill her with my seed.

I collapse on top of her and wrap my arms around her back, pulling her to me as I shift us to our sides. Both of us are gasping for air, her hair a tangled mess all over us. I hold her close and tuck her head under my chin, pushing all that hair away from my face and hers.

I time my breaths with hers, waiting for them to calm before I ask, "How do you feel?"

She snuggles closer into me. "Amazing," she sighs out.

"Really?" I sound incredulous, because I am. I expected her to say sore. "You're not still hurt?"

"A little. But it's not that bad. Just achy right now."

I smile, unable to stop it, thinking about what's next. "I have a cure for that."

~Claire~

186

"Is this better than prom?" Noah asks as he caresses my waist. His light touches are already making me want more of what we had earlier.

Earlier … was euphoric, like a dream. I don't think it has hit me yet that I'm not a virgin anymore. Or maybe it's that I thought I should feel differently somehow, like it's a rite of passage that should have accompanied a whole ceremony, maybe a blessing to Artemis. Instead, I feel like I do every other day.

I turn my head to the side to look at him sitting behind me in the Jacuzzi. "This is so much better." I lean back and kiss his chin, which is starting to get bristly. I think it adds to his appeal. "Thank you."

Noah's gaze is intense when he says, "You never have to thank me for making you happy. It's my job."

I laugh. "It's a waiter's job to serve food, but we still thank them."

"Touché."

I sink down farther into the water and against Noah's chest, causing his hand to shift from my waist to my breasts. The warm water is very soothing to my soreness, which isn't really that bad. In any case, not as bad as I imagined it would be. I'm glad, too, because I want to have sex again. It's only been once, and I'm already addicted.

Noah massages one breast, his other arm wrapped around my hips to keep me against him. I feel his lips softly tickle my ear and sigh at the sensations. Then I drop my head back against his shoulder when he pinches my nipple, moaning at the sensation. Like my moan was an invitation, Noah cups between my legs where I am already aroused and sensitive. I gasp when he slides a finger between my folds, caressing. I can't help myself from undulating against his hand.

"Again already, Claire?" His voice is husky at my ear, his lips caressing as he speaks, causing delicious shivers to run down my back.

I arch into his hand. "Yes."

I grab Noah's knees as a finger slips inside. There is a mild burn at the intrusion, but it's not enough to make me want to stop.

"You okay?"

I gasp, "Yes," as he slips his finger in deeper, while his thumb works miracles. It feels so good.

Another finger is added, and I gasp out, biting my lip to keep from moaning as I press myself closer to Noah, gripping his legs even tighter. His hand at my breasts is still teasing and massaging, moving from one to the other. His mouth remains at my ear, his breathing escalating in tandem with my own. He sounds so sexy. Just him breathing like that is a turn on.

"I could do this all day. I love touching you, hearing you lose control, watching you come."

I would let him.

I'm about to come now, the heat rising to my face, my lower body coiling tight, when Noah pulls his hand away. *No!*

"Turn around, angel."

I turn, kneeling in front of him, the water sloshing around at my movement. His eyes hold mine for a moment before dropping to my breasts. He grabs my waist and pulls me to him, his mouth latching on to one, sucking eagerly. I gasp his name, feeling him part my legs and lift them over his until I am straddling him. I take that as an opportunity to rub myself against him, rising and falling against his length.

Noah moans against my chest, stopping all attention to my breasts. "More," is all he gets out before lifting me up until I am poised over his manhood.

For once, he is looking up at me. It makes me feel empowered. Instinctually, I know what to do. I brace my hands on Noah's shoulders, lowering myself on his length as he continues to grasp my waist.

As we feel him enter, both of us tighten our grasps as I sink farther down until I can go no further. We are both unmoving, gasping for air now, holding steady, eyes connected in passion, eyelids lowered in arousal.

Noah is the first to move, moving his mouth to mine as he gasps out, "You're so beautiful."

The passion escalates as our lips connect hungrily. Then I start to move, feeling him full inside of me as we continue to kiss and grope and pull and squeeze. We can't get close enough.

Then Noah breaks the kiss, wrapping his arms around my lower back and holding me close to him as his mouth returns to my breasts. His hold on me has him hitting a spot inside that feels so pleasantly delicious. I want to move faster, have him go deeper, my desire increasing.

I arch my back, thrusting my breasts out, making the sensation he's causing by hitting that spot grow. Gasping for breath, moaning and calling out his name, he responds by squeezing me tighter.

I close my eyes and tilt my head back, my hair floating across the water. Noah's voice reaches me as he tells me how much he adores me, how good I feel, how he can't get enough. Dirty talk is thrown in there about what I feel like to him, that he can feel me tightening around him, squeezing him. His words build the arising climax until it happens.

Spots burst forth behind my eyelids. My body quakes with the release, and I can't control my movements anymore. I grow tight then limp in his hold as the pulsing contractions take over.

I'm barely cognizant when I feel Noah sit up and lift me, still connected. He places me on the edge of the tub then starts driving into me as he kisses me all over my face before he rests his forehead on my collarbone. I hear the water sloshing all around the tub with his movements and the slap of our bodies with every thrust.

I wrap my legs around his waist, crossing them at the ankle, then set my elbows on his shoulder and cradle his head with both arms. Both of us remain in this position, gasping, moaning, groaning, and him grunting until he slams into me once more and stills only moments later.

He slowly slips out of me, then lifts his head and stares at me with this indescribable look in his eyes. Then he rests his forehead against mine and closes his eyes.

I continue to keep my arms around his head, playing with his wet hair.

"I don't ever want to lose you," Noah says before giving me a closed mouth kiss then returning his forehead to mine. "Can you promise me I won't?"

His words frighten me, because he says them with so much passion. He sounds so scared, so worried. I don't like it. I don't like him feeling this way. I don't want to lose him, either.

"I'm not going anywhere," I promise him.

"I love and adore you so much, angel, so fucking much. You're my ... gravity, keeping my universe from falling apart and spiraling out of control. If I lost you, I would have nothing—"

"Don't talk like that." This is not something I'm used to hearing from Noah. Never Noah. Noah is always so in control and self-assured. To know he thinks I could tear his world apart like that frightens me. "Nothing is going to happen, and you won't ever lose me. But what if I lost you?"

Noah looks at me then, his eyes declaring that that would never happen, but I continue.

"What if you left me? Do you know that scares *me*? That you might get bored of me and go back to your old ways. Leave me ..." I can't even get the words out.

Noah shakes his head as I keep talking.

"I would still live, but I wouldn't be happy. I don't think I could ever be happy again if I lost you. You came into my life so unexpectedly, and I was drawn to you from the first second I saw you. I tried to fight the attraction. I was determined to stick to my plan: finish school, tutor for ungodly hours, and leave this town behind me. But you captured me and haven't let me go ... yet. So, I ask myself all the time: When is Noah going to let go?"

"Never," Noah growls.

I look at him sadly. "I wish I could believe that, but I still have my doubts. I always will, until it happens, or ..." I shrug and look away, not knowing how I am supposed to end that sentence. Not knowing what that "or" could be.

"I have the same fears, angel." Noah brushes away hair that is stuck to my face. Then he lifts the guitar pick pendant and kisses it. "We'll have to prove to each other that we won't." He smiles, and I return it, understanding his promise.

"I promise," I repeat back to him.

Chapter 16

Graduation

~Noah~

Nineteen years old. Done with high school. Have no interest in college. Have a beautiful girl I would do anything for, who I can't live without, who I will be spending the entire summer with before moving back to the city together. Now I just have to get through this weekend with my parents, who surprised me by showing up last night, and things will be perfect.

My parents are sitting next to Katy, Mark, Signora Gelardi, and Jonathan, who they seem to really like. Claire, well, my mom isn't too keen on my girlfriend going to Music Conservatory. That's not a "real" college to her. And singing isn't a "real" occupation. Wait until she hears where I am not going to college. That will make Claire look like the angel she is in my mom's book.

Kyle is standing in front of me, a big smile on his face as he bounces on his feet, waiting for his name to be called so he can walk up and get his diploma. Claire is all the way near the back of the line, looking uncomfortable. I watch and wait until she looks up, then give her a reassuring smile. She grimaces back at me.

Poor angel. She's so nervous about our families having lunch together—an invitation from my mother. I should have gotten Claire off before we left. That would have calmed her down. And it would have been so simple to push her dress up, spread her legs, move I should have gotten Claire off her panties to the side, and all while she sat at her vanity, putting on her makeup. I imagined. I even offered. But she protested that someone could walk in at any time. No one did. It was a waste of an opportunity, something we didn't seem to have enough time for.

Between finals, the band, and Claire's tutoring with Gelardi, who only just tolerates me now, which basically means she acts like I'm not there instead of demeaning me, we haven't had much time for getting personal. That doesn't mean Claire doesn't jump me, and vice versa, during those few precious moments we do have together.

Shit, I have chub now thinking about it.

Of course that's when names start to be called.

As I watch some of these people saunter up to get their diplomas, I can't help hoping this is the last time I have to see them. Then Troy goes up, and I have to say I'm happy he will be gone next week, though he did seem to turn around in the end. However, I don't think this will be the last time I see his face. I have a feeling he will always weasel his way into Claire's life, and thus, mine.

When Kyle's name is called, the dumbass practically runs to get his diploma, hugging everyone enthusiastically and making himself look like a jackass. He's going to the state school only a couple towns over, living the dorm life. We grew close this year, something I admit I'm grateful for. Even though he drives me insane and always says the wrong things, when I look back on this year, I can now laugh at his antics. I'm really going to miss him.

I give Claire a wink when my name is called, and then go through the process of shaking hands and taking my diploma, before proceeding off the stage and to my designated seat, where I focus on Claire as she slowly makes her way to the head of the line.

Some of the people surrounding her are talking to her, a rare occurrence. Hopefully, they are only sharing congratulations because of graduation and the fact that she was nominated to sing "Star Spangled Banner" at the graduation commencement. However, she looks extremely awkward as the kids look my way before saying something else to her, which she responds to.

I want to run up there and punch them all in the face for making her feel uncomfortable. I want to jump on that stage, take the microphone, and scream at the entire school for being such asses to the sweetest girl in existence. I want to call out all the catty girls and perverted guys, and let them all know what pieces of shit they all are.

Instead, I sit there, watching, waiting as their group moves up in line, assessing Claire's comfort level. Watching as, when they finally get closer, they all stop talking, and I see Claire take a deep breath and close her eyes. Then she is walking across the stage, beaming a smile at the superintendent, principal, vice principal, the counselor, and lastly, Mayor Couer, the guest of honor and Troy's dad.

He holds her hand longer than the others, saying something to her. But it can't be bad, because she's still smiling and even gives him a little hug before she walks off the stage, waving at our families before she grins and winks at me, the relief on her face so obvious.

I want to get up and go to her. I want to share in the joy she is exuding, feel her excitement.

Soon. Soon this will be over, and then I can join her.

And then I do.

Graduates are crowding all around, people who never spoke to each other during school now congratulate each other while trying to locate their thrown graduation caps, as I head in Claire's direction, looking for her short frame in the sea of white and black robes. It's not easy since everyone is running around frantically and families have started to converge. But then I see her, still sitting calmly in her seat, smiling up at me.

"Took you long enough," she teases.

I pointedly look around at the crowd, then arch a brow at her.

Her smile widens. "Point taken."

She holds her hand out, and I take it, helping her out of her seat. Then I wrap her in my arms, which effectively knocks the cap off her head, and kiss her. "Congratulations, angel."

"You, too, Noah." She smiles up at me.

Then our families find us, congratulating us and Kyle, passing hugs and back slaps around, talking about "that next step" in our lives.

~

"Which schools did you hear back from?" my mother inquires of me when the food is set down before us.

Claire, who was saying something to her father, stops mid-sentence, interest blooming on her face. We never talked about where I would be, or not be, going to college. The subject never came up. All we have talked about is what we will do in the city; how busy we will be. So, I'm about to get attacked from all sides.

I meet my mother's eyes. "None. I didn't apply." No point sugarcoating it.

I watch as my mother's face turns red. Yep, she's fuming.

"Why not? I packed the applications when we left. You had plenty of time to fill them out and mail them off. I mean, my God, Noah, I had already completed half the paperwork for you. How can you be so irresponsible? We raised—"

"Sarah," my dad's soothing voice, along with his pointed look, checks my mother. They start their heated whispers, belittling me the entire time.

I feel a hand on my thigh and look over at Claire.

"How have we never talked about this? You're not going to college?"

"It's not really my thing. Maybe someday," I give her, just to get the disappointed look off her face, but then I feel really self-conscious about my choice. Disappointing Claire is so much harder than disappointing my parents. "Right now, I want a break from school."

"But …" She hesitates, at a loss of what to say. I see a million thoughts going through her head all at once. She starts nervously playing with the bracelet she gave me. "What's your plan? I assumed we would both be in college, you going to your mom's school or another university."

I give her hand a squeeze. "I want a break, maybe focus on music for a while, before—"

"Great. That's just great, Noah," my mother fumes before I can say anything else, throwing her napkin on the table and abruptly standing up. "Music? Dear God." She glances at Claire before looking at my father. "Can you believe this?" Her eyes implore him to say something.

"Sit down, Sarah. You're causing a scene."

My mother dutifully listens to my father, subtly glancing around at the other patrons, who didn't seem to notice her outburst.

"I don't want to jump into a family argument," Jonathan chimes in, "but taking a year off before college isn't always a bad thing. I, myself, took a year off before finishing law school. It made focusing a lot easier after feeling burned out."

"Yes, but you were what, twenty-two, twenty-three? Noah is still a kid. He's not mature enough to make that kind of a decision yet. He needs college to learn balance. If he doesn't start now, he'll never …"

I let their voices fade out as I play with the condensation on my water glass, still holding Claire's hand with my other one as she strokes her thumb across the back. I'm used to blocking out my parents after years of listening to their conversations like I wasn't there. Funny that, for once, the talk is about me.

My mom might have a point with not being mature enough to make that decision. The whole reason I am so against school is because I don't want to be like them. I want the freedom to live my life, with stupid mistakes. I want to start at the bottom and work my way up. Do I want to play music for the rest of my life? Yes, I do. But I don't expect to make a career out of it. I just want to play at night while making an honest living during the day.

I already have a job set up back in the city, working with my bandmate Chris at his family's auto body shop, and that's all I want right now. Something easy, simple. Not back to studying all the time, dealing with all the lectures. I just got done with school; why the hell would I want to jump into more? Maybe in a few years I will change my mind. Today, nope.

"I don't think this the appropriate time to be discussing this," Jonathan cuts through my thoughts. He skims a sympathetic glance my way before smiling at Abby, who looks up from her coloring book.

"Yes, dear, I agree with Jonathan. This is a family matter." My dad takes my mom's hand to lessen the blow.

"Fine." She levels me with her professor, no-nonsense glare. "But we will continue this discussion when we're back in the city."

"I'm not going with you." I drop the second bomb.

My mom stares at me with her eyebrows furrowed. Then she looks around the table at Katy, Mark, settling on my dad for a moment, before looking back at me. "Why not?" She points at Claire. "*She's* going to the city. Where are you going?"

I sit back and have a stare down with my mom, daring her to retort before I even start. "Claire isn't leaving for a couple of months. I'm staying here until she leaves."

"Are you being presumptuous that Mark and Katy will allow you to stay, or do you plan on living elsewhere? Because, I'm telling you right now, you're nineteen, you graduated, you have no plans to go to college, so I have no plans on supporting you further."

"Noah has already asked us to extend his stay," Aunt Katy speaks up. "And we're fine with that."

Mom cuts her eyes to her like she wishes lasers would burst from them and burn Katy. "And you decided this without consulting me first? He's my son!"

"And, like you pointed out, he's an adult. We felt he could make that decision without your approval, as he did graduate today." Katy has more grace than my mother. She does not once raise her voice or speak in the scalding manner my mother uses.

"Fine. I give up. It's not like he's ever home when he is there, carousing around with all those Jezebels." Only my mom would use a savory term for whore.

Meanwhile, I cringe, and Claire locks up next to me, her hand growing cold in mine. Jonathan's mask breaks, and he looks extremely uncomfortable. Katy's face turns red in anger as she glances quickly at Claire before grabbing her glass and finishing off her drink. Mark narrows his eyes. Kyle covers his mouth with his hand, looking more shocked than amused. And Abby whisper-shouts, "What's a jazzabell, Mama? Is that a fairy like Tinkerbell?"

"Sarah," Dad scolds, looking embarrassed for me or for my mom, I don't know. "I think it's time to go."

Happy graduation to us.

~Claire~

This day went from a day of celebration to a nightmare.

During the diploma line up, some of the kids from my class cornered me, all interested to learn what was going to happen to my and Noah's relationship. When I told them we were going to the city together … Oh, man, I wish I had a camera to capture their expressions. They swiveled their heads between me and Noah, expressions in varying forms of shock, before asking more questions. Where are we going to school? Are we moving in together? Am I pregnant? That last one was hurtful, though considering that happened to Chelsea, I couldn't really blame them for asking.

Then it was time to get my diploma. I couldn't help my smile as I walked across that stage, accepting the congratulations and best wishes of the school staff. Then there was Mayor Couer, who expressed his happiness for me, gushing about how he couldn't be prouder if I was his own daughter, no mention of his son who was heading off to Marine boot camp next week.

I was on cloud nine, and then I wasn't.

Finding out Noah isn't going to college was a shock to say the least—still is. I can't get over how we never talked about it. I feel like a bad, selfish girlfriend for not knowing. In my defense, I honestly thought he was all set, knowing how his parents are. I thought Noah was a shoe-in, no questions asked, no acceptance needed; you want to go to college, then go. I thought it was that easy for him. Then, to hear that his mom had packed applications for him ... I never saw one, which tells me that he probably burned them as soon as he got here.

After the disaster that was the graduation luncheon, Dad, Noah, and I went back to our place while everyone else went back to Mark and Katy's. Noah needs a break from his parents, and they just got here yesterday. Doubt they will stay past today now.

"Your parents will get over it eventually," Dad tells Noah as we all head up to the house.

"It doesn't matter." Noah shakes off the incident like he's used to it, which makes me sad.

"*We do not remember days, we remember moments.* And Noah, back there was a moment you won't forget. It will fester inside until you confront your parents. You may not see it, but they do care about you. They don't take the right approach." Dad grumbles, "Obviously," which makes me grin as I unlock the front door. "But that's on them, not you. Think about talking to them. Get it all out, because chances diminish with age."

We are now in the foyer. Noah is nodding his head at what Dad is saying, looking down like he is in deep thought. I lay my purse down on the entry table and kick my heels off, waiting to hear what is going to be said next.

Noah is silent for no more than ten seconds before he straightens up and looks at my dad, no expression on his face to tell me what he could possibly be thinking. "Thank you, Jonathan. I'll, uh, try to do that. Try being the applicable word. Frankly, I don't think it will amount to much, but at least I can say I tried." He shrugs then, like that's that.

After hanging out with my dad for a little while, we head upstairs to my room. I want to have some privacy when I talk to him about this college thing.

I don't even know how I feel about, if I should feel anything. This is Noah's choice, his life. If he doesn't want to go to college, or if he wants to take a break, that is his decision. Still, I can't help wondering why.

"You want to talk about it, don't you?" Noah gets right down to it, no holding back. He is a give-it-to-you straight person and demands the same from others.

I shrug as I throw my shoes into my closet. My closet is a mess, unlike the rest of my room. I have all the standard furniture, in white since this is the same furniture I have had since I was four years old, plus an antique vanity that is about as messy as my closet. The floors are hardwood with a rug that spans most of my room in blues and creams.

"I'm surprised more than anything … for not knowing," I answer him. "And mad at myself that we have been together practically this entire year, talked about everything from the stars to the taste of dirt"—true story—"yet we never talked about where you are or aren't going to school." I walk up to him and wrap my arms around his waist. "I feel bad, is all. I'm sorry."

Noah wraps his arms around me, caressing both hands up and down my back. "Nothing to apologize for. I think … maybe I was afraid to bring it up; that I would disappoint you."

"You can't disappoint me." I look up at his face, arms still wrapped around him. "Definitely not about your decision not to go to college. My only question is: why? You're so smart, and you have a photographic memory, so it's not like you have to try as hard. I don't understand why you wouldn't."

Noah removes his arms from around me and takes my hand, walking us over to the bed where we lie down, facing each other, heads propped up by our hands, all the while telling me, "It's because of who my parents are that I don't want to go to college. Well, partly. And I want something simple, easy right now. I don't want pressure for a while, you know. I want to be able to work an honest job, play music, and be with you when you need me."

I mumble, "I always need you," as he continues like he didn't hear me.

"I don't know what I want to study *if* I ever do go to school. What if I pick something, go to school for it for what, two, four, six years, and then I get to the job and discover I hate it? That's years of working for something that doesn't work for me. I'm not ready to make a decision or mistake like that.

"And who knows, maybe I will like working as a mechanic with Chris and decide that's what makes me happy. On the job experience like that is better than what I would learn from a textbook. How would you feel if I chose that route?"

I shrug one shoulder, my answer immediate. "If you're happy, that's all that matters to me."

"Really, though? Will you really be happy with a mechanic boyfriend when you are this famous diva, travelling the world and singing to the rich and famous?"

I roll my eyes. "Like that will ever happen, but yes." I place my hand over his heart. "As long as you are still you, I don't care what job, career, college—whatever your plans are, I want to share it with you. And as for college, I just wanted to know, to finally have this talk with you. I don't care, Noah, I really don't." I smile reassuringly, hoping he sees that I mean it.

He rests his head on his bicep and gives me a small smile in return. "I adore you."

I lean over and give him a little kiss. "Ditto. I'll always be on your side, Noah."

Chapter 17

Blindfolds and Airplanes

~Noah~

Claire and I are leaving in the morning to check out her school for a few days. The plan is to come back, pack up all our stuff, and then drive back to the city in a few weeks, giving Claire a week before school starts up.

I took Jonathan's advice the same night he gave it and had a sit down with my parents. I told them everything on my mind, cutting them off and telling them I would walk away and not finish the discussion if they didn't let me say my piece for once. They listened. For the first time in my life, they listened.

I told them what I wanted in the immediate future, letting them know college wasn't completely off the table; it just was *for now*. When I knew with absolute certainty what I wanted, then we could discuss it again, even if what I wanted didn't include college. Of course there was the whole "you can decide that while you go to school" speech. Again, I cut them off. This was my decision.

Then I brought up Claire and how my mother treated her. I confronted her. I confided to her. I told her everything I have seen and know about Claire. I shared our relationship with her and my feelings.

I talked to both my parents about what the last year has meant to me. We talked about how they always talk like I'm not there. We talked about things in the past that should be long forgotten. We talked.

And in the end, I had this weight lifted off my chest I never realized was there. I'm not going to say we were all smiles, happiness, and love. That's not us. What I can say is that there is this … lightness when we communicate now, like before there was this heavy cloud surrounding us, and we were all bearing it, holding the rain at bay.

The rest of the weekend was a lot calmer after that. I think everyone could tell the difference. We ended up having an okay time, hanging out, having dinners together. And Mom was more friendly with Claire, telling her about some of the operas her and my dad had gone to in the city. She even went shopping with Katy, Claire, and Abby. And when they came back, Claire had this shell-shocked look on her face. I asked her what happened, and she said, "Your mom hugged me." I almost laughed at that, but I was too shocked myself.

Claire's a nervous ball of energy right now, squirming in the seat next to me as we take my aunt's truck to a surprise location. There is something I have always wanted to do, and this may be my last chance to do it, and I want to share it with Claire.

She is blindfolded once again, something she has become accustomed to, especially between the sheets. She loves playing games like that, a detail I learned through the course of the summer while absorbing every intimate thing about her: her likes and don't likes, the way she reacts to every touch, her endurance, lack of patience. The woman wants to try everything; insatiable. Just thinking about it makes my dick throb.

I grin, holding back a chuckle, as Claire tilts her head back, trying to see from beneath the blindfold.

"No cheating."

Her broad smile drops to a fake pout as she crosses her arms in mock indignation. "I'm not." She sticks her tongue out in my general direction.

"Yeah, okay."

I glance at her every few moments as I drive, watching as she continues to peek, unable to stop myself from chuckling after a while because she is being so damn obvious.

Finally, she sighs. "Are we there yet?"

I bite my bottom lip to keep silent, not wanting to laugh outright at the childish way she questioned that. "Soon."

A few more minutes go by, then, "Are we close now?"

"Sure," I give her. She didn't ask *how* soon. Is twenty minutes soon?

I start singing low to the song on the radio when, "How 'bout now?"

"Yep."

Claire softly counts to three hundred as she taps out a beat on the door. "Now?"

I glance at the clock. "Count to one thousand."

"Noah! That's not soon." She gives out a huff and crosses her arms once again.

I ignore her outburst, knowing she's being playful. She's too excited about what new surprise I have in store for her. Instead, I think back to this past summer.

It went by quickly, filled with days of doing whatever the hell we wanted. We spent time with my family; took Abby out to the park and movies, and taught her how to roller skate at the rink in town. We hung out with Max and Cyn, and I got a new tattoo on the inside of my wrist where the bracelet Claire gave me covers it. It's an outline of a guitar pick with Claire's birthdate. Cheesy, I know. And permanent. Again, yes, I know. However, so are we. And if there is the off chance that we aren't—not jinxing here—then at least I will always have the memory of the first girl I ever loved. That somehow, no matter what, I will always love.

Claire wasn't with me when I got the tattoo. She was off with Cyn getting her hair cut. She didn't do anything too drastic. However, it's a lot shorter than it was. Where before her hair was touching her ass when she tilted her head back, now it's barely covering her breasts in the front. It makes her look taller, more mature, and she seems to be happy with it. I'm just a tad bit nervous about the change, like it signifies something major. Other than that, I think she's still as beautiful as ever.

The band continues to play every Friday night, sometimes Saturdays, and sometimes during the week when they need someone to fill in. The crowd is always packed. The other bands have been working out well for Jeremy. And with my departure coming up, Cyn has already set herself up with another band. I encouraged Kyle to start a new band when he gets settled in college. He's so talented that he shouldn't stop playing.

Most of all, this summer has only been about me and Claire, hanging out at her house, walking in the woods that I love so much, planning surprise trips like this one, making love under the trees, in her bed, in the storage room at Jeremy's where we had our first conversation … just about everywhere.

A noteworthy event was Troy's departure. Though he came into my life in a big, threatening matter, he faded to the background quickly, and now he is gone. Of course, he couldn't leave without seeing Claire, trying once again to mend their relationship. He also apologized to Jonathan; in which, Jonathan forgave him. Not my finest moment, with my teeth grinding, my hands balled into fists. I'm all for forgiveness, but there are some sins that can never be forgotten.

"Three thousand," Claire sings.

It's twilight now, the sun already setting. The sky is orange on the horizon, a midnight blue above us, with stars starting to speckle the darkening sky. This is one thing I'm going to miss back in the city. In the city, you forget there are infinite stars above you. You forget there are sunsets and sunrises. Out here, you appreciate the beauty of the little things you never even knew to appreciate.

I turn into the place of our destination, then back up to the fence line and put the truck in park before turning toward Claire. "No peeking. No getting out of the cab. No questions. Got it?" I tap gently on her nose, emphasizing each instruction.

"Got it." She bounces in her seat, a huge grin showcasing her baby-sized, white teeth.

I watch her as I back out of the cab and shut the door, seeing her still bouncing in her seat, facing forward now, with her hands clenched together in her lap. I move to the back of the truck and hop on, arranging the blankets and pillows I packed back there. I even packed a cooler, filled with finger foods and drinks.

With everything set up, I make my way to Claire's side of the truck, open the door, and help her out.

"All right, we are going to spend the night hanging out in the back of the truck. I know it sounds lame, but I promise this will be epic."

Just then, I hear the sound of engines moving closer.

"Shit!" I practically rip the blindfold off Claire's face and hurry her to the inside of the truck's bed. "Lie down. Quick." I push her onto her back and lie down next to her.

She lifts her head and stares straight ahead at the runway in front of us, her eyes going wide. The noise of the engines makes it too loud to hear anything else at this point, but I read her mouth as she says, "Oh, shit."

I laugh my ass off, never expecting it when Claire swears.

The plane flies above us, the wind from its speed blowing her hair around her face. She laughs freely, the sound lost to the wind and roar. I grasp her hand as the plane flies over the airfield, landing with a squeal of tires burning rubber.

With the plane now a quarter mile away, I tell her, "I saw this in a movie once. I think it lived up to its supposed coolness."

"Oh, yeah, which movie?" she asks, turning toward me.

I try to hide a smile, wanting to keep a straight face for what's about to come out of my mouth.

"*Wayne's World*," I deadpan.

She burst into laughter, and when her laughter subsides into giggles, she says, "Oh, my God, that was definitely cool."

"Yeah. But my timing wasn't."

"No, it really was. It was perfect. The adrenaline of getting up here, hearing the jet and not knowing what was happening … It was *perfect* timing."

I bring our clasped hands up to my lips and kiss the back of hers. "I guess it was."

We stay silent for a while, looking up as the stars start to pop out one by one.

After a while, with no more sounds of approaching jets, I point out, "I guess that really was good timing. This airport gets no action."

Claire laughs and rolls over onto me. "We can give it some action."

"Mmm … I like the way you think, angel."

~Claire~

I feel like I have grown so much over the summer. Or, well, since becoming intimate with Noah. It's like this huge veil was lifted from me. Surprise! And someone else was hidden behind it for years. I don't feel awkward anymore, which is weird, because I never thought I felt that way before. However, there was an awkward girl under that veil. Also one who was constantly anxious, timid, humorless, overly sensitive, and not really alive.

Now, I feel alive. I feel fun and flirty and like I have nothing to be ashamed of when I'm with Noah. I'm more open to other people, like Cyn, who has become a wild friend I love to pieces. Max has also been someone I can depend on, always ready with amazing advice. Then there is Kyle, who shares laughs with me, mostly at Noah's or my own expense; but I learned that's how he is, always so ready to joke and be playful. Katy has also become a good friend/adopted mother. All these people have opened their arms to me, and it's all because of Noah.

I can't wait to leave with him, but it's bittersweet because of all the people we will leave behind, all our family and new friends. Of course they will still be a part of our lives. In fact, Cyn and Max can't wait for us to settle down in the city so they can visit. And we will be back when there are breaks from school.

My dad shocked me by giving me a list of apartments to look over for my graduation present. I couldn't believe it. It never even crossed my mind that I would live anywhere but at student housing. And my dad found a roommate program through the school.

We interviewed my new roommate earlier this summer, Dare Medina. She is from Spain but grew up in the States. She is a cellist, full of high energy and is very entertaining. Our chat sessions over the summer had us both in a fit of laughter.

Troy did leave for boot camp the week after school let out, and not a day later. He had all year to warm up to the idea, and by the way he was fidgeting when it was time to get on the bus, yeah, he was excited. I was there. I had to be. Troy had hurt me, scared me, and ruined our friendship, but he had once been such a big part of my life. The least I could do was send him off.

We talked while we waited for his bus. He told me about Chelsea, who is due any day now; how he felt the baby kick, how they decided on a name, and how they went shopping for the baby together and bought everything she needed and more. And now he is gone.

Noah and I make love in the back of the truck, disregarding the jets flying over us. We are probably giving them quite a show. It's a wonder security hasn't shown up and kicked us out yet.

I love the way we feel together. The way sex feels new and different every time. The way we can be serious one minute, completely in the moment, and then laughing at each other the next. The way we both take care of the other, giving each other what the other needs. There are no insecurities, both of us baring body and soul together tenderly, hard—whatever the need is.

Noah is always full of surprises. It's like he goes off this handbook on what to do. He took me to a pond in the middle of the woods, where we went skinny dipping. We played paintball once, and Noah kicked everyone's butt, having played before. He taught me how to drive his motorcycle, which scared me half to death. It took a week to learn and a lot of crying from me and patience from him. I was so afraid to hurt his bike, but he didn't seem bothered by it. I think he was wearing his poker face because I *know* how much his bike means to him. It's a testament to his love that he even let me ride it solo. Nevertheless, I will never willingly drive one again. Never.

"What are you thinking about?" I ask Noah as he stares up at the stars while crickets and cicadas chirp and sing around us. We have been lying here silently for a while now. He is dressed back in his shorts, and I am wearing my tank top and panties, lying on my stomach, caressing the lines of the tattoo he got on his wrist.

I still can't believe he would do something so permanent as to put my birthdate on his wrist, an almost replica of my pendant. It could be worse, though. It could have been my name or initials.

"I saw this show once—I don't remember what it was about—but it had this shot of the earth from the moon … I was thinking how insignificant we really are, that we aren't even a dot on the planet like the stars are a dot in the sky."

Noah has always been a deep thinker. Some of the things we have talked about are subjects I would have never thought on my own, like this one. It's no wonder he would put Socrates on his side: *The unexamined life is not worth living.* Is he thinking about that now? Examining his life up to this moment?

I stop playing with his wrist and resituate myself so I can focus on him. "That's a bit macabre," I tell him, tracing my fingers over the freckles that have sprouted back across his nose with the warm weather.

Noah shrugs one shoulder, his arms folded behind his head. "You asked." He glances at me then looks back up. "It has me thinking how some people would do anything to stand out amongst billions. Yet, in the grand scheme of the entire universe, it means nothing."

He grows quiet after that, and I think about what he says. He is right. With how vast the universe is, how little our time on earth is in the limitlessness of time, what is the point? But then I think that there must be a point. There is a point to everything, isn't there? I would like to think so.

Those people who did stand out stood out for a reason. They effected change—physical, mental, spiritual. They left an impression on the world, changed dynamics, motivated people. We had our villains, too. But by fighting against them, we brought people together.

Instead of voicing all these thoughts, I flip over to my back and look up at the stars with him. I don't care to stand out. I would hate it if Noah did, that selfish side of me thinks. The only thing I care about right now is that I am happy. Noah is happy. My dad, my friends, I want them to be happy. I may not be a dot on the planet, but I am living, alive, and I want what all people want in the end: contentment, love, comfort.

"You mean something to me," I finally voice.

Noah takes my hand, lacing our fingers together, before bringing them up and brushing his lips across my fingers. "You mean something to me, too."

Part Two

"Confession is not betrayal.
What you say or do doesn't matter; only feelings matter.
If they could make me stop loving you, that would be the real
betrayal."
~ George Orwell, *1984*

New York City. It used to be a place I loved and missed with an ache
in my gut. It was home. The place where I grew up, where I had fun,
where I had my friends, where life was as good as I knew it to be.
Then I returned. And once I was there, it didn't feel right anymore.
Nothing was right anymore. Nothing was the same. I hated it. I hated
everything. I didn't want to be in that place anymore. So, I left.
~ Noah Gish

Chapter 18

New York City

~Claire~

I love, love, absolutely love the city! It's everything I expected it to be. There is so much to see, so many things to try, so many places on my list I want to visit. I can imagine me and Noah doing one thing a day and still not managing to scratch half the list.

Saying good-bye to everyone back home was hard. Dad seemed okay with letting go. He didn't choke up when we left, but he did give me a longer than usual hug, kissed my head, and told me he was just a phone call away. I was grateful he made it seem so simple, like I was going on a weekend trip.

Our trip to New York became an adventure, a two-day journey turning into five because Noah insisted on the scenic route and stopping at every landmark we came across. We saw waterfalls and two-hundred-year-old bridges. We learned how marbles were made, and visited a ghost town. We went swimming in natural pools and ate at famous diners. It was an experience I will always remember, and obviously one Noah planned. I love his surprises.

When we got to the city, we went straight to Noah's parents' house and crashed. The next day, I wanted to sightsee right away, but Noah, being more practical, reminded me that we had a whole car to unload. Therefore, we did that, and then I picked out bedroom furniture, waiting for Dare before picking out furniture for the rest of the place since it is technically half hers.

Noah picked out my bed, and then he wouldn't help with the decision process at all, saying it was *my* place. That caused an argument, where I told him it was as much his, and he told me it's not, practically breaking my heart when he told me he planned on staying with his parents until he started working. In his eyes, he thinks he is doing me a favor, giving me freedom to explore myself. However, his argument makes me feel restricted. I don't have the courage to explore if he isn't with me.

Nevertheless, we have been here for a week now, and Noah hasn't left me once. My bedroom is mostly set up. Well, not really. I have been too distracted by the life outside my windows, dragging Noah to museums, going to the beach for the first time, or standing across the street of my new school and staring at it in awe.

I tried to get him to take me to the Central Park Zoo, but that was a resounding no. More like a "motherfucking hell no" with three exclamation points. Even after I assured him the animals were all caged, he would not budge. Laughing, I swore to him that, one day, I will get him to the zoo. His retort was to swear that, if I did, it would mean his death because, he swears the day he steps foot in a zoo is the day an animal will break loose and maul him to death. Poor Noah.

Instead of the zoo, Noah took me to meet his band. They are a crazy bunch who shared too much of Noah's past that I would rather not hear. Chris, the drummer, seems the most down-to-earth and smarter than the other two guys. He got the other guys to shut up about their reminiscences and directed the talk to what the past year has been like instead. Both Noah and I were grateful for that. That meeting lasted hours as Noah played for them most of the songs he wrote while working with the Characters.

"When does your roommate arrive again?" Noah is reclined on my messy bed while I put the last finishing touches on my makeup.

"Yesterday," I reply sullenly. Her stuff has already been shipped and is stacked in either her room or in the living room.

I talked to her three days ago, and she told me when she was flying in, which was early yesterday afternoon. I wanted to pick her up from the airport, but she insisted she already had someone doing that. Then I waited until ten o'clock last night before trying to call her, wanting to make sure she was okay. No answer.

I try to push the anxiety over her away because I have something else to be nervous about. Today is the social meet and greet at the school before the semester starts.

I look down at the simple dress I'm wearing. It's blue with little white and yellow flowers, spaghetti straps, and the hem is right above my knees. Heeled sandals dress my feet. Meanwhile, Noah is dressed in a simple white button down and black slacks with his boots. This is the most dressed up he ever gets.

"Ready?" I ask as I grab my purse.

Noah swings his legs off the bed and quickly stands up. A man of few words, he holds my hand as he leads us out the door, locking and double-checking the locks when we leave. "Can never be too careful," and a shrug is his response to my raised eyebrow at his second time checking the locks. Then he kisses me tenderly before pulling me down the stairs.

Outside, we get on his bike, and then drive the many blocks up and two streets away to my school. It's located right on Broadway and surrounded by other school, with Colombia right around the corner. The central building is where the luncheon is being held.

Noah and I make our way in after checking my name on the roster, and then he is leading me through a buffet line before finding us our designated seats. Noah's plate is stacked inches high, while I only grabbed some crackers and carrots. My stomach is too unsettled to eat. My hands have been shaking since before we left the house and now my legs are in the same position. I feel sick to my stomach, lightly sweating in my nervousness.

Noah keeps his hand interlocked with mine, stroking gentle circles along the inside of my wrist as he eats and I ignore my food. I'm too busy looking around the room, studying the people who will be my competition. I'm not a competitive person by nature, but this school means making or breaking, and my dream is to make it.

"You need to eat, angel."

"I'm not hungry," I tell him as I drop a half-nibbled carrot onto the plate and push it away.

Noah purses his lips at the plate before moving his eyes to mine. "You haven't eaten all day."

I ignore him, and instead squeeze his hand and tell him, "Thank you for being here. It means the world to me."

Noah smiles, reaching out with his free hand to stroke down my cheek. "Anything for you, an—"

"Claire!"

My head snaps to the left at hearing my name in a crowded room of people I don't know. The voice has a bit of an accent, and I know before I see her who it is.

"Is that …?" Noah wonders.

Dare practically skips over to us as I rise from my seat. She throws her arms around me like we have known each other for years, and Noah has to let go of my hand when she lifts me off my feet and spins me around, teasing me about how small I am.

If she didn't think I was so little, then I didn't think she was so tall. Dare must easily be six-feet, almost as tall as Noah. She has a rounded figure; shoulder length, black hair; and brown eyes behind black-framed glasses.

She looks behind me and spots Noah, moving to give him a hug. They have met "in passing," if you can call it that. Since Noah and I have been inseparable all summer, he was there for a lot of me and Dare's Skype conversations.

"When did you get here?" I ask as Noah maneuvers out of Dare's embrace and sits back down. I join him, and Dare sits on my other side.

"Yesterday." At my questioning look, she continues, "I know, I know. I haven't been to the condo yet. I stayed with a friend." She points somewhere across the room, but I don't look. "He's been here a few years. A singer, like you. You should come meet him. We are going to karaoke tonight!"

I want to be peeved that she had me so worried, but her energetic, happy vibes consume me. Instead of dwelling on it, we sit and talk for a while. Then Noah and I are introduced to her friend and his friends.

After an hour, an administrator and some senior students start talking, so everyone moves back to their seats as we listen to what is expected this year. Then, all too soon, that is over, and Dare and everyone we met are back. We make plans and talk like we have all known each other all our lives. And just like that, my nerves are gone, and I am having the best time.

~Noah~

I hate this city. I hate how taken by it Claire is. I hate how what used to be my home, felt like home, is now a living nightmare. I hate how you can't see the stars here. I hate the constant noise, the busyness, the crowds, the people. I hate the smell of shit, food, and exhaust.

I miss the quiet peace of Claire's hometown. I miss the quiet woods, quiet drives, quiet, quiet, quiet.

Peace. I want my peace back.

Jealousy courses through me as I watch Claire talk to her new classmates. She has come alive since being in city, and I love watching it, watching her. However, seeing her happily talk to other men, men who share the same passion as her, men who will be spending countless hours with her, terrifies the shit out of me.

We went from being inseparable all summer—most of the past year—and now I have to share her with the city, with her school, her roommate, her new peers. She went from having only me to all *this*, and I don't know how I'm going to handle that. In fact, I don't like how I wonder how I'm going to handle it.

We are in my town, my world, where I'm back with my friends, my life. The band, we have picked up from where we left off last summer, with gigs lined up and a busy schedule. Moreover, I'm already starting my job on Monday. I should be thinking about how busy I'm going to be. Too busy to stress over Claire and her newfound freedom; freedom from her own insecurity, from a small-town stigma, freedom to be herself for once. And I should be happy she will have someone and something to occupy her time when we can't be together

I need to shake off this crushing fear of failing, because that's what this is. Fear. I fear change. I fear the inevitable. I fear Claire is going to wake up one day and realize she is too good for me. I fear what being in the city will do to us; the opportunity she now has to see what else is out there, beyond her small town. I fear who I was will catch up to who I want to be now. I fear she won't like the changes this means to me. I fear.

"Noah." Claire puts her hand on my arm, snapping me out of my

213

dark thoughts. Then she leans in and drops her voice. "I think it would be fun to try karaoke. We don't have other plans tonight, do we?"

My fear tells me to make up an excuse for why we can't go. Maybe call my parents and surprise them by telling them we are coming for dinner—anything to keep her to myself and get out of going out with this preppy-looking lot.

I can feel the guys sizing me up. The assholes have been ogling my girl for the past hour.

Flash images of Claire with one of them comes unbidden to the forefront of my mind. Her in her girlish blue dress, standing arm in arm with one of them in their posh suits, hair combed over in that aristocratic style only those who grew up with old money can pull off. It's enough to make me run to the nearest bathroom and hurl.

I realize my hands are clenched in fists and release them from their aching grip, joints popping and loosening as they stretch out. Then I lift one up and move a stray hair that is brushing Claire's cheek to behind her ear. "Anything you want, angel. As long as you sing a duet with me."

I can feel my eyes soften as a blush moves into her cheeks. It will always amaze me that the simplest gesture, a simple endearment, moves her in such a way.

"I can do that." She grins up at me, a blazing smile that always knocks me back a step.

I can tell the other guys are just as affected, their eyes not leaving her even though they are talking amongst themselves now, showing false pretenses that our conversation is our own.

"Then I'm game, but"—I lean down to whisper in her ear—"I get you for the rest of the weekend … alone."

She turns her head away, but I see that telltale blush even deeper now. She tries to play off her affect by telling Dare we are in. Then we are off, a whole entourage following in our wake as we make it to the parking garage.

Claire talks a mile a minute into my ear on the way to the karaoke bar. She's really excited about working with one of the professors who was supposedly a big deal in the opera world a few years back until she retired.

When we get to the place, we are the first ones there, so I turn around on the bike and keep it propped up between my legs as I gaze at my angel. She is still talking about everything and anything, so animated in her excitement. I try to listen to her, but it's the little things that garner my attention, like the freckles on her knees that I want to get intimate with later.

I pull my attention back to her face, staring at her eyes so she thinks I'm listening as I caress my fingertips along the edge of her dress which has ridden up her thighs from the drive. She's still straddling the bike with her feet propped up on the foot pedals, her legs open, her dress hiding all her goodies that are mine alone. For good measure, I pull her dress down some.

I have had too many gloomy thoughts all day, and her chatter is making me wallow in the disparaging fear even more. She's too animated, too excited, too … different. Asshole thing of me to say, I know. But it's suddenly too much, especially with the added background noise of cars speeding by, honking—all the noise of the city. I miss the quiet.

"You seem like a different person," I blurt out, instantly regretting it.

She doesn't miss a beat, unfazed or unaware of my mood. "I feel like a different person."

"It scares me."

She looks at me in confusion, her brilliant smile wilting.

Am I that selfish that I have to bring her down with me? That's not right. I love her. I adore her so goddamn much. I should be able to smile through someone ripping my guts out, holding a gun to my head, gasping my last breath, just so she doesn't hurt.

"I'm afraid we'll drift apart," the acidic words keep spewing out. "You're finding yourself, and we won't fit anymore."

"Noah—"

"Let me finish." I pause, inching closer until my thighs are tucked under hers. "You're in a new place, starting your life away from all the cynics from your home. You're free to be you, around people just like you, people who understand you. You're coming into yourself, and I'm afraid I won't fit anymore. I'm afraid you'll see that, and where will that leave me?"

"Noah—"

"I'm selfish, Claire. So damn selfish when it comes to you."

She urgently crushes her mouth to mine. Then she licks my lips, enticing me to open to her, which I do, kissing her with all I have as she does the same. When she pulls away just as quickly as her assault came on, she looks deeply into my eyes.

"I'm selfish, too, Noah. And I want you forever."

"Forever?" I can't help asking.

"Forever," she whispers the promise.

I can't believe, when Claire sheds her insecurity, I find mine. How can she be so sure of forever? I thought I was sure. In Breckinridge, I was sure. There, I had no doubt that we were forever. Here, my surety is waning. Too much change too fast, and it is leaving me doubting everything. My sanity feels like it's slipping, and I fear our relationship will fall with it, because of it.

We remain staring into each other's eyes, saying everything we need to say through them. I show her my fears, and she shows me her confidence in us, her support in me. And then her new friends arrive.

She kisses me again before indicating she wants to get off the bike, so I help her, and once we are standing next to it, she asks, "Better?"

I nod, lying, but promising myself that I will slap myself out of my funk.

The night goes smoothly after that. I lose myself in simply watching Claire and Dare sing song after song, freeing my mind of any negativity. Dare can't sing for shit. However, that's not the point. The point is the smile on Claire's face, the twinkle in her eyes, and the laughter that bubbles out of her. It's all music to my ears.

Some of the guys start up a conversation with me, seeming more interested when they hear I am in a band. We talk music for hours; how can we not when a group of musically talented people get together? It relaxing, enjoyable even. I swipe my fears away and simply live in the moment.

~

Alone in Claire's condo, since Dare is once again spending the night with her friend, I lock the doors then move to the windows to make sure they are secured before closing the curtains.

Claire has this thing with curtains. She is obsessed with overly long ones that flow across the floor. I tried to deter her from buying them, telling her she's going to end up vacuuming them up, but she insisted, saying one day, when we have our dream house, they will go perfectly with hardwood floors in our majestic dining room, or some shit like that. I forgot my argument the second she mentioned a future with me.

With the house secured, I make my way to Claire's bedroom where she is pulling the dress over her head. Her waist is taut and her ass and breast are pushed out as she pulls the fabric up then throws it in the direction of the laundry basket.

I lean against the doorframe and watch as she turns away from me and unclasps her dark blue bra from the back. Her ass is fully exposed in a dark blue, lacy thong, enticing in the way it jiggles softly as she steps toward her dresser to put her bra away.

When she turns back around, she finally sees me and startles, but then she schools her features. I grin as she tries to ignore me, pulling the pins out of the side of her hair before grabbing her pajamas. Before she has the chance to cover herself back up, though, I have her over my shoulder, the nightgown on the ground, and I am kicking the door shut.

Within minutes, I have Claire gasping for breath and moaning, her body quivering in need, her hips keeping up with my rhythm. When I hear her breath hitching and feel her legs tauten, I know she's close, so I stop.

Nothing like delayed gratification.

"Noah …"

Before she can finish her complaint, I tell her to, "Wrap your arms around me."

She does, and then I lift her until she is sitting on my thighs. She gasps as she sinks even farther down, and I devour her moans with my lips, kissing her, searing my soul with hers. My need to rid myself of this jealousy has me wanting to brand her.

I hold her weight up, using my desperation to feverishly thrust into her. She keeps her arms wrapped tightly around my neck as she arches away from me. That makes it feel like I am even more deeply inside her, imprinting myself in a place where no one else has before.

When I pull her down on me as I thrust up, a sexy as sin groan comes out of her, and she stabs her nails into my shoulders as she tightens her hold on me. She has her head thrown back, and her breasts thrust up. All I have to do is move my head a few inches and one will be in my mouth. I don't, though. I'm too busy watching the pleasure on her face as I ride her on me.

"That feels ... so goo—" she moans, a gasp cutting off her words as her hips collide with mine and she shatters.

With her legs shaking around me, I lay her back down on the bed and slow my movements, listening to her mewls and watching her come back down. Then, when she's fully recovered, I start pounding away again, which seems to pick up on the remnants of her orgasm and makes her tighten on my dick. I cuss as it happens, not wanting to come yet.

I lick up the side of her neck to her ear then whisper, "Give me another, angel."

I let out a groan as her walls squeeze my cock again, sucking in air between my teeth as I try to hold off. That has her going. A few more thrusts and some cries from her, and her head tips back, her legs tighten around me once more, and she raises those hips into mine, coming on another cry.

The pleasure of her walls tightening around me is too much. I thrust urgently, no longer in command of my body. It's primal instinct now. My body demands I drive into her with everything I am until my essence releases from my body and into hers, marking her, claiming her, the only one to ever have her.

I bury my face in her neck, gasping, my sweat mixing with hers, our hair entwined and sticking to our damp skin. Then I blow on her neck when I recover, trying to cool her down. I am still inside her, pulsating as she is, not wanting to move. I could pass out right where I am, but I roll over, taking her with me, and I slip out.

I'm still hard as a rock. How, after that release, I don't know. Damn thing is perpetually hard in Claire's presence. It doesn't matter how much we have sex.

Claire straddles my lap, looking enticingly tousled, with her long locks in disarray. She grins down at me, lust-filled eyes looking at me playfully.

Shit. She wants to go again already?

"What's that look for?" I'm acting petulant. It's a game we play. I act like the tired, I-just-got-laid-so-leave-me-alone prick, and she acts like a sex goddess, always ready to seduce.

She pouts playfully. "I want more."

I chuckle and cover my face with my arm so she can't see the grin that's inerasable right now. That's not how I usually play the game, but damn, she's too cute.

She wiggles her ass, maneuvering herself until she is just *there*, and I peek out from under my arm to see her grind on me, and ... Oh, God. If there was ever a time I was going to experience premature ejaculation, this would be it.

She starts imitating what she would do if she were on my cock, slowly moving up and down, rocking her hips back and forth, while I lie back and enjoy the show, placing my arms behind my head. She's really getting into it, too, looking down at me the entire time, her mouth formed into the perfect *O* that I want to push my dick inside.

Right as I start to move my arms to take control and slam her down on me, she does just that. Now, with my dick inside her, she repeats her routine, a little bit more unsteady this time around.

"Touch me, Noah," she begs breathlessly, her breath already hitching in her telling way.

I oblige, using my fingers, moving them with the motion of her hips. And when she moves faster, I press harder, which makes her move against them even faster. Suddenly, she bucks, calling out my name.

Unable to bear her weight anymore, she collapses on top of me, her cheek pressed against my chest, gulping in air as she quivers. I hold her for a few minutes, brushing her sweaty hair out from her face. Then, when she is no longer panting, it's my turn to take over.

With each bruising thrust, my crushing fear that has been choking me since we arrived in the city relents a little bit more. Regardless, somehow, someway, I know forever will end. I don't know when or how or why, but it will happen. I hope it is nothing we can't see our way out of. For now, though, this, being with her, just her, melts away the fear as I show my angel how brutal and gentle and devoting my love is for her.

Chapter 19

The Beginning of the End

~Noah~

Claire is sitting on the couch in the band's practice room, studiously reading one of her textbooks. This is a routine that has become familiar over the past month. When she can make it to one of the band practices, she usually finds something to do and separates herself from the other guys' girlfriends, or whoever they are sleeping with now.

The other girls are sitting next to her, whispering and giggling as they point at us. It sets my teeth on edge. I hate them being here. Always have. This is supposed to be a band practice, not a showing off to get laid act.

Trey and Shaun are always goofing off, making out with one of the girls instead of spending our minimal practice time actually practicing. I would insist on banning girls from practice, but then Claire couldn't be here, and between my work and her school, we don't get much time together anymore.

This summer spoiled the shit out of me, being with her practically twenty-four seven, all the little adventures we went on. Now I'm usually passed out or she is by the time we are together at night. I have decent hours at the shop, but when I'm not working, I'm usually practicing since Claire is still at school or rehearsals in the afternoon.

I sat in the wings a few times to watch her rehearsals. Not much really happens, and I don't get too many peeps of her. Most of the cast is usually in the wings while the leads are on stage. Still, I do get glimpses of her talking to her new peers.

She is so much more open with them than she was with the high school kids. Finally, she has people who understand her. I'm happy for her, but so jealous at the same time I make myself sick. I have to constantly remind myself that it's me she comes home to every night.

I still have a place with my parents, but I'm never there. I always crash at Claire's. I don't like the idea of her being alone in that condo. Yeah, she has Dare, but Dare is never home. That girl has slept at the condo only a handful of times.

I whistle to get the guys' attention, and then we start in on a new song. I notice Claire tapping her foot to the beat, lip-syncing as she reads her book. She doesn't know it, but that little gesture warms my heart. I feel like I have a cheerleader, someone who is rooting just for me, someone who is proud of me.

When the song is over, with a wary glance at the girls next to her, Claire packs up her bag then comes up to me.

"I'm heading out."

I look at the two girls on the couch who are watching our every move, then look back at Claire. "What did they say?"

Claire shakes her head. "It doesn't matter, Noah."

Her reluctance to tell me pisses me off. I saw the looks they were giving me. I saw the petty, jealous hatred they shot toward Claire. I know it matters. If it didn't matter, Claire wouldn't want to run away like she always does when I know she really wants to confront someone. I love and hate how she always wants to be good, how she is always the peacekeeper.

"It matters to me, Claire. *You* matter. And if they are saying something that makes you uncomfortable, then I'll kick them out. *They* should be the ones to leave, not you."

She reaches up on her tiptoes and gives me a quick peck on the lips. "I have to go, anyway. I didn't bring my laptop, and I have read everything I can here. I need to do some research online and start a paper. I'll see you when you get home, okay?"

I grab the back of her head and pull her toward me. After a more satisfying kiss, I linger against her lips, telling her, "I adore you."

"I know."

With a last brush of her lips, she leaves.

When the door shuts behind her, I turn to glare at the two girls. Both are dressed like prostitutes. I don't know what hole the guys dragged them out of. They all look the same to me these days. I can't even believe I used to notice them, fuck them. I disgust myself.

Turning my back on the girls, I start to play our new song again. Shaun has been a beat behind on it, and we have to get it down before tomorrow night's show.

This is one of those moments I wish I were back with Kyle and Cyn. The three of us clicked in a way me and these guys don't. Our music was always in synch; our practices were in a controlled environment, not like here where it seems like anyone can come in. How can someone miss a place they were so determined to hate?

When band practice is finished, Trey and Shaun head out with their dates. I pack up my guitar then sit back on the couch in the same place Claire was sitting earlier, a bottle of water in my hand.

Chris comes over and sits down next to me, offering me a beer. I shake my head then lean back against the couch, staring up at the water-stained ceiling.

"What's up with you, man?" Chris sets the beer he offered me down and opens a second one.

"Nothing." Everything, it seems.

"Bullshit. Something's bothering you." He chugs down the beer while I cut my eyes over at him, watching as his throat works the drink down.

I sit up and put my elbows on my knees, looking down into my grasped hands. "Do you think Claire is too good for me?" I'm not one to open up to anyone, but if I had to—which I apparently do right now—it would be to Chris.

He is the closest person I have ever had to a friend. We went to high school together. He was the one who encouraged us to put a band together, finding Shaun and Trey through a music store ad. He is the one who sets up all the gigs and holds this band together.

Chris pauses in grabbing the second beer. "Honestly … yeah." Then he hurries to say, "You're better with her, though. A better person. And I don't think you could be with anybody else. Claire— from the small amount of time I've known her—seems the same way. I can't see her with anyone else, either."

I barely hear what he says after the, "*Honestly … yeah.*" My mind is tuned into those two words. Two words that choke me and send my heart into a cardiac arrest speed.

Honestly ... yeah.

Honestly ... yeah.

Honestly ... yeah.

I knew it was true, yet hearing someone admit it is different than my conscience telling me it's true. It's eye opening, making me question what the hell I am doing to Claire, how I could be bringing her down, ruining her.

The look on her face earlier when she left, those girls and their comments that sent her away, she doesn't have to deal with that. She *shouldn't* have to deal with that.

What can I do to be more worthy of her? Should I drop the band, quit working for Chris's family, and go back to school? Can I be that type of person? But if I change my mind and do the college thing, would it make me more worthy? She wouldn't have to worry about the girls so much.

"Noah, man, I see those wheels turning," Chris cuts into my thoughts, and I focus back on him, seeing wariness in his eyes, and pity. "I'm sorry, but you asked. I think you two are great together, and Claire is a sweet chick. Hotter than Hades, too." He grins at that. "You're lucky as hell to have her. Don't hurt her by thinking you're less than you are."

He reclines on the couch, resting his arm along the back. "You're not the same person from a year ago. You changed—for the better. Just don't take what I said in the direction I know you're going. Don't think down on yourself, and get Claire off that pedestal you put her on. When you get her down, you'll see that she's just a girl, and you're just a boy, and the two of you have a chemical reaction that is simply nature." He shrugs. "You two balance each other out, and you need to accept it as it is and not think the whys or hows. It. Just. Is. Accept that and forget the rest. It just is."

I'm speechless. That is the most philosophical piece of advice I have ever heard from him, and that's coming from a guy I once watched drink a fifth of whiskey, pass out puking, just to wake up two hours later and start hitting it again. And all the while, he was

224

screaming about bears and fucking every skirt in sight. I don't know where this Chris has been hiding, but I am extremely grateful for him. "Thanks, man."

"Anytime, Noah. And if I need to kick your ass someday for fucking it all up, I will ... gladly." He smirks again before opening the cap of the second beer and once again gulping it down in five chugs.

~Claire~

Once at home, I drop my bag down on the couch and head toward the kitchen to make a coffee. I have been so exhausted lately from studying, rehearsals, and trying to find the time to spend with Noah. Juggling everything is starting to wear me out. I never thought college would be so time consuming. It's rewarding, too; I do have to admit that. The sense of accomplishment. The contentment of coming home at night and just *being*.

I love where my life is right now and where it is going. I can't wait to see where life takes me and how everything will turn out. So far, it seems like a happily ever after fantasy. I am finally able to leave the nightmare of high school behind me. I have friends with like interests, and a crazy roommate that, though I rarely see her, still gives me little bursts of happiness whenever she does come around. Then there is Noah.

Noah's band is as good as Characters were in Breckenridge. However, they don't always seem as serious, and they pay too much attention to the fame side than their music.

Those girls who were over there today have no interest in Shaun and Trey, who were the ones that invited them. They were more concerned with *my* boyfriend, talking about what they were going to do to attract his attention, and then what they were going to do when they got it. It was like Chelsea and Nikki all over again.

There is a knock at the front door as I wait for the coffeemaker. I run over to look through the peephole, not recognizing the man standing there. He is dressed in a suit, older, with salt and pepper hair. I have never seen him a day in my life, and I am too nervous to answer the door when I am home alone.

"Who is it?" I hear from behind me and startle, turning around with my hand over my heart as I watch Dare approach. Thank God she is home for once.

"I don't know." I step away from the door, and she looks through the peephole.

She shrugs. "Never seen him before. Answer it. Could be a solicitor or could be a representative from some big production company," she says the last part excitedly, her eyes getting a dreamy quality to them. "Let's see," she says as she opens the door with a flourish.

I stand behind Dare, almost invisible behind her tall frame as the man asks, "Hello? Are you Claire Sawyer?"

Dare crosses her arms over her chest. "Who's asking?"

The man digs a card out of the side of his briefcase and hands it to Dare. "I am the representative of Tiffany Jacobs-Sawyer-Roberts—"

"My mother," I gasp.

The man finally sees me and gives me an almost sad smile. "I take it you're Claire Diane Sawyer? Father is District Attorney Jonathan Sawyer?"

"Yes, sir," I say, now moving from behind Dare. "What is this about my mother?"

"May I come in?" He gestures toward his briefcase like that is the answer to my question.

Dare opens the door wider for the man, and he steps in, looking around the apartment with approval.

"Please, take a seat." I move to one of the chairs as Dare closes the front door and the lawyer puts his briefcase down before unbuttoning his jacket and sitting down.

"You need me out here?" Dare asks, concern and wariness in her eyes.

I shake my head, nervously playing with my necklace. I am scared to death of what this is about. Scenarios are running through my head, and none of them are good.

"I'll be in my room if you need me, okay?"

I smile nervously up at Dare, showing her I appreciate her gesture and concern.

She gives the man an eye over before turning and heading down the hall.

Then the man clears his throat. "I am Trevor Jameson, by the way."

I don't say anything. I don't know what to say. I don't know what to think. Well, that's not true. I'm thinking a lot, but all my thoughts are jumbled together.

Does my mom want to see me? Where has she been? What could possibly bring this man here to see me? How did he know where to find me? Does that mean my mother knows where I am? How?

I wish Noah were here, or my dad. They would know what questions to ask. They would know what to say to get this man to say what he came here for and leave.

I don't think I even want to hear about my mom. I have been over her abandonment for years. In any case, that's what I tell myself. But deep inside, deep in the caverns of my heart, a small, teeny tiny part of me does want her here; wishes it had been her at my door. I don't like that small part of me.

I startle out of my thoughts as Trevor moves, sitting up on the coach and clasping his hands in front of him. "Ms. Sawyer, this is never easy to say. Your mother is a dear friend of mine." He pauses, looking right at me. "Your mother is sick. Dying. She's in the hospital, and she would very much like to see you ..."

The next hour is the most gut-wrenching one I have ever experienced. I pretend to listen, not really hearing much beyond, *"Your mother is sick. Dying."* I don't know how to feel about that. I want to cry. Why do I want to cry? How can someone cry for someone they don't even know? Is it the tragedy of the situation you cry for?

I learn that my mother divorced the man she ran away with years ago, my dad's ex-best friend. She never had kids, besides me. She had a decent job here, in the city, only streets away. Her apartment is north of here. She is leaving everything to me, her only daughter, her only kin. My mom is dying alone in a hospital, and I am her only family.

At one point, Dare comes out of her bedroom and sits at my side as Trevor hands over paperwork regarding her estate and information on bank accounts she set up in my name years ago. He also hands me a manila envelope filled with newspaper articles of me, and a small box with my mother's prized jewelry. It's like she is already dead.

Trevor then tells me she only has days, maybe a week or two to live, that she waited until the last possible moment before asking Trevor to reach out to me.

She wants to see me. She wants to see me, and I don't know if I can see her. I'm too numb right now to make that kind of decision. I wish Noah was here. I wish my dad was here.

"Keep my card. If you lose it, I'm listed. Call me when you make your decision on whether you want to see her or not." He pats my hand as he stands up. I can only imagine what I look like right now as I see the pity in his eyes. "Your mom's been a good friend. I don't know why she waited so long to see you, but when she reached out to me, I could see the longing in her eyes for you." When I don't say anything, he picks up his briefcase and sees himself out.

What was I thinking earlier? That my life seems like a happily ever after fantasy. That I love where my life is right now and where it is going. How I couldn't wait to see where life takes me and how everything will turn out. It's so sad how life can throw a one-eighty at you in the blink of an eye.

~Noah~

When I get home, I immediately hear Claire crying and follow the sounds to Dare's bedroom where I find Claire with her head in Dare's lap while Dare softly strokes her hair, cooing promises of everything being all right.

"What's going on?" I ask, wondering if this has to do with earlier and those girls, or if something happened back home. Whatever it is, it must be bad, because Claire rarely, if ever, cries. I definitely haven't see her cry like this: blotchy face, eyes swollen, tears pouring out unceasingly.

At my voice, Claire immediately jumps from Dare's bed and into my arms.

I swing her up, cradling her as she wraps her arms around me, now crying into my neck. I feel her tears soaking my collar in seconds. God, I want to know what is wrong.

Carrying her into her room, Dare follows, telling me, "Her mother's lawyer came by. She's in the hospital. He said she's dying and wants Claire to see—"

"Wait," I cut her off, sitting on the bed then lying back with Claire still cradled in my arms. "Let me settle her down. I'll be out in a few."

"Okay." Dare turns around and leaves, shutting the door softly behind her.

I can't imagine what this is doing to Claire. I can *see* it, but what is going on in her mind?

"Do you want to talk about it?" I ask, brushing my lips along her hair. Her sobs have turned into sniffles after five minutes of full-out, gasping-for-breath crying.

Claire shakes her head, hiccupping, "What … is there … to talk … about?"

I know it's a rhetorical question, but I answer, anyway.

"Well, how you feel, for one. Do you know what's wrong with your mom? Do you want to see her? You can start by telling me what happened after you left earlier."

Claire sniffles again then backs up so we are both lying on our sides, facing each other. She tells me all about Mr. Jameson's visit; how it felt like her mother was already dead, and she didn't know how to feel about it; if she can even work up the nerve to visit her mom; if she even wants to do that. I listen to it all, wiping the tears away, wishing I had been here, my mind racing over all the information.

"Why now? That's all I keep thinking. Why wait until the end?" Claire gestures with her hand toward the door. "It's obvious she thought about me over the years—kept pictures and articles about me—so why didn't she come see me, be a part of my life? Why wait until it's too late?"

I don't have an answer for her. It doesn't make sense to me, either. All I can think is that her mom was too ashamed before, and now is her chance since it *is* the end.

I have to give the woman some respect because she is trying. Maybe too late. Almost way too late, but at least the olive branch is out there. All Claire has to do is take it or not. She can obtain all her answers or live the rest of her days without them.

I can't allow the latter to happen, so I tell her, "You should ask her that." She starts to object—I can see it in her eyes—but I press my index finger to her lips to hush her. "It's not the ideal situation; but otherwise, you are going to beat yourself up over wondering this for the rest of your life, and I won't let you." Her eyes narrow at that as I continue, "You'll regret it, Claire. You know you will. You crying like this tells me that you care. You want this opportunity, but you want to hurt her like she hurt you."

Again, she starts to object. "I don't want—"

"It may not be there in the forefront of your mind," I talk over her, "but how can you not? The woman left you." And here is when she starts crying again. Nailed it. "You were a newborn, and she walked away. Better yet, she left your dad ... for his best friend. Who does that?" I nod as she starts sobbing again. "You want to find out. You deserve to know why. Why would a mother—your own mother—walk away from you and your dad?"

"Stop it, Noah," Claire sobs out, and it breaks my heart, but she needs to hear this. She needs to put an end to that chapter of her life. She needs answers, and she needs to tell her mother how she feels. She is one of few who has that chance.

"No, Claire. I have never not told you the truth or sugarcoated shit for you, and I'm not going to do it now." My chest feels tight at the look of heartbreak on her face, at having to hurt her to heal her. "You need to see that woman and find out why. Get your answers and put this to rest—put her to rest ... Find peace within yourself. *You know.* You know you have to do this."

Claire nods, relenting, still sobbing.

I pull her back to me and let her cry it out. She needs this like I needed to tell her the truth, even if I hurt her more in the process. I'm not about to let my angel suffer years of torture of not knowing when the last opportunity is right in front of her.

Chapter 20

God Damn You

~Claire~

These past two months have been a nightmare. Trevor said my mom had days to maybe a week to live, but she managed to hold on for six weeks. Reluctantly, I took Noah's advice and went to see her. It was surreal. Here was the woman who gave birth to me, dying, a shell of a woman. It seemed poetic for her to meet me at my birth, only for me to meet her at her death.

My mother was in the last stages of brain cancer. It started off with headaches, then fainting spells, loss of memory, a pins and needles feeling all over her body. And when the vomiting started, she went to her doctor. By then, it was too late. The tumor was inoperable, embedded too deeply in her brain.

When I walked into her room for the first time, she cried, and I cried—mostly because I was terrified and she was crying. I didn't know what to do, what to say. I simply held on tightly to Noah's hand, needing him to ground me. I honestly didn't know what I was doing there.

Then she weakly held out her arms to me like she wanted to hug me, tears streaking down her face, a sob bubbling out. Again, I didn't know what to do. I wanted to hug her back because she seemed to need it and I wanted to comfort her—she was dying; I was her daughter. However, she was also the woman who had left me. I didn't know her.

Terrified, I let Noah guide me to her. Then I let Noah place my hand in hers, and she gripped that hand with both of hers, raising it to her face, holding it against her cheek. By that point, I was a sobbing mess. Still, I didn't know what to do, what to say. I simply stood there, shaking so badly that Noah had to hold me up.

Noah pulled stayed there throughout the first meeting as we both listened to my mom talk, her voice getting hoarser by the minute. She was a blabbering mess the entire time, telling me her regrets, her fears. She wasn't making excuses—she pointed that out often. She was merely trying to find understanding, but I couldn't give her that.

I sat there and simply listened, not commenting, not giving her anything in return. Meanwhile, my mind was screaming at her, wanting to tell her how selfish she was, that I didn't understand running away from your child because you felt you were too young, that your life felt final, over.

Regardless of my feelings, I gave her the closure she needed before she died. I couldn't let her leave this life thinking she meant nothing to me. She gave me life, and I loved my life. I had to be thankful for that. She gave me such a wonderful father, I lived to fulfill dreams some people would sin for, and I was alive to meet Noah.

After I first talked to my mom, I called my dad, who dropped everything to fly up. I would have called him sooner, but I didn't know how to tell him, or if I should. My mom left him almost nineteen years ago; what if I caused him pain by reviving memories of what could have been? Nonetheless, I selfishly needed my daddy's support.

He stayed a few days, visiting my mother every one of those days, and then came back to my apartment looking aged. I shouldn't have told him. I told him that, but he assured me he needed this. They both needed to clear the air. Still, I felt terrible.

I continued to visit my mom almost every day of those six weeks that she held on. Some days, she never woke up. Some days, I would talk freely to her and answer all her questions about me and my life. It hurt my heart to see her smile at some of the things she missed out on. And some days, we would cry until she fell asleep, which was often. Every time she fell asleep, I wondered if it would be the time she didn't wake up. It was a confusing experience.

On top of that, my grades are falling from spending so much time yet not enough time at the hospital. I missed so much rehearsal time that, though they said they understood, I got pushed back to an understudy, not like I had a major role in the first place. And I am exhausted all the time, but I haven't had time for more than five to six hours of sleep.

It all makes me realize that this is life. This is adulthood. All my childhood playtime is over. This past summer was the last of it, and now the real world is knocking, and there are so many responsibilities with not enough time to do them all.

I can't eat, can't sleep, can't concentrate or focus. Thankfully, I have Noah to remind me of those mundane things. He has been my hero in all this, using all his free time to be with me, simply being there for support. At night, when he comes home to find me still studying, he simply closes the books and guides me to bed, ignoring my protests, not saying a word.

Just the other week, when I was at my worst, he brought home a kitten. A beautiful, white fur ball of Persian sweetness. She is the most exquisite kitty I have ever seen.

I cried again when I saw her scamper into my room, a pink bow tied around her neck. I sat up in bed, and the little thing clawed her way up my bed and into my lap, giving me a soft meow. I was in insta-love.

Noah named her Angel, saying his angel needed one, too.

Then, a few days ago, my mom fell into a coma. And yesterday, while I was trying to study, the hospital called me seventy minutes after I left her room, telling me she had passed away. Thankfully, Noah was home and Dare was gone.

I cried, deep sobbing, uncontrollable tears. I missed the moment she fell asleep, never to wake up again. I missed the moment she took her last breath. I was just there. I didn't understand how life could change, be gone, in the blink of an eye.

I can only imagine what it would have been like if I was there. Her chest rising, the respirator whooshing, the heart monitor beeping steadily. Then, her chest falling, the respirator depressurizing, the heart monitor screaming that there was no sign of life. That image haunts me.

Trevor dropped a few boxes off earlier. He said it was my mother's wish for me to have them as soon as she was gone. I still need to go through her apartment and figure out what I want to do with all her stuff, but that can wait. Trevor is taking care of the funeral for me, and he already has all the financial stuff out of the way.

Now I am reading letters, so many letters my mom left for me over the years. She bought me a card or wrote me a letter for every occasion. Then she also wrote me a letter on days when she thought about me and had to write down what she was thinking. Some of them have me in tears and some parts make me laugh out loud. My mom had quite the sense of humor.

As I am unwrapping the gift she got me for my thirteenth birthday, there is a knock on my door. I hesitate to answer it, not wanting to be disrupted right now.

Dare took her boyfriend Victor, or Vick as he likes to be called, to Noah's show. They asked me to come, and Noah begged me to be there, but after Trevor showed up with the boxes, Dare knew I wouldn't. I called Noah and made an excuse about needing to study, not wanting to tell him the truth, knowing he would worry.

There is more going on here than I can tell him right now. I need the time to work it out in my own head. I'm already so stressed out with everything else. I don't want to add to that tension by stressing Noah out, too. I need to believe everything will work out for the best. It should, right?

I decide to get up and at least check to see who is at the door. Noah's parents stop by all the time, more so now than the first month we lived here. I know he stops by his parents often enough to grab clothes.

His mom has been a huge support for me. She was a shoulder to cry on those first few weeks when I started to see my mom. She even came to the hospital with me once, wanting to meet her. She has given me lots of study tips, too, knowing I hardly have time.

Looking through the peephole, I quickly step back. Troy? What is he doing here? Last I heard, he was still in training. He must be on leave. But why would he come here? Why isn't he with Chelsea and their baby?

Curious more than anything, I open the door.

He is standing there in his uniform, looking so completely different from last time I saw him. I look him up and down twice, trying to put my finger on why he looks so different. He seems more mature, wiser—I can't figure it out. He seems different ... in a good way.

"Hi," I finally get out, holding the door cracked open.

"Hey, Claire."

We both stand there for a minute, not saying anything. I'm still taking in how much he has changed. His eyes are wiser, older. His build is even more muscled than before. He's holding himself taller, more self-assured. I wonder if I look different to him, too.

His expression changes from wariness to concern. "Have you been crying?"

I reach up and swipe my fingertips under each eye, making sure mascara isn't smeared. "Yeah, um ..." I can feel my lip quiver. "My mom ... She just ... Um ... My mom passed away last night."

Troy's brows draw down, looking confused, and he should be. He knows I never knew my mom.

I open the door wider. "Do you want to come in?" I can't not let him in. He's here, where he knows no one. I only hope he has somewhere to stay, because Noah will not like him staying here.

Troy nods and steps inside, closing the door behind him as he looks around. Then Angel comes in and introduces herself by rubbing against his legs. My sweet girl loves attention.

He reaches down, petting her under her chin, as he looks up at me. "She yours?"

I nod. "Yeah, Noah just got her for me. He's been trying to cheer me up with"—I let out a sigh—"everything that's been happening."

Troy nods, not even looking bothered that I mentioned Noah. He surprises me more by saying, "Noah's a good guy." He sees the look of disbelief on my face. "I know. Shocking, right? But it's true."

I gesture for him to sit on the couch, and he does. I take a seat on the chair, curling up into it with my legs tucked under me. Angel comes up and starts butting her head under my hand, so I start petting her. Troy continues talking throughout all this.

"A year ago, I hated to admit it. Angry at it. But ... yeah, he's been good to you. Anyone with eyes can see that. I'm happy for you, Claire."

"Thanks," I mumble, mixed emotions running through me:

shocked that he is being so mature about this; happy that he seems happy, content, compliant; sad because I'm still sad at recent events; scared for the same reasons; and again, shocked by how much has changed.

He looks over and sees the boxes and the letters scattered around. Then he looks back at me, somehow inferring they are from my mom. "So, your mom, huh? Want to tell me what happened?"

I do. I tell him everything that has happened since he left. I tell him about moving to the city; how happy and excited I was, how everything was starting to settle down and become this content routine. Then I tell him about the past six weeks; how scared I have been, sad, hurt. I tell him everything, not realizing I needed someone who didn't live through it with me to know. It's cathartic.

When my tirade about the most recent and fearful part of all is said, I can't calm down. Troy gets up and pulls me in for a hug, telling me that things will get better. And I cling to him, ruining his beautiful uniform with my tears. Selfishly, I'm not sorry. I needed this so badly, and I didn't even realize.

At this moment, I am so thankful to have my best friend back. It's like how we were when we were kids. We hug, and I reminisce all the times he was there for me. All those times I got hurt, and he was my hero, making it all better, even kissing my boo-boos, though he thought girls were yucky. All those summers and after school playdates. All the hours we spent hanging out and keeping each other company. I missed my friend.

When I finally settle down, I apologize, and then promptly ask Troy to fill me in on him. And he tells me stories about his training, all the friends he made, where he is getting stationed. He already has Chelsea and Tori's place all set. He got them a three-bedroom apartment for times he wants to crash there, but he is going to live in the barracks for the most part. Chelsea is going to start school in January, just taking a few classes. She already has interviews for part-time work set up, and the base where he is stationed has daycare for their daughter.

I smile the whole time he talks, so happy for him, and even for Chelsea. It doesn't even sound like he is talking about the same girl.

Honestly, it doesn't seem like I am talking to the same guy. It's all surreal.

Then Troy leaves, asking if he can stop by tomorrow. I tell him yes and, as I close the door, I realize it's almost one o'clock in the morning and Noah isn't back yet. His set should have been over a couple of hours ago. Maybe he decided to stay at his parents? But that isn't his normal routine. He wouldn't leave me alone the night after my mom died, not after not leaving me alone for the past six weeks. Would he?

I try to call him, but it goes to voicemail, which isn't like him. He always answers my call. Where is he?

Troy comes back up to the door, and when I answer, thinking it's Noah and he lost or forgot his keys or something, I see Troy holding Noah's guitar case. Why would he have that?

Troy tells me he found it on the sidewalk, outside the building.

Frantic now, not knowing what to think, I thank Troy, practically slam the door on his face, and call Dare. She tells me the guys were breaking down the stage when she left, that Noah looked fine. He even told her he was coming right home to be with me after she divulged the boxes of my mom's stuff to him.

I don't know what to think. Why was he fine a couple of hours ago, and then disappeared from practically right outside my door …?

I look at the window behind the chair I was sitting on, and then I look at the couch. He couldn't have seen Troy here. And besides, he knows Troy isn't a threat, right? Oh, my God, what if he got mugged?

I don't know what to do, so I call Dare back. She tells me to wait until morning, and then call Noah's friends and his parents. Maybe Noah went somewhere with his friends, and his friends dropped his guitar off as a joke. Maybe he *is* staying with his parents.

I don't believe any of that. All I can think is that Noah heard everything I said to Troy and freaked out. He can't take dealing with me anymore. I became a burden to him. We are both so young, yet life threw us too much too fast, and he bailed. I know it.

~Noah~

237

Ever since finding out about her mom, Claire's been in a funk. She has no appetite, lost considerable weight on her already tiny frame, and is falling behind at school. I don't know how to get her out of this depression. She is slipping further away from me, and there is nothing I can do to bring her back.

Now I am rushing to get to her, but the damn taxi driver is moving slow as shit. It's too cold and my guitar case is too heavy to ride my bike, which has been in my parents' garage for a couple of weeks now.

When we finally get to Claire's building, I jump out of the car before handing over the cab fare and grabbing my guitar case and the lily I bought her. It's not much, but I hope it brings a little joy to her. Seeing her eyes light up, even for a second, gives me reassurance that she will be okay soon.

Turning away from the cab, I look up at the second-story window and freeze, my guitar and the flower dropping from my hand. My thoughts freeze, my stomach somersaults, my heart stops then starts pounding like it's trying to escape my chest. I feel like I'm going to be sick.

I stumble—I fucking stumble—backward and slip off the curve, landing on my ass. I'm going to be sick.

All that negativity, all those dark thoughts I have had since we arrived in the city, my fear … It's my worst nightmare, my biggest fear. I'm going to be sick.

Bent over the gutter, I hurl. My stomach clenches and relaxes then clenches again as everything I ate today comes up. Throat burning, vile taste. Even then, when there is nothing left, my stomach still seizes. Dry heaves, convulsing.

I can't believe it. I just can't believe it.

I look up again, and … Yep.

I continue to dry heave. My stomach hurts now. It doesn't only feel sick; it hurts.

My chest hurts. It's burning. I feel like I can't breathe.

I feel like my heart is being torn from my chest. It hurts. Goddamn, does it hurt. Burning, searing, ripping, fist clenching agony.

I bring my hand up to my chest where my heart is pounding. I feel like I need to hold it in, hold my heart's pieces back together. I need to press it back into my chest.

No other thoughts are hitting me yet. All I can think about is my body's responses, wondering if I am having heart failure, a stroke—something other than heart break.

I cough, and it hurts. I sniff, and it hurts.

Why? How? Since when? Thoughts are back online, and I want them gone!

Goddamn, motherfucker. Goddammit. Jesus!

No, dammit. Just ... no! Fuuuuucccckkkk!

I get off my hands and knees and stumble to a stand. I feel drunk. I'm dizzy, nauseous, and my head feels like it is floating above my body. Detached. My head's detached. My heart's detached. My limbs ...

I move my right arm and bring it up to my mouth, biting down on the soft leather of my jacket to stop myself from screaming while breathing deeply through my nose.

I can't look up again. I need to get in control of myself. I need to get out of here. I need to get far, far away. No, I need answers!

No! To hell with that shit. Seeing is believing, and I have seen enough. I don't need to deal with bullshit excuses. I don't need to subject myself to all this shit. I hate drama. Hate it.

To hell with this shit! No one should put up with it.

Just walk away. The end.

I pull out the sleeve of my shirt and wipe my nose off.

I'm not crying. Fuck that. It's the damn November cold. It's sensitive to my nose.

Claire ...

Heart pounding anew, thundering in my own ears. Lack of breath. Sucking in air, gasping.

No, dammit. Get ahold of yourself!

Deep breath in. Blow it out. Shake it off.

It doesn't work.

God damn you, Claire!

I bite down on my jacket again to stop the scream, forever marking my jacket.

I need to go. I need to just leave. I need to get as far away from

Claire Diane Sawyer as possible.

Chapter 21

It Will Get Easier

~Claire~

February 14, 2011
Noah,
I have not passed the angry stage, but I thought,
as today is Valentine's Day, I should write in
remembrance of happy times. Our first and last
Valentine's day: breakfast in bed, lilies, piano
playing at dinner, and dreams that that night would
be our night. Alas, you held out for months and
months later. I thank you for that.

Thank you for all those precious memories. I
have a lifetime of forever to look back on and to share
each beautiful memory when the time is right. I will
never forget our Valentine's Day.

I think I will hold on to my anger for a long time
to come. I can't move on to bargaining when I have
no idea why.

Why did you leave? Are you really the coward I
now think you are? I can't believe that. And I can't
move to depression because I am already there, have
been there since you never showed up that night, have
been there since before you never showed up.

How could you [...]
Claire

It's been three months since Noah disappeared. No sign of him
from anyone—*anyone*. Not his parents, nor Mark, Katy, and Kyle. Not

241

his friends, his bandmates. No one. Why? Is he in trouble? Did he run away from me? From us? Did he somehow get amnesia? I have no answers, just his beloved guitar and a crushed lily outside my door. But I do have a world of pain in my soul.

I know he left town. I called his parents the next day, and they said it looked like he quickly packed up his clothes, his backup guitar, and took his bike. His mom, Sarah, told me that his room was trashed. They didn't even hear him come in.

His band members are angry that he left them to fulfill shows with no lead man. Chris is especially livid since it left his family short a man at the auto repair shop. He has been by my place on a regular basis, making sure I'm okay, asking if there has been any word, holding vigilance, it seems. We both call and call Noah, until one day, his phone is disconnected. Last connection to him ... gone.

The heartache is nauseating. Most days, I get so sick at speculating what went wrong, why he would run, that I can't keep anything down. Headaches bombard me daily, increasing in intensity, debilitating me to the point I moan and writhe in bed, trying to run away from my own body. Sleep doesn't even ease the pain because the headaches don't allow me to sleep.

However, as people always say, time heals all wounds. That may be true in some aspects, but the pain from the hole I feel in my heart won't lessen. I haven't even taken a deep breath since the last time I saw him. And I don't think that is going to change any time soon.

You know what I don't get? I haven't cried. Not once. I used up so many tears for my mom that I don't have it in me to cry anymore. It's like I simply accepted that life sucks, and we were put on this earth to deal with it, bear it, find the moments of happiness and simply savor them, because life ... is pain.

And the more I think back on that, the more I realize that I felt that pain, the loneliness, the isolation all my life. I forgot about it the year I was with Noah ... up until Trevor Jameson came to my door. Now ... Now that my year of happiness, my year of perfection, my year that, looking back, feels like a forever yet forever ago is over, all those memories and feelings have come back.

Life is so very painful, but I am grasping the moments when I can laugh, smile, feel my heart lighten a bit. I hold them in my heart, savoring the feel of something other than pain.

With no more unanswered phones calls to Noah that leaves me to taking up my mom's medium of contact—writing letters upon letters to him. My mom poured her heart out in those letters to me, writing like it was more of a diary than to her daughter. I don't think she ever expected me to read them.

Now I write the same way, addressing the letters to Noah, but writing more for myself, fearing Noah will never read them. He will never want to. He will never look back and think of me. If he will, then he wouldn't have left in the first place. Regardless, if he does one day, then he will know my heartache. He will see a journey I went on without him.

I never thought Noah was a coward before. He was always ready to face any obstacle; get in the face of any adversary and fight back. Never would I have thought he would run from me. But he must have. There is no other explanation. It's too much of a coincidence that he would run the same day Troy came to visit. And now I must face what fate has thrown my way alone.

> *I hate you, you cowardly bastard. I hate that, when I need you the most, you're not here. All those dreams, all those promises, and you left, damn you! What am I supposed to do now?*

Well, I guess this is going to be another hate letter, then.

I bang my head several times on the kitchen counter before resting it there, taking several deep breaths to control my newfound anger. I don't know what to do. I want to escape my own skin.

I feel someone stroke down then up my back before strong hands knead my shoulders. "It will get easier, Claire. I promise you; it will get easier."

"When, Dare?" I ask with my head still resting on the kitchen counter. "Why did he leave?" It's the same question I ask everyone.

"I don't know, sweetie. But when I get my hands on him, I will rip his cock off, and then get the answer for you."

I laugh at the venom in her voice. Dare, my cheerleader, and the very best friend I have ever had … Well, besides Noah, who turned out not to be such a good friend after all. She has been such a rock for me.

"I want to rip his ... cock off myself," I admit timidly, not comfortable with the use of that word.

Dare starts to pull all my hair back and braid it. "That's my girl. But, since he's not here, we can burn his guitar and everything else you have of his. That's what you're supposed to do once you hit the anger stage."

I sigh, finally lifting my head up and staring at the words of my most recent letter to him. "I can't. I have to keep everything."

Now Dare sighs, hers more out of anger than my melancholy. "I know, I know." Braid done, she wraps a hair tie around the end. "It was just a thought ... and a wish."

"I wish, too."

A knock on the door interrupts our conversation.

I look at Dare in desperation, telling her, "Not today." I don't want anyone else giving me the pitying looks. I have had enough of that from everyone, even my own father.

"I'll tell them you're sleeping," she assures, patting my shoulder before turning toward the door.

I smile, feeling so grateful for my cheerleader. "Thanks, Dare."

She looks over her shoulder at me from the door, hand on the handle, and smiles. Then she cracks the door open and asks who it is.

Hm, so it's not someone we know. That makes me curious, and then I hear his voice.

I jump up from the chair and rush toward the door as Dare starts to tell him I'm sleeping. I grab the door and swing it open, finding not only Max, but Cyn, too.

Me and Cyn squeal and laugh, throwing ourselves into each other's arms. I am wearing the biggest smile on my face, and it feels so good. That bubble of happiness seeps into my chest, warming my heart and covering over the hole that Noah left behind. I know it's only temporary, that as soon as the adrenaline and surprise is over, the hole will appear again. For now, though, I savor the warmth, exhilarated that two people who mean so much to me are here.

"What are you doing here?" I ask as I release Cyn and move to hug Max, comforted by his large, protective frame.

I missed Max. The big teddy bear is a wise, wise man, and one of only few who I know will do anything for me. Just as I would do anything for him.

I guide them into the apartment and shut the door as Cyn says, "We told you we would visit. And, well, after ... you know ... we made it a priority. As soon as Max could get away, we left. Sorry it took so long." Cyn gives me that pitying smile I'm used to.

I ignore the smile and shrug with one shoulder. "I'm glad you guys finally made it." I beam another smile, not wanting them to see how much I still hurt, not wanting them to bring it up.

Think I'm happy and don't mention the bad, I silently tell them.

I introduce them to Dare, who has been at my side, smiling at us. Then we all sit around and talk. I ask them if they want to stay here, but they already checked into a hotel. I ask them what's been going on back home, and they fill me in, telling me about work, Cyn's new band, how Kyle comes by often. The boy has gone wild with tattoos, getting a new one almost every week. I ask about Sassy because I can't help myself, and they tell me she got married last week, which throws me off.

After a couple of hours of talking, Dare excuses herself. She has orchestra practice tonight in preparation for the spring recital, another something I was pushed into an understudy role.

I swear, my life is falling to the pits. With everything that hit me this school year, I am genuinely thinking about dropping the program for a while. Everyone thinks I should, including my program chair and school counselor. I can't put all the focus I need into my work. My grades are better, more than better; but rehearsals ... I'm not there. It's like my voice is gone. My concentration is shot.

When Dare leaves, Max gets up and makes some excuse about needing to run errands. I know this is a setup. He is leaving so Cyn and I can talk in private, which makes me fear they know something about Noah.

I look at her warily as I make my way back to the couch and curl up in the corner, pulling a throw blanket over me.

She maneuvers herself into the same position, then bluntly asks,

"How are you really doing?"

I sigh and close my eyes. Then I open them and ask outright, needing to get this over with, "Have you heard from him? Know something about him?"

Cyn immediately shakes her head, taking away my fear. "Not a word. Nothing." She clears her throat and sits up straight, indicating whatever she is about to say is important. "Max has been scouring databases, trying to get a hit on him. No traffic violations, no credit hits—"

My mouth drops open before I yell out, "He broke into his bank account?"

She scoots up the couch, making her way toward me, and grabs my cold hand. "Claire, Max is pissed. And confused. This is hitting him hard ... The way the two of you were, and with how this happened, it doesn't make sense. Plus, the man is really big on devotion and brotherhood." She rolls her eyes.

"Anyway, he's torn between foul play and ..." She doesn't finish, just shakes her head. "Either way, he's angry and wants answers—for you, for himself, for everyone involved. It doesn't make sense." That's what I have been thinking for months. "So, yes, he is using any means necessary to track Noah down. You want to know why, right?"

"Of course, but not at the risk of Max getting in trouble."

Cyn smiles. "Max is too good for that. He's using a detective he knows for that kind of information. They are old friends from college. Max does all his tats."

I sigh in relief. "Good grief. I thought he was some kind of hacker or something." Wouldn't surprise me.

"No," Cyn says. "The man is genius material, but networking genomes is easier for him. His friend lets him use the FBI database. Anyway, we want to ask you if you know how Noah is getting around. If you are aware of how he is paying for stuff."

I have no clue. Noah always had money, but I don't where it came from. I always assumed it was an allowance or savings or something. And he got a job with Chris when we moved here. Plus, he got measly pay for playing at bars and clubs around town.

When I tell her this, she says, "Claire, the morning after he disappeared, he withdrew ten thousand dollars from a bank across town." As I gasp in shock, not realizing he had that kind of money, she continues, "He's been gone for three months, so Max figures, if he's paying cash for everything, he will run out soon and make another withdraw. Max will be ready to drive to wherever that is and track him down. However, if you can tell his parents about this, we hope they may be able to freeze his account, forcing him to come back. Well, if it's not foul play. Which brings me to telling you that we don't think it was."

I hold my breath, waiting for the bomb I know she's been hesitating to drop. I can see her reluctance.

"Claire, Noah is sitting on a lot of money. It's not a fortune, but if he wants to, he can live off it for quite a while." She pulls out a slip of paper from her pocket and hands it to me. The dollar amount on it surprises me.

How did I not know this? Why didn't he tell me?

"If this was foul play, wouldn't the culprit have had him withdraw all the money?" Cyn asks rhetorically.

All I can do is stare at the figure; more evidence that Noah left of his own free will. More evidence that he did abandon me. Still, it's not evidence that he left because of me. It could still be because of something else. But what? He was fine at the show, and then came home before he disappeared. All my instincts tell me this is because of Troy. He saw something or heard something that made him run.

After Cyn leaves with plans to meet up in the morning for breakfast, I call Sarah, telling her what Max found. But I don't tell her about the plan to freeze his accounts. I'm not about to let him starve and be homeless. I adore him too much for that. I love him enough to accept that he left and let him go physically, but never emotionally. There is still too much between us to do that.

Before I even ask about where it came from, she tells me the money was his inheritance from her father, something she regrets releasing to him now since it gave him the means to disappear. But, like me, she can't deny him. I'm surprised she knew, knew that is what he is living on. I'm hurt she didn't tell me.

It doesn't change anything. Noah left, and I'm not about to force him to come back.

He needs time. He just needs time, I keep telling myself.

February 28, 2011

[...]

Do you realize how worried your parents are? Yeah, I know. It's a surprise to me, too. But there it is. Your parents have been really supportive, actually.

I'm being kicked out of school. Well, kind of. Earlier today, I had a meeting with my counselor, when she "strongly recommend I take a break [...]" I was planning on it, anyway.

I lost my voice. I have no concentration. Therefore, I have until the end of the semester, and then I will be home. Not the place I want to be, especially under these circumstances.

Like I said earlier, your parents are being supportive. Your mom is retiring early and opened their home to me. But I can't do that. I can't be anywhere where there are reminds of you. See? Still in the angry stage. And I am depressed ... all the time.

[...]

248

Chapter 22

Apologies from the Past

~Claire~

May 19, 2011
School is over. I don't know how I got through this year—the hardest year of my life. As sad as I am to leave, I am happier to go. Too many memories, in the apartment, at local places we used to visit, the people who stop by less frequently now. Not that going home is going to be much better.

I had to close my eyes and take a deep breath at that thought.

I won't be there long, though. And soon I will have new memories to make there [...] And Katy and Abby are so excited. I'm glad they will be there. I miss them so much.

So, this will be my last letter from New York. Good-bye all my hopes and dreams, and the future that should have been. (Morose, huh?) It's time to move on to the next step of adulthood—accepting. This is life with all its good and bad. And sometimes there is good with the bad. I'm happy with the good. The bad is hard, but rewarding in the end.

[...]

In other news, Dad is here, talking to Trevor about selling my mom's condo. We're shipping her furniture and personal belongings home to put away in storage until I can sort through it. I haven't had time this year to do it. Too much going on. Dare is going to continue to stay at the condo. I talked her into it. Plus, we found another roommate for her, and her boyfriend is moving in. I'm glad I'm not leaving her alone. She has come to mean a lot to me. Of course, she can't wait to take over my room. They promised to visit this summer [...]. I'm glad she's been such a good friend to me.

The spring recital was amazing. I was an understudy, but I spent most of the time with the composer. That was an avenue I never considered, and I am thankful for the opportunity to learn from him. I know how to read music; I know how to play the piano; but I didn't know how to compose. I can't say I can now do that, but I'm starting, learning more about that aspect because I have an idea that's never been done before. That's my new focus for now while I wait for my voice to come back.

You have been gone for six months now. I wish I knew if you were okay. Even alive. Your parents, your friends, me—we are worried about you. I feel like I need to keep telling you that. We want to know that you are safe and not lying in a ditch somewhere. Where are you, Noah?

I will keep writing to you, knowing that if you are alive, you have to surface sometime, and then your parents or aunt Katy will forward my letters to you.

[...]
I need to end this now. Dad came back.
Claire
P.S. Oh, and Angel says a hi meow. She's sprawled out on the table now, smacking the pen around whenever it comes near her.

It has now been almost a year since Noah left, and I still write him letters a few times a month. The pain from missing him is fading, but there are times when I feel it so poignantly that I simply shatter.

No, there is nothing simple about it. I literally break down, asking myself all the whys and what ifs. I go from missing him so deeply that my very soul seems to rip in half to hating him so much I feel fire running through my veins. It's not pretty.

The only evidence he is still alive is another withdraw made in the southeast back in June. By the time Max got there, there was no sign of him. He hit up all the motels in town; bars, in case he is playing—everywhere. No one recognized him. He must have been passing through.

Dad even hired a private detective to track him down, but it's like Noah disappeared off the face of the planet.

On top of … well, everything, Max passed away. He had a genetic heart disease, which explains his study in genetics. He was riding his motorcycle and … his heart simply gave out.

Cyn is beyond beside herself. She is both grieving and mad at him. She can't understand how he never told her what he was dealing with. They apparently fought a lot about marriage and children, Max telling her he couldn't commit to those two things. Now we know why. We think he knew his time was near, and he didn't want to pass his disorder down to their children. So much grieving.

With all this sadness surrounding me, I am visiting Chelsea, Troy, and baby Tori right now before heading out of the country. There comes a point in everyone's life when they want to run away. They don't always follow through, but they want it. Well, I am following through. Except, unlike most everyone else, I have the backing of all the people who matter to me.

My cat is coming with me when I move, and so is Noah's guitar. I need to keep his reminders with me, even though I hate to. But Angel is like my baby, and Noah's guitar … well, someone else may want that one day.

Tori is fifteen months old and cute as a button. She is dressed up in a cute sailor outfit, her blonde hair in little pigtails, and she has a ruffled romper that is too adorable for words. The child is simply precious.

Chelsea is doing a great job as a mommy. I can't help taking note of all the changes in her. However, I'm still wary on why she wanted to see me. We have been dancing around each other for two days now, making small talk. It's been more than awkward.

"No, no, Victoria, you can't put that in your mouth." Chelsea sighs as she takes the phone from Tori and wipes off the drool. Tori immediately tears up. "Oh, God," Chelsea whines. "Karma is kicking me in the butt." She picks up her daughter and sits her in her lap so they are facing each other. "Unless you want Karma to bite you in the booty one day, I suggest you cut that out right now. You can't have everything you want; trust me. Take a lesson from your mama."

The little girl finally giggles at the tone her mother uses, and then reaches out and grabs her hair. "Air."

"Yes, baby, that's Mama's hair. Ouch." She opens Tori's hand to release her hair then gives a toy mirror to her. "Play with this, sweetie," she says as she puts her on her feet, back on the floor.

The little girl teeters over to her toy box, then plops down on her butt to make faces at herself in the mirror. I giggle. It seems like such a Chelsea thing to do.

I can't believe Chelsea is a mommy, and such a good one. I hate thinking that, but knowing her all my life, I am amazed at how much she has turned around. She is no longer the mean girl. She is content, happy, and mature.

I shake my head in bewilderment every time I think how much having a baby can change people. Both her and Troy are better people, grounded. Not once have I seen their old selves. In fact, I sometimes feel like I am with strangers.

"So, when are you heading overseas?" Chelsea finally turns her attention to me, still wearing her mommy smile that transforms her whole face.

We are sitting on the couch together, practically at opposite ends, back to the small talk.

"Oh, four weeks." I shake my head, thinking about all the things I need to do before we leave. "We got delayed ... so we aren't leaving until the first week in November now."

"And Italy ...?" There is a glint of the old Chelsea in her eye. It makes me nervous. Is this when she starts in on the last conversation we had, accusing me of stealing all the attention away from her?

"Yeah ..." I clear my throat. "Signora Gelardi is moving back to her family home. We'll be living with her. My dad is beside himself." That's an understatement. Dad put his foot down at first, until I reminded him that I was an adult now, a few months' shy of twenty.

Once I explained to Dad that I wouldn't let the circumstances of last year deter me from my dream, he finally gave in and accepted that I needed to do what was best for me. And he adamantly agreed that leaving the country was the best thing to separate my past from my future.

I think my dad is as heartbroken about Noah's disappearance as I am. Dad's faith in Noah is broken, and I don't think, if Noah ever does turn up, Dad will ever forgive him. Some things you simply can't salvage.

"I'm so jealous," Chelsea admits, her eyes straying to Tori. "But I understand wanting to do what's best with what life hands you."

That's an understatement. So much in my life has changed since last year. With my mom dying, Noah leaving, school career ending, not to mention everything else, I realized that I need a major change in my life. Therefore, I took up Signora Gelardi's offer to move to Italy and take up work in her old opera house.

I'm working myself up to the idea. I hate leaving my dad and everyone, especially Cyn now, but I have responsibilities, and working is one of them. I can't rely on people anymore. I did too much of that before.

I hid behind people, always needing someone to rely on. As a kid, it was my dad. Then Troy. Then Noah. When Noah left, Dare babied me, and then back to Daddy. Now I need to step up and be a real woman. I need to be the one someone can depend on.

I notice Chelsea's eyes return to mine and a glint of excitement shines through them before she announces, "Troy and I are engaged!"

I genuinely smile, admittedly not the least bit shocked since they have been sharing a room while I have been here. Though, last I heard, they decided to do this co-parenting thing separate, and Troy said they both agreed they weren't meant to be. He never mentioned starting a romantic relationship with Chelsea. He's been home from a tour overseas for four months now.

Happy for them and thinking this must be why she wanted to see me, I tell her, "That's great! Troy can never stop talking about you and Tori. He seems more peaceful now."

"Yeah, tell me about it." Chelsea rolls her eyes. "I think the Marines burned out all that extra testosterone in him." She giggles. "And the sex helps."

I blush, which makes Chelsea laugh, which in turn makes Tori giggle and run over to her mama.

Chelsea has never been one to hold back, using any ammunition to embarrass me. I guess some things never change, despite how much the people themselves have.

"You are such a prude," she says, and I can't tell if she's saying it as a tease or not.

She picks Tori up and blows a raspberry on her belly before setting her back down again. Then, still watching her daughter, she tells me, "I want to apologize for the way I treated you for all those years." I start to object, not wanting to rehash old tortures, but she cuts me off. "Claire," she sighs out, "I was a major bitch. I get that now. Then ... not so much. I didn't care if I hurt you. I *wanted* to hurt you. I blamed you for everything wrong in my life. Even my boyfriend being gay." She scoffs at that. "That's how egotistical I was. But none of it was your fault. You weren't even a part of my world. I was so jealous of your self-confidence—"

"I wasn't that confident," I mumble.

"—your talent, your beauty, how you didn't seem to need popularity or a boyfriend to feel complete. You didn't seem to need anything, whereas I thought I had to have it all. Yet, that never worked.

"I thought that, if I hurt and embarrassed you, you wouldn't walk around looking like Little Miss Perfect. I thought guys would stop staring at you ... I would stop wanting to *be* you." She sniffs and wipes away a stray tear. "I was wrong, and I am sorry." She finally looks me in the eye. "I'm sorry, Claire."

She lets out a weak laugh and wipes her nose with the back of her hand. "Looking back, I hate myself for the way I treated you. Man, I was pathetic." I again try to interrupt her, not liking the self-loathing talk, and again she talks over me. "I was. And if it wasn't for Tori ...

Well, let's be real. I probably would have ended up in the same circumstances I did. And that's okay." She smiles with real warmth in her eyes. "I regret how I treated you, but I can't regret where that led me.

"Now I feel like it's my chance to make it all up to you, and I will. If you ever need anything, call. I want to try to be friends. I can't promise anything, only that I can try." She shakes her head adamantly, saying, "I don't want to go back to being that person. I want to be someone people can look up to."

I smile back at her in wonderment, touched by her honesty, until she throws me off by asking, "So, what was Noah like in bed?"

"Chelsea!" I gasp then laugh at how she broke the seriousness of the moment. She laughs with me as I sputter out, "I-I …" I can't talk about that.

Just the mention of Noah has me holding my breath. I don't want to relive my year with Noah. I try not to think about him around other people at all. It puts me in panic mode. I hate and love him so much it physically hurts, still, after almost a year. Time does not heal all wounds.

"Come … on," she goads, trying to wipe off her makeup smeared by tears. "We're both adults now. Shit, this is what all the girls talked about in high school! There's nothing to be ashamed of when you know *everyone* does it."

True, but …

I get up to get her a tissue. "When are you and Troy getting marri—"

"No, uh-uh, you are not changing the subject. And it's at Christmas. Now spill it." She looks a little too eager, making me remember back to when she flirted with Noah, trying to sit on his lap in the cafeteria, the party I heard about where she slept with Kyle since Noah bailed.

I'm afraid telling her anything about Noah will come back to bite me later. I know she apologized and spilled her guts to me, but what if she uses something I say to attack me later?

Then, when I look around the room, at her, Tori, thinking about how she said she's marrying Troy, how Noah is never coming back, I decide that nothing I say can be used to hurt me anymore. Noah might as well be dead. We will never see him again.

I sit back down beside her, handing her a couple of tissues and baby wipes, before I look over at her to gauge her expression when I admit, "He held out until prom night."

"Are you kidding me!" she screeches. She starts laughing hysterically, and I nod, turning my attention to a stuffed bunny on the floor, a small smile on my lips.

"But I remember that motorcycle incident—" She cuts herself off at the look I shoot her.

"He did," I continue. "There were so many times I thought we would ... do it, but he held out. He said he wanted to prove he wanted something more, something forever with me."

Chelsea scoffs. "Yeah, well, look how that turned out. Asshole." She huffs again. "I admit, I was totally jealous. Noah is gorgeous, the total package. Any girl would give her right breast to be with him, but to do what he did ..." She shakes her head, looking down.

"Yeah," I sigh. "I never saw it coming."

"Right?" Chelsea relaxes back into the sofa. "Continue," she says like the queen bee she used to be, and I laugh a little at that.

"Um ..." I try to get my thoughts back to that first night. "So, prom night. We skipped; went right to a hotel room. He took his time while I was feverish. I don't think I was ever nervous," I muse. "I mean, I was, but it was Noah. He had already made me feel worshipped for months, so I had little to no insecurities. I can't say the same now."

"It will get better," Chelsea assures, placing her hand on mine.

I tear up at her thoughtfulness and give her a tight smile.

"Anyway, I always looked for opportunities after that." I smile at the memories, especially thinking about all the times we made love in the back of Katy's truck.

God, people are right when they say the high school years are the best. My senior year made up for the other three years I can barely recall. So many memories fit into one perfect year.

Chelsea gives me a devilish grin. "Want to hear about sex with Troy?"

"Not really," I squeak out, making Chelsea laugh again.

"I won't talk about it. All I will say is that you missed out on a massive—"

I slam my hand none too gently against her mouth in my eagerness to shut her up, and she bursts out laughing again.

I remove my hand and sit back, mumbling out, "Noah's was pretty impressive," which makes her laugh even more.

"I can imagine." She sighs then says, "Things happen for a reason. I needed to have a baby to grow up. Having Tori made Troy grow up, too. He's so wonderful now. Such a good father." She shakes her head. "Mama brain. Back on track. The point is, you didn't need anything to make you grow up, but maybe you need Noah gone to learn how to stand up for yourself, be by yourself. You know?"

It's like she read my mind.

Neither Chelsea or Troy mentioned Noah for the rest of the visit. Troy took me to the beach one day where we walked up and down the shoreline for a few hours, reminiscing about the past, laughing and simply enjoying our time together. It felt like old time.

Chelsea took me shopping a lot, insisting Italy didn't have this or that so I had to get it now. That trip was the opposite of the peaceful beach trip, wrangling around baby stuff, strollers, shopping bags. I don't enjoy going out with a baby.

Overall, it was a nice good-bye to the States. I got to patch things up with Chelsea, have Troy back in my life, and end that chapter of my life, knowing I don't have to worry about them anymore. The only one I will worry over is my dad, but him and Noah's family have grown close. I know Mark and Katy will look after my dad. I wish he didn't live alone. That's the part that hurts the worst.

Chapter 23

Having No One

~Claire~

Merry Christmas, Noah.

[...] Dad flew in for Christmas and brought me a surprise. Kyle! It was so good to see him. He's doing well in school. You should see the sleeves on his arms. The guy looks like a work of art. All Max's studio art, of course, in commemoration of him. Still no girlfriend, but he and Signora Gelardi's granddaughter, Giuliana, were eyeing each other over dinner tonight, much to Signora Gelardi's disappointment. It was funny to watch all the tension at the table.

And I had a date tonight. I hate to admit that it's the first one since you left, but it is what it is. I want to say it's because I've been too busy, but I could never lie to you. And maybe I'm hoping that, by telling you, you will rush in like a knight in shining armor and rescue me, and then we can live happily ever after. But fairy tales aren't real.

His name is Jesse. He's British, which I can't help loving his accent. And he works with me. The date went well, just a walk along the river and stopping to hear the Christmas bells from the churches. I loved that part. Magical. He is the composer's intern, and I haven't made company yet at the opera house, so we weren't needed at work tonight. I kind of like not having responsibilities like that.

You should be happy to hear that while the date went well, and he did kiss me at the end of it, I couldn't help hurrying to my room to write to you ...

March 14, 2012
When are you going to show up? When are you going to put us out of our misery and let us know if you are alive or dead? I am so conflicted right now and could use my best friend: you. Despite everything, you are still my best friend. I will always, always love you ...
It's more than that ...
I slept with Jesse last night, and now I feel so damn guilty, and I have no reason to be. No. Reason! You *left* me. You *are probably sleeping with hundreds of women and not* me. *So why do I feel like I am cheating on you? Why can I not feel any of the passion I felt with you with him? What makes you so damn special!*

May 1, 2012
Happy 21ˢᵗ Birthday, Noah!
How does it feel to be able to drink legally? Not that you were ever much of a drinker before, but, who knows? Times change, right? People change. Like me. I love wine now. How can you live in Italy and not appreciate it?
I wish you all the happiness in the world for your birthday. Be safe.
Loves,
Claire

October 2, 2012
[...] Jesse proposed, but I couldn't go through with it. I love him, but I'm not in love with him. His

gesture was so romantic, too. He got down on his knee in the middle of the road and asked in front of a crowd of people, and all I could do was shake my head, holding back tears of embarrassment and sorrow that I couldn't say yes. I couldn't. Something held me back. I don't know ...

After the boos, which Jesse came to my defense and told everyone we had just started dating, lying to save me, he took me into a café where we had a serious conversation. He made me keep the ring, saying when I was ready to just wear it, but I don't know if that will ever be possible. I told him that, yet the man is stubborn and now things are back to how they were before the proposal.

The ring sits on my desk, in front of me right now. It's beautiful, exactly something I would pick for myself. But how can I put on an engagement ring when I still wear the pendant you gave me? [...] I can't. I simply cannot.

September 27, 2012. Remember that date as the day another man asked me to marry him. A man worthy, yet I am not. How can I be true to him when you are still in my heart? [...]

Claire

P.S. Is it a sign that Angel knocked the ring off my desk and now I can't find it?

November 22, 2012
Happy Thanksgiving!

Time is slipping by. The opera is mid-season, and we've had a great year. Everyone is saying that the numbers are double from previous years, and I got moved up to lead! I can't believe it! I want to throw up whenever I'm on stage, but I am LEAD!

The downfall is that I don't have a lot of fans in the company. Being the newest and youngest member,

260

not too many lifers are happy. However, I commit to being thoughtful to all and hope for the best. Kill them with kindness, right? It's working for the most part. And it helps that Jesse has been with the company for years and is supportive. [...] It will get better. I know it.

And I have been interviewed by newspapers and magazines from all over the world! Do you know how nerve-racking that is? Signora Gelardi has a friend who works in PR who has been teaching me what to say. It's all so exciting yet nauseating at the same time. I'm also afraid to mess up, and I never have "me time" anymore.

In fact, I must go on stage in half an hour.

March 3, 2013
We finished the season last night. It was the best one in over a decade. I'm on such a high right now! I'm literally shaking just writing this. I smiled brighter than I have in years. My face literally hurts from the smiling. I can't believe I went from dropping out of the Manhattan School of Music to this! I don't care if I ever get to sing on a bigger stage; I am too happy here. I wish my dad was closer. Your family, too.

Before I forget; my dad started seeing someone. He hasn't told me anything, but Katy saw him on a date a few weeks back. I keep forgetting to mention it. I am so happy for him. I hope she's nice, cares for him. I don't want him to be alone anymore.

July 25, 2013
Signora Gelardi passed away. I know I mentioned it before, but she's been sick for a long time now. She kept fading away, leaving the house less and less, leaving her chair less and less, yelling

at everyone less and less. Giuliana found her. [...]
That was over a month ago.

I couldn't stay in her family's home anymore, so
I am renting my own place now. We were never
supposed stay there forever. Just too busy to move.
Now I feel like I don't belong. Signora Gelardi's son
insisted we stay, but I can't. So, once again I feel like
I'm running away from ghosts.

Her service was lovely. She would have liked it.
So many people showed up. Famous ones, too. Yeah,
Signora Gelardi would have been very pleased. God,
I miss her.

Dad flew in for it and stayed a week. I can't tell
you how good it was to see him. It's been since
Christmas. You know Dad, he can never get away
from work.

I did get the details on his love life. He has been
dating, but there hasn't been a woman who appeals
to him. He's enjoying the dating scene. In fact, he's
gone on quite a few dates and has even brought some
of them to those fancy dinners he used to drag me to.
He seems happy, which makes me happy. At least
there is some good news in this letter.

Wishing you were here.

December 15, 2013
Kyle is staying with us for the rest of the month.
Him and Giuliana are pretty close now. I've accepted
the fact that he doesn't come here to see us anymore,
just Giuliana. He's staying with me this time, though.
No more crashing at the Gelardi's house. Giuliana is
at my place most of the time, anyway ...

I have been with the Italian Opera House for over two years now,
which has been such a great fit for me. Years of singing Italian meant
mastering the language in no time. I feel like a native, conversing with

the best of them. And the food, the culture, the history, it makes living here a dream. I feel like I made the best decision when I took up Signora Gelardi's offer to move here.

She was back to being my tutor, never going soft on me, something I admire and am grateful for. I don't want anyone being gentle with me. I want the criticism. I want the hard hand and hard words. I would take a whipping if it meant I became a stronger person. And I do feel stronger every day, musically and as a person. I am finally able to stand by myself, never behind someone. Chelsea was right; it was a good thing Noah walked away.

However, now Signora Gelardi is dead. It's been six months, and I am still so heartbroken. Both my mother and the woman who was a mother to me are dead. I can't get over it.

After sitting back and playing understudy for a year, all my hard work and Signora Gelardi's grueling tutoring paid off. I am in my second year of being the lead, singing several nights a week, working several different operas in one year. It's above and beyond rewarding, and time consuming. So time consuming. Signora Gelardi made my dreams come true.

Then there is Jesse Page to contend with. Jesse is the opposite of Noah in every way. Physically, he is auburn-haired, green eyes, tall, and thin yet muscled. He comes from an old English family, aristocrats, and has manners imbedded in him. He is sweet, but a tad spoiled. We met as soon as I moved here and slowly started a relationship while working together on a project I started back in college.

When he proposed to me, I wanted to throw up. While we were in a relationship, a physical one at that, I didn't think I was giving him the I'm-serious-about-you vibes. We never talked about where we wanted to go. We never even said how we felt about each other. Therefore, him proposing completely blindsided me. I'm not there yet. And I don't think I will ever be there with Jesse.

He is great, takes care of me, we work well together, but marriage? I'm only twenty-one—was twenty when he proposed—I don't want to think of marriage right now. I have a career to focus on, responsibilities. I can't make that kind of a decision, especially with someone I know I can't live with. There is too much stacked against him in my mind.

While having sex with Jesse, I realized something. Sex can be good with him, but it's not great, because it's not with Noah. Sex with someone you don't love isn't the all-consuming, powerful, encompassing passion you read about in books unless it's with the one you feel all consuming, powerful, encompassing love with. I never understood that before. Noah was my first, so I thought sex was always that good. But it's not. The sex you read about in books is between two people who have the love me and Noah had.

It's now going on thirty-eight months of no word or sign of Noah. I think the unspoken concession is that he is dead. I don't believe it, though. Not Noah. He is out there somewhere. I don't know what he is doing, but he is out there.

Everyone stopped looking for him once Max's lead went cold. I don't even mention him anymore. It's been over three years. I'm supposed to be over it by now, forgotten about him. That's what everyone wants for me. But I haven't.

My heart still aches for him, though I will never admit that out loud. No one needs to know how weak I still am over that man. Or, well, the dream of him. How I wake up crying into my pillow after dreams of all we lost. How I think how different life would be if we were still together.

One word, Noah. Just one word and maybe this pain will go away.

I still religiously write to him. Sometimes I won't write for a couple of weeks, sometimes I write a few times a week. That's my only link to him. It feels robotic yet therapeutic to write to him.

The memory of him is slipping away, and my feelings are changing, like he is only a dream I chase around, but now the dream is fading and reality has set in. I look back all the time, reliving our year that felt like a forever in my mind. So many memories ... One year in my twenty-one years of life, but God, it seems like a lifetime. Remembering the way his eyes lit up on his birthday when he saw I had a present for him; the longing stares in our senior year classroom, waiting to get out of school and just be the two of us; the way his mouth quirked up on one side on the rare occasions he told a joke; the laughter that lit up his whole face when my laughing was addicting and he would catch it; the heat in his eyes when we made love …

God, I miss him. I miss the idea of him. I miss all the times we would fall asleep in each other's arms, entwined, his leg between mine, mine between his, his arm as my pillow, one resting on my hip, my hand over his heart, feeling each thump, while my other arm fell asleep beneath me. Waking up with him on me, the opposite of how we fell asleep, his face buried in my neck, his hand cupping my breast, my arms wrapped around his back, our legs still entwined. Always entwined.

I miss the whispering conversations whenever someone was around, lost in each other and our talks of life—past, present, future—our dreams, memories, daily events, likes and dislikes, movies, TV, books, music, and so much more. We talked about everything, never afraid to share anything with one another.

I miss our adventures. Our walks in the woods, camping, swimming in lakes, splashing through creeks, teaching Noah how to fish, riding his bike, sitting in Aunt Katy's truck and watching the clouds pass by, staring at the sun. God, those days were so innocent.

Then New York. Noah taking me everywhere, sometimes more than once, showing me his old haunts; watching him perform, tinges of jealousy at the rabid girls wanting his attention, the beautiful satisfaction and glee when he came straight to me every time, no one else in his eyes, no one else getting a second glance. I could breathe more freely after that, never noticing I held my breath every time he finished a set and made his way off the stage and through the crowd … to me. I smile now, thinking about the adoring look in his eyes.

At this point, I'm afraid of him returning. So much has changed. I have changed. Noah must have changed. What if, if he does come back, we will never get to that place we were before? I know we can't, so I don't know why I still hope. Well, I do know why. Still, it will all be different, and that thought scares me in ways that nothing in my life scared me before.

"Earth to Claire."

I look up to see Jesse waving his hand in my face. I haven't heard a word he said since he came in, distracted with trying to finish up dinner and picking up around the house. I was aware of him following me around, his energy high, but I am too distracted.

Working, domesticating, and trying to sustain a relationship is getting to be too much. I can't give up the first two, which means the third needs to end. However, I don't know how to do this. Jesse is great, but he isn't for me. How do I tell him that without hurting him? I can't cut him out of my life completely. I work with him. He's become a part of my little family.

This is so hard.

I toss a bunch of things in a designated bin in the living room before rushing back to the kitchen to check the casserole, Jesse still following me.

"Have you heard anything I said?" he asks with this excited exasperation in his voice that makes me finally look at him.

I close the oven then lean back against the cabinets, giving him my undivided attention. He looks more excited than I have ever seen him; a wide smile on his face, his eyes animated. What did I miss?

I place my hands behind me, gripping the edge of the counter. "I must have zoned out. What did you say?"

He mistakes my actual confusion for shock, thinking whatever news he gave me has befuddled me. I can tell by the way his smile grows, by the way he reaches out and holds my biceps like he needs to support me.

"I said," he says slowly, "the Metropolis Opera House wants to buy our idea—your idea," he quickly corrects himself, "and they want you to lead the auditions. They want you to produce the opera. They want you to market and promote the idea. They want you, Claire." He laughs then, joy bursting out of him. "The largest, most famous opera house in the world wants us!"

He has my complete and undivided attention now.

I am shocked stupid, confused. How did they hear about my idea? How are they aware of—

"What did you do?" I accuse, all the pieces fitting together.

We have been working on a new opera together for the past two years. It's an idea I came up with in college for a class. I started writing

266

the music myself during my free time, using the piano, something I dove into after Noah left. I remember once having a conversation about it with him that always stuck with me.

"*I bet you're being modest.*"

"*No, really. I can't even play by memorization. I have to read the music. And songs that should be fast are slow because I don't have the dexterity to make my hands do two separate things at once.*"

"*So, you can't pat your head and rub your tummy?*"

Ever since that conversation, and after seeing Noah's relationship with his guitar, I always wanted to expand my music and learn more. The piano was my goal, and I am doing great. Then Jesse stepped in and took over the composition while I worked on scenes and lyrics.

The focus of the opera is to get kids involved in the art. My sales pitch is, if we can bring in the kids, then we can bring in the parents, expanding the range of audience. Right now, and for a long time now, only a certain clientele came to the opera, mostly a populace of fifty years and older. Getting kids interested builds our viewers and will put opera back in the public's eye.

Therefore, our opera is bringing fairy tales back to life. And I'm not talking about the princess type of fairy tales portrayed on television. I worked with the original ones that everyone has forgotten. Sarah and Anthony helped a lot with that. They introduced me to stories from different cultures they came across over the years. Old stories that you can only find in the depths of history. Every scene is based off a different story. There are so many, we can write and compose an entire series, something we have already started. We have three so far, but the goal is ten. That's how many I have outlined.

We agreed to wait until we were done with all ten before discussing what we would do with them, but now I realize that Jesse didn't go home to visit his parents two months ago. He didn't leave this past weekend to visit his sister in France, either. He went to New York. He took my idea to sell it.

I feel downright betrayed. Not only did he sell my idea, he kept it from me. Lied to me. Why? Because he knew I would be upset. This is my baby, and he took it and ran with it without talking to me.

Before he can say a word, I turn off the oven and walk away, pain shooting throughout my head.

"How can you be upset with this?" Jesse accuses as he follows me into the bathroom where I fill a glass with water to down the little pill I desperately need right now.

I swallow the pill then sigh, trying to calm down. "How can I not? Jesse, you went behind my back. It's not even ready—"

"It's ready enough," he practically whines, following me to the laundry room where I take a load of towels out of the drier. Angel curls around my leg before she heads toward her food. "You have all the scenes laid out, lyrics done. Now other people can finish the rest. You don't have to worry about this in your free time anymore. It's sold!"

His last words freeze me in my tracks.

"It's what?" I put my hands up like I'm telling him to back off. "You said, they *want* us. They *want* our idea." I pause, at a loss of words. "Now you're saying it's sold? You sold it!"

Jesse doesn't have much going for him right now, but at least he looks sheepish. Guess he didn't mean for that to come out of his mouth.

"Yeah," he says quietly, looking intently into my eyes, that spoiled, selfish side coming out, daring me to tell him no. "I closed the deal this weekend; negotiated to finish the season with our company. We are due in New York by April."

"You son of a bitch." I'm seething, so angry at him. Never has he pulled something like this.

Greed. That's what this is. He is tired of being an intern, and I get that. But forcing me back to that city ... He has no idea what he has done to me.

"Claire ..." He deflates. Good. I hope he realizes how much he messed up. "This is going to be such a great thing. Why aren't you happy? Don't you want to go home? Be closer to your dad, your friends? What is this about?"

For starters, you haven't even apologized, I want to say. Instead, I tell him, "I don't want to be in that city. I like it here. We're happy here." This is my life, my idea, I can be as stubborn as I want.

Jesse gets this inquisitive look in his eyes before he asks, "Is this about—"

268

"Partly," I admit, knowing what he was about to ask. He asks it all the time, whenever I get in one of my moods, whenever the past catches up to me. "Mostly it's that this is home for me now. We're happy here."

Giving up on getting laundry done since this conversation has wiped me of all energy, I make my way back to the living room where I sink onto the couch.

Jesse is still following, still trying to argue his case, talking about the paperwork I need to sign, the apartment I still have that we can stay in. On and on and on, and no apology yet. I can't listen to him.

"Jesse," I sigh, turning toward him where he sits next to me. "I can't do this with you anymore. What you did ... I ... I have no words. You broke my trust." He tries to cut me off, but I talk over him. "What's done is done. I'll go with you to New York. I will read over the paperwork. I will even move there and do what needs to be done." Not like I have much a choice since he already sold it, and backing out now, just to turn around in a few years and try then won't promise anything. They will more than likely shut me down for shutting them down now.

"You're right; this is my dream, and thank you for making it happen, even prematurely. But ..." God, why is this so hard? "You're not living with us. I don't want to continue a relationship with you. I'm sorry."

I say sorry, but I don't feel sorry. I'm not sorry for ending it. Hurting him, yes. Now, though, I can't feel it. He went too far with this. And it was a long time coming. Relief is all I feel.

He gave me the out I needed.

~Noah~

I am losing my shit. Three years without seeing Claire, and after the first six months, I wanted to turn around, beg her to take me back, apologize until my throat bled, and grovel and worship at her feet. I am the biggest asshole. The stupidest, gutless, most selfish son of a bitch.

When I saw Claire and Troy hugging in that window, I felt

betrayed. At the time, I thought she needed a night to be alone with her mother's things. Then I saw Troy, and the only thought in my head was she lied to me about coming to my show so she could hide the fact she was with him.

After months of stewing, running from my nightmares of Claire by going back to my old ways, doing things I can't even admit to myself, I realized how wrong I was. Claire wouldn't lie to me. Troy being there was a coincidence. He probably surprised her as much as he did me. Their embrace wasn't romantic. It was comfort. Claire was grieving, and her friend was there to console her. I'm the biggest idiot in the world.

I took advantage of the misunderstanding. I let my fear control me. I threw away what Chris told me, about how Claire and I balance each other out, how we are perfect together, how I needed to accept it as it is and not think the whys or hows. I twisted his words around until all I could see was that I wasn't right for her. Then I proved it by taking off, screwing around, drowning in my selfishness.

I drove and drove for months, never staying in one place for more than a few weeks. I got solo gigs set up wherever I went, sometimes even playing street corners. Then, six months after I left, I cashed out the rest of my money and headed west, all the way west, as far from temptation as I could get.

Once there, I straightened myself out. I started school, not that I knew what I wanted to do. I wanted to be better, not accept the easy life. I also continued performing solo under a different name and got a job on campus to help pay for tuition.

For the next two years, my world revolved around school. Associate's in General Education was out of the way, and I was on to my Bachelors. No parties. No drinking. No drugs. No girls.

Then, this past summer, my world changed again. I was playing at a spot I frequented, a small bar right off campus, when a man in a business suit came right up, shook my hand, and introduced himself as a representative to the biggest music label in the business. Blown away is an understatement.

Turns out that the guy had followed me for years after hearing me months after I moved out here. He found out my schedule, showed up to multiple shows, took note of all my songs, and invited some executives to listen to me play. One set and they told him to bring me on.

Here's the kicker. I didn't want to be in a band anymore. I played for me these days. The extra money didn't hurt, but I didn't want to compete in an ever-changing business. Therefore, we settled for songwriting.

Karma never felt more real. I can't help touching the bracelet at that thought.

I signed a contract, went into their gigantic, awe-inspiring building, into one of their dream studios, and recorded every one of my songs, even the ones from back in high school. In weeks, I was receiving contracts, setting up royalty payments from artists who couldn't get enough of my stuff. All those songs I wrote about Claire, our relationship, our breakup, missing her, how I feel about her, everyone got that shit and wanted to sing about it themselves.

I was so happy I wanted to call Claire, have her share in my joy, my success. I picked up the phone to do that, just to get slammed back to reality that we weren't like that anymore. I didn't even know where she was, what she was doing. I didn't know anything about her anymore, if she even had the same number.

I couldn't call anyone. I had isolated myself from my family and friends for so long that I was afraid they didn't even want to hear from me anymore. I was all alone. I only had my music. So, I wrote about my feelings.

I sold my feelings for the world to hear what a piece of shit I am, how I threw away the best thing that had happened to me, the person who knew me better than anyone. I sold my feelings about running from my family because I was afraid of what they thought of the mistakes I had made. I sold my feelings about the bandmates I had left behind. About little Abby who was probably all grown up now. I wrote and wrote and continued to sell pieces of my soul. And that's where I am today.

I continue with school, now studying music production since I have the start of a career in it. I still live in the same shithole I rented a room from when I moved here, living with three other guys. I'm never home. I never socialize with them. I don't even eat there. It's only a place to sleep at night. I spend all my free time in the studio, and sometimes I crash there, too. Their couch is much more comfortable than my bed.

I don't know where to go from here, if there is anywhere else to go. I know I need to go home soon, let everyone know I am alive. I owe them that much. I don't know what to do about Claire.

Did she finish her degree in three years like she planned? Did she get picked up by a company? Has she moved on?

I want to look her up so badly; see if there is any news of her. Maybe she's on social media now? I can't bring myself to look. I'm scared shitless of what I will find. I have regular nightmares of finding out she ended up with Troy after all, that I pushed them together. I left her when she was at her lowest, the day after she had lost her mom. What if one of her guy friends became a comfort to her when I wasn't there? Shit, what if she turned to one my own bandmates? If I find that her and Chris hooked up, I would probably puke.

Nevertheless, one of these days, I need to get up the nerve to go home and find out. I need to face my mistakes, and then learn how to move on. I need to apologize for worrying everyone, for disappearing like I did, for not even making one phone call. I have a lot to make up for, but today is not the day. Tomorrow won't be either.

Soon.

Chapter 24

He Was There

~Claire~

June 16, 2014

I googled your name and finally got a hit. Honestly, I've googled your name often for the past four years. It's been a while now since last time I did. You start to lose hope after four years of nothing.

I heard a song on the radio that was a different rendition of one you used to play forever ago. I couldn't believe it when I heard it. I called Chris right away (yeah, I still talk to him once a while), and he turned on the radio to listen. I don't have to tell you how pissed off he was. Especially because the band slowly dissolved in the first year you left.

Chris now co-owns his dad's garage. He's doing good. Practically gave up on music altogether, but you can still hear him playing the drums occasionally. I don't know what happened to Trey and Shaun. When the band gave up, they all went their separate ways.

Anyway, I am so proud of you and hate you at the same time. I can't believe you wrote a song for your favorite band. I still remember going to their concert with you, my first one. Well, my only one. I thought most of those bands wrote their own songs. Regardless, it's still pretty cool. Congratulations, Noah.

And now the hating you part...

I'm moving on, as much as I can since I still

write to you like a total stalker. But there is still this ache where my heart is. And then I see you in a group picture with the band, smiling, shaking hands, recording together, and I hate that you can smile like that, like you can move on, *move on. Like you're a selfish asshole when I know you're not. At least, you used to not be.*

Good luck to you, Noah.

~Noah~

My songs started hitting the radio this summer, and that's when the money started coming in. I make a percentage for every album sold, every time someone downloads my songs, every concert where my song is played, and propaganda that advertises my songs. It's a small percentage each, but everyone listens to music and my songs are spanned out in a lot of genres, so I am constantly making money. It's insane. And it's only a matter of time before my family finds out, which is why I am making my way to Uncle Mark and Aunt Katy's right now and hoping I don't run into Jonathan, Kyle, Max, or Cyn.

I rented a car for this visit. My poor bike broke down months ago—too many miles on her. I will get a new one soon, when more money comes in. I want to hit a certain amount and never let my account get lower than that. That's what my dad taught me years ago: always have a cushion. Well, I lost my previous cushion four semesters ago, so I'm raising the bar and waiting.

Right outside of town, I pull into a gas station. Really, I'm procrastinating. Ten minutes away, and my heart is already racing. I haven't eaten all day, too nauseated to stomach anything. I don't know what kind of reception to expect. They are my family, but I know they thought of Claire as family, too. And when one family member hurts another, the family is divided. Since I wasn't there to have anyone on my side, I'm guessing they are all on Team Claire.

As I notch the gas pump into my rental, I hear, "Well, look who we have here." I know that voice. I forgot all about the person.

I look over my shoulder toward her. "How are you doing, Sassy?"

274

She ignores my question, eyeing me up and down. "You haven't changed much. You look older … sexier. I like the rugged look you got going on." She indicates the fact that I haven't shaved since I left yesterday morning.

I wish I could say the same about her. These past four years have not been kind to her. She looks drugged up, lost weight, and she has track marks up her arms.

I need to get out of here quick. I have had enough experience with junkies to know not to linger.

Since I didn't need gas in the first place, I quickly return the nozzle to the gas pump.

"Good to see you," I tell her, quickly getting back into the car.

I almost have the door shut when she asks, "Are you here with Claire?"

God, simply hearing her name is like a knife to the chest and makes my blood sing. No one has said that name to me in four years. Sometimes, when I hear someone else say it in public, my heart starts racing, and I twist my neck trying to locate her, both afraid and desperate to catch a glimpse of her.

Ignoring Sassy, I let the door slam shut and drive off, heading toward my family's home. I briefly wonder if Sassy is still in contact with Max, if she will call him and tell him I'm in town. Then I wonder if he is still with Cyn and whether they still talk to Claire. Regardless, I made the decision to come here, knowing someone may mention it to her. It's time to face my past and all the mistakes I made.

At Mark and Katy's house, I knock on the door. It feels weird to do that, but it's the right thing to do.

An older Abby answers. God, how old she is now? Eight? I can't believe how much she has grown in four years. She still has those big, innocent brown eyes, but her brown ringlets are now straight, and she's dressed like a miniature teenager in skinny jeans and a tank top.

"Noah?" she asks in a little voice that brings a smile to my face. I was afraid she forgot about me.

"Hey, Abby."

"It's Abigail now," she tells me with some sass that makes my smile broader. "Where's Nico?" That makes my smile diminish some.

Who?

Before I can ask, Katy walks up from behind her. "Noah," she says breathlessly, like she can't believe what she is seeing. She smiles widely, opening the door wider before pulling me in for a hug. "Oh, my God, it's so good to see you. I can't believe you're here. Does your mom know?" She seems to realize the answer to that because then she says, "She's going to be so relieved to know you are okay." Then she pulls back and smacks my arm. "Don't ever, ever disappear like that again."

She leads me into the house, all the while berating me for disappearing, telling me that everyone thought I was dead, and how Jonathan had an investigator looking for me the first year. She never mentions Claire, and I don't, either.

When she notices that Abby has quietly followed us into the kitchen, she tells her, "Abigail, let me talk to Noah in private really quick."

Instead of listening, Abby runs up to me and wraps her arms around my waist, a wide smile on her face. Meanwhile, Katy looks like she's about to have a heart attack. Is it because I am here? Does she hate me to the point she doesn't want her kid around me?

"I missed you, Noah."

I rub her back as I tell her, "I missed you, too."

She smiles as she backs away, then turns around at the hallway and presumably goes to her room.

I can't get over how much she has grown. No more No-ie. I'm simply Noah to her now. I miss the little girl she used to be. So much has changed. What else have I missed?

I turn my attention back to Katy, and she immediately wipes the worry from her face and plasters on a fake smile. She returns to preparing the dinner she must have been making when I got here, talking about this and that. I answer every question she asks, but I'm not really paying too much attention to her. I'm taking in the house and noting the changes.

I see some of my baby pictures on the refrigerator door and think they must have really missed me to resort to putting them up. It seems a bit too much if you ask me.

When I look back at Katy to answer another of her questions, she has this strange look on her face that I can't place. She swallows hard, and it makes me uncomfortable. Then she looks down at my left wrist, noting the fact I still hold a torch for my ex-girlfriend.

"Oh, Noah," she sighs. She comes around the kitchen island toward me. "Please tell me what happened. Why did you run?"

My happy reunion mood deflates. I shouldn't have let her see it, but I can't take it off. Even when I convinced myself that Claire broke my heart, I never took off the leather bracelet she gave me. I never tattooed over her birthdate on my wrist. I never let go of anything us. It's all I have left.

"She hasn't let go, either," Katy tells me, reaching into the drawer beside me and pulling out a newspaper clipping.

Katy hands me the piece of paper, and I see Claire's face smiling. I immediately close my eyes to block the image out. It hurts too much to look at her.

"Look." I feel Katy stab at the paper in my hands, and I open my eyes to see what she is pointing at.

Claire is wearing the pendant I gave her, and it's a recent picture. The date is from this month.

I feel my brow furrow as I study the image. Why is she in the news? Before I can figure that out, I see the guy in the image next to her, his arm wrapped around her shoulders. Automatically, all those years of fearing this moment makes me stiffen and hold my breath.

Katy feels the change in me and explains, "That's Jesse. They met in Italy. They aren't together anymore, but they did collaborate on a project that is bringing them worldwide media coverage. You haven't heard?" I hear the confusion in her voice.

"No," I croak out then clear my throat. "I've been too afraid to look." Because I don't want to know that she moved on. I don't want to know that I'm the only one always looking back. But, am I? That pendant says otherwise.

"Oh, Noah." Katy shakes her head. "Between the two of you, it's a wonder I haven't died of heartache myself."

I look away from the image that is already seared into my brain. Her excited smile. The blue svelte dress she is wearing. Her brown hair that looks windblown; still long, wavy, and halfway down her back once again. She hasn't changed much in these four years. And *him*. The skinny, little shit with the smug smile. The guy looks like he has a stick up his ass. What did Claire see in him?

Katy takes the paper from me and sets it back in the drawer. Then she proceeds to make coffee, telling me to sit down. I listen, robotically sitting at the kitchen table, lost in thought as Katy tells me about Claire's opera. I don't know how to feel about it. I think I'm still shocked from seeing her image again. My memories didn't do her justice at all.

Katy sets a cup in front of me and asks again, "Why did you walk away? Do you know how worried we have all been? God, Noah." She shakes her head.

"It was a mistake," I mumble absently. "I saw Claire with Troy." Rubbing my forehead, feeling a headache coming on, I tell her what I saw that night and admit what I built it up to be, finding an excuse to walk away.

It was too much too soon: the move from the quiet town to loud city, Claire's newfound friends, not having the time together that we used to have, school, jobs, gigs, rehearsals, her mom dying. It was all too much at once, and I cracked.

I hate change. I can't jump into something. I need time and quiet and peace to accept something different. I don't know why. Maybe because my parents carted me off to extremely different environments growing up. Who knows? Whatever the case may be, I wasn't prepared when Claire and I moved to New York.

I didn't think it would be so different than when we were together at her hometown. I didn't account for Claire making new friends so fast. I didn't account for her excitement and adventurous spirit, wanting to see and do everything at once. Everything was simply too fast. That's my only excuse.

"Noah." Aunt Katy puts her hand over mine on the table and squeezes. "You should have said you needed a break, not disappear for years. I wish I could tell you—"

At that moment, her cell phone rings.

She gets up from the table and walks to where it sits on the counter. Looking at the screen, she tells me, "It's Kyle."

Shit. I wonder if this is an impromptu call or if he somehow knows I'm here.

Katy answers, and then I get my answer when she hands the phone to me. "It's for you." She looks sad, which tells me Kyle is not too happy to hear from me.

Shit. I don't know if I'm ready for this.

With my eyes closed, bracing myself, I put the phone to me ear. "Hello?"

"You son of a bitch!"

For the next two minutes, I don't get a word in while he verbally strikes out at me, repeatedly hitting me where it hurts. He yells at me about Claire's suffering; how she dropped out after her first year and had to leave the country to escape me. "Not to mention other shit I'm not at liberty tell you, fucker!"

He yells about how his parents and my parents mourned for a year. How Max flew across the country to find me, and then passed away soon after, which leaves me striking out at him because the self-hatred and guilt shatters me. I had no idea Max was gone. The last words I said to Max are now something I will regret for the rest of my life.

Then Kyle goes on to spout how worthless I am, how he hates me for what I did to everyone, how he wishes I had stayed gone. By that point, I am done, regretting ever coming here.

I storm out the door, needing to get away from here. Again, too much at one time. I need to get away and cool down. I need quiet. Kyle words are still screaming in my head.

"Noah, wait!" Katy calls, and I hear her running after me.

I stop before I reach my rental and turn around to face her. She is carrying a box.

"Take this with you." She holds out the box to me, but I don't take it.

"What is it?" I can tell by the wary look on her face that it's not what I think it is.

"Letters."

I visibly gulp. "From whom?"

She gives me a look in answer, and now I am shaking.

When I don't take the box right away, she thrusts it into my hand. "You *owe* her this. Just read the letters, Noah, and you will understand why everyone is so angry with you."

I raise my brow at her like *it can't be that bad*, and she raises one back at me like *you have no idea*. That makes me clear my throat, return my face to neutral, and grip the box tighter.

Glancing into the box, I see that it's not just letters. There are smaller boxes with wrapping paper, manila envelopes with bulges, thumb drives.

I'm speechless that she would do all this. I don't know what to say or do, so I put the box in the backseat and hand Katy my card with my business number and P.O. Box, courtesy of the record label.

Katy looks at the card and smiles softly. "Congratulations, Noah."

I nod then get in the car and leave.

I thought I was ready for this visit. But glancing back at that box, I *know* I'm not ready to face Claire. Not yet.

~Claire~

I have been back in New York for almost six months now. I didn't know what I would do for a place to stay since Dare and her roommate still lived at my place. She broke up with Victor years ago and was now dating a guy named Neil who owns his own restaurant.

I called her days after breaking up with Jesse and told her I was coming back to town. After screaming with joy, she told me how great that was because she wanted to move in with Neil but didn't know how or when since she was renting from me and didn't want to add more to my plate. It all worked out, and she took her roommate with her to Neil's.

I bought all new furniture for the place, using a lot of my mom's since she had nice stuff. I didn't want the place to look anything like it did when I last lived there. However, I did put up my old curtains. I couldn't let go of them. Stupid, I know.

Giuliana, Signora Gelardi's granddaughter, who is the same age as me, moved to the States with me. She stayed in Dare's old room for a few months. Then Kyle moved here over the summer, and she moved in with him once he got settled into a new job and found a small place for himself. He quit school after getting his associates, and then worked on his EMT certifications. Now he is a paramedic, and in a city this large, he is constantly busy.

The opera house has been insane. I have been burning the candle at both ends with this new job. There's so much to do with rehearsals, costumes, background sets, composition, marketing, advertising. We have completely revamped our target audience, which has gotten us a lot of attention. The media is literally following me everywhere. When all I want to do is hide my private life, they make it difficult. Hence, Giuliana's involvement, as she works for me.

Next week, we are going on a statewide tour. Next month, we are hitting the nation, stopping at major cities around the country. By the time that's over, the season will start. The investors are expecting weeks of sold out tickets. It's exhausting.

But I knew—I *knew*—this idea would take off. And as mad as I am at Jesse for jumping the gun, I have calmed down and am now grateful. At the same time, I wasn't ready for this. I hardly have time to myself with everything that needs to be done. How can I produce and lead? I can't. It's not possible. Therefore, I'm only singing for all the promotional bits. I don't know how Jesse or the investors thought I could do both, never mind wanting to do it.

Jesse was too excited over this opportunity to be heartbroken for long after I broke up with him. He sulked for a week before talking nonstop about this new prospect. I'm hurt and simultaneously relieved. Did I mean so little to him that a week was enough time to get over me? And what does that say about me and my four-year long sulk over Noah?

Nevertheless, every time it's questioned in interviews whether we are an item, Jesse likes to throw his arm over my shoulder and smile like that's answer enough, before I smile politely and comment, "We're just friends."

I don't know, nor do I care, if Jesse is doing it to boost ratings by making us some power couple. I do know I don't appreciate it. It feels like high school with Troy all over again.

To prove a point, I date often. Most dates don't last past the first one, but there is still a lot of networking potential and some dates I stay in contact with as friends. Then I have PR setting me up with celebrities for functions and charities. It's for a good cause. Plus, it stops speculations about me and Jesse. However, Dare is always throwing another smut magazine at me with rumors I'm with so and so: dancers, violinists, actors, even an Olympic runner. It's publicity. How fast it is all happening is another story.

Like Noah. I used to google his name on a weekly basis, just to see, never expecting anything. Then, with the move back to the States, time slipped by. Then I heard one of his songs on the radio. I know I looked him up when we were still in Italy, which means that in six-months' time, he was nowhere to all over the place.

As staggering as it was to sing along to the lyrics one minute then pausing with a *what the hell?* expression the next, I thoughtlessly called Chris in my eagerness to share the news. To say he was pissed is an understatement.

Now I'm at the theater, checking props at the last minute, when Kyle shows up in his paramedic uniform. I think it's odd since I know he's at the beginning of his shift. Plus, he storms in here like someone is chasing him.

I watch him worriedly as he briskly walks down the long aisle toward the stage. When we meet, he is out of breath, even sweating a bit. It is still hot outside, though we are at the end of September. However, the out of breath has me worried that someone is hurt. Did he bring someone we know to the hospital?

"What's wrong?" I ask, my heart starting to beat frantically. "Is it—"

"No. No, everyone is fine," he quickly assures.

I take a deep breath, putting a hand to my chest as my heart goes from skyrocketing to calming beats. "God, you had me so worried."

"Sorry. Um … You got a minute? I need to tell you something." He looks more anxious than upset now.

"Want to sit down?" I gesture toward the auditorium seats. He looks like he needs to. Oh, my God, maybe he's going to propose to

Giuliana and needs advice or a favor.

Kyle and I have grown close over the years. He is like a brother to me. He's not the joking kid he once was. Now he is too serious sometimes.

He nods and leads the way. Then, when we sit down, Kyle takes a deep breath.

Wow, whatever this is, it's hard for him.

Concerned once again, I put my hand on his shoulder. "Kyle, what is? You're starting to scare me."

"I … I don't know how to say this. I was pissed. Really pissed. Remembering how messed up you were when he left." My heart stops and starts pounding again at his words. "I wanted to kill him. But seeing you now …" He shakes his head and looks down.

"Kyle, what are you talking about?" I let my hand fall from his shoulder. It's shaking now as I grip my pendant like a lifeline. My whole body is shaking, and I suddenly feel cold. "What happened? Why are you bringing up"—I swallow a deep breath—"Noah?"

You will always remember your first love, but life carries on. Memories, feelings, life—it all changes. The emotions you felt at the beginning of a relationship fade, whether you are still with that person or not. Well, not fade, just … turn into something else. A happy memory, something good and uplifting to look back on fondly. Yet, speaking his name, all the feelings I ever associated with Noah spark anew, and I feel something I haven't felt in years. Hope.

Kyle looks up from his lap and right into my eyes. "I talked to him … Not twenty minutes ago." He starts talking a mile a minute, and I try to keep up, all the while feeling relief that Noah is alive. "Cyn called me. She got a call from Max's old friend Calvin, who got a call from Sassy. She ran into him at a gas station in town. *Our* town, Claire. I called Mom. Noah was there. He was there," he seethes, "talking to my mom. I got him on the phone and laid into him. I was so mad. And then he hung up on me. By the time I got my mom back on the phone, he was gone."

Something is stuck in my throat, my heart feels like someone has reached into my chest and is squeezing it, and my stomach churns with acid. I am cold. So cold I start to shiver.

Kyle sees what is happening to me and goes into EMT mode. He takes off and quickly comes back with some fabric. I think it's part of one of our costumes. He drapes it over me and starts rubbing my arms, causing friction. I hear him yell at someone to get me some water, and then a bottle is thrust under my nose. He pulls out one of my pills, telling me he knew this would happen so he came prepared. All this takes place from a spectator's view.

Inside, I am reeling. Noah is alive. Noah went to see Katy. Is he coming here? Four years of waiting, and now I am scared to death of the idea.

Wait.

"Letters," I gasp out, pushing the water bottle out of my face. I search the crowd of people surrounding me, overwhelming me, looking for Kyle's face. He's right in front of me, looking back at everyone and telling them I'm fine. "Kyle." I grab his arm, and he turns back to face me. "Did he ... get the letters?"

Kyle nods. "Yeah, Claire. Mom gave them to him."

I can't help the sob that escapes. Relief and fear and joy and hope override my emotions, causing me to smile wanly while tears cascade from my eyes and body-racking sobs immobilize me. I fall into Kyle's lap, thinking that Noah will know soon. Noah will know. I want him to know more than anything.

Kyle continue to holds me, repeatedly telling me that he is sorry for making Noah run off again, sorry for losing his cool. He wishes he would have waited until he saw him in person and punched him instead. That makes me sob out a laugh.

At least he finally got the letters.

Chapter 25

Did You Tell Him?

~Claire~

It's been seven months since Kyle told me about Noah showing up. I called Katy as soon as I got ahold of my emotions, soaking up every detail she gave me. Then my dad called me after hearing about it—small towns talk. He wanted to take off after him, but I convinced him not to. Noah had the letters, and I was now sending the ones I often wrote directly to his P.O. Box. I figured, soon enough he would contact me.

After one call, we realized the number he left Katy was the corporate number when a secretary answered. Sarah left a message, but Noah never returned the call. That channel was declared a dead end.

Then month after month slipped by, and I lost all hope once more. My feelings began to fade once again. My flare of hope burned out. And I went back to my routine. Life as it has been.

He ran again, and I induced that my letters had him running harder and farther away. I can't blame him. Well, I can, but I sympathize, knowing he needs time to come to terms with the facts.

I thought about confronting him myself, knocking on his door and demanding he speak to me. I couldn't do it. Again and again, I told myself no. No, if Noah wants what I offered him, he will come. And if he doesn't, then he will stay away.

Meanwhile, the show must go on, and it did. Wow, did it ever.

Deutsch Märchen, the first production of fairy tale stories based on German lore, was a hit of epic proportions. Opening night was like a movie premiere: red carpet, media outlets everywhere, fans cheering, celebrities galore. The investors spared no expense to make sure it was a hit. And opening night was bigger than any Broadway production in history. Overnight, people who never heard an opera in their life were buying tickets, selling out the season in less than a week.

Now I divide my time between the warehouse where all the scenes and costumes are designed for next year, at the theater for rehearsals, and at the main office where we finalize the scripts. I am worn to the bone, feeling aged beyond my years.

Now, with it being the end of the season, I requested a week off. Everyone can see how worn down I am. The bags under my eyes cause everyone to question how I am feeling, and I tell the truth. I'm tired.

After two days of lying around the house, something I haven't done in so long I can't remember when, Giuliana decides I need a girls' night out. And so, after a quick trip to Sarah and Anthony's house, I meet up with Dare and Giuliana at her and Kyle's place, where we hail a cab to a new club across town.

Dare's boyfriend, Neil, told us about the club. He's always into all the happenings around town. He was raving about the old speakeasy feel of the place, so we made sure to dress the part in 1920's flapper dresses and hairstyles, making sure to paint our lips scarlet red.

It's fun. We laugh and tease each other as time passes, reminiscing about "old times" like so much time has passed, like we aren't only twenty-one and twenty-two years old. Then again, so much has happened in the years we have known each other, especially Dare and I.

God, I can't believe Dare is about to graduate in a month. I'm so shocked by the thought, I say it out loud.

"I know!" Dare squeals, drawing the attention of the group next to us. "I have no idea what I am going to do next." Her face turns sour, and she pouts. "I got an offer, but I can't take it. Neil has his business here, and I don't want to leave him." She picks up her shot glass and throws it back.

"You want me to talk to Henry?" I offer. "I can see if we need another cellist. I think one of ours is retiring soon. I can throw the suggestion out there and get some feelers at least."

"Oh, my God, would you?" Dare asks dramatically. The girl is already wasted. She wouldn't say anything otherwise, which kind of sucks because I would love to pay her back for everything she has done and continues to do for me.

I smile encouragingly. "I'll ask first thing when I go back to work."

"Yeah, because I won't let you try any earlier than that. You, my dear friend, need a break." Giuliana points at me and narrows her eyes in warning.

Giuliana is like my own PA. She is constantly reminding me of everything. And she has some of her grandmother's spunk, not taking any excuses from me. If she thinks I'm working too many hours, she will literally pull me away. Though, really, it's the incentive she brings with her that sways me.

We continue to talk and laugh, the drinks never running dry. It's a comfortable atmosphere. The club is more of a bar, with circular booths along the walls, and high tables spaced out around the bar. There is a dance floor in front of the stage where a jazz band plays serenely, the pianist the foreman. As the night wears on, though, the music picks up tempo and couples crowd the dance floor to perform the foxtrot, the Charleston, and some dances I'm not familiar with. This is a place I can see myself coming back to.

While Giuliana is telling us a story about Kyle and his EMT adventures, I feel eyes on me. I glance up, looking around the bar, watching the dancers for a moment before my eyes skirt away to across the room where I see Chris heading toward me.

I smile brightly at him, delighted to run into him. I haven't talked to him in weeks, and it's about time to catch up. But the expression on his face has my smile faltering. What happened? Why does he look … guilty?

"Hey, Claire," he says as he stops right in front of me, a little too close if you ask me.

The girls both cheer his name, and he smiles at them, leaning over for hugs from my two very intoxicated friends.

"What are you doing here?" I ask stupidly, like this can't be a fortunate coincidence.

Chris looks guilty again. "Same as you, I guess."

"What's wrong?" I ask point-blank.

He takes on this carefree attitude and answers with, "Nothing. I saw you here and came over to say hello." He smiles widely, a little too fake in my opinion.

"Uh-huh." I'm not buying it, but I keep a teasing nature to my tone. I try to look over his shoulder, asking, "Who are you here with?" but he blocks me. Now I am really suspicious. "What?"

"What, what?" Chris smiles. Then he ignores me and asks the girls, "So, how long have you ladies been here?"

I try to look over his shoulder again, and again he intercepts me. Is he hiding a girlfriend or something? I will be thrilled if he has a decent girlfriend. Chris hasn't dated anyone for longer than two months in the years I have known him. I get the feeling he's hiding a cougar or something.

I give up and turn away from him, seeing Dare pull out her phone and glance at the time. "Three hours so far," she answers, which means it's after midnight. "We should leave soon. I have class at eleven in the morning." She crinkles her nose at that. I know she is dying to finish school.

"You want me to call you guys a cab, or is Kyle picking you ladies up?"

Now I'm getting irritated. Why is he trying to get us to leave?

Turning to Chris with narrowed eyes, I start in on him, "What are you—"

"Good evening, everyone."

The entire world stops spinning at those words.

"Oh, God," I exclaim, whipping around in my seat, at the same time Chris says, "Shit," and Dare says, "You have got to be kidding me," followed by Giuliana asking, "What?" When no one answers her, she follows our eyes to the stage, her eyes widening, and then she says, "Oh, my God, is that …?"

In his classic way, he doesn't waste time with words; the guy starts playing a borrowed guitar, taking a rock song and jazzing it up for the audience.

I can't believe my eyes, my ears. He looks more rugged, older, no more boyishness, not that I ever thought he looked like that, but seeing him now, I can see what I couldn't see then.

He is dressed down in his normal jeans and boots, but has on a buttoned-up shirt. His eyes look older, wiser, world-weary. He has the shadow of a beard, his lips looking more pronounced, his jaw firmer, his body so much more toned. When I catch sight on the leather bracelet still adorned on his wrist, I close my eyes as my throat tightens.

"Claire, he still doesn't know," I hear Chris tell me as my body remains paralyzed.

I keep my body turned toward the stage, but force my eyes open and to Chris. "He hasn't read the letters?" I ask in confusion.

Why the not? He's had them for seven months now. What is he waiting for? Why is he here if he hasn't read them?

Chris shakes his head in answer, and I turn back to the stage.

Oh, God, he's playing one of my favorite songs, about not wanting memories, but the actual person. About looking back to what was, fearing their feelings then. And now waiting for a glimpse if nothing else, waiting for the person to come to them, hoping to have back what was. It's a song that rips me apart and pulls out my guts.

"Claire," I hear my name being called, but I don't know by whom. All I know is that I am running out the door. I don't even know how it happens. Then I am getting sick in an alley while Chris, Dare, and Giuliana are standing around me.

I wipe my mouth off with the back of my hand then turn to glare at Chris. "How could you not tell me?" I accuse, realizing he knew Noah was here. But for how long?

Chris holds his hands up as if to ward me off. "He asked me not to."

I glare at him, crossing my arms and gripping my shoulders, tears stinging my eyes, but I refuse to let them fall. "Why?"

Now both Dare and Giuliana are glaring at him, too.

Chris sighs and drops his hands. "He's been back since January. I found out last month when I ran into him." I gasp as he continues, "Yeah, surprised the hell out of me, too, which is why I haven't been around much. I took a swing at him when I saw him, yelled at him for so many things. That's when I realized he didn't know anything about anyone. When I settled down enough, we went for a couple beers. I told him about you and—"

"Did you tell him about—"

"No! God, no. You made us all swear, and I wouldn't break your trust like that. Jesus, Claire." When I give him a grateful, sad smile, he says, "He didn't know Kyle moved here, so then I told him about Giuliana, and about Dare and Neil. I told him about his parents, and what I knew of Shaun and Trey." He shrugs. "I caught him up with everything before asking about the letters. He wanted to know how I knew about them, and I told him everyone knows, that we all have been writing to him. He seemed taken aback by that, saying he thought they were all from you and he hasn't had the courage to read them yet. I think it's time to make him finally do it."

"Thanks, Chris. I'm sorry I yelled at you."

He holds his arms out, and I walk into his embrace. "I'm here for ya, little chick."

No one feels in the mood to party any longer, so Chris goes back inside to Noah, and the girls and I share a cab back to our respective homes. I can't go back in that club and face him. I can't. I appreciate the gesture he made, but I don't know what to say to him.

What do you say during a situation like this? "Hi, where the hell have you been?" Or maybe a classic slap across the face? Or do you act like nothing happened, like he didn't emotionally scar me, worry me, and make me wonder what happened and where he's been for four years? "Hi, I'm so glad you're back. What have you been up to for the past four and half years?"

I stop at Sarah and Anthony's before going home. I didn't plan on going back to their place, but Sarah is still up, and they deserve to know as soon as possible. Then I head home with my precious cargo, my heavy heart, and fall asleep hoping the dreams stay at bay.

~Noah~

Well, that didn't go as planned. Not that I expected some romantic, forget the past four and a half years, and let's live happily ever after reunion. Still, I didn't expect her to run out the door, not even looking back once. I must admit, that hurts, and then I was stuck finishing the song.

For a sliver of a moment, I thought about running after her, but then I got a peek at the look of warning in Chris's eyes, the glare of pure hatred from Dare, and some accusations coming from the other woman. Yeah, it was safer in here where we wouldn't cause a scene. I must brave the storm and see Claire directly, privately … someday.

I came here tonight with Chris. We have been trying to repair our friendship over the past month. It hasn't been easy, but it's getting better. I can tell he is still holding a lot of shit back. It isn't going to get easier until he man's up and gets it all off his chest. In the meantime, I'm being patient.

I transferred studios a while back, wanting to come here where I thought it would be easier to make that leap to talk to Claire. It hasn't been. Instead, I am locked in the studio for longer hours than before, writing my heart out. A positive to all this angst? It makes great writing material. I barely finish a song before someone is snatching it up.

For the last two hours, I sat across the room from her, mostly hidden by the booth partition, watching her laugh and talk with her friends. She looks the same yet older. Her body is slimmer, toner, yet she is even bustier. That silver and pink flapper dress she was wearing didn't hide that from me. Her brown hair was in soft waves on the top and pinned back in a bun. Her blue eyes no longer hold that innocence I used to love about them. Now they look jaded, even laughing.

Chris spent the time I stared at her trying to talk me out of staying here. He wanted to leave right away. When he wasn't talking about leaving, he made small talk about his family's business. I only half-listened, happy he seemed to like taking over for his dad. He has been bugging me about jamming together like the old days, and I was suspicious at first, thinking it was his attempt to restart a band. But, with the way he talks about expanding his dad's business, I don't think that's where he wants to go. He simply wants to reminisce, and I'm cool with that. Then he kept bringing up those damn letters and how I needed to read them before talking to her.

Why? He filled me in on everything. I know she dropped out of school, moved to Italy, dated that Jesse guy for about three years, and now you can't go anywhere without knowing who Claire Sawyer is. Why are the letters so damn important?

I can't believe what she has done to the entertainment world. She has everyone buzzing. I'm even getting requests to make the choruses more opera-worthy, pop stars wanting a piece of the action. Even grown, hardcore rockers are coming out with noteworthy ballads that dance on the line of arias. Little girls want to be opera singers now. Claire has the whole world eating out of her hands.

As I watched her, I made a spontaneous decision. I remember everything about Claire Diane Sawyer, and one of those things is her love for sappy songs, one in particular that summed up what I was thinking and feeling at the moment.

Without a word, I headed for the stage, not once looking at her. If I did, I didn't know what I would have done.

Chris comes back inside after following Claire and her friends out. It's hard not to notice that he is alone. I feel my whole body and soul deflate at that. Why would Claire write so many damn letters just to run away the minute we are in the same vicinity?

"Not cool, Noah. That was not cool at all," he seethes.

I agree. The timing and execution were all wrong. What the hell was I thinking? I know what I was thinking. I wanted her to *know* how I feel, that I am sorry, so sorry. That I can't stop looking back. That I can't look forward without seeing her.

"Yeah, I know," I finally answer, staring into the bottom of a shot glass. How cliché.

I need another drink.

"Look," Chris starts, folding his hands on the table like he is getting down to business. He leans in and fixes me with determined eyes, a layer of anger in their depths. "There are things going on with Claire that you don't understand. I'm going to keep drilling this into your thick skull until you finally do it. You need. To read. The letters," he says slowly and precisely. "You can't go to her until you do. Otherwise, you are going to be blindsided … and you're going to want to run again. That's what everyone thinks, anyway. Especially Claire. And she doesn't deserve that. So, you need to read those damn letters before you decide to make another fucked up attempt to see her.

Because, if you do, and then you run again, me and everyone else who cares about her will hunt you down."

"What's going on with her?" I ask as calmly as I can while inside my heart is thundering. What is going on with Claire that I need to prepare myself for?

Chris sits back, blowing out a deep breath. "I can't tell you. No one will. Claire needs to be the one to tell you, and she's been trying since right after you left." He shakes his head in disappointment before rubbing his face. "All I can tell you is that, the night you left, Claire found out ... something. She was already going through all that shit with her mom, then this, and then you left ... Noah, Claire was a mess. She needed you. We were all there for her, but she really needed *you*.

"She needs you there now, because no one else can help her the way she needs you to. I don't know how she has gone on this long." He raises his glass at the passing waitress, indicating we need new drinks before fixing me with his determined stare again. "That woman is brave and determined. She's conquered so much in a few years. You don't deserve her, but you need to read those letters so you can be there for her now, because that's all she wants. She is bound and determined, and so hopeful ... so damn hopeful to have you back in her life in some aspect. Just read those damn letters and determine what you want to do, because I won't let you get her hopes up just to finish her off. You stay or you go. You won't get to do both."

Claire is sick. Claire is dying. That's all I can induce from his cryptic talk. And if that's true, then what the hell am I going to do about it? Does she have brain cancer like her mom? Is that shit hereditary?

I try to remain calm, but I notice my hands shaking as I reach for the shot glass the waitress sets down. What the hell have I done? I took off for years while Claire has been suffering, dying. How much time does she have left? That thought has my heart thrashing at epic speeds. I need to read those letters. But do I want to know the truth? Will I be able to handle it? God, I don't know.

I do know that I want to be there for her. If Claire wants me, it's the least I can do. I adore the memory of her with every fiber of my being. I don't know her now to know how I feel about her, but I want to believe that the feelings I had extend to the her she is now. I know I would lay down my life for hers.

God, please don't take Claire.

I suddenly stand up from the table, and Chris turns in his seat, looking at me in confusion.

"Where are you going?"

"To read those damn letters."

~

I lied. I don't leave to go back to my place and dig out that box of letters; those letters I look at all the time yet never want to read. I have contemplated it so many times, but the minute I put my hand on one, start to peel back the flap on the envelope, I drop it like it burned me. I don't want to read about how much she hates me. I don't want to see that word directed at me.

Instead of going to my place, I walk up and down Claire's street. I can't believe she still has the same place. At least, per the return address from the last year, she does.

I pause and look up at her living room window, the lights still on, seeing those same curtains from forever ago, verifying that she does still live there. It makes me wonder how much in there is the same. Does she live alone?

Continuing another trek down the street, I keep going once I pass the street, making my way down two more streets. This is my third pass already, reliving walking this street years before, making grocery stops, finding a place to dine after late nights when Claire or I finally come home to find the other hadn't eaten yet. I remember back to when Claire first moved here and how she never sat still long enough to relax, wanting to see everything, experience everything. It's all bittersweet memories.

Looking back, I can't believe how selfish I was. How I wanted to keep her all to myself. God, I hate myself.

A cab passes me, and then, when I hit the fourth block down, I do an about face and start walking back toward her apartment. I don't know why I am doing this. I made the decision to read those letters, so why am I procrastinating once again?

I can't stop thinking about what Claire needs me to know. I'm scared to death of finding out, reading about what she has been going through. I hate the idea that I came here, finally facing my demons, just to lose her anyway. It makes me sick to my stomach. A world without Claire? What kind of world would that be? Not one worth living in.

Then a random thought strikes me, and I chuckle to myself. How I can laugh at a moment like this can only be explained by my random thought and the alcohol burning its way into my system.

I remember back to when Claire and I first started dating. I held her off for so long, needing to prove to myself that I was in this for the long road, not like that means much now. Now, here I am, having gone longer, holding myself back. And not to prove anything. Just ... after that first six months when I left, when logic came back to me, I couldn't even look at another woman. The drinking, the drugs, they all left my system, and my single focus became being better. And not just for Claire, though she was the biggest part of it. I realized I had to expect more for myself.

Once again in front of Claire's apartment, I stop and look up. Then I stagger back.

It's like déjà vu, reliving that moment four and a half years ago when I stood in this exact spot, thinking I was seeing something that wasn't. It's that moment all over again.

My thoughts freeze, my stomach somersaults, my heart starts pounding like it's trying to escape my chest. I can't believe it. I just can't believe it.

How have I messed up this much? What the hell have I done?

My chest is burning. I feel like I can't breathe. I feel like my heart is being shoved back into my chest. I bring my hand up to my chest where my heart is pounding. It hurts.

I know what I must look like right now, standing here, staring, gawking.

I can't believe what I have missed. How? How did I not know? Why? Why didn't anyone tell me? Not Katy. Not Chris. What the hell? This isn't something you not tell someone! Shit!

I'm biggest asshole this universe has ever spit out. What the hell! Claire ...

Heart pounding, thundering in my own ears. Lack of breath. Sucking in air, gasping.

I need to get out of here. I need to get to those letters. I need to catch up on Claire, so I can catch up with Claire … before it's too late. It's already too late for so much.

No, dammit. Get ahold of yourself!

Deep breath in. Blow it out. Shake it off.

God damn me!

Chapter 26

The Damn Letters

~Noah~

Back at my sorry excuse for an apartment, I charge inside, slamming the door shut, already making my way to my bedroom where I keep the box of letters at the back of my closet, out of sight. Grabbing the first stack, I rip off the rubber band, snapping it in half in my haste.

My hands are shaking and my breaths are rushed as I reach for the first letter and tear it open. The salutation alone makes me nauseous. God, I knew this would suck.

January 30, 2011

Coward,

I hate you, you cowardly bastard. I hate that, when I need you the most, you're not here. All those dreams, all those promises, and you left, damn you! What am I supposed to do now?

Why did you leave? If you never speak to me again, at least have the decency to answer me that.

We're having a baby, Noah. A baby! Is that why you left? Did you overhear me talking about it and freak out? It's okay to freak out; I did, too. Trust me; I wanted to run away, too, but I can't run from my own body. And I thought you would be here to tell me it will all be okay, to be that pillar of strength you always were to me. And I thought I would be yours.

Please, Noah, please come back. I promise we will fight and scream, and you can punch as many

holes into walls as you want, but please be here with
me. I don't want to be alone. I don't think I can do
this alone.
>*Stop running and be here, damn you!*
>*Pissed off, hormonal, mother-to-be.*

An ugly knot forms in my throat. Her begging, her news, the lost and hopeless feelings permeating from her first few angry letters make me hate myself so much more than I thought possible.

Then there's Jonathan's letter, addressing me as son, telling me there is nothing in life worth running away from. He is never mean or judging, just quoting the facts of life and conquering fears. Those letters stab another knife through my chest.

>*February 14, 2011*
>*I have not passed the angry stage, but I thought,*
>*as today is Valentine's Day, I should write today in*
>*remembrance of happy times. [...]*
>*How could you leave me the day I found out we*
>*were having our baby? It should have been a happy*
>*day. Instead, you tarnished it. I was scared, Noah,*
>*damn you. I will have no regrets, though. You can*
>*have them all. I will not regret what fate has given me.*
>*It might be hard to deal with, but I will make the best*
>*of our circumstances.*
>*I don't know what the future holds, but I do know*
>*I will stop at nothing to show our child that they are*
>*loved and provide everything they could ever want.*

>*February 28, 2011*
>*Chicken shit,*
>*I'm being kicked out of school. Well, kind of.*
>*Earlier today, I had a meeting with my counselor,*
>*where she "strongly recommend I take a break due to*
>*my condition." A condition YOU helped with, you*
>*selfish, heartless, scared, immature brat! I was*

planning on it, anyway. I lost my voice. I have no concentration. Therefore, I have until the end of the semester, and then I will be home. Not the place I want to be, especially under these circumstances.

Like I said earlier, your parents are supportive. Your mom is retiring early and opened their home to me. But I can't do that. I can't be anywhere where there are reminds of you. See, still in the angry stage. And I am depressed ... all the time. This baby is going to be the saddest kid alive.

Baby news. You are having a son. If this is why you left, which is the only reason I can think of, then I hope he becomes more real to you now. And, one day, I hope you can love him as I already do.

I will never tell him why you left us. You will always be a fond memory. And he will never know otherwise that he isn't loved by us. Do you hear me, Noah! He will never know otherwise!

If you someday decide you want to accept your responsibility, the door is always open to you. I will NEVER keep your son from you.

Ides of March, 2011

Your son is six months into gestation today. So, happy minor birthday to him. The doctor tells me he is very healthy and is going to be a big baby.

Since today is such a mile marker, I decided to name him. Nicholas Julian Gish-Sawyer. There, that is the first time I have written his name or even said it. I wanted you to be the first to know. I will give this letter a week to hopefully reach you before I tell anyone else.

I got lots and lots of ultrasound pictures of our precious Nicholas. I have enclosed today's for you and had the doctor mark his legs, feet, hands, head, and sex for you. Isn't he beautiful already?

I hope he looks exactly like you. He already has
your height. ;)
Until next time, Noah.

Staring down at the first image of my son opens the floodgates. Tears silently stream down my face, blurring the black and white image of my boy. I can't believe the sight, the thought that this tiny, precious creature came from our union. Long legs curled up, arms down to his side, I can see his heart, his spine, his unproportioned head.

How is it even possible? Claire was on birth control. I know she would never in a million years plan this. She was always so set on her goals. We talked about kids once, both agreeing that kids were something we wouldn't think about until we were pushing thirty. Honestly, I would have been happier much sooner than that. I wanted to seal her to me in every way possible. Regardless, we were young and it was Claire—I went with whatever she wanted.

Wiping my face dry, I move on to the other letters.

May 1, 2011
Happy birthday, Noah!

Enclosed is a picture of Claire with "Happy birthday, Daddy" written on her belly. Dare's hand is in corner of the picture, flipping me off. A laugh-sob leaves me at that. I can't believe her belly. She looks so stunning.

May 19, 2011
School is over. I don't know how I got through
this year—the hardest year of my life. As sad as I am
to leave, I am happier to go. Too many memories in
the apartment, at local places we used to visit, the
people who stop by less frequently now. Not that
going home is going to be much better.
I had to close my eyes and take a deep breath at
that thought.

I won't be there long, though. And soon I will have new memories to make there, and the baby will know where we fell in love, where I grew up. And Katy and Abby are so excited. I'm glad they will be there. I miss them so much.

[...]

Two more months of this pregnancy left, and wow, am I huge. I feel like an elephant. My feet and ankles are swollen, my fingers are swollen, and my belly is most definitely swollen. See enclosed picture, and there will be no way you can deny that.

I look at the picture she is referring to, but I can't agree with her. She looks perfect in the side view, wearing a dress, her belly protruding out, smiling at the camera. I hate that I missed this. This is about the time I woke up and realized how much of an asshole I am.

God, Claire ... I'm sorry.

[...]

I am still mad at you and confused, but my promise is set in stone. Whenever you are ready to meet your son, he will be waiting for you.

I must end this now. Dad came back.

Claire

P.S. Oh, and Angel says a hi meow. She's sprawled out on the table now, smacking the pen around whenever it comes near her.

The image she paints makes me smile a bit. I forgot about that cat. I wonder if she still has her.

June 4, 2011

I am going out of my mind at home. I can't wait for this baby to come so I can have my body back. I feel like I have been invaded. I guess I kind of have.

The baby is kicking so much now; there is no

room for him. Plus, I'm eating like crazy. I am huge, though my doctor and Katy say I still haven't gained enough. I don't understand how when I can't even see my feet.

Troy called the other day. You might remember him, because a feeling tells me he is why you ran. It's just a feeling, but I'm trusting it. I don't know what you thought you saw, or if it's what you heard, but it gave you no right to run. That's not even you. Well, not the you I thought I knew. I'm not getting into that right now. I'm too close to the end of this pregnancy to risk the baby by getting angry. My blood pressure is already too high as it is.

Anyway, Troy called, saying Chelsea wants to talk to me. I must say that I was rendered speechless at that. Last time I talked to Chelsea, she yelled at me, hit me, cried. That's the picture of her that has stayed in my head. I told Troy that I would visit, though. Who knows, maybe she saw you or something and wants to pass a message? I don't know. I do want to see their baby.

Troy has grown up a lot; has his anger under control. He is in a much, much better place now. He was overseas for the past six months. After training, he had one month to get settled at his new command before they shipped him off. Poor guy. I can't imagine going that long without seeing your baby.

After our baby is born, and after a few months of getting into a routine with him, I will be flying out to visit Troy, Chelsea, and Tori. I'm torn between excitement and nervousness about that. I hope Chelsea isn't setting a trap. I'm positive Troy won't let her. Keep your fingers crossed.

News of Troy doesn't simmer my blood like it used to. And once I read through more letters about him, I find that I am genuinely happy that he is happy. I learn that him and Chelsea got married, which shocks the hell out of me, but good for them. They have another kid together, too. And Chelsea reads like someone I have never met before, not the mean, callous bitch I knew back in high school.

> *July 12, 2011*
> *I wish you were here right now. I am so scared. My dad rushed me to the hospital because I was cramping so badly. It hurt. Oh, my God, did it hurt. And Dad ... My poor dad. He shouldn't have to go through this.*

I stop reading right away. The dagger in my chest is twisting, making me close my eyes to blot out the pain.

God, Claire. I wish I had been there, angel.

> *I'm in the hospital now, getting testing done. They want me to stay overnight for now until they can get more tests done. I'm contracting every ten to twelve minutes right now. If the baby comes, he will only be a few weeks early so that's a relief.*
>
> *I'm scared, anxious, want to puke with nerves, but so excited and relieved to be near the end. I can't wait to meet him.*
>
> *Okay, the doctor came back in and told me I can go home in the morning. The baby is okay. His vitals are strong and normal. Thank God. The doctor thinks I am just having strong Braxton Hicks contractions. I shake my head at that. That must mean I am weak, unable to handle a little pain.*
>
> *I know I am weak, because I don't want to do this without you. I hate, hate, hate making all these baby decisions and not having your input. I see a cute outfit and know you will hate it. I stop and think, "I should buy it because of that." Then I think, "But maybe I'm wrong, and he would love it." I mean, I thought you*

would never leave, but you did. I'm being bitter again, I know. I hate this, Noah. I hate you.

Anyway, Nicholas's bedroom is all set up next to mine. Katy and Abby helped me purchase everything he will need, and Dad set everything up. He had a terrible time building the crib, but he did it with a smile on his face. I love my daddy. He can't wait for his grandbaby.

I can't think of anything else to say for now, so ... until next time.

That was supposed to be my job. That's all I can think about. All of it—everything. I was supposed to be there.

Gritting my teeth, I continue reading through a lot of hate mail from Cyn and Dare. They never mention the baby, just how much of an asshole I am. In fact, one letter from Dare says just that: *Asshole*, in letters cut out of magazines like a ransom note. That girl had too much time on her hands and too much hatred in her heart.

July 26, 2011

Here it is, Noah. The day of your son's birth. I am lying in the hospital bed right now, contractions two minutes apart. Within a couple of hours, your son will be coming into the world.

I wish you were here, dammit. I'm so scared. I NEED you, Noah. I can't do this alone. I don't want to do this alone. I need you. Nicholas needs you. I want our son to know his daddy.

Claire

P.S. This is Cyn. I will castrate you when I find you!

There are tearstains all over that note, and the next one right underneath it.

I add my own to the mix.

To the new daddy,

Today is the most significant day of my life. Your son is here. I can't stop crying right now. Sorry for all the watermarks on this page. I'm so tired, and happy, and so incredibly sad you are missing this. That you aren't here to meet your son. That you will miss so much of ... everything.

God, Noah, he looks JUST like you. His hair is so black and so full, though everyone tells me his color could change. His eyes are still the newborn bluish-gray, but his natural color will become more prominent in the next few months. He has the longest legs. It's so funny. He's going to be tall like his daddy. Thank God. Poor kid doesn't need my little height. His nose is a little squished, but it's adorable. His ears are so little. They are definitely your ears. I don't know, there is something about him that screams Noah.

I have a lifetime of photos for you. Seriously, I need to put them on a drive because there are so many. Everyone was snapping away. I felt like the paparazzi was attacking me.

I pick up the sim card that is in the envelope and leave the closet to find my laptop. Then I spend the next hour pouring over every picture, unable to stop examining every nuance, every expression my son makes: from his screaming, angry face to the look of wonderment when he meets his mom for the first time. I can't pull my eyes away.

They are both so beautiful. Claire, even sweating, tears streaming down her red face, not a speck of makeup on, her hair clinging to her profile, she is more lovely than I ever saw her.

I see her in a different light. She's a mom. She's a single mom, who moved to another country with a newborn, worked her ass off to fulfill her dreams, all the while taking care of this little creature. I am in awe of her, and my heart expands at the level of adoration I have for both them, for the son I have never met.

Then I come across a video at the end, and my eyes become a broken dam. I watch the video three times because I miss so much the first two. Claire giving birth.

I wish there was more shown than there is. I wish I could see my son making his first appearance, but the first I see of him is when the doctor holds him up, bloody and naked, the umbilical cord still attached. I watch as Cyn cuts it, smiling as she cries and laughs at the same time, telling Claire how proud she is of her, how handsome our baby is.

Then the camera is back on Claire, and I watch as my own mother wipes her face, telling Claire how well she did, crying herself. It's so weird to see my mom like that: comforting, proud, so happy and loving and supportive. It makes me miss her. I want to thank her for being there.

A nurse moves into the frame, and Dare coos from behind the camera, getting Claire's attention. She smiles at the camera, or Dare, and then all her attention goes right to the baby in the nurse's arms. She tries to scoot up in the bed, but a doctor out of view tells her not to move as the nurse places baby Nicholas into her arms.

Claire starts to sob as she looks at him, which makes me sob and smile simultaneously. This is the part I still can't make it through, when Nicholas quiets down as soon as he catches sight of his mother for the first time. It's a beautiful moment as Nicholas simply watches her as she coos at him, telling him how much she loves him, how perfect he is.

I soak in everything about them, not seeing anything else. And when I finish watching the video, I finally return to the closet and the letters, bringing my laptop with me.

He's perfect, Noah. I wish you were here to see him. I imagine you carrying him around the room, already teaching him music and promising to teach him how to play the guitar one day ...

Oh, so stats. Okay, he was born twenty-three and a half inches tall, weighing eight pounds four ounces. You probably aren't aware of this, but that's a big baby. It's a miracle considering he came out of me. Which, the labor was pretty easy.

I went in for my weekly exam, and the doctor said I was already four centimeters dilated. Her words: "You're going to have a baby today." And sure enough, Nicholas Julian Gish-Sawyer was born five hours later.

Honestly, the doctor said that was the easiest labor she ever had the pleasure of being a part of. As soon as my body was ready, I pushed twice, and he was out, screaming bloody murder, too.

I cried, and cried, and cried. Dad cried. Katy cried. Cyn cried. Even Dare.

He is so beautiful, Noah. He is lying in his hospital bassinet right now, his hand in his mouth, sucking away.

I got distracted watching him for a while.

So, yeah, Katy, your mom, Dare, and Cyn stayed in the room with me during the delivery. Dad, Anthony, Mark, Max, Kyle, and Abby waited in the hall. Dare videotaped most of it, so I'm attaching that in this letter. I told her not to film the gross stuff. I don't want to see it, so I don't want you to see it. Serves you right if you did, though.

Cyn and Max are going to be Nicholas's godparents. Kyle is claiming the uncle role, which means Abby is the unofficial aunt. And this kid has more grandparents than I ever thought a child of mine would since Katy and Mark are declaring themselves a part of that role.

I'm sorry. I'm crying again, feeling all the love these people are giving us. I'm so happy, yet I miss you so much right now. You should be HERE, dammit, with me, with Nicholas.

I can't write anymore right now. It's too hard. New mommy.

August 7, 2011

This first few days at home from the hospital were fantastic. Now, not so much. Nicholas has the appetite of a bear. Your mom tells me you were the same way. I find comfort in that.

He wakes up every two hours to be fed. Then he falls asleep in my arms. Your mom told me not to feed him in my bed because he will become accustomed to it and it will be hard to break him from it later. But I am so tired, trying to sleep when he does, and he feels so good in my arms. I can't help cuddling him. We both seem to sleep better that way.

With the aftermath of the pregnancy, depression has set in again. Just being with Nico (oh, that's what Signora Gelardi has nicknamed him and it kind of stuck) and thinking about all his firsts and that you won't be here to share that breaks my heart. I get so damn angry and frustrated when I am so tired and want to skip one feeding, have someone else take care of him for once. Those moments, I hate you and think it would be better if I knew you were dead instead of abandoning us for your own selfish reasons. That's what I end up telling myself. That you are dead. And these letters are just a way to connect with you, to feel like you are still here.

I'm getting off topic.

Your mom and dad left today. Your mom is wrapping up her release for retirement and mentioned every hour, it seemed, how she would love to have us stay with them. It brings tears to my eyes how much she cares. You should see her look at Nico. There is an ocean of regret in her eyes. I think she misses having you as her little boy and now realizes how much she missed out on.

I don't know what I am going to do next. I'm

focusing on being a new mommy for now. Signora Gelardi has a few ideas, but I told her to wait until Nico is four months old before she starts pestering me about them.

I hope you're safe, but I can't hope you're happy. Knowing you are happy somewhere without us would feel like a betrayal to our son.

August 20, 2011
This is the first time I've had the chance to write to you in weeks.

Max passed away. I'm sorry if this is how you are finding out. He was out for a ride and just ... his heart gave out. It was a genetic disease, something he kept from everyone, including Cyn, who is beyond herself with guilt.

I don't know what to do for her. She is keeping to herself, locking herself in their room day and night. She came out only for the funeral, which was a closed casket due to the severity of his injuries, having crashed his bike when the heart attack hit him. It was horrible, Noah. So horrible.

Max was one of the bestest friends I could ask for. He was like a big brother, you know? He always looked out for me, for you, for everyone. I will miss him so, so much.

I hope you are safe. Now I fear every moment that could have been you on your bike.

Something no one seems to know, and I don't plan on telling anyone, is that Max did find me. I don't know why he lied and said he didn't. Well, yes, I do.

I was a mess when he showed up in my motel room. It was about a month after I started sobering up, hating myself for leaving, feeling too much at once. All the nastiness I had filled myself with were still leaving my body. My thoughts were not always my own. I was still in the stage of wanting to go home, yet too scared that people would see through me.

Seeing myself through Max's eyes scared the shit out of me. In his expression, I saw all the ugliness I had allowed into my life. I saw everyone's disappointment, and that was when I decided I couldn't go home. So, I lashed out.

I told Max about all the shit I had done, who I had done. I told him lies to send him off, not wanting to see his pity, his concern. I told him I hated him, hated my family, hated Claire. I lied and lied, throwing shit, hurting myself, being the worst version of myself so he would leave, so I wouldn't have to see that disappointment.

That's why Max lied and said he didn't find me. That's why I will live with the regret that the last thing I ever said to him was that I hated him. That's why I lashed out at Kyle when I first heard about Max's death. That's why I don't know if I could ever face Cyn again. That's why it took me so long to come back.

September 1, 2011
I don't have much to say this time. I'm basically
writing this to send you some things that speak better
than my words do.
Missing you,

Inside is another sim card. Every letter since Nico's birthday has one or two pictures in it, but this one has a whole a lot more. I plug it into my laptop and scroll through them all, seeing Nico held by everyone, seeing Nico lying in a bouncy chair, seeing him sleeping. She has a lot of pictures of him sleeping. There are some professional photos of the two of them, and some of just him. A month later and he still has a head full of dark hair, and his eyes are changing colors, looking muddier now.

September 26, 2011
Asshole,
Yes, I'm back to being angry! Our son is two
months old today, and instead of getting easier, it gets

harder and harder. And you're not here to help, damn you! You are going to miss his first crawl, step, teething, potty training—everything! And I HATE you for it! I will NEVER, EVER forgive you for being so selfish!

I hope you regret never knowing what it feels like to have your son depend on you, to have him hold on so tightly to your finger, snuggling up to your warmth, looking for your protection and security. I hope you regret not knowing how it feels when he studies your face as intently as you study his, memorizing everything.

Damn you, Noah!

I don't think I have it in me to ever forgive you. That's how tired and angry and sad I feel today.

Regardless, he is YOUR son ... I can't talk about it anymore right now.

Nico and I are going to visit Troy, Chelsea, and their baby, Tori. Then I will be leaving the States with Nico. At this moment, I need to get as far away from you as possible. Two more months, and I will be far, far away from every reminder of you. Well, except for our son ... and your guitar. I'm taking that with us for Nico. He needs a part of his daddy by him.

Melancholy Mommy

That letter makes me cringe, and guilt festers inside of me.

November 9, 2011

If and when you ever get these letters, me and Nico are in Pisa, Italy now. We are living with your most favorite person in the world, Signora Gelardi.

December 25, 2011

Merry Christmas, Noah.

I wanted to send you these pictures I took of Nico

*today. For only being five months old, he has a handle
on this Christmas tradition. Of course, he thinks the
papers and boxes are more exciting than the gifts
themselves.*

I stop reading to flip through the pictures, smiling as I see my boy sitting up on his own, fists full of paper in his hands, not even interested in the toys surrounding him. Gelardi is the in the background, sitting in an old-fashioned rocking chair, looking at Nico with a small smile on her face. Jonathan and, surprisingly, Kyle are there, too, laughing at something in the one picture they are in, standing in the background behind Claire, who is holding a squirming Nico in her arms.

*Dad flew in for Christmas and brought me a
surprise—Kyle! It was so good to see him. He's doing
well in school. Still no girlfriend, but he and Signora
Gelardi's granddaughter were eyeing each other
over dinner tonight, much to Signora Gelardi's
disappointment. It was funny to watch all the tension
at the table.*

And I had a date tonight.

I almost stop reading right there, already knowing where this is going.

*I hate to admit that it's the first one since you
left, but it is what it is. I want to say it's because I've
been too busy, but I could never lie to you. And maybe
I'm hoping by telling you that you will rush in like a
knight in shining armor and rescue me, and we can
live happily ever after. But fairy tales aren't real.*

*His name is Jesse. He's British, which I can't
help loving his accent. And he works with me. The
date went well, just a walk along the river and
stopping to hear the Christmas bells from the*

churches. I loved that part. Really magical. Neither of
us have made company yet, so we weren't needed at
work tonight. I kind of like not having responsibilities
like that.

You should be happy to hear that while the date
went well, and he did kiss me at the end of it, I
couldn't help hurrying to my room to write to you ...

I rip the letter to smithereens, frustration and anger at myself
welling up.

January 1, 2012
Happy new year, Noah

Enclosed is a picture of Nico with a party hat on, staring up at the
fireworks in awe. The kid is so handsome. His eyes are brown now.
He looks just like me, which makes me realize the pictures Katy had
on her refrigerator weren't my baby pics; they were Nico's. The truth
was staring me right in the face the entire time, and I was too stupid to
see it.

March 14, 2012
When are you going to show up? When are you
going to put us out of our misery and let us know if
you are alive or dead? I am so conflicted right now
and could use my best friend: you. Despite everything,
you are still my best friend. I will always, always love
you. You are the father of our child, how can I not?
It's more than that ...
I slept with Jesse last night. And now I feel so
damn guilty, and I have no reason to be. No. Reason!
You *left* me. You *are probably sleeping with*
hundreds of women and not me. *So why do I feel like*
I am cheating on you? Why can I not feel any of the
passion I felt with you with him? What makes you so
damn special!

Nothing. I'm not special at all. I am a broken, messed up person who leaves the woman they love pregnant and alone, without a word, for over four years.

I'm sorry, Claire.

I walk away for a while after reading that letter and turn back to the pictures of Nico. It puts me in a better mood before I can return to the letters, reading some from my family and used-to-be friends before going back to hers.

> *March 22, 2012*
>
> *I am sorry for my last letter. It was uncalled for, and I shouldn't have even sent it, but I made a promise to myself that I would send everything to you: the good, the bad, the despicable. That last letter was the latter.*
>
> *Today, I write about happy times.*
>
> *Nico started walking! Signora Gelardi videotaped it since I was at work when it happened. I cried when I found out. She called me right away, and I ran home to see him. Literally.*
>
> *I enclosed too many pictures for you, but this is such a huge milestone, and I wanted you to have as many pieces of it as you can, however you can.*

My throat lumps up again at thinking this is something we share: missing his first steps. The video isn't attached, but I do go through the pictures, sharing in the joy of the milestone. I am so damn proud of the little guy who looks proud of himself; a big, toothy smile on his face.

> *April 13, 2012*
>
> *Enclosed is a CD of videos of all Nico's firsts up until now. Also, he's been saying Dada since yesterday, which is on here. I thought that marked the perfect time to consolidate all the videos and send*

them to you.
Happy early birthday.

I rush to get the card in my laptop, making sure to save the previous card's pictures and videos on my hard drive. Then I spend an unknown amount of time watching video after video, replaying some of them.

The sun is coming up by now, but I'm not tired in the least.

> *May 1, 2012*
> *Happy 21ˢᵗ Birthday, Noah!*
> *How does it feel to be able to drink legally? Not that you were ever much of a drinker before, but who knows now? Times change, right? People change. Like me. I love wine now. How can you live in Italy and not appreciate it?*
> *I wish you all the happiness in the world for your birthday. Be safe.*
> *Loves,*

Enclosed are more pictures of Nico and Claire, obviously taken by someone else with them at the opera house. Claire carries him around, pointing at different things. I can imagine her explaining everything to him. And he looks like he is holding on to every word, either staring intently at what she is pointing at or watching her as she talks to him.

> *June 11, 2012*
> *Some updates, since it's been over a month since I last wrote to you. Sorry about that. I'm enclosing lots of more pictures to make up for it. It's down season, so Signora Gelardi took us around Italy for some sightseeing, as you can see from the pictures.*
> *Nico continues to grow and grow. I can't believe he's already almost a year old. Another year you have missed. He's running around everywhere now and*

baby gates are a thing of the past since he is climbing over them. Scares me to death! Your mom tells me this is a trait I have you to thank for.

She and your dad were here for a couple of weeks. They got us into parts of the Coliseum that are blocked off from tourist. Jesse bought Nico a wooden sword and plastic shield in remembrance of that memory. He didn't care for the shield, but he loves his wooden sword and uses it to strike out at everyone when he has a tantrum ...

I laugh at that, hoping he hit Jesse where it counts.

... so Mummy (as he calls me; picked up from Jesse's accent, no doubt) had to put it away and replace it with a foam one, which he is NOT happy about. Oh well. Bad mummy.

And our baby is bilingual. I try to speak as much English as I can, but with as much Italian as he is around, he picks up more of that.

I have three more weeks before auditions for this season starts. Signora Gelardi was kind enough to give me a break. Actually, I don't think it was out of kindness. I think she is sick, but the stubborn woman won't admit it.

Jesse is doing well. It feels so weird to write that. However, you should know since he's around your son so much. We've been together for six months now. He's a wonderful man. Kind, caring, gentle, smart. I can't help comparing him to you, though. He doesn't get me the way you do. He doesn't hold me the same. I blame that on me more than him.

You see, I'm not the same as I once was. I used to cry in front of others; not anymore. I used to be able to tell you all my secrets; now I hold everything inside. I can't give that piece of myself away anymore.

I used to love with reckless abandon; now I fear giving away so much. I used to laugh until I had tears running down my face, dance naked in the snow, trust; now those childhood fancies are gone. Now I look at everything critically, weighing the pros and cons before taking a step. I have learned that's how it is to be an adult.

Hugs and kisses from your son. (I show him your picture, and he kisses it goodnight every night, saying "nigh nigh, Dada.")

Once again, I am walking away. I go into the kitchen and grab a beer, finishing it before taking a breath. I rest my head against the refrigerator door and take more deep breaths.

It hurts. This really, really hurts.

Claire has been such a great mom. Anyone can see that from the pictures alone. The fact that Nico knows about me … I can't even put into words how that makes me feel. It's painful, but a wonderful pain, if that makes any sense.

Tossing my empty beer bottle in the trash, I then pour myself a glass of water and head back to the closet, noting that it's now past seven in the morning.

> *July 26, 2012*
> *I hate you. Dramatic, I know. But I do. I really, really do.*
>
> *I was sitting here, drinking by myself after I put Nico to bed on his first birthday, and I started to cry at the loss of you. Not my loss. Oh, no. I'm over that. Yep,* way *over it. No, I'm talking about Nico's loss.*
>
> *He called Jesse daddy today! Jesse! Jesse is NOT his daddy. You are, dammit! Wherever the hell you are, you need to get here and BE the daddy! Get over yourself and take responsibility!*

Well, that has been the hardest thing I have read so far.

I sit back and stare at the wall in front of me, trying to clear my mind of that letter. I thought the worse thing I would read is her telling me she hates me, which I have read plenty of, but reading *that* is so much worse. I want to beat Jesse's face in, snatch up my kid, and ... I don't know what.

Taking another break from Claire's letters, I read some of my family's. Mom and Dad write about things they are doing. Katy writes about life with her, Mark, and Abby, and how things are going with Kyle. I guess he got serious with that Giuliana around this time, getting his associate degree before enrolling in EMT certifications. Mark and Katy were a bit disappointed at first, but then they warmed up to it after hearing Kyle gush about his job.

He writes to me about moving to Italy for a while, about Giuliana and what he thinks about her. It's weird reading this side of Kyle. He was such a goof-off when last I knew him. Now he's this serious, life-saving, in love guy I don't even know anymore. Another stab to the heart.

After I read a year's worth of letters from my family, I get the nerve to go back to Claire.

September 17, 2012

I'm sorry it's been so long since I wrote. After my last letter, I kind of lost it. I wish you knew how hard it's been raising a child and trying to keep up the appearance of their daddy who is never here. I never want our son to know his daddy walked out on us; do you hear me? I'm more convinced now than I was in the early days that you overheard my conversation to Troy and ran because of Nico. I won't tolerate him ever thinking that. I would rather you were dead than have him know you left us like the scared shitless kid you obviously were. Still must be.

I didn't like someone else being called daddy by Nico, and Jesse and I had a blowout over it. He doesn't understand why it matters, and I can't blame him. It might be neurotic, but I still have hope that

318

Nico will have a relationship with you one day.
As my apology for thinking I could cut you out of
our lives (hence the two months' radio silence from
me), I have enclosed this letter in a big package for
you. In it you will find Nico's binkie, his first outfit, a
copy of his hand and footprints from the hospital, a
copy of his birth certificate, which I did name you as
his daddy, something I debated on for almost eight
months. Also, there is an up-to-date video copy, and
lots more pictures. You should be able to fill up album
after album from all the pictures I have sent you. I
know I have.
We are in the beginning of this year's season, so
unless something important happens, I won't be able
to write as much. I have a minor role now and am the
understudy for the lead. Much excitement!

I look for the corresponding box she is referring to and go through it. Claire is right; the amount of pictures she sent takes over an hour to go through.

I save the best for last, holding Nico's binkie, caressing his first outfit, study his hand and footprints, and then I read every word of his birth certificate, getting emotional all over again at seeing Claire and my name side by side, seeing Nico's hyphenated last name and wondering what could have been if I had never left.

By this point, I'm hungry, but I have no appetite. I finally move out of the closet, though, and pack everything into the living room before making myself a sandwich and forcing myself to eat it. I feel exhausted, but I want to finish reading everything.

I replay all the videos, putting them on repeat so it runs through each video, and lie down on the couch. Around the time I'm watching Nico eat his first birthday cake, I fall into a dreamless sleep and wake up when the sun is setting.

The videos are now on Nico's birth again. I let it continue to run as I get up and shower. I shave, get dressed, then head into the kitchen to find something to eat. Finding nothing, I order Chinese take-out then return to the letters.

October 2, 2012
Nico decided he wants to be a piano player when
he grows up. Too soon? Yeah, maybe, but he sure
does love banging away on that thing. Signora
Gelardi is content to let him sit on her lap and pound
away for hours. And let me tell you, that little guy is
persistent. He gets this sound in his head and doesn't
seem to give up until he gets it the way he wants it.
Then he looks up at you with such pride on his face
and the biggest smile! Love it.
What I really want to tell you in this letter is that
Jesse proposed, but I couldn't go through with it. I
love him, but I'm not in love with him.

I sigh and toss the letter down. I don't want to read this shit. Then I think about how much I owe it to her. So, I suck it up and pick the damning letter back up. I know she doesn't marry the guy.

[...]
How can I put on an engagement ring when I still
wear the pendant you gave me? How can I marry one
man when I have a baby with another, who might not
even know it? I can't. I simply cannot.
September 27, 2012. Remember that date as the
day another man asked me to marry him. A man
worthy, yet I'm not.
How can I be true to him when you are still in
my heart? I mean, I carried your seed inside me, and
we created beauty out of it. We created a miracle
together. How do you move on from that?

I read some more letters from her and the others before the Chinese delivery guys shows up. Then I stop to eat, replaying Nico's baby videos. I can't get enough of the little guy. And seeing Claire like that, being able to watch her, it's addicting.

There are videos where Nico says, "Hi, Daddy," and I lose all appetite at that, feeling angst and love simultaneously. Another video is shot where Nico doesn't know he is being observed, playing my guitar that sits on the floor in front of him. He plucks at the strings, humming some unknown song in his head. Another video shows him and Jesse at the zoo. The kid has awe all over his face as he feeds the farm animals or looks at wonder at the African animals, pointing and speaking gibberish in his excitement. I cringe at those, hating those wild animals.

> *July 25, 2013*
> *Signora Gelardi passed away.*

Well, damn, that sucks. I wasn't her biggest fan, and she wasn't mine, but I know how much she meant to Claire.

> *I know I mentioned it before, but she's been sick*
> *for a long time now. She kept fading away, leaving the*
> *house less and less, leaving her chair less and less,*
> *yelling at everyone less and less. Giuliana found her.*
> *Thank God it wasn't Nico, whose second birthday is*
> *tomorrow. He usually wakes up before me and crawls*
> *into her lap for morning cuddles. For once, maybe*
> *God's intervention, he slept in the day she passed*
> *away. That was over a month ago. [...]*

I doubt Nico would remember something like that, but I know my own childhood scars and thank whoever was watching out for him that he didn't find her like that.

> *December 15, 2013*
> *Kyle is staying with us for the rest of the month.*
> *Him and Giuliana are pretty close now. I've accepted*
> *the fact that he doesn't come here to see us anymore,*
> *just Giuliana. He's staying with me this time, though.*

No more crashing at the Gelardi's house. Giuliana is at my place most of the time, anyway, since she's claimed the position as Nico's nanny. That's what she wants in life, so I pay her for it.

She brings him to the opera house to visit me during the day so I can see more of him. Everyone loves Nico. He's such a great kid. I can't even call him a baby anymore. Over two years old, and already he is a little man. Just thinking about it has me hoping once again that you are finally getting my letters and reading about what an amazing kid he is. I hope it sends you running to us. Nico knows you're his daddy. He's waiting for you.

We love you, Noah ... still.

She hasn't written that in a while. It warms my soul and gives me hope that after three years she still felt that way.

I read through more letters of the day-to-day activities, and then I get to one from right after I visited Katy.

September 29, 2014,

I'm hurt and angry again. You went to see Mark and Katy and not me? What did I do wrong? Is it the letters? No, of course not. You just got them. Ugh. I wish I knew!

Katy told me about the bracelet, Noah. If you hate me so much, why do you still wear it?

And the business card? What does it mean? I have half a mind to stalk you and make a scene. Dare would love that. She's all for getting the pitch forks.

June 16, 2014

I googled your name and finally got a hit. Honestly, I've googled your name often for the past four years. It's been a while now since last time I did. You start to lose hope after four years of nothing.

I heard a song on the radio that was a different rendition of one you used to play forever ago. I couldn't believe it when I heard it. I called Chris right away (yeah, I still talk to him once a while), and he turned on the radio to listen. I don't think I need to tell you how pissed off he was, especially because the band slowly dissolved in the first year you left.

Chris now co-owns his dad's garage. He's doing good. Practically gave up on music altogether, but you can still hear him playing the drums occasionally. I don't know what happened to Trey and Shaun. When the band gave up, they all went their separate ways.

Anyway, I am so proud of you and hate you at the same time. I can't believe you wrote a song for your favorite band. I still remember going to their concert with you, my first one. Well, my only one. I thought most of those bands wrote their own songs. Regardless, it's still pretty cool. Congratulations, Noah.

And now the hating you part. I'm moving on, as much as I can since I still write to you like a total stalker. But there is still this ache where my heart is. And then I see you in a group picture with the band, smiling, shaking hands, recording together, and I hate that you can smile like that, like you can move on *move on. Like you're a selfish asshole when I know you're not. At least, you used to not be.*

Good luck to you, Noah.

After that letter, I can't take anymore. It seems like too much of a good-bye.

Chapter 27

Does This Mean ...?

~Claire~

A couple days' worth of rest, and then running into Noah two nights ago, and I am back to being more tired than before.

Angel jumps up onto my lap and curls herself into a ball on my lap. I pet her with one hand, holding a glass of wine with the other, as I stare out into the night. There isn't much to look at, just another building across the street, but it is raining and the lights from passing cars make interesting shadows and color displays on the building.

Really, I'm not even paying attention. I see it, but it doesn't register. All I see are flash images of the other night, seeing Noah up on stage again, thinking about the subtle changes in him. I compare him from then to now and think about all the in-between.

Almost six years from the time I first saw him to now. So much has changed.

And then my mind circles back to the big questions. When will Noah read the letters? Will he ever? If or when he does, will he show up, or will he stay away, run again?

Either way, my heart speeds up. If he runs, then he will never know his son, the little boy who is sleeping right now in Dare's old bedroom. And if he shows up ... I can't even think of what I will say to him.

I rehearse what I would say all the time. All. The damn. Time. I literally have conversations going on in my head. I stay up at night, thinking about it repeatedly. Constant conversations that always end with me in tears. No matter what, I know it will not end well.

If or when the showdown occurs, it's going to be the most emotional experience of my life.

After the run-in with Noah, and fearing he will try to reach out again, I took Nico to the one place I know Noah will never go, not willingly—the zoo.

I laugh thinking about that, which unsettles Angel, who lifts her head to give me that annoyed cat look.

Thinking of Nico has me getting up to check on him. I head down the hall to his room and silently open his door. His room is a typical little boy's room, with toys scattered around from where he left them in the middle of playing. He has a single bed against one wall with a small table next to his bed that has his nightlight, an illumination of the constellations projected on his walls and ceiling. There is a low table across the room where he plays with his figurines and cars, building miniature cities that turn into battlefields. And then there is Noah's guitar, set in a stand in one corner of the room, no toys near it, like it's a shrine to his father.

My little Nicholas. He was a total surprise, one that scared me to death. I thought my life was over when I found out I was pregnant the day after my mother died. And, for a while, it really felt like my life was ending. But really, it was just beginning, like the pregnancy was the cocoon, and when Nico arrived, I became a butterfly. At that moment, all the hard work and motivation I thought I always put into my goals became mediocre. It didn't compare to the determination I had when my son was laid in my arms.

When Noah and I first moved to New York, there was so much going on, and then with the chaos of school, and my mom dying ... Time slipped on by, and before I knew it, I was two months pregnant. I was due for a birth control shot in August, the same time we moved. Hence, I forgot to get my booster injection. I didn't even think about getting a new doctor in the city. I don't know if I thought I would wait until I went home for the holidays or what. I wasn't thinking.

Nevertheless, that's in the past, everything worked out well—for the most part—and I have a healthy, beautiful almost four-year-old now.

Nico is a wonder I keep a secret in my professional life. Not many people outside of my immediate family and friends know about him. I already have my dating life splashed all over the news, I don't need my son showcased, too.

I lean down over him, swiping his wavy brown hair away from his forehead before kissing it. He is the exact replica of Noah. If you held up their two baby pictures together, you couldn't tell the difference. Same hair, same dark brown eyes, full lips, long legs, tall—everything Noah. He also has Noah's photographic memory.

He plays with Noah's guitar all the time, but he doesn't know how to play. Basically, it's this really cool toy from his daddy.

Nico knows who his father is. I don't keep that from my son. He sees pictures of him all the time. I even keep some out around the home, wanting Nico to know he does have a daddy, just …

Daddy has a lot of work to do.

Daddy can't get away from work.

I don't know when Daddy will come.

The older he gets, the harder it is to keep up the charade. That's why I want Noah to finally come here, commit to his son, be a part of his life.

Noah's songs on the radio help to drive home that "Daddy's working" lie. I can always tell which one are his, and even look it up when I hear one to verify.

Nico gets so excited when he hears one, so proud of his father. He knows all the words to all Noah's songs, singing at the top of his lungs, even the bad words, which I chastise every single time.

Kids. You want to laugh, yet you know that's not right.

I leave his room, securing the door shut, before walking back into the living room. I pick up the wine glass, finish it off, and then set it down before snuggling back into the corner of the couch.

Tap, tap, tap. I hear a gentle knock on my door and sit up. The movement has Angel leaping off the couch, where she lands on the floor, sits, and proceeds to groom herself like that was her intention all along.

Tiptoeing toward the door, I look through the peephole and lose my breath.

~Noah~

My hands shake as I tap on Claire's door. It's late, but her light is on. I don't know if she keeps the lights on all night, yet I figure it wouldn't hurt to try. That's why I simply tap on her door. I don't want to wake my son up, and if Claire is up and in the living room, she will hear it. If not, well, then I will have to find the nerve once again tomorrow morning.

I spent all day finishing the letters before I ran an errand then went to visit my parents, something I should have done four months— shit, four years ago. That was hard, but nothing compared to this moment. My mom cried, and my dad wouldn't let me go, hugging me harder than ever as I apologized and explained everything as best I could. I felt like a little kid again.

I called Jonathan, too. More apologizing. There was silence on the other end of the line for so long when I told him it was me that I thought he hung up on me. Then he used that tone he always used on me, telling me he was glad I was safe, but I had a responsibility to Claire and myself to let her know I was alive and own up to my mistakes. I agreed and informed him that I was on my way to her as we talked. I only got off the line with him when I was in front of her apartment.

I hear the door lock click, and my heart stops, just to start galloping, pounding against my chest. I can hear that shit in my ears it's thumping so hard. And my hands tremble harder, not knowing what to expect, what to say, if I will even be allowed in. This is the scariest moment of my life.

~Claire~

I can't believe he's here. He came. Does this mean …? Did he read the letters? Does he know?

I look through the peephole again to see Noah looking down, looking nervous. His hair is styled different, something I didn't notice the other night. It's shorter, more put together and not the messiness of long ago. He is dressed the same. I don't think his style will ever change much, no matter how many years pass. Noah will still be wearing those boots and jeans even when he is an old man.

In one hand, he holds a few pieces of paper. My letters? In his other hand, he holds a superhero action figure. Nico's favorite, as a matter of fact, and one he doesn't have.

I lose my breath again as I think about what this means.

He knows. He knows, and he came here.

I feel tension I never knew I carried leave my body. At the same time, my chest constricts, something feels like it gets lodged in my throat, and my whole body feels exhausted beyond comprehension.

Taking steadying breaths, my heart erratic, hands trembling, I reach out to the top lock.

~Noah~

The seconds feel like minutes as I listen closely to the sound of another lock clicking, the door handle jangling, and then the release of air as the door slowly opens. And there is Claire, half concealed behind the door, holding it wide open for me with trepidation in her wide eyes, looking like she wants to run more than she wants me here.

She is dressed for bed, wearing a tank top that stretches over her breasts, satin pajama shorts that show off her glorious legs, and a long wrap sweater that she pulls around her, covering everything up when she sees me looking her over. Her hair is piled up in a messy bun, and her face is free of makeup, with dark shadows under her eyes. It's the pendant settled low on her chest that captures my attention the most.

I close my eyes briefly and relieve myself of the breath I was holding. I can't believe she is still wearing that after everything.

"Hey," I say softly, not knowing what else to say. I want to start by apologizing, but words aren't enough. It won't send us back in time. It won't erase the past four plus years. It won't help or change anything. So, *hey* is all I have, until I can act an apology out, prove I'm not going anywhere ever again. I want to know my son … and Claire again, if that is even possible.

I know I don't deserve it. I don't even deserve the fact that she opened her door. Nevertheless, I am still selfish; that hasn't changed. I'm going to grasp on tightly to whatever mediocre thing, act, or words she gives me, and I won't back down.

"Hey," she chokes out then clears her throat before looking down, trying to hide the glimmer of tears in her eyes, the nervous flush of her cheeks.

God, so beautiful. And I am a bastard for even thinking that right now.

She clears her throat again before looking back up then away, gesturing to the living room that has changed quite a bit since the last time I was here. "Come in?"

I don't say anything as I watch my foot pass over the threshold, a vise choking my throat as I step back into the one place I have longed to come home to for four long, miserable years.

I stop inside the door and look around as I hear Claire shut the door behind me. Nothing in this place is the same, everything is new … except those damn curtains. There are Legos, cars, books, figurines, and a bunch of other toys piled in bins along one wall, and I smile sadly when I see those before glancing at the couch, hoping that by some chance Nico is there, but he is not.

I glance down the hall to where his bedroom must be as Claire passes me and makes her way to the galley kitchen. I remain where I am, still holding some of her letters and my childhood favorite superhero as I watch her pour us both a glass of wine. That is a weird sight for me since Claire was never much of a drinker when we were kids. I know now from her letters that has changed.

She walks out of the kitchen, holding both glasses, and pauses at the sight of me. Her wrap is open again, flowing down her sides and exposing her scant clothing. Her face is impassive when she starts to move again, but I didn't miss the flashes of emotions on her face when she paused: fear, hope, sadness, disbelief.

She sets the glasses down on the coffee table before giving me a look like, *well, are you going to sit?* Then she sits herself down, close to the edge, ramrod straight. She feels the same anxiety that is in me.

I make my way to the couch, keeping distance between us when I sit, wanting to be closer, yet knowing she doesn't. Then I set Nico's gift down on the table and pick up the glass and take a sip.

Putting the glass back down, I face the wall in front of us, noting Claire is doing the same.

Why does this have to be so awkward? I expected it, while hoping we would somehow slip into how it used to be.

From the first time I met Claire, words simply flowed. Now, I have nothing.

"I don't know what to say," Claire finally says.

Picking up the glass of wine again, I chuckle, and not with humor, before downing the entire thing, hoping for some liquid courage. "Me, neither."

Deciding one glass won't be enough, I hold the cup out to her and ask, "May I?" gesturing toward the kitchen.

She nods, and I get up, hearing her take a deep breath as I head into the kitchen, pour myself another glass, and then chug that one down before refilling. I should have gotten tipsy before coming here.

"I do know one thing I have to say," Claire starts as I head back into living room, a brand new, just opened bottle in my hands. I give her a raised brow to continue, and she does. "All I really want to know is"—she swallows, and I know how hard this is for her—"why."

That is the one thing I hoped we wouldn't have to get into tonight. I don't want to do this right now.

I scold myself at that thought. I might be selfish, but when it comes to Claire's needs, I have always been considerate. Well, except when it came to the no sex thing. That was for her, though. Everything else, I was—and still am—putty in her hands.

"Claire …"

"No, don't use that tone with me," she snaps, surprising the hell out of me.

I look over at her face to see a fury there I have never seen before. Tears cascade down her face in anger as she starts in, escalating my own anger, anger at myself.

"Over four years, Noah. No calls. No texts. You disconnected your phone. We didn't know if you were dead or alive, and for what?" she screams the last word.

Too irritated to sit still any longer, I stand up and start pacing. This is not how I planned this to go.

"I was a kid! Fuck, Claire—"

"You ripped my heart out—"

"—I was so scared. And I wasn't ever good enough for you."

"—and I've been so empty since you left, with this gaping hole, right here!" She pounds on her chest, right over her heart. Then she takes a deep breath and closes her eyes as I continue, the words flowing now, coming out angry, but not at her.

"I saw a way out, and I took it. I *wanted* to believe you were cheating on me. I needed to get away before you realized how worthless I was, that you could do so much better. You were surrounded by all these people that were like you, and I'd look back and see my band, the groupies, the drugs, the alcohol. I thought, *how can we make this work, make this last? Me on the bottom, with you, standing on some high pedestal with all these rich, beautiful people.* It never made sense to me how you could love me. So"—I pause my pacing, facing her, looking at her closed eyes—"I thought I saw something, and I went with it. And I'm so fucking sorry!"

She opens her eyes and continues on a whisper like she didn't hear me. "It hurts, Noah. It hurts so badly, and I want it to go away." She gasps, clutching her waist now. "Why won't it go away? Why couldn't I let you go and move on? How did you make it look so easy? How could you …?"

I don't know what to do. I want so much to go to her, hold her, take that pain away and have it taken from me. I want to soothe each other. I want to rewind the past. I want to go back to the way it was. But I fear her rejection. I expect it, but I fear it.

Taking that chance, tired of fearing and not acting after holding back for so damn long, I move toward her, presuming the minute I touch her, or she feels the couch dip, she will run, push me away. She doesn't disappoint.

The second I put my hand on her back, my ass not even on the couch yet, she attacks.

She beats on my chest, my arms, my legs, tears running in torrents down her face, cursing me like she has never cursed before. And I take it, letting her get it all out, feeling each blow and word she spouts like a stab to the heart. I let her do her worse until she weakens, and then I am holding her, my arms wrapped around her. And she sobs into my chest, her arms tight around her own waist.

My throat tightens, my chest feels like it's about to explode, and I can feel my own tears trying to force their way out as I rock her in my arms, apologizing repeatedly. It's all I can say.

"I'm sorry. I'm sorry. I'm so sorry."

It's a mantra, matching the furious beat of my heart.

And that's when our son walks in.

"Mommy?"

My head whips in his direction, and Claire quickly pulls away from me, pushing me back at the same time she swings her legs to the ground and frantically wipes away her tears.

Nico stares at us with confusion as Angel—I can't believe I forgot about that cat again—wraps around his little legs. His head is tilted to the side, looking from his mom to me. I see another emotion hit him when his eyes widen. He looks from me to the wall then to me again before warily shuffling around the coffee table to his mom's side, all the while still staring at me.

He climbs up onto Claire's lap and burrows against her, his head fitting under her chin as she wraps her arms around him. Still, he stares at me before looking at the wall again then back at me.

I follow his gaze to a picture of Claire and me. It was taken one of the times we went to the lake with Kyle and Abby. Kyle took the picture when we weren't paying attention. Claire and I had just gotten out of the water, our hair drenched, and I had wrapped a towel around her, my hands on her arms as she looks up at me, laughing at something.

I look back at Nico, realizing he recognizes me, yet he doesn't know how to react to my presence. I don't, either. I'm so shocked to see him. It's like looking at a mini-me, which I don't know how to take. It's bizarre.

I have a kid. With Claire. That shock is hitting me all over again.

"Hey, Nico," I finally say, not knowing what else to say. Poor little guy is probably scared and confused as hell.

That tightening in my throat is happening once again, choking me.

"Hi," he says, barely a whisper. The next thing he says breaks me. "You're my daddy."

I feel my eyes well up, and I let out a gasping breath as that hold on my throat becomes too much to bear.

"Yeah, Nico, I'm your daddy," I manage to choke out before I feel the tears win their battle to escape.

I lose all thought process as I scoot closer to the two of them and pull Nico into my arms and hold on for dear life, crying into his little neck and shoulder as he grips me back as fiercely. My whole body shakes as I lose my shit, sobbing as I try to hide my face in his little neck. I feel him pat my shoulders, his hand so little for such a manly gesture.

Then I hear Claire start to sob again, and I pull back from Nico, still holding on to him tightly, as I look at her and spout, "I'm so sorry, Claire. God forgive me, I didn't know. I didn't know."

She doesn't respond, just cries harder, covering her face with her hands. And all I can do is cry with her.

~Claire~

By now, Nico is crying, too, gripping Noah as he whimpers. My heart breaks at that, more so than it's already broken. How can a heart sustain so much pain?

Finding out Noah left because he felt unworthy, using the excuse of cheating, that hurts, but not as much as if I found out it was because of Nico. That would have killed me. It was something I feared for so long now that, now that I know, I don't know how to take this. I need a moment, or two, or five.

I make my way to my bedroom, leaving Noah and Nico to have their moment. I need to think. I need to be alone to calm myself down, because every time I see Noah back in my home, I break apart all over again. I can't believe he is here. He knows, and he is here, holding his son, seemingly happy yet remorseful to be doing so. He cares. That's all I wanted. That's all I need—my son knowing his daddy, his daddy being in his life. I feel like I completed a life mission.

I hear Noah sniff and let out a deep breath as I walk into my room. Closing the door, I then hear him tell Nico, "I'm sorry for crying, little man. I'm so happy to see you."

333

More tears spill down my cheeks at that, and I rest my head against the closed door, inhaling deep breaths.

My emotions are all over the place. I'm so happy for them both that I fear my heart will burst, while sadness sits in my stomach. So many years lost.

My head is splitting. Too much tension in the past half hour. Too many emotions and holding in my anger, my despair, my nervousness of seeing Noah. It's all too much too fast.

Knowing I shouldn't because of the wine, I make my way to the vanity and pull out my bottle of pills, shaking one out into my hand. Then I grab a bottle of water that always sits on my nightstand and swallow down the pill. I fear I will live with these headaches for the rest of my life.

I sit on my bed, giving myself and the guys some alone time. I don't want to cry anymore, not tonight, not ever. I can't even remember if Nico has ever seen my cry. Poor kid. I probably scared him. Not to mention Noah's appearance.

I hope to God he stays. *Please don't put my son through what you put me through.*

But now what? Where do we go from here? How do we do this?

When you are young, you never plan on co-parenting. You never think, *when I grow up, I want to be a single parent and my ex-lover will have my kids on weekends and every other holiday.*

Then I think about the way Noah looked at me from the minute he saw me opening my front door. It was the look of a man appraising and wanting. And when he held me as I cried … it felt like home.

Not needing to go there with my thoughts, I head back out into the living room to see Noah and Nico looking over the superhero toy Noah brought him. Noah is telling Nico it was his favorite superhero when he was a kid, and Nico beams at him, telling him, "Me, too." They both have red-rimmed eyes, but they seem to have gotten past the crying.

I can't believe Noah even cried. I can't remember him ever showing strong emotions. Shock, rarely. Happy, definitely. Sad, not much. Crying? Never. He was always so stoic. It took a lot to get him emotional. I guess facing past mistakes was a breaking point for him.

And his son.

I sit away from them and watch as they interact. Noah is leaning back against the couch with Nico still in his lap, facing each other. They both are so tentative, dancing around the other, asking and answering questions with caution. Nico wants to know where he has been, tells him about the songs on the radio, asks to see where music is made, while Noah asks him what his favorite things are.

Occasionally, Noah will look up at me and give me a smile that is equal parts grateful and reticent. I can see the questions in his every glance. Is this real? How long will it last? How much will you give me of him? I can see he doesn't want to let go, which equally relieves and worries me. There is still so much to talk about.

Eventually, Nico yawns, and I look at the clock to see it's after midnight. Poor little guy.

He curls up against Noah's chest, asking, "Will I see you when I wake up?"

Noah looks at me questioningly. I see him swallow hard. Then I see a look come into his eyes that is half-determination and half-defiance. I know what he is going to say, and it makes my heart flutter in a way that it hasn't fluttered in years.

He looks back at Nico and promises, "I will be here when you wake up."

Chapter 28

Just Headaches

~Claire~

I awake early the next morning. Too early for how much sleep I didn't get. How could I sleep after all the emotional turmoil from the night before? Noah was here. Nico met his father. Noah is back, and he knows. He read the letters.

Just thinking that has me getting out bed, wanting to see if he is still here.

Last night, I let Noah put Nico back to bed while I stood at the door and watched. The moment hit a tender spot for me, with Noah promising him repeatedly that he isn't going anywhere, that he will be on the couch when Nico woke up, and then they could spend the day together. I wanted to cry again at the sight of the two of them, but I promised myself I wouldn't, so I sucked in a deep breath and smiled gently at Nico, telling him goodnight.

When Noah was done, we just stood there in the hallway. I couldn't look at him, and I didn't know what to say. For Nico's sake, I was glad he was staying, but I was conflicted—still am—on him being in my home. Between us, there is only Nico. Noah took away the luxury of comfort between us.

For years, I held on to hope that he would come back, and I always told myself it was for Nico's sake, but I could never lie to myself.

I hoped he would come back for me, too.

That's why it never worked between me and Jesse. I couldn't let go of the past. I couldn't stop comparing Jesse and all other men to Noah. I told myself I couldn't move on because I didn't have closure, when I couldn't move on because I knew in my heart that Noah was the only man for me.

However, our happy ending was crushed. I can't forgive that. I can't forget. The ill feelings still linger and probably always will. Therefore, hoping he came back for me … it's a dream, a fantasy I played and replayed in my mind. Now that he is back, reality checks in and tells me that dreams are meant to be just that—a contemplation of possibilities that one has during sleep or an indulgence used as a distraction. Dreams aren't meant to mix with reality. It's the thoughts one has of promises that aren't meant to be real.

The reality is that I don't trust him not to repeat history the next time he thinks less of himself or things get too hard. Raising a kid is not easy; made even less so when you are Noah and missed out on the first almost four years. He's about to get a reality check on what being a parent means, and he may not be able to handle it.

I will steel myself for the moment he breaks and runs again. I will not fall into the hole I climbed out of the day Nico was born. I will not put myself through those emotions again. I will not expect anything from him, but will be grateful for whatever he gives. I will not let hope weigh me down. I will be strong for my son.

I grab my wrap sweater, sliding my arms through the sleeves and closing it over my torso, not that it likes to stay there. Then I head to the bathroom to take care of business before peeking in on Nico.

He's not there, and that has my heart pounding. For a split second, I fear Noah left with him, or Noah left and Nico went looking for him. Then I calm down when I step into the living room and see them both on the couch.

Noah is sprawled out on his back, one knee bent off the couch, one arm flung over his eyes, while his other arm is curled around our son. Nico is using Noah's arm as a pillow, his body curled in on himself, nestled into Noah's side. He has his superhero figurine hugged tightly against him. Both are sleeping peacefully, their chests rising and falling in tandem.

I turn around, heading back to my room for my camera. Pictures are an image that portray so much. This moment, them lying side by side, I want to have proof of the testament that they share a bond.

I snap a couple of pictures, moving soundlessly around them, trying to capture them at different angles. Neither one of them move. Neither of them hear the soft clicks of the images snapping off. It's then that I notice a few things.

One, Noah is shirtless, and his chest is more defined than it once was. The next thing I notice is the Karma bracelet Noah wears on his left wrist. I lose my breath and lower the camera at seeing that. I can't believe he still has it, that he still wears it, and that does something funny to my insides that I don't want to think about. The third thing I notice is the bandage wrapped around his right wrist. The funny feeling goes away and in its place is dread. What did Noah do, or try to do?

Not wanting to wake him up and risk waking Nico, I set the camera down on the coffee table then make my way back down the hall and into the bathroom. This is the time I would be making breakfast for Nico, but I don't want to wake them by making too much noise. Instead, I take a shower and get dressed, giving them more time to sleep.

Back in my room, I run out of things to do and not even an hour has passed. I still don't hear anything from the living room, meaning they are still asleep, but with nothing else to do, it's time to make breakfast.

Trying to be as quiet as possible, I make pancakes for Nico and omelets for Noah and myself. I remember how Noah used to favor them and think to myself, *why am I doing this?* as I make his favorite then find some fruit to add to the side.

As I flip a pancake over, I sense someone behind me. Turning around, Noah's sleepy eyes and bedhead hair greet me. I look over his shoulder to see Nico restlessly moving around, about to wake up, too.

I don't give Noah another look before turning back around and resuming flipping pancakes. I can't look at him right now. He is still shirtless, and his disheveled state reminds me of too many times waking up beside him when he looked that exact same way.

I shut my eyes tightly, trying to squeeze the imagery out of my mind. This is not the past, and the present is no comparison.

"I, uh, made you an omelet." I gesture toward the little dinette set off the kitchen where I already set out plates, utensils, and the fruit.

When I don't hear a response, I look over my shoulder to see Noah hasn't moved. He is still standing on the other side of the breakfast bar, watching me with a look I am all too familiar with, never thought I would see directed at me again, and one I feel equal parts flustered and ... flattered to see.

It can't be denied. Noah is gorgeous, and any girl would want to see that look from him, and a lot probably have in the past four years.

That thought has my flattered feeling turning to ire. He has no right giving me that look.

I ignore him, happy when Nico wakes up fully and snags Noah's attention. I hear them talk about getting dressed and ready for breakfast. It's too surreal.

God, I hope Noah doesn't leave again and hurt my son. I can't stop that prayer from echoing in my head, in my heart.

While the boys get dressed, I finish cooking and setting the table. I'm getting Nico some juice when I hear them come back in, Nico talking a mile a minute, asking question after question. I smile as I look at him. He is so happy to have his father here. Then my smile slips as I once again think how that can go away.

"What?" I hear Noah ask, and when Nico doesn't reply, I look up to see he is watching me again.

"I'm sorry. What?" I place Nico's cup in front of him before taking my seat.

Noah sits down on the other side of Nico, saying, "You were smiling, and then ... you weren't." His eyes seem to penetrate mine when I look back at him. They snare me in until I quickly look away again. It's too hard to look at him.

"Just thinking," I excuse, rubbing my temples as I feel another debilitating headache coming on. Too much stress.

Happy thoughts.

"Mama, you got another head hurt?" Nico asks, fork poised at his mouth as he looks at me with the puppy dog eye of concern only a toddler can pull off.

I quickly remove my hands from my head and shoot him a smile before digging in to some fruit and placing it on my plate. "I'm fine, baby."

Nico's concerned look drops from his face, and he concentrates on his pancakes, shoving a piece in his mouth while happily swinging his feet. Noah, on the other hand, doesn't fall for it. He stares at me with concern swirling in those dark depths of his.

I continue to ignore him, popping a blueberry in my mouth.

Breakfast continues with Nico's banter, him asking Noah about the most random things like: why cats purr, where do the stars go in the daytime, will he take him trick-or-treating. Then there are the awkward questions like: are you going to live here now, and are you and Mommy going to get married, because the kids on TV all have mommies and daddies that are married. Noah sidelines those questions by asking him something or telling him he wants to see his toys. It makes the tension in my head worse, and my heart feels wrung out.

Then Nico asks, "What happened to your arm?" and now my attention is fully on Noah, wanting to know the same thing.

I stop placing the dishes in the dishwasher to look toward where they now sit in the living room.

Noah's eyes meet mine for a second before he looks back at Nico. "You want to see it?"

I hold my breath at that, now knowing it can't be something bad if he offers to show it to an almost four-year-old.

Nico nods eagerly, and then Noah starts to shove the bandage to the side.

Nico leans over to get a closer look. "What's that?"

"That's your birthdate."

"Oh," Nico states, sounding a little disappointed. He probably expected a battle wound or something equally gruesome.

Meanwhile, my heart skips a beat.

~Noah~

I laugh at the expression on Nico's face. This kid … It's so bizarre to simply look at him.

When I look up at Claire, I see she is rubbing her head again. That and the fact that Nico implied she gets headaches all the time has me worried that there is still more I don't know. Was I right in my previous assumption that Claire is sick? Her mother said she had headaches before she was diagnosed with brain cancer. Has Claire been checked out? Is history repeating itself here?

Nico snags my attention as he tells me we have to go to his room to see all his toys. I follow the little guy down the hall and into his room, which has transformed quite a bit since Dare used to live here. I glance in Claire's bedroom on the way, noting her room is completely different, too. Why is everything so different? I wouldn't think that much could change in four years.

Nico immediately guides me to a familiar sight. My old guitar, the one I dropped when I told myself I saw Claire cheating. I don't know how I missed that last night, and the shock of seeing it has me stunned.

I pick the thing up then sit on the edge of Noah's bed, thrumming the strings and finding it dreadfully out of tune. As I rectify that, I tell Nico, "I learned how to play on this guitar. I wanted one—this one— for a long, long time before your grandparents finally broke down and got it for me when I was eleven. I played every day, almost all day. I used to watch videos to see how guitarists play, mimicking their moves. Then I played in a band. Did your mom tell you that?"

Nico nods. "Mommy has pictures." He jumps up at that and runs out of the room, coming back seconds later with a book that looks so big in his little arms. He sits back on the bed, facing me and crisscrossing his legs with the big book set in front of him.

I put the guitar down and kneel beside him on the floor as he starts flipping through the pages.

"See?" He points to an image of Kyle, Cyn, and me at Jeremy's.

I look at the picture, not recognizing it. I don't remember Claire ever taking pictures at one of our gigs. I wonder if she got this from someone else.

I tell Nico stories about what was going on as he flips through the pages, not remembering who had the camera for most of the pictures.

As we scan images of Claire and my short time together in the city and come across pictures of my old band here, Nico asks, "Will you teach me how to play?" The little guy looks so hopeful I can't deny him.

341

"Of course."

Then his expression turns sad so suddenly it's kind of funny, but before I can even grin, he says, "You don't have to leave for work again, right? You get to stay here now? Because Mommy is really sad. We want you to stay."

I don't know what to say to that. Claire and I haven't talked about what we are going to do. We haven't talked about anything, and I don't know when we will get the chance since I doubt neither one of us want to get into it with Nico here. I wish I could stay here, in their home, but that's wishful thinking. The reality is so much more complicated.

His comment about Claire worries me. I don't know how to feel about that. Does she miss *me*, or miss me for Nico? I can't fathom her wanting what I want after everything. I messed up too much to kindle any hope for that.

"I'm not going anywhere," I promise him. "But I can't stay here, either." I point at the floor, indicating their home. "I live across the city, but I can see you whenever you want. And you can stay with me sometimes." I sit back on the bed and hold my arm out to him, and he quickly crawls over the photo album and into my lap. "I still have a lot to talk to your mom about it, but I promise I won't leave again.

"I work here now; did you know that?" When he shakes his head, looking up at me, I tell him, "You can come with me and see my studio. There are guitars, drums, and lots of other instruments there."

His eyes get wide at that, and I let out a chuckle, mussing up his hair. Then I hear a noise outside his room that has me placing him back on his bed.

"I have to go talk to your mom now, okay? Can you stay in here so I can talk to her?"

He nods. "You're going to come back, right?"

God, that question kills me. How much have I damaged my kid already? A kid so young shouldn't be afraid of people leaving him. Or … maybe it's me he is worried about.

I rub my chest, feeling an ache start. "Yeah, I won't leave until you're ready for me to leave, okay?"

Nico nods again, looking completely miserable, which makes me feel completely miserable. *I'm sorry, Nico.*

I kiss his little head then get up in search of the woman who unknowingly owns every part of me, finding her in her bedroom.

When I saw her earlier, cooking at the stove, dressed in a loose tank top, skinny jeans, her long hair cascading down her back, I thought I was back in time. I almost walked around the bar and slipped behind her, pulling her into me. Now I am hesitant, peering through her cracked open door, watching as she stands by her vanity, her back to me. She pops something—a pill—into her mouth then picks up a bottle of water and chugs down a gulp. I can't see the expression on her face, but her body is taut, like she is strung up too tightly. Worried? In pain? I don't know, but I'm going to find out.

Slipping inside, I close the door behind me and, at the sound, she whirls around, her eyes wide. I know I startled her, but is it because she's hiding something?

She quickly schools her features then asks, "Where's Nico?"

"In his room." I watch her face closely as I tell her, "I told him we have to talk and to stay in his room for a while."

She nods. "Yeah, we didn't really get to hash things out last night."

"Not really," I mutter before diving in, wanting to get to the bottom of her headaches before I drive myself crazy. "What are the pills for? Headaches? How often? Are you sick like your mom was?"

Claire stands there with her mouth slightly open. She doesn't say anything for a long time as we face each other. Eventually, she deflates, squeezes her eyes shut, and starts massaging her forehead. "Can we take this conversation into the living room? I don't really feel comfortable with you in here."

My heart stutters at that, not expecting it. I knew it, but it's different hearing it.

"Yeah, okay. You're right." I try to play off the hurt, acting unaffected as I turn around and open the door.

In the living room, I notice she picked up my makeshift bed and feel guilty for not cleaning it up myself.

When we sit down on the couch, Claire dives in, "So, Nico goes to preschool for a few hours—"

"Claire, your headaches. We were talking about your headaches."

I'm not letting her deter me from this. I need but don't want to know what's wrong with her; scared to death of what she will say.

"They're just headaches, Noah. Tension headaches caused by stress. I started getting them when I was pregnant, and the doctors told me that was normal." She scoffs. "Yeah, a headache that can incapacitate you for weeks isn't normal. Then they continued, and after a year, a doctor prescribed me muscle relaxers instead of pain relievers."

"So, you don't have a tumor?"

"No, no tumor. Just stress. Lots and lots of stress."

The relief I feel at hearing that is astounding. All rigidity leaves my body, and I sink back into the cushions. "Is there anything I can do to help?"

She gives me this perplexing look as she says, "Don't leave again. Don't hurt Nico."

"I promise I won't."

"I remember you promising me once that you would never leave me." She shrugs, a move that looks callous on her with the sardonic tone she uses. "See how that turned out."

My blood boils at that. This is not the same Claire I left. The before Claire would never say something so coldhearted. She always thought of the most rational approach as to not hurt someone's feelings. Her remark was meant to burn.

Fists clenched, white knuckled, I tell her, "I remember that conversation, but like I said last night, I was scared. I made a mistake—the biggest mistake of my life—and I know it doesn't matter now, but I am sorry. If I could go back, I would."

"No regrets. Another conversation we once had." She's talking about my first tattoo. *The unexamined life is not worth living.*

"Yeah, well"—I stretch out my legs, groaning as the muscles in my back loosen—"I have too many regrets now. There's been a lot of shit I haven't thought through. Like that night." I shake my head, talking to myself out loud. "I wish I had stayed at my parents' for a while." I cut off that thought, shaking my head and sitting back up, staring down at the ground between my legs. "It wouldn't have mattered. I still would have run. I remember where my head was then, and it was all about me needing to prove something to myself."

I look up at her. "I went to school." Seeing the wide-eyed surprise on her face, I look away and continue, "Yeah, I didn't know what the hell I wanted to do; I just knew I had to do something. I had to prove something. Then the record company scout found me, and you know all about that. I still went to school, though. I took time off when I came here, but I only have maybe two semesters left."

God, I'm talking to her how I used to, pouring all my internal bullshit onto her lap. I don't know how or why only Claire does that to me.

Sitting back again, I turn slightly toward her. "I regret how I left you. I regret being stubborn and even too scared to check in; see how everyone was doing. I regret not knowing about Nico, you having to do this all alone. But … I have to wonder if what we went through was for the better." I see her lips tighten and hurry to say, "I know it's a shitty thing to say, or even think, but I don't think we would be where we are today if it didn't happen. I don't …" Knowing I'm saying this wrong, I stop to think before I continue to upset her. "If I had stayed, do you know where I see us?"

She shakes her head.

"I see you never going to Italy, never being there when Gelardi died, never starting your career there. I see you still here, trying to finish school, and then never getting picked up because of Nico. I see myself still working with Chris, staying out late hours, and never having *us time* because we would be back to the same routine as before, but now we would have Nico, too.

"Back then, I thought that life was okay, but it wouldn't have been. It would have been suffocating—the same routine day in and day out. You were meant for more, and if I hadn't left, you would have held yourself back and never fought for more."

She starts to cut me off, but I speak over her. "I read your letters, Claire. Every one. Before Nico, you were waiting around. You didn't have any motivation to continue. I saw that with my own eyes before I even left. And I know shit—too much shit—was going on. You were sinking, and I couldn't pull you out. I knew that, and maybe that's one of the reasons I left—back to not being good enough.

"The point is ..." I sigh and scrub my face. "I don't know what the point is, just that shit happens for a reason. What I did was messed up. I'll regret that for the rest of my life. But, looking back, knowing what I know now, I can't regret everything. I can't regret where my actions got us. I can only regret not being here for Nico. I'm sorry, but that's the truth.

"Us. I wish there was a way we could have continued that and still be where we are today, but that's not possible. I ..." I stop myself from saying what I want to say, yet needing to get it out there and put all my cards on the table.

I scoot a tad closer to Claire, trying to look at her, but unable to meet her eyes. "Every second I was gone, I longed to come back." I watch her lips part as she inhales. "Whether I was damning you or missing you, I wanted to come back. Then, after a while, it became so hard to even wish it. Just the thought of turning around made me sick to my stomach. Still, I wanted to. My soul kept looking back, but my heart, my head told me I couldn't, that it was too late." I finally look into her eyes, seeing them watering. "Dammit, Claire, I know—I know—I can't, but I still want to."

She looks away from me and takes a deep breath, her chest rising and falling with the motion.

Neither of us say anything for a minute. I don't know what else to say. I do know whatever she says isn't something I'm going to want to hear, though.

Finally, she looks back at me, her expression resolute. "I don't trust you, Noah. God knows I wished for you to come back so many times for me, for Nico, but I don't trust you to not leave again. I'm glad you're here now but, without trust, there can't be anything else." She shakes her head sadly, her eyes welling up again before she turns her head, hiding her face from me.

Her words are nothing I didn't expect to hear. She says there can't be anything else, but how could she want me to come back if she didn't feel something for me. Even now, she can't even look at me. Like Pandora's box, once everything is let out, all there is left is hope. I hold on to that.

Chapter 29

A Reunion

~Noah~

Claire and I work out an arrangement. Every day, Claire drops Nico off at his preschool class in the morning while I record, and then I pick him up. I take him out to lunch, to the park—wherever he wants to go. Most of the time, we go back to his and Claire's place and chill out. I teach him how to play my old guitar, bringing one of my newer ones with me. He has a knack for music, not surprising.

Sometimes Claire is there when we hang out. We talk, mostly cordial and never much about the past, especially the years I was gone. I ask her a lot of questions, trying to engage her, and sometimes I make her laugh, the one thing I miss about her more than anything. There is still tension between us, but I see it easing up more and more into a resemblance of the comfort it used to be, knowing it will never be how it used to be. I don't think Claire realizes how out of the norm it is for two separated parents to get along so well. I'm not going to point it out, either. Just another point toward me.

Many days, I bring Nico to the studio if there is a project that needs finishing. He likes those days, playing with all the instruments, asking questions about the sound equipment. When it's time to work, he sits quietly in the control room and either watches or colors. My kid is awesome.

At night, we all hang out, playing games or watching some kids' movie until it's time for Nico's bedtime—another out of the norm activity I'm not pointing out. Then I say good-bye, always promising to see Nico in the morning.

Occasionally, we will all go out to dinner, to my parents', or to the movies. Other nights, when Claire works late, I take Nico over to

347

my place. I only have one room, so I give Nico my bed and sleep on the couch. My lease is up in a few months; I'm getting a bigger place for him then.

Sometimes Giuliana comes by to pick Nico up when both Claire and I have to work so he can spend some time with her new charge. She was his nanny, but since I came back, she got another nanny gig. You can tell she loves Nico with a fierceness.

Then, about once a week, Jesse comes over to pick Nico up. Meeting him was an experience I wish I could forget.

"Noah, this is Jesse. Jesse, Noah," Claire introduced us when Jesse stepped into the condo four days after I walked back into their lives.

I didn't even hold my hand out, not wanting to shake the man's hand. Meanwhile, Jesse looked at Claire, different emotions rolling over his face: confusion, surprise, anger, hurt, betrayal, and back to anger.

"Is this why …? Is he why you …?"

I could tell what he wanted to ask, but there was no way he was going to ask it in front of me. He proved that with his next words.

"Can we talk out in the hall?"

Claire nodded, and Jesse reopened the door, letting her pass while glaring daggers at me. I raised an eyebrow at him.

Creeping toward the shut door, there was no way I was missing what he had to say.

"You could have at least given me a heads-up," Jesse chastised.

"He showed up a few days ago, and we have been busy trying to sort out a schedule for Nico—"

"And at work today? Claire, we sat in the same room together for hours; you couldn't tell me then?"

First, I didn't like the way he talked to her. Second, she had said "we." That was a powerful word. Third, I didn't like the fact that they spent so much time together, but I had no rights to what that knowledge did to me.

"It wasn't really an appropriate time, was it?" Claire rebutted.

"After work would have been!" Jesse seethed, and I was so close to interceding. "Maybe when we were leaving, and I told you I was running home really quick before coming over? You could have said something then so I could prepare myself instead of getting blindsided by your ex! Blood hell, Claire. How do you think this makes me feel? Nico is like a son to me, and he feels the same—"

"You don't know how my son feels. I told you from the beginning that you are not his father. I told you I would never let Nico believe that nor keep his real father from him." I heard Claire sigh before she said, "I won't keep him from you, either, but Noah is here now, so he needs to know when you want to visit."

It was quiet for a moment, and then Jesse asked, "Is this why you broke up with me? Was it coming back here, knowing he was here? It wasn't about the contract, was it?"

After another moment of silence, I barely heard Claire mutter, "Not fully, no."

My heart hammered against my chest at that. I wasn't even able to take it in before Jesse's raised voice was heard.

"Are you kidding me?" He laughed cruelly. "I knew it." There was silence again, and then, "Three years, Claire! Three years to his one. How can you hold on to one bloody year of your life and not have a second thought to the years we were together? You let him walk back in like nothing happened, and I'm discarded—"

I couldn't help interrupting then. Him yelling at her was infuriating me.

Grabbing the handle, I yanked the door open. "According to *our* family and the tabloids, it was only two years, not three." Yeah, I did emphasize the "our" part. Whether we are together or not, and whether Nico was involved or not, my family is hers. Always will be.

That shut Jesse up quickly, whereas Claire looked embarrassed. I hadn't meant for that to happen.

In the end, Jesse made excuses to come by another time. I couldn't blame the guy. He was blindsided.

I had mixed feelings about him. On one hand, I didn't like him or the fact he had a fatherly role in my son's life. On the other hand, I had to respect him for the same thing. He was there when I wasn't. He continues to be there because he was there when I wasn't. I can begrudge him for that, but I can also accept it.

349

Take this moment for example, when Nico calls him papa and runs up to him with a big smile on his face, throwing himself into his arms. That hurts like a bitch. It hurts more than anything.

We are all gathered at my recording studio where Nico wanted to spend his fourth birthday. He invited his preschool friends, and they have been whacking away at the drums, pretending to play the guitars and other instruments set up, while a sound guy and one of my somewhat friends records them. The kids are so excited to hear themselves that they only last about twenty seconds before they run into the control room to play back their jam session. And yes, this is costing me a small fortune, but it's the first birthday I'm with my kid, so it's worth every penny.

Claire must see the hurt on my face because she comes over from where she has been recording the kids playing and lays her hand on my arm. She doesn't say anything. She doesn't have to. Her sympathy speaks more words than she could ever say.

I pat her hand back, trying to restrain myself from holding it.

Spending so much time together again has been confusing on so many levels. We get along, yet the minute I bring up my feelings or something from the past, she shuts down, turns cold even. There is an icy fortress guarding her heart from me, and I can't think of how to melt it.

I want back inside. I want my family. I want my future to be beside hers, not this arrangement we have now. I can't think of how to get past her frozen doors. Therefore, I continue to live her way, being around as much as she allows. When enough time passes, and I'm still here, I hope she will see that I'm worth giving another chance.

"It doesn't get easier … seeing them together," I finally say, realizing my hand is resting on hers. I pull it back, and she does the same, no longer touching my arm.

"I can imagine," she whispers, looking at me with a mixture of pity and sadness. She angles her body toward me, and I do the same. "I really did try to put boundaries up, but"—she looks back over to where Nico is now showing Jesse the guitar I bought him for his birthday—"after so long, it was inevitable. Jesse is all Nico knew. And he is a good man."

"I know," I reluctantly agree. "I wish ..." *I wish I could have been there. Not have missed so much.*

"Yeah," Claire says on a sigh.

"What are you two talking about?"

We both direct our attention to the woman I was not expecting to meet again. Well, not in the condition she's in.

Cyn is very much pregnant. After Max's death, and after Cyn finished college—surprisingly a journalist now—she went for artificial insemination and is expecting a daughter in two months. She shouldn't have flown in her condition, but being Nico's godparent, she didn't want to miss his birthday.

"Dinner plans," Claire lies, answering Cyn's question. "Noah wants to take everyone out, but I already made all of Nico's favorites."

Cyn rubs her belly. "Did you make those little croissant sandwiches you made last year? God, I have been craving those things like there is no tomorrow."

Claire laughs. "Yep. We're going to have a small get-together later. No kids."

"Wonderful," Cyn says, and then immediately cringes as one of the kids starts beating on a cymbal. "God, whose idea was this?" She throws an accusing look my way.

Yeah, we still aren't on speaking terms. Well, she's not speaking to me. I haven't made much attempt, either. Guilt over Max stops me from trying. I'm afraid, if I mention him, my last encounter with him will come blubbering out. Then, she will never speak to me again.

Claire laughs again and answers, "Nico. He talks about this place nonstop and wanted to show it off to his friends."

"Well," Cyn sighs out, "I guess I can't fault him for that." She gives me another glare, and I figure I'm the one she faults.

Claire then leads Cyn to the control room, telling her she needs to get off her feet. I watch them walk away, wishing Claire still had her hand on my arm.

When I swing my eyes back around to watch Nico, I catch Jonathan's eye. He's talking to my parents and Kyle's parents, but nods at me. He flew in two days ago and has been staying at my parents' house. I was so nervous when we picked him up at the airport.

He is the one man in my life I respect above anyone else, so when he hugged me instead of throwing a punch, I felt a few pounds of weight lift off me. We haven't talked much since he's been in town, but that's okay. It's another mountain to climb toward my goal.

"—zoo tomorrow." I catch the last two words of what Jesse says to Nico, and my attention zips to them.

The zoo? Why does my kid like that shit smelling place?

"Really?" Nico asks excitedly, and my heart deflates a bit.

"What?"

I startle a bit at hearing Claire's voice.

Turning toward her, surprised that she seemed to have dropped Cyn off at the couch and hurried back to me, I say, "Please don't tell me our kid is a fan of the zoo."

Claire throws her head back and laughs, garnering the attention of almost everyone in the room. God, I adore her laugh. It's so different from her voice, especially her singing voice. Her laugh is deep and throaty, and so very sexy.

When she gets herself under control, she says, "Oh, yeah. Big time fan. He can't get enough. Especially the hippos." She holds her hands out in front of her, grinning when she sees the look of what must be horror on my face. "Don't ask. I don't know why, out of all animals, that's his favorite."

The grin on her face looks painful she's smiling so wide. She knows the hippo is the animal I fear the most. Yet, I can't bring myself to care about the fact my kid loves my biggest hate, because Claire is looking at me like that. Like the way she used to when we were kids and happy, and so in love. I want, more than anything, to kiss her right now.

I take it that she sees that look when her smile falters, so I hurry to say, "I guess that's one good thing about having Jesse around—he can take Nico to the zoo." The minute I say it, I know it's a shit thing to say and wish I could take it back.

Claire brushes it right off. "I took him to the zoo the first week we moved back here. Since then, it's been a monthly trip. Well, until you—He hasn't asked to go for a while."

"It sounds like Jesse is taking him tomorrow," I hurry to say, seeing she's embarrassed for what she almost said.

"Yeah, he asked me earlier. You mentioned needing to fly out west, so I figured you wouldn't mind."

I shake my head. "No, I don't mind."

I have a meeting with the record label. What about, they didn't disclose; just asked me to fly out for a few days, so that's what I'm doing, catching the red-eye tonight and coming back Wednesday night. I will miss Nico, not having been away from him one day in the past few months. I wish I could take him with me, but since it's a business meeting and I have no one who can watch him for a few hours, I think better of it.

Kyle walks up then, giving me a chin lift. "Hey." He turns to Claire. "Can I talk to you for a minute?"

"Sure."

The two of them walk away to a corner and start a hushed conversation.

Kyle and I have been hanging out more often. In the beginning, it was rough. I let him yell and curse me. He seemed to need that. Then he asked—more like interrogated—me about everything I had been up to. Out of everyone, he seemed the most hurt that I left. Now we have a strained relationship. He tries to be amiable. We go out for drinks occasionally with Giuliana and sometimes Chris. And him and Giuliana come by the house a lot to visit with Claire and Nico. Those times, I am mostly ignored.

I am almost knocked down when forty pounds unexpectedly crashes into my legs. I regain my bearings and look down at my four-year-old jumping up and down, trying to shove a robotic dinosaur in my face.

"Look, Daddy, lookie!"

I love hearing my new title come out of his mouth.

I kneel at his level as he thrusts the toy at me, demanding I release the T-rex from his packaged bindings. He must have gotten the gift from Jesse since that was the last person to show up and the last person I saw him talking to. I look over to where they were, but Jesse is no longer there. In fact, I don't see him anywhere. Did he leave already?

I start massacring the packaging, forgetting about Jesse, as Nico's nonstop chatter catches up with me. "What's your favorite dinosaur, Daddy?"

I look up at him, seeing the excited glint in his eyes. "I like the triceratops." Honestly, it's the first dinosaur that came to me.

"That's the one with three horns!" he declares, grabbing the T-rex that I hand him and immediately setting it down. He hits a button, and the thing roars, swaying from side to side as it takes baby steps forward. Nico squeals in delight as he crouches down and mimics the thing, watching it in fascination.

I laugh as I stand back up and look for a place to discard the trash.

Claire comes back over to me, holding a black trash bag, a happy smile on her face.

"What was that about?" I ask, referring to Kyle with a head nod in his direction as I stuff the trash in the bag.

Eyes brimming with happiness, she tells me, "I'll tell you later."

Setting the bag down against the wall, she remains by my side for the rest of the day. It's the best feeling in the world.

~Claire~

Today has been a very good day. Nico is happier than I have ever seen him, all my friends and family are here, and Noah ... I'm happy that he is finally here to share in Nico's birthday. I think it showed a little too much, but I couldn't help remaining close to him. I haven't allowed myself that in the past few months he has been back.

Usually, I try to nonchalantly move away from him whenever he is close. It must be a defense reflex. Today, I feel like we should stay close, like a united front or something. I don't know how to explain it. I feel a closeness to him since today is the anniversary of when we— or rather I—brought our child into the world. The anniversary of when our lives forever interlinked with the coming of one little person.

Everyone has left now except my dad, who is putting Nico to bed, with Angel following behind, and Noah, who is helping me clean up. Dad is staying with Sarah and Anthony, while Cyn is staying with Kyle and Giuliana. I offered to let Cyn stay here where she could have my bed, but she declined. Her pregnancy has her moody, and that's something I can do nothing about, except to constantly ask if there is any way I can help, which she always says no. Just once I would like to repay her for all the times she was there for me.

"So, what was that thing with Kyle earlier? He looked anxious about something," Noah asks as he loads the dishwasher.

I snap a lid onto one of the Tupperware containers then lean over the counter to see down the hall, making sure my dad isn't in hearing. Then I lean toward Noah and quietly yet excitedly tell him, "Kyle is going to propose."

Noah's eyes dart up to mine as he straightens up from depositing a plate. "No shit? Wow."

"Yeah," I start to jabber, keeping my voice low. "He's irrationally nervous, thinking she will say no. He needed some assurance. I know for a fact that Giuliana will say yes."

"I'm heading out now. Nicholas is asleep."

Hearing Dad's voice makes me jump. I look over to see him watching Noah and I from the other side of the breakfast bar.

Dad never warmed up to Nico's nickname, always insisting on calling him by his proper name.

" 'Kay, Dad." I walk out of the kitchen to meet him by the front door.

He leans in and whispers to me, "Is there something I need to know?" He jerks his head in Noah's direction.

I never knew how my dad felt about what happened between me and Noah. In the beginning, he was concerned, using connections to find Noah. Then he dropped the subject altogether like Noah never existed. I know he wrote to him occasionally because Katy told me, but Dad never gave me a hint as to how he felt.

I wonder what the letters said and make a note to ask Noah some time.

Instead of answering my dad right away, I open the door and step out. He follows, and when I close the door, I tell him, "We are in a good place right now. This is what I want—for Nico to have his father. That's all there is, Dad."

He doesn't give anything away when he asks, "Are you sure? I don't want to see you hurt again." When I give a frustrated sigh, he continues, "I watched you two today, and it doesn't look like that's all there is."

It's the same thing everyone implied today. People pulled me aside left and right to ask what was going on between us. And my answer was the same to all of them: absolutely nothing. That's the truth. I'm happy and content that Noah is here for our son, that he is spending every available moment and then some to simply be what he is—a father. He's taking his role seriously, more seriously than I could have dreamed, and I am ecstatic about that. For the first time in almost five years, I feel at peace.

"That's all there is, Dad," I promise.

His face falls for a moment, and I realize he wasn't asking for the reason I thought he was. Just as quickly, he wipes the expression away, so then I second-guess myself.

"Okay. I'll see you tomorrow, kiddo."

"Bye, Dad," I call out to him as he makes his way down the flight of stairs. Then I make my way back inside where Noah is cutting into a slice of cake. The kitchen is clean now, all dishes and food put away.

"Want some?" he asks, glancing up at me. "I noticed you didn't have any earlier."

I was too busy cutting everyone else a piece earlier, and then cleaning up all the food from dinner. I have been moving since I woke up, and now that the house is quiet and everything is done, I would love to sit down with a piece of cake and a whole bottle of wine.

Wine used to be a self-medication, but lately, I noticed that my headaches have come less and less frequently. As a matter of fact, I can't remember the last time I had one. Huh.

"I would love some," I tell Noah as I head into the kitchen to open a bottle as he cuts another piece and sets it on a dessert plate.

I hold an empty glass out to him, silently asking if he wants some, and am struck stupid as I watch him lick a dollop of icing off his thumb.

Wow, it's been too long since I had sex.

Diverting my eyes and hoping he didn't see me staring, I croak out, "Want a glass?"

"Sure." Noah shrugs, and I breathe easier at his seeming

ignorance, assured he didn't catch me. Then he grins that heart-stopping grin of his and winks before popping his whole finger in his mouth and sucking off the rest of the icing.

I feel myself blushing before I roll my eyes and carry our glasses out to the living room. I try to act unaffected, telling myself I am, as Noah puts in a disk and turns on the TV.

"What are we watching?" I ask, curling up on the couch before setting my glass down on the side table.

"I compiled all those videos you sent." Picking up our plates and handing me one before sitting next to me, he shrugs, not making eye contact. "I like watching them, and today is one of those days when there is an excuse to watch them, I think."

Feeling moved by that, I tell him, "I haven't even watched them all."

He swivels his head so fast in my direction I'm surprised he didn't snap his neck. "Seriously?"

Mouth full of cake, I shake my head. Then I take a sip of wine, quickly discovering red wine and chocolate cake are not a good combination, and say, "I was there. Those videos were mainly for you." I feel bad for saying that, but I don't mean it as a cutting remark. It's true.

Noah doesn't seem put off by the comment. "Well, thank you, because I can't get enough of them."

I see how sincere he looks when he says that, and already he is watching the screen, enraptured by Nico's birth. I remember every second of that day: the fear; the hope that Noah would burst through the door, grab my hand, and tell me everything will be okay; the love that instantly consumed my heart when I laid eyes on our son; the tears, both happy and sad.

I don't need to watch the video to relive it, so I watch Noah instead, seeing so many emotions cross his face as I recall what was going on by listening.

We continue to watch the videos as we finish our slices of cake and finish off the wine while I tell him stories about what else was going on during the scenes or what I was thinking. Eventually, I get too tired to talk anymore and simply watch, feeling emotions swell inside me, like when Signora Gelardi is filmed. I miss her.

It's amazing how much joy can fill so little years of life, yet still have all the pain that was buried deep inside me. Watching the videos, I feel like I'm seeing someone who isn't me. I'm seeing the me everyone else saw, not the me I am. It's surreal. Made more surreal as the video mixes with dreams.

~

I wake to find myself entwined with Noah, like how we used to be: legs tangled, my head on his chest, his arms around me, me gripping his shirt. I know he's awake because he is caressing a patch of exposed skin on my lower back. I don't know how I feel about this.

Instead of jumping up instantly, mortified, I continue to feign sleep, savoring the nostalgia of the moment, trying to convince myself that the last few years never happened and we are back in the past. I don't want to move, don't want the contentment to end. Is it so wrong to pretend?

Then Noah kisses the top of my head, like so many times before, and I squeeze my eyes shut, holding back the pain. Because the past did happen. I can't pretend otherwise.

"You awake, angel?"

Why, Noah? Why do you make everything so much harder for me?

I tighten my grip on his shirt, wanting to continue pretending and knowing I can't. I look up at him, inches from his face, and take him in.

He needs to shave, a morning shadow covering the bottom half of his face, making his lips stand out. I notice for the first time that he no longer has those freckles that used to be splattered across his nose. His eyes are alert, telling me he's been awake for a while now. They look down at me warmly as he tilts his head to see me better.

I am arrested, transfixed by him. I tell myself to move, to get up, to get far away from him, but my body is frozen in place. A sense of déjà vu overcomes me, except I know I have been here before, in this same position, looking up at him as he looks down at me. One of those perfect moments in my memory that haunts me.

Noah's eyes soften as he moves his hand to my face, cupping my cheek. I want to lean into the touch, yet I remain still. He whispers my name reverently as he leans toward me, his hand twitching against my cheek. Then he closes his eyes, and I follow, closing mine also, before I feel his soft lips touch mine, pressing gently, nothing more.

My mind completely shuts down, instincts and yearning taking over. I part my lips, pressing another kiss to his bottom lip, and Noah shudders all over yet doesn't take over, only remaining still.

Breathing harder, I slip my tongue out and lick along the seam of his lips. When he still doesn't move, I press one last kiss to his lips before pulling away, confused to what this was.

I watch his eyes slowly open. They are filled with so much pain and longing, so tender as he looks back at me. So why didn't he kiss me back? I can feel the evidence of his arousal against my knee. I know he wants me, or this.

Is that it? Just a moment of weakness? Is that what it is for me, too?

No. I won't lie to myself. Regardless, I know it's not right. Maybe that's why Noah stopped the minute he started. He realized this was a mistake before I did.

I pull away from him and sit up, scooting down the couch so temptation doesn't pull me in again.

"Claire—"

"It's okay, Noah. It was a moment of weakness … for both of us. I get it."

We have been so comfortable with each other for the past few months, falling into a domestic routine without the physical. Then yesterday, I was probably sending too many mixed signals. Probably have been for a while. Even sending mixed signals to myself. Happy that he is here, but not just for Nico. I'm so confused.

"I don't think you do," Noah says, and I look back at him. He's now sitting up, legs stretched out along the couch. "I want more. I want *everything*." His eyes bore into mine, getting his message across. "But this"—he gestures between us—"it's too soon. I have too—"

"I don't think that's ever going to happen," I hurry to cut him off.

He purses his lips, looking at me contemplatively. "What was that, then? You kissed me back." His voice is soft, mellow, like a school teacher trying to get his student to think more deeply on the subject, see it from another perspective.

"I ..." I stop, looking away from him and thinking about my actions. What was I thinking in that moment? Truth is, I wasn't. My body was on autopilot, muscle memory looking back into the past, into a similar moment. "I'm sorry." It's all I can say, thinking we need some time apart.

I need to get my head back to reality. I need to remember this is the man who hurt me more than anyone else has before. More than Troy when he forced himself on me. More than the years I lived with the knowledge that my mother left me. More than when I dropped out of school, thought all my dreams were lost. And he could do it again, at any time.

"Claire." My name from his lips has me looking back at him. "You want to know what I think?" When I don't respond, he continues, "I think you want to fight us, but I don't think you can. You know, as much as I do, that our story doesn't end this way." He leans forward, legs crisscrossed, hands holding himself up. "Eventually— and I can promise you that—I will be inside you again. Your heart, your every thought ... your body. And I will *never* leave them."

Tears flood my eyes as I whisper, "Your promises don't mean anything."

He nods slowly. "Not yet, but my actions will prove otherwise. Maybe not this year or the next, but eventually, I will earn your trust again. And every promise I make will mean something again."

Resting back, he folds his arms over his chest. "I don't forget anything. And everything I ever told you is still true, Claire. Bliss wrapped in hell; do you remember that conversation?" When I nod, he says, "That sums up our entire relationship up until now."

He's right about that.

"It's the bliss that I'd rather hold on to. Who wouldn't?" He shrugs. "It's easier for me to say that because I'm the one at fault here. I know you hold on to the hell instead. No one can blame you for that. I put you through hell, and I will tell you I'm sorry for the rest of my life for that."

Every word from his lips has me transfixed. He's right, which is why I can't let go. Sadly, I want him to hurt for as many years as he hurt me.

"I didn't want to have this conversation yet," Noah continues, and I watch his mouth as it moves. "I wanted to wait much longer for it, but I can see you're pulling away, so I'm going to tell you now that I'm not going to stop fighting for us. You're going to tell me to make myself sparse for a while, and I'm going to do the opposite. I'm going to buy you flowers and chocolate and all that sappy shit you love, and you're going to try to ignore it, but it's going to keep on coming, reminding you of me every second of every day. You're going to come home, and I'm going to be here, treating you like the angel you are, pampering you until your little heart's content while our son beams at us, showing us how happy he is because I am happy and you are happy. And he's going to see us together and know this is how it's supposed to be.

"You're going to push and pull, and I'm going to boomerang back, even after you admit defeat and welcome me back into your heart. And, Claire, I know I never left." He reaches over and touches my pendant. "The same as you know you never left mine." Then he touches the bracelet I gave him forever ago. "This is it for us. This is meant to be. Claire and Noah. Noah and Claire. There isn't meant to be anything else. Our fates were intertwined long before we met."

Tears continue to spill down my cheeks, and I suck in a breath before gasping out, "I can't," running away from him and to my room where I lock myself in.

~Noah~

Claire slamming her door wakes up Nico, who sleepily makes his way to me and curls up on my lap as he slowly wakes up. After snuggling with the little guy for a while, I go about the routine of making him breakfast before sending him off to get dressed and get ready for Jesse to pick him up. He is so excited to be off to the zoo that he doesn't even think about the absence of his mother.

After another awkward greeting with Jesse, he asks where Claire is, and I lie, telling him she had errands to run. I'm playing dirty now.

He thinks nothing of it, taking Nico's hand and leaving, telling me they will be back by one. Good thing, too, because Nico has a lot of company in town who still want to spend time with him. Right now, though, it's my time with Claire, something I'm going to make more of.

Walking to her door, I knock. "Jesse just left with Nico."

She doesn't respond.

Figuring she fell back asleep, yet not ready to leave, I grab the bag I stashed in Nico's closet for times I end up sleeping over and make my way into the hall bathroom where I shave and take a shower. When I come out, Claire is leaning against her doorframe, arms crossed.

"What did you do after you left?"

I know what she's doing. She's trying to justify her reasoning for keeping me at arm's length, reminding herself that I am only Nico's father and nothing else. If that were true, though, then why would she allow me into her life so much—letting me stay over, hanging out with me when Nico is asleep. Couples with nothing left don't do that shit. No, they drop off and pick their kids up at the door, barely saying more than a few words to each other. They meet up for holidays and birthdays and nothing else.

She may have kept me at arm's length physically, but even that was broken last night and this morning. How easy that happened scares the shit out of her, but I have seen it happening ever so slowly, falling back into our easy comfort, talking like we used to, even laughing a lot. It came as no surprise to me, yet it must have been a slap to the face for her. I get that. It doesn't mean I'm going to allow her to pull away.

I smooth my hand over my wet hair, wiping the droplets off on my jeans, as I answer her honestly, "I self-destructed. Then I got my shit together. End of." Simply saying that initiates flashes of images of the shit I remember during those first six months. It's not pretty. Truth is, it's downright ugly, disgusting, dirty, and nothing I want tarnishing her.

Claire steps up to me, looking up at my face, her arms still crossed, and demands, "More."

"*More*? More what?" The shit I did? Not happening. "No."

Further defiant, she says, "You owe me this. You said you're going to fight for us … Well, this is one of the battles. I want to know where you were, what you did. I want to know what you went through before you 'got your shit together.' " She makes air quotes before crossing her arms again, stepping even closer to me, her head tilted so far back it looks painful. "Then I want to know what you did after that. I want everything spelled out for me. I want a visual."

Angry at myself and at her for pushing this, I seethe, "You don't want that shit in your head."

"Yes. I. Do."

"Ignorance is bliss. Not always, but in this case, it is. Trust me on that."

"I don't trust you at all," she grits out. Immediately, tears come to her eyes. She looks shocked and hurt at herself, washing away the anger she used to say that.

Knowing her words are true, I still take a step back, catching myself against the bathroom's doorframe. "I know," comes out on a whisper.

We stare at each other for a minute before she whirls away from me, going back to her room. I follow, stopping in her doorway and watching as she takes one of her muscle relaxers then gulps the pill down with water.

"I did a lot of that," I tell her, shocked at myself for saying anything. She's right, though. This is a battle I need to win, and not just for her, but for myself, too. A confessional where I can admit all my sins in hopes of getting absolved.

She spins around like she's surprised I'm there, and I indicate the pill bottle.

"During those first six months, there were a lot of drugs."

"But … you hated drugs."

I shrug. "I never felt any which way about them before. I preferred alcohol. But after I left, I needed an escape that alcohol couldn't provide. Someone offered me something, and for a little while, I didn't feel anything. I still remembered, but the grief wasn't there. It was like seeing it from the outside. So, I did it again and again.

"I'm not going to horrify you with the details. Just know that things got bad enough to scare me, so I cleaned up. I didn't even drink for a year so I wouldn't lose my inhibition and pick up more drugs."

"Where were you? Where did the drugs come from?" she asks as she sinks onto her bed.

I figured, since she's getting comfortable, then I will, too, so I take a seat at her vanity. "I headed south from here, driving along the coast, stopping whenever I got tired. Sometimes I would linger in a town if it held appeal. No more than a week, though. I was too restless. I felt like I *had* to keep running.

"The first place I stayed at more than a day, I ran into someone who offered to get me high. I can barely remember what we did for the next couple of days." It was a girl about my age who let me crash at her place. We fucked and got wasted for days, too high to leave the house—pot, cocaine, ecstasy, liquor. The party ended when her boyfriend came home and found us. I got out of there before they finished yelling and headed south again. "Then I was on the road again, looking for the next party."

"How did you pay for that? We—"

"That's where most of the money went."

"But where did you sleep? Eat? We calculated how long it would be before you made another withdrawal."

I raise an eyebrow at that, wondering who the "we" are. "Motels are cheap, especially in smaller towns. And food ... I didn't have much of an appetite." I didn't sleep in a motel often. There always seemed to be a woman who wanted to take me home. And food? Yeah, I wasn't lying about that. Sometimes I went days without eating, too out of it to remember.

Claire is quiet, looking down at her hands in her lap. "That's it, then? Just sex, drugs, and alcohol?"

"I never said anything about sex."

She gives me a look that seems to ask if I think she is stupid. "You don't have to. I can read between the lines."

"Then, yeah, that's all there was. I stayed in New Orleans for longer than most places, played in a few clubs. That was when I 'woke up,' I guess you could say. I looked back over the shit I had done, reevaluated what I thought I saw that night, and then concluded I was an idiot but you wouldn't want me back because I had been gone for so long." I want to tell her about Max finding me, but so many things stop me from that. One, Max didn't tell her, so now that he is gone, it feels like a betrayal to him. That was between us. Two, the things I said to him, the way I acted ... Yeah, it's best to leave that in the past, locked away, like all the other details of my six months of hell.

After a few silent moments, she asks, "What happened next?"

I sigh, already emotionally tired of this conversation. "You know what happened next. I went to L.A., went to school, got picked up by the record company, and eventually made my way back here."

"And the drugs? The women?"

I close my eyes, not wanting to admit this next part, yet owing it to her. I owe her everything; she was right about that, too. "The drugs stopped in New Orleans. The drinking, too. I drank on occasion after a year without, needing to prove to myself that I could. The women ..." I don't know if I'm embarrassed or what about this next part. "I haven't been with anyone since I quit the drugs." God, I can feel my face warm with admitting that. I can't even look up to see Claire's response, and she doesn't say anything. I get so uncomfortable that I almost leave the room, but then she says something else.

"Now tell me why you really left."

I lift my head at that, looking at her in confusion. "I told you why. I thought I saw—"

"No, I don't want to hear the excuse you told yourself. I want to know why. Everything between us seemed fine. I mean, I know it was hard for a while because of my mom, but then you left the day after she passed away. You weren't even there for the funeral. For all you knew, things were about to turn around for us. I wouldn't need to spend so much time at the hospital. We would have had more time for us to go out, to hang out with friends together, go to all your shows. We would have been happy again, like how it was when we first moved here." Her voice lowers on her last line, turning wistful.

"*I* wasn't happy here," I admit to her, hoping this is the truth she wanted. "In fact, I was miserable. I hated seeing you here, sharing you with everyone." My voice rises as old scars from that time devour me.

I get up and start pacing her room. "I hated this city and how much it captivated you. I wanted to run back home, take you back to Breckenridge, and live there, where it was quiet, peaceful. I wanted things to go back to how they were.

"I felt on edge all the time. All the noises, the excitement—it was too much for me. And you changed. You went from this quiet, shy girl who only spoke freely to me to being animated all the time, suddenly having all these friends who took your attention away from me.

"And yeah, dammit, I know how messed up that makes me sound, but that's the truth. That's how I felt. Add to that the fact that I saw where you were going and where I was going, and how total opposites they were—I freaked out.

"That's why I ran. That's why I did the drugs, the women. Because that's where I saw myself going. I went all the way to the bottom, where I felt like I already was, where I could look up and see you all the way at the top, because that's what you deserve. I felt like I would only hold you back, which is what I did … for a while, anyway."

"And now?" she asks, neither her voice or expression giving anything away to how my words make her feel.

"It's different now. I guess I grew up, matured, stopped thinking about myself—I don't know. I'm happy being a part of your life again—however much I can be—and being here with Nico. My world ends and begins with you two. All the chaos from before doesn't touch me anymore.

"Coming back to New York again was scary, but it felt like finally coming home. Last time, it didn't feel like that. Last time, after the excitement of showing you around, it felt like there was something crawling all over me. I was itching to get away from here, not you. Not at first … Now, I don't know if it's because this is my home, or because you and Nico are here, but that feeling never came. I don't want to run anymore. I don't feel overwhelmed. Here"—I indicate her condo, sitting back down on her vanity seat—"I feel like I'm finally at home."

"And what about next time? What happens the next time you get overwhelmed and have an itch to run away?"

I want to tell her that I will take her and Nico with me. However, that's not what she wants to hear. Then again, I need to be as honest as I can. "*If* there's a next time, then I won't bottle that shit up again. I will talk to you about it. *If* there's a next time and talking doesn't help, I will grab my family and go until I find peace again."

Claire's lip twitches. I can't tell if she's fighting back a smile or what. I highly doubt it's a smile since there is nothing funny about this shit. Talking about it, telling her about the darkness I went through, my heart is pounding, my nerves are shot, and I am full of shame. If she *can* find any humor in that, then she can have it.

Claire gets up from the bed and walks over to me, stopping when her legs hit mine. I look up at her, which isn't by much since she's so short, and she leans down, surprising the shit out of me when she presses her lips to mine, not moving, not going any further, like how I did with her earlier. When she's done, she pulls away, and it takes all my restraint not to follow her, not to grab her and pull her back.

"Thank you. I think you needed to say that as much as I needed to hear it."

All I can do is nod.

Chapter 30

Looking Back at Mistakes

~Claire~

Hearing what Noah felt right before he disappeared, I saw him in a different light. It's like he finally tore down this barrier I never knew he had. I never knew his jealousy ran so deeply that he could be jealous of a thing and not just people.

As he talked, I remembered back to when we first came to New York. I remember him telling me his fears then, but I never listened.

"You seem like a different person."

"It scares me."

"I'm afraid we'll drift apart. You're finding yourself, and we won't fit anymore."

"I'm afraid I won't fit anymore. I'm afraid you'll see that, and where will that leave me?"

"I'm selfish, Claire. So damn selfish when it comes to you."

I was too caught up in the excitement, too happy to be away from my hometown, living with Noah, being on my own, looking forward to the future, school, new friends. I didn't see then how scared Noah was. I brushed off his fears, thinking it was fleeting.

Then I thought back to the last weeks of my mom's life, when I wasn't having fun and hanging out with new friends. Noah was there for me in a way no one else could, and he seemed happier than he had been before I found out about my mom. We were closer, like we had been before coming to the city. That's why it hit me so hard when he disappeared. And now I can see perfectly clear what I didn't before.

Noah's words, him telling me what he will do if there is a next time when his nature gets the best of him, almost made me smile. Not because of what he said, but how he said it, like a petulant child who was being taught a lesson by their parent. It reminded me so much of Nico.

As for his comments about things being different this time in the city, I can see that. This time, there is no excitement and changes. I have been settled in for a long time, and Noah had months to settle himself in before we ran into each other at that bar. He read the letters. He had time to prepare himself for the changes, which makes me wonder if I instinctively knew he would need that. Living apart—mostly—he can go home and get away from me and Nico if it's too much, though he hasn't.

He kept true to his promise to me. For the past five months, he has been randomly sending me flowers and little gifts. It gets embarrassing sometimes, like when he sends them to the theater. That's not really me. I don't need those things, though it is nice to know I am thought of on a regular basis.

What I love are the little things, like how Nico and Noah always have dinner waiting for me when I get home. Or sometimes they pick me up from the theater and take me out. I love watching the two of them interact; that's the kind of gift I want. Or the fun times, like when Noah is relentless in his pursuit to rub my feet, which turns into a huge tickling fight that includes Nico jumping on the both of us, taking my side and attacking Noah with me. Or the mornings when I wake up to find Nico had found his way to sleep with his daddy on the couch. I swear Noah stays at our house more than his.

Sometimes Noah has me meet him somewhere while Nico is with Giuliana. I was a little uncomfortable with that at first, being tricked, thinking Nico would be there, too, but I'm used to it now. The first time he set me up was a week after Nico's birthday and after our talk and kisses.

I asked him what he was doing with the whole wooing and dinner thing, and his response was, "You're the one who kissed me back." I couldn't argue that, but I still told him it was a bad idea. In the end, he convinced me to take a night off, stating I was already there, so I might as well take advantage.

He kept the conversations on Nico, asking about our time in Italy. I'm sure this was to make me comfortable. It was a nice time, and then he dropped me off at home and went back to his place.

The sneak attacks became a game after that. I went out with him and Nico so much that I never knew when Nico wouldn't be there. The times Nico wasn't, I would sigh and shake my head at Noah before leaving it alone and enjoying the night.

Truth is, I am slowly falling in love with Noah again, and I adore every minute of it. I don't want the game to end.

However, there is one more test I want to put Noah through. It was a sore spot in the beginning of our first relationship. It seems like the same game is being played, yet I haven't voiced any complaint because I have been playing it back on him. That's going to change soon. It's going to be the game changer.

All our "dates," the months of spending time as a family, we have not been physical. The mood hasn't been like that. It's more of a friendly nature, though I know we both want to cross that bridge. Noah finds ways to cuddle on the couch. Fall asleep there, too. Sometimes we hold hands, which he always initiates. We always sit close to each other, finding ourselves in our own little world and forgetting our surroundings and the people watching us. I never realized this until it was brought to my attention when we went to my dad's house for Christmas.

I only had three days to be home before having to return to work. Unbeknownst to Noah, my dad has been spending Christmases with his family. Either his family goes to Dad's house or he goes to Mark and Katy's. Except for when I was in Italy and couldn't get away, then my dad and Kyle went to visit me there. This year, my dad held Christmas and all our family was there, plus Giuliana, who I guess is practically family now since Kyle proposed to her a few months ago.

Christmas morning, everyone gathered together for a morning brunch, and then we watched as Nico and Abigail tore into their gifts; too many gifts if you ask me. Being the only babies, they were both spoiled.

Noah gave me a locket with my birthstone in the center and Nico's at the top. Diamonds were scattered around the rest of it. It looked like an antique, and I loved it. Noah explained to me why he got it, what everything meant, opening the locket to show a single picture of Nico, both of us having one of those moments when we were lost in our own world.

Katy pointed this out to me later, asking me what was going on. I told her we were just friends, while inside I yearned for more.

My doubts and insecurities were fast being locked in a box. Seeing Noah with Nico, my heart told me he would never leave us. He would never leave his son. However, Katy's concern had let a bit of doubt seep back in.

She told me I had missed all the looks everyone was shooting at each other while we were in our bubble. Everyone was afraid of Noah running off again. They were afraid of what would happen to me, to Nico, if he did. No one trusted him anymore.

I stood up for Noah, telling her that wasn't going to happen again. I told her I was more aware of him now than I ever was. That we were older, life was more settled. We weren't kids anymore. Noah was a father, and he was doing everything possible to prove that we could depend on him. And Noah overheard.

He stopped in the doorway of my dad's office, having come to look for me. I knew he was there, though Katy didn't. When I was done with my tirade, he walked away, and I followed after him. I knew that look on his face, and I didn't need him to feel the self-loathing I saw there. He needed to know his family was as concerned to lose him as they were of Nico and I being left behind.

I knew now how he ticked in a way I never knew before. Maybe I was too young then to see it. I know I was certainly in my own world then. Now I knew better. Age and experience had taught me—opened my eyes—to pay attention to those around me. And I watched Noah incessantly.

Catching up to him, I led him into the solarium at the back of the house. I thought of ways to explain to him what everyone was thinking, making excuses for them, but in the end, I simply told him, "*I* trust you," and then I kissed him. Just like that. It was the only thing I knew to give him to turn around his mood. Not the kiss, but the words. Because, it was true. It didn't take years, as I thought it would. It only took months.

And Noah kissed me back. *He* kissed *me* back. And it was like everything I remembered, plus more.

He cupped my face with both hands, using almost bruising force, and I tangled my hands in his hair, holding him to me. It was several moments before we broke apart, me ending up on a table with him between my legs, both of us out of breath. We were inseparable after that.

Noah and I went from having a love at first sight, practically dive right into a relationship the first time, to building trust and establishing friendship this go-around. Love has always been there. How could it not? He was my first love, and we created a child together. I couldn't let go of that. There was also a lot of pain attached to that, and years of never letting go, dwelling on the bad, never forgetting the good.

I hope tonight we can get past all of that and continue to bury the bad with all the good. Noah has to give me one more thing. I am being the selfish one now.

After dragging our suitcases in and Noah gets a sleepy Nico to bed, he grabs his bag and starts to empty out some of Nico's Christmas gifts that wouldn't fit in the extra suitcase my dad let us borrow. I wasn't kidding about the spoiling this year. It was too much.

"You think I should take these with me so he has more to play with at my place?"

I look up from uploading the Christmas pictures onto my laptop, seeing Noah look at the extra suitcase then at the bin of toys that keeps residence in the living room.

I bite my lip, not knowing how to answer that. I want to tell him no. I want to tell him that I don't want Nico staying at his place anymore. I don't want Noah staying at his own place anymore. I want him here. I hold my tongue, though, because that won't happen anytime soon.

Noah bought a bigger place a few months ago. I must say, he makes a lot more money than I ever will. His condo is gorgeous with its open floorplan, hardwood floors, and four bedrooms. It's about four times the size of my dinky apartment. I don't know why he would buy it when he spends all his time here. He hasn't even completely furnished the place yet. Last time I was there, all he had were the basics, besides Nico's room. That's the only room that seems finished.

"Yeah, I guess," I answer, looking away from him. I don't want him to see the disappointment in my eyes.

He doesn't say anything, which makes me look up at him again from my position on the couch. He's studying me in that way of his. His head is tilted to the side, his eyes penetrating. I know it's because I'm sending mixed signals again, but so is he.

He stays here so often, yet he acts like he's getting ready to leave. Our flight didn't come in until after eleven p.m., and now it's closing in on one o'clock in the morning, so why does he seem like he is in a hurry to get out of here? I thought we hit some pinnacle after our kiss at my dad's house.

"Well, I'm going to head out. I'll see you tomorrow." Noah stands, bag in hand.

Before he can take a step, I stand, too, and say, "Wait." He remains where he is as I walk up to him, arms folded across my chest in a protective stance. "Why are you leaving?" comes out more timorous than I wanted it to.

Noah shifts in place, looking down and avoiding eye contact before searing me with one look. "Because I want to sleep in a bed for once."

"Oh." I feel like a bitch now. Noah sleeps on my couch more than he sleeps in his own bed, and while my couch is pretty comfy, it doesn't compare to an actual bed. If he leaves, though, I can't proceed with my plan. "Um, you want to take my bed?"

Noah shakes his head. "No, Claire, I'm not going to take your bed from you." Now he looks tortured.

Tightening my arms around myself, my toes curling and relaxing in a nervous habit, I take a deep breath and sputter, "I mean … with me." I close my eyes after saying that, unable to believe how foolish I sound. I haven't initiated anything in a long time. Not at all with Jesse. He was always the one to go there. Noah was the only one, but that seems like forever ago. I feel inexperienced once again.

Just imagining what sharing a bed with Noah used to be like causes liquid heat to pool between my thighs. I clench at the memory and open my eyes, seeing the arousal I feel reflected back at me.

"Are you sure?" Noah asks, his eyes smoldering, his entire body so taut that it vibrates.

Maintaining eye contact, I answer, "Yes."

Quicker than I can compute, Noah drops his bag and, in the next second, he grips my hips and hauls me up his body. I instinctively wrap my legs around his waist then rest my arms on his shoulders, staring eye level with him as he carries me down the hall and into the bathroom.

I am visually shaking with nerves at this point. I want this. I need this. And by the eagerness in Noah's movements, he wants this, too. By the yearning in his eyes, he needs this. By the wariness in the way he watches me, he can't believe this is real.

"Um ... Why the bathroom?" I ask when he sets me down on the vanity.

"Because it will give me time to reacquaint myself with your body while washing off all that airport funk," he says, sounding out of breath and visibly shaking as much as me.

I giggle, more out of nervousness than humor. "I forgot about *that* phobia."

Noah turns on the shower then steps toward me, peeling off his socks with each step. "Why do you say it like that? *That* phobia," he mocks, grabbing the hem of my off-the-shoulder sweater and peeling it up my body. I unsteadily raise my hands in the air. It feels like prom night all over again, just a vastly different setting.

Smiling like an idiot, I say, "Well, there's your animal phobia— I will never forget that one. Your 'dude' phobia, kissing the rest of the world pho—"

Noah kisses me, thrusting his tongue into my mouth, and I moan, feeling him slip his fingers into my waistband before he presses his thumb right *there*, through my comfy leggings.

"Oh, God," I moan, already so close to climaxing after working myself up all day thinking about this moment.

Noah removes his thumb, and then I feel both his hands at my waist. "Lift up," he orders, and I brace myself on the counter, lifting my hips so Noah can peel my leggings and panties down.

The tease doesn't touch me again as I watch him take off the rest of his clothes, adding them to the growing pile on the floor at our feet.

His body is so much different than it used to be. Broader, more filled out, yet still so familiar. I wonder what he sees when he looks at me, if he sees differences in me, too.

Never taking his eyes off me, he then steps toward me again, reaching up to unfasten my hair from the many pins holding my messy bun in place. I hear them *chink* on the countertop before he runs his hands through my hair, massaging my scalp and checking for any more pins. Another moan escapes me at the feel of his hands, and I shut my eyes at the ecstasy of it.

"I miss your hair being long," he whispers as he caresses his lips along my forehead and down one cheek. The hot steam from the shower is already drenching my skin, perspiring the counter, the mirror, making everything a slick surface.

I open my eyes, seeing his chest in front of me. Reaching out, I rove the back of both hands down his chest, down his waist, his hips, before circling one hand around the engorged part of him.

My breaths quickening, I stroke him, a small smile coming to my lips when I hear his sharp intake of air. Then he is pulling away from me, bracing his hands on either side of me on the counter, bent over and taking gasping breaths.

"Not yet," he stresses, whereas my body demands differently. I need him inside me unlike I have ever needed anything else.

On shaky legs, I hop off the counter, forcing him to straighten and back away as he eyes me warily, probably wondering what I am about to do.

Instead of giving in to my body's needs, I turn and step into the shower. The hot water is painful to every sensitive nerve ending, making my need so much more pronounced.

I feel Noah step in behind me, and then I feel his hands at my hips, pulling me back until our bodies are pressed close. He wraps his arms around me, holding me tightly as the water sprays down on us.

"Jesus, Claire, I never thought we would be here again. I hoped and prayed, but ..."

"Hush," I tell him, turning in his embrace and wrapping my arms around his waist.

I feel him against my abdomen, but before I can move to attend to our needs, he again steps away from me.

He can be so frustrating. It's starting to feel like the same game all over again, yet on a much bigger scale here.

I feel my face heating further at the annoyance, until he lathers his hands, and then they are everywhere: my breasts, my waist, between my legs … I tremble from the most delicious feel of him touching me everywhere I have longed for.

As he kneels in front of me, I grip his hair, watching as he stares at the most private part of me. He licks his lips as he slides his hand up the inside of my thigh. When he reaches his target, he looks up at me, watching me react to the play of his talented fingers. The desire in his eyes alone makes me want to release.

Needing to brace myself from the orgasm already near the surface, I lean against the wall, closing my eyes as I tilt my head back, focusing on touch alone—his touch. I can hardly bear it, my hips moving of their own accord, thrusting into his touch. Then his mouth joins in, and I am done, biting my lip and bearing down against his ministrations as I hold a scream in check, breathing unsteadily through my nose. Noah continues as my body wrings out every sap of energy I have and then some, until I feel another climax coming.

Out of fear of my own body, unable to stand the sensations any longer, I try to move away from him, but he grabs one of my legs and holds it over his shoulder, which gives him even more access. This time, I can't hold back the shout of surprise when my body tightens and releases with another orgasm. I call out his name repeatedly as my body fights to get closer to him and what he is doing to me. I can't control my own thoughts; simple pleasure overrides every action.

Finally, *finally*, Noah gives up his torture, sinuously rising from his knees. His eyes are so dark with lust, fervid with desire. It's a look I missed, though I barely remember. At any rate, my memory didn't do the look justice.

He braces his hands on the wall beside my head then leans over until we are eye level, our lips so close that, when he talks, they brush against mine, eliciting another moan from me.

"I need to get cleaned up. Why don't you dry off and wait for me?"

Reaching for his erection, I say, "Why don't I return the favor instead?"

Chuckling, a grin tips up half his lips. "Angel, you already did." When I look at him in confusion, my brows furrowing, he explains, "It's, uh ... been a while, so ..."

Understanding dawns, and I blush. I try to cover it by looking down, seeing that, despite that, he is still hard. I bite my lip before looking back at him, grinning in excitement that I have that effect on him. I didn't even need to touch him.

"I'll check on Nico while you finish." I grimace, thinking about our kid possibly hearing me. "I hope I didn't wake him."

Noah chuckles again before pressing a kiss to my lips, and then I'm slipping past him.

~Noah~

Faster than I ever have before, I quickly lather my body and rinse off, thinking back to my determination to win Claire over.

For the past five months, her sweet kisses and thank you after I told her my reasoning for leaving took over everything else. All my songwriting went into that time we spent in her bedroom, writing about letting go of the past, admitting to mistakes. And my determination finally paid off when she told me she trusted me.

No words have ever sounded sweeter. Not words of love, exculpation, adoration. Hearing her say she trusted me after working so hard to earn that trust means more to me than anything else. And when she kissed me, I felt spiritually exalted. I took that kiss and filled in all the years we spent apart. I wanted her to feel how much regret, self-hatred, and loss I felt before I found my way back. And how much adoration, gratefulness, and fortitude I feel to be back and to make sure to never wander a separate path from hers again. Because she is where I belong. She is my home.

She is the only one who has ever made me feel cherished, important. She is the only woman who can bring me to my knees. She is the only one who makes me feel like I matter. And I know I do ... to her, to Nico, and that's all that matters to me. They are my entire world.

Stepping out of the shower, I briskly dry myself off. Then I walk out of the bathroom, steam rolling out with me until it meets its end with the cooler temperature. I press my ear against Nico's door, not hearing anything. I don't want to go in there, knowing Claire probably did already. Too much risk waking him up.

In Claire's bedroom, a place I hardly ever step foot in, I find her combing her hair on the edge of the bed, wearing a silk robe I once bought her long ago in Chinatown. She loved that little adventure.

I silently watch as she runs the comb through her long locks, and then soaks up the water at the ends with a towel before repeating the combing process. I remember how she always hated to sleep with wet hair, how she would wait until morning to wash it, and then spend half an hour blowing it out, though it never seemed to dry all the way. I always loved watching her routine. Watching her like I am now, watching as she gets lost in her own thoughts, looking at the wall but not seeing it, seeing something I am not privy to.

I shut the door, locking it, and then walk over to her. She finally notices me, turning her head to watch me as I once again kneel at the feet of my angel.

The comb slips from her fingers as I part her robe, finding her still completely bare and now open to me. I run my hands along her hips, digging my fingers in as I slide her back farther onto the bed then follow her up. The towel slips off my waist as I maneuver her, situating her back against the pillows before shadowing over her, covering her body with mine.

"Are you sure?" I hate that the words slip out, but I have to know. This is like the first time all over again, and I don't want her to have any regrets.

When she nods, I blow out a relieved breath then start trailing kisses over her breasts that are fuller than they were when she was eighteen. I then suck one peak into my mouth, earning a gasp and the arching of her back, pressing her breast more firmly against my mouth.

My dick is already pressing against where it wants to be as Claire rotates her hips, rubbing herself off on it, trying to notch it in place. My dick is telling me foreplay is over. That happened back in the shower. And it seems that Claire is thinking along the same lines.

Kissing and nipping my way up her neck, I finally press my lips against Claire's, mimicking our kiss from this past summer, waiting for her move. She doesn't disappoint.

Claire opens to me, one hand in my hair, holding my head where she wants it. Her other hand moves from my ass to my cock, where she lines it up, tilts her hips and, using her legs wrapped around me, slams me into her while pushing her hips up. We both groan and gasp into each other's mouths.

The sensation of being inside her is so overwhelming I almost come again. My entire body shudders at the sensation, and then my eyes meet hers as I pull back, using my forearms to balance myself over her.

I watch as a tear escapes the side of her eye, running down to disappear in her hairline.

"I want to stay like this, but I need you to move, and I need it as hard as you can give."

Brows drawn in, I ask, "Why?"

She licks her lips, and then I watch her mouth as she speaks. "Because there's still too many angry and resentful emotions between us to be any other way. I want to get it all out before we move on."

Understanding what she is asking for, I give her a look that I hope says she asked for it. Then, summing up all the self-hatred I have for myself, I pull back until the tip of my cock is in her before pounding back into her, and I don't stop.

This is nothing like our first time when I was as gentle and careful as I could be. No, this time around, it's bruising, uncontrollable, painful. It's invigorating, embodying, heartbreaking. It's a battle against all the pain I caused her and all the pain I caused myself. I pound away my insecurities into her, and then she takes control and rides all her anger out on me. It's cleansing.

After she takes an orgasm from me, she collapses on my chest, sweat and maybe even residual shower droplets sucking our skin together. I roll her over, still inside her, and back to the position we started in. Locking her arms against her sides with mine, I brace myself so I don't put too much weight on her.

Smoothing back all her matted hair, I ask, "Is that what you wanted?"

Her eyes closed, she hums her assent.

I grin, softly kissing her lips. She opens her eyes as I pull back, and my grin falls as I look back at her, the impact of what is happening hitting me.

"You're so damn beautiful." I wonder if she even knows she's as beautiful inside. Only an angel would give me a second chance.

Her eyes soften at my words. Then she wiggles her hips, getting comfortable, and I groan at how it feels inside of her, closing my eyes as I feel my dick twitch and swell.

"I want to make love to you this time."

She smirks, giving me a seductive look with her half-lidded eyes. "This time?"

I nod.

She's clenching her inner muscles, which makes it hard to articulate anything. I already feel myself hardening. Soon, if not already, she will feel it, too.

"This time, and then again."

Her eyes widen at that. "How many times do you plan on having sex tonight?"

"As many times as we can until Nico wakes up." I am totally serious. I have years to make up for, which leads me to another thought. "Birth control?"

Claire sobers up at that, her smirk fading. "Same as last time, but I keep up with my appointments." She pauses. "I guess it's too late to ask, but are you—"

"I'm clean," I tell her while nodding. "I would have told you otherwise before the whole trying-to-get-you-back mission."

" 'Kay." She smiles back at me, but it doesn't reach her eyes.

Playing with a strand of her hair, I start, "I—Claire … I can't tell you enough—"

"Shh …" She lifts her head and presses a kiss to my lips. "Leave it in the past now, Noah. That's all I want. That's all we can do if we want to move forward. 'Kay?" When I nod, adoration for this angel making my chest feel like it's going to burst, she wraps her arms around my neck, her legs around my waist, and whispers against my lips, "Make love to me now."

I don't even hesitate. With my body sensitive to every touch, my heart pounding, and my soul soaring, I make good on my promise. I make love to her all night, taking my time, memorizing her body again. And when dawn breaks over the horizon, I hold her to me for a couple of hours, not letting sleep take me with her. I simply hold her, watching her peaceful, contented face, listening to her even breaths. Then I get up, get dressed, and wait for our son to wake up so I can share breakfast with him.

Such simple and mundane tasks follow me for the rest of the day, yet it's the best day I have ever had, because it's the first day I spend as an authentic family.

Chapter 31

Secrets and Surprises

~Claire~

Noah has been leaving me some cryptic messages this past week. I don't know what's up with him, but I know I am going to find out today.

It all started when he left Thursday morning. Nico and I dropped him off at the airport, and as he got out of the car, he asked me, "Do you love me?"

"Yes ...?" I answered, making it sound like a query in my confusion over his question and the nervous look on his face.

"And you still trust me?"

To that, my eyes narrowed.

We have been more than great lately. Top of the world, delirious with happiness, and bursting with joy are more appropriate terms. I thought Noah was open with me when we dated previously, but it's been nothing like now. Maybe it's more that he knows himself better, as do I. Whatever it is, we are closer than we were before, and much happier.

Not to say that we don't argue sometimes, like when Noah again and again gets that look on his face. It's the sorry, regretful look he gets sometimes when he stares at me or watches Nico. I want to vanquish the look from ever appearing on his face. Instead, I always tell him, "Don't," and he always says, "I can't help it." Then he goes into this whole monologue of self-abasement and remorse. It kills me.

I wonder if he will ever get past it. I wonder if I will ever get past it. I don't say anything to him. It's not going to change anything, so why bother? I would rather look at the happier memories. And the times Noah wasn't there? Well, I have the image of him watching those videos I sent him; his face showing emotions I don't even have names for as he watches our son grow. That's a good memory I will always hold on to. It's also a pastime Noah has taken on—recording all our special moments so he can watch them when the moment strikes.

So, the question was: Why was he asking all this?

"What's going on, Noah?" I asked him warily, my eyes still narrowed at his guilty face.

Getting back in the car, he grabbed my hand, looking straight into my eyes. "Nothing ... bad. I don't want to worry you—"

"It's too late for that," I told him, my heart pounding in fear, my head following suit. I hadn't had a tension headache in months. That streak ended.

Noah got to within inches from my face, cupping both my cheeks. "I swear, on anything you ask me to, I'm not running. I ..." I watched as he struggled for words, and my breaths became faster, hysteria taking over. "I need you in my corner right now, okay? I'll explain everything when I get back, but for now, I need to trust you, and I need you to trust me." Then he seemed to collect himself, taking a deep breath. "Stay away from all media, okay?"

I nodded, unable to speak. I was confused, overwhelmed with negativity. I didn't understand where this was coming from. What was he talking about? Why would he get so serious like that? What was happening in L.A. that would have him needing to ask me to stay away from the media? All I could think about was that the studio was making him escort some bombshell somewhere, and that hurt.

Nico had gone with him for a few trips, saying they stayed at a hotel, and he got to meet some nice men. Noah also took him to Disneyland once, and to the beach back when it was still warm. He asked if I wanted to go, too, but I haven't had the time off to do so. Now that the season is ending, I should be able to go.

Before Noah left to catch his flight, he whispered, "I adore you," and gave me a searing kiss. Then he gave Nico a hug and was off. And I was left wondering how a few words could make my happiness sink into depression.

Things have seemed so good lately. So much better than it was thirteen months ago, when Noah first walked back into my life. Even better than five months ago, when we finally shared a bed together again. In fact, Nico and I moved in with him after he asked a month ago, saying, "I want your curtains hanging in our windows." I couldn't resist that, surprised that he remembered such a little thing.

I love living at his place, yet I was sad to leave mine. We made a trip back home to go through my mother's things, finding furniture to add to our place. The condo is nowhere near finished, but we have the essentials there. All of Nico's and my stuff is out of my condo, and the place is up on the market. Nico's room is completely done. Most of the master bedroom, and the kitchen and living room, too. The two extra rooms are trashed, boxes and extra furniture everywhere. We are taking our time setting everything up. The curtains were the first things Noah hung up, and then we had to buy more because he has a lot more windows than I was prepared for.

Noah called me when he arrived in L.A, making me promise again not to look at any media. He sounded so nervous that it made me nervous. I was sick with it. Then, the next day when he called, he asked, "What would you say if I told you I was entertaining the idea of forming my own band?"

I squealed in excitement. I have always wanted that for Noah. He is too talented to hide behind simply songwriting. With his voice, style, and looks, he should be in the limelight. I had wanted to tell him so many times not to hide his talent, but I know he has always struggled with sharing his music.

"Christ, Claire," Noah breathed out in obvious relief at my excitement. "That took a load off my chest. I swear, I was shaving years off my life, worrying about your response."

"That's what that was all about yesterday when I dropped you off?" I asked, all my fears melting away.

"Yeah. Sorry about that. What did you think it was?"

Sighing in relief, I told him, "I had so many scenarios playing out in my head. Most of them centered on you being seen with another woman."

"Fuck that," he said vehemently.

"Yeah, well, trust me when I say PR will do anything to get

attention. I had to be seen with many different people while promoting *Deutsch Märchen.*"

"Don't remind me," he grumbled into the phone.

After that conversation, my fears were put to rest, but I was still curious as to why he asked me to stay away from media coverage. I kept my promise, though I wanted to look him up so badly and figure out why was being so secretive.

Now today is the day he is coming home.

I take out my phone and look at the time. I met Dare for her lunch break, but I need to leave soon to pick Nico up from Giuliana and Kyle's before heading to the airport. Noah's flight arrives in an hour, and I promised Nico we would pick him up as a surprise to Noah.

He's only been gone for five days, but it feels like so much longer.

I tell Dare that I need to head out, and we leave. She heads back to practice, where she did get a job after I put in a recommendation for her, and I make my way to the parking garage where Noah's Land Rover is parked. We hardly ever use the car, but since the airport is such a journey, I decided today would be a good day to use it.

Noah bought himself another bike a while back and uses that whenever he is flying solo, which is basically to work and back. If he has Nico or I am coming, too, we usually hire a cab. No car is safe in the city.

Pulling out of the garage, I flip on the radio. It takes me a full thirty seconds before I realize what I am listening to.

Oh, my God.

Pulling over at a curb, I sit in silence, eyes brimming with tears. My hands automatically start playing with my necklace, the two pendants—the guitar pick and birthstones locket—vigorously sawing back and forth in my excitement.

Noah, you little sneak. I laugh as tears spill down my cheeks as I hear the DJ come over the speakers.

"That was from the new band, Looking Backward. Their debut song came out today. Lead singer/songwriter Noah Gish, as some of you may know, has written many hits that have come to us over the past two years. You're not going to want to miss this band, people.

And next we have ..."

I can't believe he hid this from me. Why? This is such good news. Why would he tell me he was entertaining the idea when it's already happening?

Oh, Noah, you self-conscious, depreciating man.

He's been flying out to L.A. for ten months; is this what he has been doing? Well, I guess that is apparent now.

I laugh again, excited energy zipping through my body. I even have goose bumps.

When I think most of the excitement is out of my system, I pull back onto the road and head toward Giuliana and Kyle's.

I practically run up the steps to their apartment when I get there, knocking on the door frantically and probably scaring them. When Kyle opens the door, I bounce on my toes, throwing my arms around his neck and breaking out into laughs again.

Kyle grunts at the impact then asks, "What the hell has you so excited?"

I break away from him, looking around the room. "Where's your computer?"

Giving me a questioning look, he says, "In my room. Why?"

"You need to get it, please." I remove my sweater as Nico runs up to me, hugging me around my waist.

"Hey, baby." I run my hand through his hair before kneeling and giving him a kiss, asking him what he did today and trying to leave my excitement behind for a few seconds.

Kyle leaves to get his computer as Giuliana comes out of the kitchen, handing Nico a sandwich wrapped in a napkin. I tell him he has time to eat it at the table when I see Kyle come out of his room, laptop in hand.

Too excited to wait, I skip over to him, snag the computer, and make my way over to where Nico is eating his lunch, taking the seat next to him. I pull up the internet search and type in the band name, totally squealing like a fan girl when their website comes up.

"Is that ...?" Kyle starts, leaning over me from behind. "Son of a bitch," he says in awe before looking at me. "You didn't know, did you?"

Shaking my head and grinning like an idiot, I tell him, "No! I heard him on the way here!" Then realization hits me. "You're not mad, are you?" When Kyle gives me a puzzled look, I clarify, "I mean, you ... the band—"

Kyle scoffs and waves me off. "Creating music is the best, but it was never anything I foresaw as a long-term thing. Noah has always been the one with talent. I found my calling." Smiling, he indicates to the EMT uniform he is already dressed in. Then he plays back the debut song.

I feel like I am about to cry again. I can't even explain how happy I am. That buzzing energy is all around me, making me feel anxious in the best way possible.

I notice Nico bobbing his head up and down to the beat, and I swear he is lip-synching the lyrics like he knows the song, but then Kyle distracts me as he pulls out his cell phone.

"He's on the plane," I tell him

He nods, putting the phone to his ear. "I'm calling Mom and Dad."

"That's Daddy's band and new friends," Nico says like it's old news to him, hands on the table as he leans over to see the screen.

"How—"

"Why didn't he tell you?" Giuliana asks, patting Nico's bottom so he takes the hint to sit down.

I shake my head. "No idea."

Nico points at the screen. "That's Mr. North. He reads to me sometimes. He says he wanted to be a school teacher. And that's Lucky. He's funny. He calls his guitar Dolly. Isn't that funny, Momma? Mr. Jack"—he points to the guy holding a bass guitar— "looks scary, but Daddy says that's his thinking face."

"You knew about this?" I ask the obvious, wondering for how long Nico knew and didn't say anything.

Nico sits back in his chair and shrugs before taking a big bite of his sandwich. "I told Daddy secrets are bad, but he said it was a good secret, and we can keep good secrets. Is Daddy right, Momma?"

I give him a reassuring smile. "Daddy wouldn't lie to you." Then I jump up and turn to see the time on the stove. "We have to go."

Giuliana hurriedly wraps Nico's sandwich back in the napkin, telling him to put his shoes on and grab his bag.

I put my sweater back on and grab my purse. The Giuliana hands the sandwich to me.

"Good luck," she tells me as we head out the door, and I beam at her then wave good-bye to Kyle as he tells his parents the news. Soon, Noah's parents and my dad are going to call for the details. Details I don't have.

"Daddy famous now?" Nico asks as I strap him into his booster seat.

"I think so," I answer then close his door and get myself into the car.

On the way to the airport, I incessantly scan the stations, listening for any more news on Noah and his band. I miss the end of the song on one, but the DJ doesn't come back on before the next song plays. My phone has been ringing incessantly, but I ignore all the calls from my dad, Sarah, and even Cyn.

We get to the airport with only five minutes to spare. Parking in the garage, I help Nico out of the car, and then we quickly make our way to the arrival gates. There is madness everywhere as I find the schedule of arriving flights then find the ones coming out of L.A. He has already landed.

I look toward the gate again, hoping we didn't miss him, spotting some paparazzi standing around. Crap. They seem to always be waiting to catch a glimpse of someone famous. They haven't been so bad this year as they were last year, but I still don't want to draw attention to myself and, most importantly, to Nico.

I look down at him, trying to decide what to do, when he suddenly yells out, "Daddy!" and rips his hand from mine, running toward his father.

~Noah~

I have been hiding something from Claire since my trip to L.A. right after Nico's last birthday. At first, it didn't feel like a big deal, so I didn't feel like I had anything to tell. Over the past few months, though, the news has grown. Honestly, I don't know how Claire has even missed the gossip about it. Nevertheless, I am at the airport, back in New York, on my way back to her, sweating bullets.

When I flew out to L.A. and the executives threw the idea out there, I was in immediate rejection mode. Then one of them talked about my songs on a personal level, explaining the level of depth that song hit him. It brought back the conversation Claire and I had when she told me how people personalize the songs for themselves and not me, the singer. With her words in mind, I agreed.

After that was a whirlwind. Within weeks, I was flying back out to L.A., with Nico that time, listening to demos sent in from all over the country. After a few days of narrowing down the artists to a couple dozen, we flew them out for auditions.

Jack, Lucky, and North were the three I could see myself working with. All three have completely different personalities, but all three have one thing in common: when it comes time to work, they work. That was my main concern in wading through the contestants.

Is Claire going to be mad at me for not telling her? Will she downplay it, pretending to be excited at first? And I still need to talk to her about all the travel that's about to occur. How is she going to take that news? Nico starts school this year; how are we going to work our way through that? Maybe this was a bad idea.

So many thoughts fry my brain. I haven't been this nervous since the night I knocked on her door over a year ago. God, so much has changed since then, and I'm hoping that so much more is about to change. And I don't mean with this music shit.

I was so nervous when I asked Claire to move in with me. I didn't think she would want to give up her apartment. That place felt more like home than any other place, but I wanted something that was ours. Not hers, not mine, but ours. I wanted to finally be able to say that, yes, we do live together.

The second she said yes, I started packing. And I do mean literally. Claire thought I was joking. I wasn't. It took an hour of me packing her room before she realized I was serious and wanted them in our home that night. I even added her name to the property the very next day.

Simply moving in together, I feel closer to Claire. Making love in our bedroom, finally having something that belongs to us both, I am happier, yet constantly fear this happiness will get taken away.

I know Claire sees it. When she does, she talks about the future, getting my mind off the past. And I hint at marriage by playing with her ring finger, trying to gauge what she thinks about that aspect of the future.

Claire gives nothing away. I honestly think she is oblivious to my hints, which makes me wonder if that is even something she wants. She used to, but then I was a fuck-up. Not knowing, not being able to bring the subject up without outright asking, indescribable fear of rejection compresses my throat, a fear I feel at this very moment.

I step out of the arrivals gate and immediately hear the second sweetest voice in the world call out, "Daddy!"

Surprised since Claire didn't mention picking me up, I look around for my son and see him barging his way toward me. Before I can even look for my angel, I manage to bend over and barely have my arms open before Nico is jumping into them.

I pick him up and look around for Claire, seeing her coming toward us. Nico is talking, yet I can't understand what he is saying, all my focus is on her.

She knows, but instead of being upset at me like I worried, she is beaming at me, until she sees the fear in my eyes, then her eyes soften.

I put Nico down as she finishes her trek toward me. Then I wrap her in my arms, Nico smooshed between us, clasping my leg, as I whisper in her ear, "I'm sorry."

She looks up at me, showing me pure joy. "I am so, so proud of you. Don't be sorry for doing something you should have done long ago." She playfully smacks my abdomen, smiling widely once again. "But you could have told me."

I smile back at her. "I know. Trust me; I know. I wanted to. I almost did when you dropped me off, but I lost my nerve. How did you find out?"

"I heard you on the radio and had to immediately pull over," she gushes. "By the way, Kyle and the rest of the family know by now. My phone has been ringing off the hook. I'm sure you have plenty of messages, too."

"Daddy's famous!" Nico squeals from below us. Then he says with an air of exhaustion, "I'm so glad I don't have to keep that secret anymore," earning an amused grin from me as I look down at him, seeing him beaming at me.

Claire rolls her eyes and scoffs before she giggles. "Daddy's *been* famous. Now everyone can put a face to the name. We should go out tonight and celebrate," she directs to me.

I immediately shake my head. "No. This week has been insane already." Press releases, interviews, photo ops—things I wasn't prepared for at all. "I want a quiet night in with you and Nico."

Claire nods. "Okay, but I don't know how quiet it's going to be with everyone calling." She starts to turn away, but I stop her, needing to do this now before I lose my nerve.

"Claire?"

She turns back around and her face turns to worry at whatever she sees on my face. "What?" She reaches up and feels my forehead. "You look sick all of sudden, and you're cold and sweaty; no fever. What's wrong, Noah? Is there more news? What is it? You're freaking me out."

I must be because she is rambling, something she only does when she is worried or excited.

Hand shaking, I grab hers and pull it up to my lips, pressing my lips to the back of it. "I ... Claire, you ..." Jesus Christ, I can't do this.

"Noah, you are scaring me. What is it?"

Shit, I am making this so much worse. I need to breathe and get through this scariest moment of my life.

"You ... You once said you wish you could believe that I will never leave you. That"—I swallow before I can continue—"you would doubt me until I did, *or* ..." I pull out the ring I bought her longer ago than I care to admit. "This is your or, Claire." I try to look into her eyes as she looks down at the ring. "So, what do you say? Wanna sing a duet with me?"

I watch as she simply stares at it, her mouth open.

This is the part I feared the most. It's the unknown. I don't know if I am going to get the yes I desperately hope for, the yes I have wanted forever; if I'm going to get a flat out no, rejected and left to feel like she stabbed me in the heart; or if she will give me a not now, wanting to wait until some unknown future time. I need the first, will die with second, and may still die with the third.

I need this security, our happiness, our happily ever after like I need my next breath, which I am currently holding. I don't know if I can move on with my career choice if she's not tied to me. So much of me depends on her.

Seconds feel like an eternity as she blinks at the ring then glances up at me before riveting her attention back on the ring. Nico is looking at us both with confusion, still plastered to my leg with one arm while playing with Claire's pants pocket with his free hand.

"Claire?" I prompt, my voice cracking.

Distantly, I hear Nico ask her what's wrong. It's then that I see she is crying, twin tears spilling from each eye, trailing separate paths down her cheeks while her shoulders start to shake.

My heart seizes, and my legs almost fold.

It's a no. I asked too soon, in the wrong moment, in the wrong place.

For months, I have been daydreaming of the moment to ask her. I thought of doing something special, like a quiet dinner. I thought of doing something she would like, like Nico offering the ring. I thought of doing it when our family was around, making a huge announcement. Nothing felt right. It was too cheesy for me, though I think Claire would have loved the quiet dinner. At the same time, she would have known something was up. That's why I decided to do it at random, taking us both by surprise. And this is it.

I never pictured the rejection hurting so damn much.

I try to swallow against the knot in my throat, feeling sick to my stomach, as I turn her hand over and place the ring in her palm. "It's still yours regardless." Then I take Nico's hand and start leading him toward the car, not knowing what is going to happen now, wanting to be alone to lick my wounds.

"Noah," Claire chokes out from behind me, and I turn back toward her, my whole body feeling like the weight of the universe is on me.

"Yeah?" I ask, lifting my eyes from the ground to see her tear-stained face. Her tear-brimmed eyes gleam back at me before more tears fall.

I watch, feeling sorrow heavy in my gut, as she uses her right hand to pick up the ring from the palm of her left. To me, her every action seems to happening in slow motion. I can hardly bear to watch. I don't want to look at that ring ever again.

That ring signifies every battle I fought to come back to her, to Nico, to find my place in this world. It gave me comfort, strength. It filled me with longing and loss. It gave me hope. And it kicked my ass like the One Ring kicked Frodo's.

Sobbing now, she places the ring on the corresponding finger and gasps out, "Yes."

Now I do collapse to my knees, my body acknowledging her words before my brain does. My lungs deflate as my breath exhales in a rush.

Before I even gasp my next breath, Claire is straddling my thighs, lifting my heavy head until I meet her eyes.

"I want you forever, Noah. You shouldn't doubt that."

"Forever?" I can't help asking, wrapping my arms around her and holding her so tightly I'm sure she can scarcely breathe.

"Forever," she whispers into my neck.

I feel like I have completed a journey. What started as love at first sight changed into a tragedy, just to change again into a love filled with warmth, family, and a constant.

Looking back, I can see now that our passion for each other was the only thing that never changed. It's what motivated both of us: my fight to come back to her, and her continuing on without me. In the end, it's what brought us to this moment, another memory in the story of our forever.

Librettist and Rock Star Engaged, Plus Their Secret Love Child

Sunday, May, 15th, 2016

Fans were shocked today when songwriter Noah Gish was greeted today by his secret girlfriend, Claire Sawyer, and their four-year-old son.

Noah Gish is making news because of his recent rise to fame with an unexpected album release due out next week. The studio hired Gish a couple years ago, and his songs quickly climbed the charts, making him the most desired and highest paid songwriter in the industry. With the news of the release of his own album, expect to see Gish hit the charts overnight.

Many people already know Claire Sawyer. Her and her one-time boyfriend, Jesse Page, made headlines over a year ago with their sold-out operas. Their involvement around the time of Sawyer's son's birth have people speculating who the real father is, but sources have confirmed that high school sweetheart Gish is, in fact, the father.

Following the surprise of their child, in view of cameras secretly recording the event, Gish proposed to Sawyer…

Noah Gish and Claire Sawyer Married!

February 12, 2017

Mr. and Mrs. Gish were married today in a small ceremony bordering the woods outside of her father's house. Insiders told us the reception was a private affair with just under fifty people in attendance. The couple ...

Baby Prima Donna or Baby Rock Star?

December 16, 2017

A bump was spotted on the petite Claire Gish when she was seen coming out of the Met yesterday on the arm of her husband and the world's favorite musician and heartthrob, Noah Gish. When asked how far along she was, Noah Gish boasted, "Seven months!" It was clear to those surrounding them that the newlyweds were both excited.

Noah Gish is busy recording his second album after finishing his first semi-world tour where both wife and son, Nicholas Gish, were repeatedly spotted visiting him ...

World Famous Librettist Steps Down to Play Mommy to Baby Rock Star, Touring with Rock Star Daddy!

March 22, 2018

With the close of another season, Claire Gish ended the year in style, not only giving birth to her and her husband, Noah Gish's, second son, but stating that she will no longer be working at the Met on a full-time basis…

Another Baby Rock Star for Noah and Claire Gish!

January 7, 2020

Noah Gish has been making headlines all over the news, but today we are here to report his wife, one-time Prima Donna and Librettist, Claire Gish, has given birth to a baby boy. This is the third son for...

.

Rock Star Daddy, Noah Gish, Shows off His Baby Prima Donna!

April 12, 2021

A photo was leaked today, showing Rock Star Noah Gish cradling him and wife's, Claire Gish, baby girl in his arms. The couple introduced her to the world late last night…

Epilogue

~Noah~

Twelve years ago, if anyone would have asked me where I saw myself in ten to fifteen years, *this* wouldn't have been my answer. This is me, feeding my two-month-old daughter in the quiet of her nursery while my almost ten-year-old son amuses Aiden and Gabriel, my three- and one-year-old sons. My wife—God, I still get a thrill simply thinking that—is supposed to be taking a nap.

That poor angel has been nonstop. I can never get her to sit down. If she isn't working with my mom on their fable research, then she is working on songwriting—things she wrote off three years ago, yet can't manage to let go of. It's one of the many things I love about her. And when she's not working, then she is catering to the kids, which is where most of her time goes. Then here I am, demanding her attention, too. To top that all off, this is our last night in this place we have made our home. The movers are coming in the morning and almost everything is already boxed up.

Adding little Chloe Grace to our family gave me the excuse to sit out on my career for a year. I still plan to record our next album, but that time is going to be stretched out. My wife needs me. My kids need me. And there is nowhere else I would rather be.

I never realized what having a family would mean to me. Both Claire and I were an only child, so I guess it seemed fitting for us to have more than one. I missed all Nico's firsts, so I was overly excited when Claire told me she was pregnant with Aiden. I was there for every ultrasound, the birth, baby checkups, first word, crawling, walking—I refused to miss anything. Then, right after his first birthday, Claire told me she was pregnant again.

That freaked me out. We had a short tour that year. I wanted it to be over way before she gave birth, and I did manage to be there when

Gabriel came into the world. Then, the night of Nico's ninth birthday, six months after Gabriel was born, she told me she was pregnant again. *Jesus.*

This condo is already feeling too small and three of our kids are still babies. Gabriel barely graduated from sleeping in our room before his room was taken away from him in preparation for his sister, so Aiden and Gabriel are now sharing a room.

I found a house in the country, close to Claire's dad in Breckenridge. I plan to open a studio there or build one on site so I can always be close to Claire and the kids. And that house has ten rooms because, yeah, I'm not done making babies with my angel, and I know she agrees.

Everyone is excited for our move. Fifteen-year-old Abigail is already claiming the babysitter role. My parents left the city earlier this year and moved to Denver, so they will be close by. Kyle and Giuliana will probably move soon, too, with their baby girl, since no one else is left in New York. They married right before Claire and I did. Cyn lives in Denver with her daughter. She's been seeing someone new, trying to move on.

"She's asleep," Claire's soft voice comes from directly behind me.

I look up from my position in the rocker, the same rocker we used for our two youngest sons, and see her dressed in only a robe. "I know." I can't stop watching Chloe, though. She already has Claire's softer brown hair, and her eyes are still a baby blue. I hope they will stay that way.

Aiden and Gabriel are a perfect mix of the two of us, unlike Nico who is my spitting image. Aiden has Claire's hair and my eyes. Gabriel has my hair and Claire's eyes. I think he is going to have her height, too. Little guy isn't as tall as his brothers were at his age. I can already foresee him being the runt in the family. Aiden picks on him all the time, while Nico is the big protector. Family dynamics already starting.

"Aiden and Gabriel are passed out, too. They fell asleep on the couch."

I raise my eyebrow at her. "And how do you know that when

you're supposed to be sleeping?"

Claire sighs. "You know I can't sleep during the day."

I get up and place Chloe down in her crib, watching as she stirs and lifts her fist to her puckered mouth, sucking away. She's been the best baby so far. Rarely cries, doesn't wake up much throughout the night. She is the total opposite from her brothers. Aiden and Gabriel were needy, little hellions their first year. Both had a wakeup call when the next of the brood was born. Poor guys.

I turn away from the sleeping beauty to my other beauty, stepping into her space and wrapping my arms around her. She places her hands on my sides and rests her head on my chest.

Contentment. That's what this moment is. The house is as quiet as it gets around here, unless the kids are sleeping, with some kid show playing in the background.

I start softly swaying Claire in my arms to the tune stuck in my head when she states, "I adore you."

I kiss her head then whisper, "I adore you, too ... so fucking much."

The End

Acknowledgements

This is always the hardest part for me.

I want to thank my two biggest supporters: my mother, Debbie, and my best friend, Deanna. Both of you guys put up with so much Noah and Claire talk. And you both read this book more than once for me. Thank you from the bottom of my heart. Love you guys.

To my betas and author friends who gave me feedback and support (M.S. Brannon, Jamie Begley, Sarah Brianne, Jenn, Louise, Chelsea, and I hope to God I am not forgetting someone!), thank you so much for taking the time. You guys really helped a lot, and I hope you know that means the world to me. Melissa, you made me laugh so hard. I loved your enthusiasm.

Thank you to Marisa at Cover Me Darling for the gorgeous cover. I had no idea what I wanted. All I knew was that Claire's pendant and Noah's bracelet had to be on the cover. The first proofs she sent, she nailed it! Thank you!

Lastly, I want to thank my kids, The Marine and the astronomer ballerina, for putting up with a lot of my anxiety over this book and all the hours I work. Love you.